LATE SPRING

Book 1 of
To Serve Them All My Days

A novel of youth spanning two generations who
fought in two World Wars, surveying their values,
their ideals and the country they served, it sees
the period 1918–41 as a cycle of years in which
the enormous changes of the twentieth century
first became apparent. The whole theme is
expressed through the eyes of four hundred
growing boys at a remote public school in
Exmoor and of their teacher, David Powlett-Jones,
David is a miner's son, who emerges from the
horrors of Passchendaele to find a new identity
as a bridge between the Victorian–Edwardian
generation and the post-war generation seeking
new freedoms and new values. From an
unqualified history teacher, he ultimately
emerges as headmaster of Bamfylde School,
and in 1941 finds himself in exactly the same
position as his predecessor who lost nearly a
hundred of his Old Boys in the 1914–18 conflict.

This is a school novel which develops
fundamental questions about the real purpose
of education, a novel of social change in the
twentieth century, of compelling strength, and
a plea for British standards of character and
conduct which will find a strong echo in many
hearts.

Also by the same author

To Serve Them All My Days
Book 2—The Headmaster

A Horseman Riding By
Book 1—Long Summer Day
Book 2—Post of Honour
Book 3—The Green Gauntlet

The Avenue Story
Book 1—The Dreaming Suburb
Book 2—The Avenue Goes to War

God is an Englishman
Theirs was the Kingdom
Farewell, the Tranquil Mind

and available in Coronet Books

Late Spring

Book 1 of
To Serve Them All My Days

R. F. Delderfield

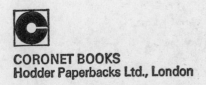

CORONET BOOKS
Hodder Paperbacks Ltd., London

Printed and bound in Great Britain for
Coronet Books,
Hodder Paperbacks Ltd,
St. Paul's House, Warwick Lane,
London, EC4P 4AH
by Hazell Watson & Viney Ltd,
Aylesbury, Bucks

ISBN 0 340 17599 0

*Dedicated to my friend and colleague
of the book world—
ROBIN DENNISTON*

A QUALIFIED DISCLAIMER

Almost every writer of fiction inserts the obligatory disclaimer in his work and some, I suspect, do it with tongue in cheek. The truth is, of course, no one ever *invented* anyone. Every character in fiction is an amalgam of factors drawn from the author's memory and imagination and this is particularly true of *To Serve Them All My Days*. No character here is a true portrait, or caricature, of any master or boy I ever encountered at my six schools and one commercial college, between 1917 and 1929, but aspects of people I met are embodied in all of them, and I have even used nicknames I recalled, as well as several scholastic backgrounds. To write fiction in any other way would be to divorce oneself from reality and what kind of book would emerge from that? In using, say, an average of six schoolmasters and six boys for every one between these pages, I intended no slight or criticism, only to portray life at school as I saw it up to 1940, when I had entered my twenty-ninth year. I was glad to leave five of the six schools but there is one I still regard with the greatest affection. I leave it to the reader to sort the wheat from the chaff.

R.F.D.
February 1971

PART ONE

INITIATE

How soon hath Time, the subtle thief of youth,
　　Stolen on his wing my three and twentieth year!
My hasting days fly on with full career,
　　But my late spring no bud or blossom shew'th.
John Milton

CHAPTER ONE

I

The guard at Exeter warned him he would have to change at Dulverton to pick up the westbound train to Bamfylde Bridge Halt, the nearest railhead to the school, but did not add that the wait between trains was an hour. It was one of those trivial circumstances that played a part in the healing process of the years ahead, for the interval on that deserted platform, set down in a rural wilderness, and buttressed by heavily timbered hills where spring lay in ambush, gave Powlett-Jones an opportunity to focus his thoughts in a way he had been unable to do for months, since the moment he had emerged from the dugout and paused, rubbing sleep from his eyes, to glance left and right down the trench.

From that moment, down long vistas of tortured, fearful and horribly confused dreams, his thoughts, if they could be recognised as thoughts, had been random pieces of a child's jigsaw, no two dovetailing, no half-handful forming a coherent pattern. Yet now, for a reason he could not divine, they coalesced and he was aware, on this account alone, of a hint of reprieve.

* * *

The shell, a coal-box, must have pitched directly on the parados of the nearest traverse, filling the air with screaming metal and raising a huge, spouting column of liquid mud. He had no real awareness of being flung backwards down the slippery steps, only a blessed certainty that this was it. Finish. Kaputt. The end of three years of half-life, beginning that grey, October dawn in 1914, when his draft had moved up through a maze of shallow ditches to a waterlogged sector held by the hard-pressed Warwickshires they were relieving.

Even then, after no more than two days in France, his sense of geography had been obliterated by desolation, by acres and acres of debris scattered by the sway of two battle-locked armies across the reeking mudflats of Picardy. There were no landmarks and not as many guidelines as later, when trench warfare became more sophisticated. The confusion, however, enlarged its grip on his mind as months and years went by, a sense of timelessness punctuated by moments of terror and unspeakable disgust, by long stretches of yammering boredom relieved by two brief respites, one in base hospital, recovering from a wound, the other when he was withdrawn for his commissioning course. Superiors, equals and underlings came and went. Thousands of khaki blurs, only a very few remaining long enough to make a lasting impression on him. Here and there he had made a friend, the kind of friend one read about in the classics, true, loyal, infinitely relished. But the mutter of the guns, the sour mists that seemed to hang over the battlefield in summer and winter, had swallowed them up as the wheels of war trundled him along, a chance survivor of a series of appalling shipwrecks.

Occasionally, just occasionally, he would be aware of conventional time. The coming of a new season. A birthday or anniversary, when his memory might be jogged by a letter from home, full of mining-village trivia. But then the fog would close in again and home and the past seemed separated from him by thousands of miles and millions of years, a brief, abstract glimpse of links with a civilisation as dead as Nineveh's.

And at the very end of it all that ultimate mortar shell, landing square on the parados and pitchforking him over the threshold of hell where, for the most part, he was unaware of his identity as a man or even a thing but floated free on a current of repetitive routines—shifts on a stretcher or in a jolting vehicle; daily dressings, carried out by faceless men and women; odd, unrelated sounds like bells and the beat of train wheels; the rumble of voices talking a language he never understood; the occasional, sustained yell that might have signified anger, pain or even animal high spirits.

The intervals of clarity and cohesion lengthened as time went on, but they were never long enough for him to get a firm grip on his senses. He learned, over the months, that he had been dug out alive, the only survivor of the blast, after being buried for several hours. Also that he had survived, God alone knew how, the long, jolting journey down the communication trenches to the dressing station, to advance base and finally to Le Havre and the hospital ferry. For a long time, however, he was unaware of being back in England, shunted from one hospital to another until he finally came to rest at Osborne, reckoned a convalescent among a thousand or more other shattered men as confused as himself.

Then, but very slowly, he became fully aware of himself again. Second Lieutenant David Powlett-Jones, 'A' Company, Third Battalion, South Wales Borderers; sometime Davy Powlett-Jones, son of Ewart and Glynnis, of No. 17 Aberglaslyn Terrace, Pontnewydd, Monmouthshire, a boy who had dreamed of scholarship and celebrity, of bringing a gleam of triumph into the eyes of a short, stocky miner who had worked all his life in a hole in the mountain and died there with two of his sons in the Pontnewydd-Powis explosion of August, 1913.

He was aware of his identity and, to some extent, of his past and present, but the future was something else. He could never attach his mind to it for more than a few seconds. The war surely would go on for ever and ever, until every human soul in the world was engulfed in it. He could never picture himself leading any different kind of life but that of trudging to and from the line, in and out of the mutter of small-arms fire and the sombre orchestra of the shells. Hospital life, as he lived it now, was no more than an interval.

Then Rugeley-Scott, the neurologist, infiltrated into his dream world. First as a white-smocked and insubstantial figure, no different from scores of predecessors who had paused, hummed and prodded during the last few months, but ultimately as a force where he could find not comfort exactly but at least relevance. For Rugeley-Scott had certain theories and persisted in putting them forward.

One was his theory of upland air and David's own Celtic roots responded to this, feeding a little vitality into the husk of his flesh and bone. For Rugeley-Scott said that a man could enjoy a sense of proportion in upland air that was denied the Lowlander, upland air being keen and stimulating and capable of clearing the fog in the brain and reanimating petrified thought-processes. It had a trick, he said, of making a man at one with his environment. Rugeley-Scott, of course, was a Highlander, whose boyhood had been spent in Sutherland and whose medical studies had taken him no farther south than Perthshire. He believed passionately in upland air in the way a primitive savage believes in the witchdoctor's bones and amulets.

Rugeley-Scott's second theory grew out of the first, close involvement in a small, tightly knit community, where a personality was encouraged to flower as it could never

flower in a city. It was concerned, also, with a specific purpose
enshrined in an ideal of some kind. In a creed, perhaps, or a
crusade. In one or other of the arts that yielded an end product. Above all, in involvement with others but not too many
others. A hundred or so, collectively breathing upland air.

David never afterwards recalled how these theories came
to centre on the profession of schoolmaster, imparting to
successive generations of the young such knowledge as a man
accumulated through books, experience, contemplation.
Yet somewhere along the line, in the first weeks of 1918, this
concentration occurred, so that David Powlett-Jones, white
hope of the Pontnewydd Elementary School, the miner's
son who had won the first local scholarship to the Grammar
School at thirteen, and had gone on to win another for
university four years later, began to see himself, a little fanci-
fully, as an usher on a rostrum, writing on a blackboard in
front of an audience of boys.

It was no more than a silhouette at first but Rugeley-Scott,
with Celtic obstinacy, persisted until a comprehensive
picture emerged. And after that, a train of minor events was
fired that involved letters and telephone calls, so that at
length, on a still afternoon in early March, seven months
after the coal-box had exploded below Pilckhem Wood,
David Powlett-Jones found himself sitting on a paint-scarred
seat on Dulverton Station, wondering who had dumped a
rail junction in such an isolated spot. He wondered too how
long he would have to order his thoughts before he boarded a
train for a place he had never heard of before Rugeley-Scott
gave him the envelope containing particulars for his interview with the Reverend Algernon Herries, Headmaster of
Bamfylde School, Devon.

He thought then, with a mixture of bitterness and humility,
"But what the hell am I doing here anyway? What headmaster in his senses would engage a wreck like me, who

jumps a foot in the air every time a door bangs? That chap Herries, whoever he is, will take one look at me and show me the door, tut-tutting all the way to the motor, providing they have motors out here."

He then drew three deep breaths of upland air and despite the memory of the ward's wry jokes about it, found that it did have a noticeable effect upon his powers of concentration. At least it enabled him to evaluate the view of those hanging woods, part evergreen, part the skeletal branches of older, heavier timber, and remark on the astounding quietude of the little station. Quiet was something he had forgotten about, along with so many other things that belonged to his child-hood and boyhood. Never once, not even on the blackest night in Flanders, had it been as quiet as this. Always there had been the scrape and shuffle of working parties, the plash of signallers slipping in flooded trenches, cursing at every traverse. And in the background, always, the guns had growled north or south of the sector, a thunderstorm roam-ing between Switzerland and the sea.

Here you could almost reach out and touch the quiet. It was a living thing that seemed to catch its breath up there in the hanging woods and then, at a wordless command, slip down the long hillside and gust over the rails to lose itself in the wood opposite. Its touch was gentle and healing, passing over his scar tissue like the fingers of a woman. He wanted to embrace it, press it into himself, swallow it, lose himself in it. And all the time the white clouds overhead kept pace with it, moving in massive formation across the blue band above the valley and the breeze smelled of resin and bracken and all manner of clean, washed, living things. No whiff of putre-faction here. And no hint of gas.

He surrendered to its benediction, and was sound asleep when the walrus-moustached stationmaster found him, studying him with the compassionate detachment of a sixty-year-old who had seen the passage of a thousand troop-trains. The long, slightly saturnine face was Celtic, one of the darker, taller, heavy-browed Celts who had little in common with West Countrymen this side of the Tamar. The limbs, relaxed now, seemed shrunken under the khaki gaberdine, the body pulled in by the worn Sam Browne belt. The face was that of a boy prematurely aged, with hollowed cheeks accentuated by deepset eyes and high cheekbones. The skin was tanned, but below the tan there was a hint of pallor. The railwayman muttered, "Osspittle. Somewhere up the line," and was tempted to let him sleep on but then, recollecting his duty, he shook him by the shoulder and said, "Tiz yer, lad. Vower minutes late. Your stop'll be fourth on, no more'n vifteen minutes."

The man's clumsy gentleness touched him. It was a long time since anyone had called him 'lad'. It was another short step on the road to resurrection.

II

The flint road wound upward through immense patches of wild rhododendron, then down again to culverts that carried a swirl of storm-water from the moor, along with a sludge of brown, decaying twigs and dead leaves. There had been no one to meet him at the halt and no sign of a convey-ance of any kind but he did not mind walking. It set forward the time of the interview by half an hour, the time he cal-culated it would take him to walk the two miles to the cross-roads marked on the map enclosed with the letter confirming his interview. The crossroads was marked as Barton Cross and when he reached it he saw that the barn or barton marked a junction of four roads that were really no more than half-surfaced cart-tracks. He thought, "Now who the devil would build a school right out here? Nothing lives here but rabbits," but then, as at the station, his awakening senses told him the wilderness was teeming with life, every kind of life, and that there was promise here, in a month or two, of an immensity of colour and movement under the touch of April.

Already the hedgerows were starred with campion and primrose, with dog violets showing among the thistles and higher up, where the rhododendrons tailed off on the edge of a little birch wood, the green spires of bluebell were pushing through a sea of rusty bracken.

He calculated the gradient at about one in six and the road kept twisting towards a brown-green summit that was the open moor. And then, coming at last to a level stretch, he saw the grey line of buildings on the southern edge of the plateau, and the twin ribbons of leafless beeches lining the two drives. He paused at a ruined five-bar gate that lacked a hinge and bulged outward. Beyond it was a playing field and on the rugby pitch a game was going on between two fifteens wearing identical red and black jerseys. The cries of the players came to him faintly on the freshening breeze and he had a sense of renewal, seeing the little figures over there not as part of the present but of a time a million years ago, when he had played in the Grammar School fifteen, and had worn a jersey rather like that, save that the stripes were red and yellow. The moment passed and he pushed on, passing up the east drive to the forecourt and pausing in front of the three-storey Gothic building that reared itself there, grey, rather gaunt and incongruous in that setting.

The façade itself was long and flattish but outbuildings straggled all the way up the slight rise to a quadrangle he could glimpse beyond an arched doorway. He remembered then that the place had been built at a period when no commercially minded architect would dream of using any but a Gothic design, a time when the missionaries of Arnold of Rugby swarmed south, carrying the Doctor's creed into every shire of the nation. You did not have to be told it was a school up there. It had, even at this distance, the smell of school, a compound of boiled greens, stale dust, steam-heat, spurned grass, sweat, socks and damp clothes. He moved along the forecourt until he came to an iron-studded door with a knocker fashioned in the shape of a dolphin. He raised the knocker, dropping it without resolution.

*　　*　　*

The Reverend Algernon Herries looked like an ageing, amiable clown. He had a cheerful, piping voice and a fruity bottlenose, lined with a network of tiny veins and clothed, as though in crude jest, by a swathe of dark, curling hairs that reminded David of the legs of an insect. White hair rose from the forehead in a clownish peak, giving a false idea of his stature that was short and thickset but still suggestive of agility and precise movement. His face was an actor's face, that might have been seamed and burnished by years of make-up routine. The mobile eyebrows were clownish, too, tufted and pointed like the hair, but below them the eyes were of piercing blueness, the one feature of the face that belonged in a world of earnestness and shrewdness, eyes, David told himself, that would miss little and were there to keep watch over tolerant excesses that could go with a face like that. The man might look eccentric but that did not mean he was anybody's fool. It therefore followed that he would not waste much time on an applicant lacking any kind of degree or experience, who had, moreover, the Twitch.

Yet the handshake was cordial, neither too firm nor too limp, and as he turned to lead the way down a stone corridor to his study he called, "Mr. Powlett-Jones, Ellie! Bring tea, m'dear!" and motioned his visitor into a room spilling over with books and dog-eared papers, indicating the one armchair beside the window, saying, "Sit you down. Ellie will be here with the tea in a jiffy. My apologies for your having to walk. We had a boneshaker until Christmas but then Stanbury, who drove it, took it into his head to do his bit and join the Army Service Corps. I do hope they don't trust him with one of those heavy Thorneycrofts you chaps use. He'll wreck it, for sure. He was always disputing passage with cromlechs and taking short cuts across patches of bog."

David began to warm towards him. It was impossible not to, for his geniality was so genuine. But there was rather more to it than that. He was the first civilian David had ever heard inject irony into that phrase 'do his bit'. For years now civilians had talked about 'doing their bit' as though they were on their way to church and wanted everybody to acknowledge their piety.

"I . . . er . . . enjoyed the walk, sir," he said, hesitantly. "The countryside . . . it's much wilder than the country around Osborne . . ." but then he stopped, biting his lip. He had been on the point of saying something bloody silly about the tortured Flanders landscape. Herries said, with unexpected gravity, "How long were you out, Mr. Powlett-Jones?"

"Three years."

"Three? Then you must have been under age when you enlisted."

"Only a week or two, sir. I went across with a Territorial draft in October. We were untrained but the regulars were badly hammered at First Ypres. I've been luckier than most."

"There's no possibility of your returning?"

"No, sir, I'm boarded." And then, with a touch of defiance, "I'd be no use to anyone out there now." He noticed dismally, that his hands had begun to shake.

Herries got up suddenly and at first David assumed the movement was an excuse to prevent him noticing the Twitch. It was not. He crossed the room and pointed to a fading sepia photograph hanging above one of the book-shelves. It was a very conventional photograph, fifteen lumpish youngsters, ranged in three rows, one lad squatting and nursing a ball.

"There's no need to feel isolated from us, least of all from me. That was our 1913 First Fifteen. Twelve are dead and one of the survivors is legless. We've lost eighty-seven to date, seventy-two of them known to me personally. My boys." He was silent a moment. Then, "On July 8th, 1916, I recorded eight names in one week's casualty list. Does that help?"

It helped but it also embarrassed. Suddenly, inexplicably, David felt his throat constrict and whipped his right hand to his eye. For nearly a minute there was silence in the cluttered room. The bell saved him, saved them both perhaps. Its harsh, clanging note filled the room and then went jangling away to the north as the ringer, relishing his work, crossed the quad towards the longest of the red-brick outbuildings. Herries said, "That's Shawe. Nobody is allowed to touch that bell but Nipper Shawe. He was the smallest boy in the school when he came here, so I had to find something to invest him with dignity. It worked, as you see. He now has the strut of the professional town-crier."

A murmur reached them, swelling rapidly to a sustained clatter, as boys began to pass the window in twos and threes, boots scuffling, voices shrill and urgent. Herries pushed open the casement and hailed the nearest of them.

"Who won, Daffy?"

A breathless boy paused under the window. "Nicolson's, sir! Eleven–five."

"*Eleven*, you say? Great Scott! Outram's were leading five-nil at half-time, weren't they?"

"Yes, sir, but Monkey scored a try early in the second half and Dodger converted. Then Hutchinson scored two more tries far out in the last five minutes!"

"He did? Well, good for Hutch! That must have rattled Outram's. Thank you, Daffy."

The boy ran on, disappearing in a stream that was flowing through the arch of the western face of the quad. Away in the distance Nipper Shawe was still swinging his handbell. Herries settled himself, reluctantly David thought, behind his littered desk.

The spate of nicknames, the obvious rapport between headmaster and boys puzzled him. In both his schools the headmaster had been a remote, austere figure. He had never heard either of them use a nickname, or address even a senior boy as a near-equal. His hands stopped shaking. He said, getting some kind of a grip on his nerves, "I've . . . er . . . no degree, sir. I was planning to go up to Cambridge in the autumn of 1914. I only agreed to this interview because the Osborne neurologist insisted. He has . . . er . . . some eccentric ideas on therapy."

"Really? Tell me."

"He said I could apply for a temporary post, and gain experience while the shortened ex-officers' courses are being arranged at Varsity. I wasn't even sure I wanted to teach. I'm certainly not equipped for the job."

The tufted eyebrows came up. "Any other career in mind?"

"No, sir."

"Then I'd say the neurologist knows what he's about."

Herries got up again. Behind a desk he seemed unable to express himself with characteristic directness. "Look," he said, suddenly, "why don't you give us a trial? As from now, and irrespective of whether that chap at Osborne is right or wrong? You'd be helping me no end. I'm stuck with a dozen tired men called out of retirement, and two C.3 trainees, rejected by the medicals twice over. Oh, they do what they can, but they come in for a lot of ragging. This overdose of jingoism we've had for so long, it's rubbed off on the boys. You'd have a distinct advantage over the rest of us there. Three years at the Front. Twice wounded. It's a flying start, man."

"I'm very far from fit, sir."

"You'll *get* fit up here. Everybody does." He expanded his barrel chest and David thought briefly of Rugeley-Scott, and his insistence on the benefits of upland air. "Besides, we'd make allowances. History is your main subject, isn't it?"

"Modern history was to have been, sir."

"Could you make a stab at English in Lower School? Ground work? Introductory stuff? As I say, we're in a rare pickle here. Every school is, of course, but out here, miles from the nearest town, we're at the very end of the queue. Just how do you feel about hanging around Osborne until those shortened courses are set up, then going up for the minimum two years?"

"Frankly the prospect terrified me, sir. It's difficult to make the necessary effort when the only people you meet are crocks, as bad or worse than yourself. They tell me it'll be much the same at Cambridge. Every man on those courses will be ex-service."

"You're afraid of becoming institutionalised? Is that it?"

"More or less. I had thought about signing away pension claims, discharging myself and going it alone somewhere."

"Anywhere particular?"

"In the Welsh mountains. I had some good times up there when I was a boy but Rugeley-Scott insists . . ."

Herries flipped the cover of a buff file.

"It's only fair to tell you I had a lengthy letter from Mr. Rugeley-Scott. He was very explicit. Would you care to see his letter?"

"No, sir. I can guess what he said."

"The bit about an enclosed community?"

"I know the clinical symptoms of severe shell-shock, I should do, after seven months in hospital."

"Let's take it as read then. As to 'going into retreat', you could do that here if you cared to. Term ends in three weeks and you could stay around and nurse yourself for a month. It's very quiet during the holidays. I could show you the country on horseback. We still have a couple of old screws the requisitioners left behind. Or you could walk solitary if you preferred it."

For the first time since he had been fully aware of his situation David came to terms with his profound reluctance to go home to Pontnewydd. His mother, who had survived worse tragedies, would stay clear of him, but who else would in a close-knit mining community, where almost everyone knew him as 'Davy-boy'? What was necessary, what was absolutely essential in the next few months, was privacy. Privacy, within a community of people cut off from the reality of what was still happening over there.

"Could you give me a moment to think it over, sir?"

"I can give you all evening. No need to pound down that road for the five-thirty. Be our guest and sleep in the President's Room—President of the Old Boys that is. We always keep a room for him, that's his privilege. I can lend you pyjamas and we'll root out a toothbrush, although I'm told they're in short supply like everything else except eggs and bacon. We're very privileged in that respect. We keep our own hens and pigs."

He opened the door and stepped out, calling to his wife Ellie for the tea. David went over to the window that opened on the quad. Behind what looked like the changing rooms the light was dying. Through a screen of leafless elms bordering the playing field he could see the orange glow of a heatless sun. Sunsets belonged to his earlier life. In the trenches the sun always set behind the British sectors. There was some kind of bath-house over there and every now and again a towel-draped boy darted across a flagged court and disappeared into a cloud of steam. It was as much a masculine world as Flanders but the difference showed in the speed of the boys' movements and their high spirits that reached him as half-heard sallies and short barks of laughter. Out there men still laughed but rarely in that way, rarely without bitterness. He thought, "It's what I need, I daresay, but how the devil do I know I could stand up to it? If any one of those kids tried it on, as boys always do with a new man, I might go berserk. Or I might crumple up and pipe my eye, as I nearly did when Herries mentioned that 1913 First Fifteen. . ."

He braced himself to take a closer look at the photograph. The boys were his contemporaries, their average age about seventeen when that picture was taken. It was even possible to fancy he could recognise one or two of them, so typical were they of all the youngsters who went west in the bloody shambles in 1916. That was the day Robin Barnes copped it two yards from the trench. And Nick Austin, too, although Nick had taken a night and a day to die, too far out to be brought in by the stretcher-bearers. A whole generation gone and here was the next, flexing their muscles for the show, looking forward to it, he wouldn't wonder. There was talk of a big Jerry offensive, with whole divisions released by the collapse of the Russian front. If things were desperate enough they might even come combing in places like this. Jerry already had. Two prisoners, brought in by trench raiders the night before he stopped the mortar blast, had been seventeen and looked much younger. He remembered them vividly, although he had never thought about them since, a pair of terrified starvelings in uniforms several sizes too big for them, their coal-scuttle helmets sitting on their shaven heads like extinguishers . . . Could anyone do anything about it at this stage? Suppose the war ended next year or the year after? Would there be anyone left to listen?

Herries and his wife came back together, the headmaster carrying a loaded tray. Mrs. Herries was four inches taller than her husband and thin as a beanpole. Her eyes were as kind and shrewd as his and he thought, as Herries introduced them, "He's holding on better than most and so is she . . . It must be a little like losing seventy-two sons . . ." and the reflection helped him to make up his mind. He said, "Could I wire for my things, sir? Enough to tide me over?" and Herries said, casually, "Better than that. We'll telephone the hospital as soon as you've had a meal and a look round. Crumpets? Why not? There are certain compensations in being marooned, my dear chap."

It was dusk in the quad when they went out. They had no electricity up here and a shuffling little man with buck teeth was lighting oil lamps suspended over the three arches and at intervals down the long, flagged corridor to the dining hall. David peeped in and made a rough calculation of numbers seated at tea. Four hundred, give or take a dozen. He followed Herries up two flights of slate steps to a landing giving access to two large dormitories, each sleeping about thirty boys. It seemed a very Spartan school. There were no floor coverings, apart from narrow strips of scuffed coconut matting, and no lockers beside the iron cots, each covered with a red blanket. Under each bed was a laundry basket and an enamel chamber-pot. It was very much like a barrack but some of the headmaster's brusque geniality had rubbed off on the fabric, enough to make it threadbare-friendly, like an old and shabby rectory. Herries, reading his thoughts, said, "We're not too well endowed and all the renovations we had in mind have been postponed for four years. The carpentry shop keeps us from disintegrating completely. Our numbers keep up, however, a third of them the sons of Old Boys. A few of their fathers were in Upper School when I came here."

"When was that, sir?"

"Summer term, 1904. I always say I came in on the radical tide. It was a year or so before a Liberal landslide. You would have been a child of eight."

"I remember for all that," David said, smiling. "You can't evade politics in the valleys. How did Bamfylde come to be built in a place as remote as this, sir?"

"Everyone asks that. It grew from a school for farmers' sons. About two dozen of them used to ride their ponies to a farmhouse a mile or so nearer the village. Most of the day boys still ride. One of Arnold's disciples was rector here and talked the local people and county authorities into founding the place, in 1853. We're a direct grant school, and about a third of our income comes from the Ministry. They leave us pretty much alone, however, and I get my way in most things. Lord Hopgood—this is part of the Hopgood estate— and the Old Boys make all the real decisions. After I've primed them, that is. Some of the Governors are Old Boys, others are local government bigwigs, a few of them local tradesmen in the area. I'll give you some registers and a prospectus to lull you to sleep after dinner. Come on down now. We've just time to view the place from my thinking post before it's dark!" and he bounced down the stairs, into the passage, across the quad and through the arch leading to the changing rooms and bath-house, moving at a half-trot.

The red-brick block behind the school was shut and silent now. Herries, bustling ahead, pointed to a row of single-storey stone buildings. "Tuck-house, stables, junkroom, armoury—we have a very flourishing O.T.C.—and the fives court. Latrines opposite. Have to do something about them

soon, war or no war. The only effective flushing we get is by
moorland brook. Well enough this time of year, when it
rains five days a week, but a problem in a dry spell. Take the
left-hand path between those two elms. That's the cricket
pavilion and swimming bath. We had the devil's own luck
there. It was finished the week war broke out. Mind the
roller—the chain-gang shouldn't have left it there. Along
under the hedge towards the plantation. I've seen that
grow. Local wiseacres said trees couldn't survive in the path
of the north-easters but they did. We now have a windbreak
I wouldn't care to be without. Here's the spot. My thinking
post!" and he stopped, giving David time to catch his
breath. Herries heard him wheezing and was instantly
apologetic. "I say, old chap, I'm sorry ... simply never
occurred to me ... I trot everywhere. Most of us do up here,
except in summer term. Have to keep the blood circulating.
But I should have remembered, you're still convalescent.
Take a breather."

Herries's thinking post was the stump of an enormous
beech, snapped off about twenty feet from the ground. He
seemed to have a great affection for it and patted it as though
it was a dog. "Getting on for three hundred years when it was
struck by lightning, in 1912. Lucky job it happened in
August, with no one about. Could have killed a dozen of us.
Took the sawyers a month to cart it away but it's still very
much alive for me. I used to climb it as a boy."

"You were a boy at Bamfylde?"

"Seventy-three to seventy-eight, but that was in Wesker's
time. Wesker was a brute. I've seen him flog a whole class for
spelling mistakes in dictation. Damned fool thing to do.
Lucky I could spell." He paused for a moment, looking down
on the scatter of orange lights some two hundred yards below.
The outline of the main buildings was just visible, a blue-
black blur, quickened by the last pulse of the winter sun. "I

very rarely flog a boy and then only for two offences. Persistent lying, and persistent bullying."

David said, suddenly, "How do you see it, sir? Education, I mean, the real purpose of it? In all that time you must have formed some conclusions."

In the dusk he saw the man smile as he stroked his thinking post.

"How? Well, certainly not as a matter of hammering information into boys. That was the general idea when I was young, before Arnold's ideas had time to flower. He was an insufferable prig, of course, and most of his disciples were worse, but they were moving in the right direction. The important thing is to adapt their theme to the twentieth century, before the commercials move in and take over. I don't really regard myself as a schoolmaster, or not any longer. I've changed direction myself a good deal since I took charge here, particularly so in the last few years. I suppose I see myself as a kind of potter at the wheel, but then, that's priggish too, wouldn't you say?"

"Not the way you mean it."

"Ah, but how *do* I mean it, precisely? It isn't easy to put these things on paper, or even convince yourself satisfactorily. Parents send their sons to a place like this for specific reasons. The main one is to get an education that will enable them to survive, I suppose. But once they settle in many other processes go to work. They learn a little tolerance, I hope, and how to see a joke against themselves, and how to stand on their own feet. But, above all, the knack of co-operating. I'm not too insistent on scholarship. Scholars are dull dogs for the most part. When I was a boy here there were no organised games to speak of. We crammed and then mooched about, devising ways of avoiding punishment, and tormenting one another out of sheer boredom."

"Isn't that what everyone's engaged in now, sir?"

"Yes, it is. But there's a well-defined end product, thank God."

"What is it, sir?"

"A second chance. You're a history man, so let me ask *you* a question. Granted my thinking post is three hundred years old, what was happening when it was a foot high?"

"The Civil War was brewing."

"Precisely. And something very practical emerged from that. Parliamentary democracy for one thing. Two steps up, and one and a half down. That's my view of history. British history, at all events."

"But we've fallen down a long flight since 1914, haven't we?"

"We've taken a tumble certainly, but that's because we were too damned cocky in the first years of the new century. I daresay we'll learn from it. Dammit, we have to unless all those youngsters were the victims of an obscene practical joke, and I can't let myself believe that they were. As I say, I saw seventy-two of them grow up, and there weren't many fools among them. And no cowards, either, not in the true sense of the word."

The man's optimism was working on him like a drug. His staying power, the strength and simplicity of his faith, was something the men out there had lost long ago, as long ago as Neuve Chapelle and Loos. But a flicker of doubt remained. He said, "As to learning from it, I take it you mean internationally? Out there everyone below the rank of field officer has had a bellyful of patriotism."

"Ah, patriotism," Herries said, affably, and although the dusk now shrouded them completely, David divined a twinkle in the eyes. "Don't forget Edith Cavell, Powlett-Jones. 'Patriotism is not enough' . . . She could have amplified that, poor soul. Patriotism is a first step, I'd say. On the road to civic maturity that is. You had three years out there.

I still believe in a Divine Purpose. You survived for a purpose, I imagine. To help head other survivors in the right direction, maybe."

Nipper Shawe was swinging his bell again. For prep probably, and its clamour terminated Herries's reverie. "Come, we'll look in on Big School and introduce you. It'll break the ice for man and beast. Then dinner. Ellie has shepherd's pie, with gooseberry fool to follow. We have fruit cages behind that copse and Ellie is a fanatical bottler."

They moved down the slight incline towards the scatter of lights and at the end of the path David barked his shin on the fender of the horse-roller. "Curse that chain-gang," Herries said, genially, "I'll have Masterson's press-gang move it in the morning. Masterson is down for Dartmouth in September. He's a natural leader of the press-gang."

CHAPTER TWO

I

Never in the past or indeed in the years ahead was he so sharply aware of that heightened sense of time that accompanies the process of self-discovery; of new faces, new experiences, new dimensions of space, shape, texture, colour and relationship that lifted him out of limbo and set his feet squarely upon virgin ground.

There was that farcical incident the first day he took the Lower Fourth, that final refuge of extravagant humorists, who regarded any new tutor, especially an inexperienced one, as legitimate prey, a blind and bumbling bear, to be baited and tested for sharpness of tooth and claw. From the first he saw the various groupings of the boys in terms of sections in a muster of infantry, halfway through his front-line service, a time when the ranks of any sizeable unit included battle-tried veterans, work-shy barrack-room lawyers and any number of nervous eighteen-year olds, fresh from school and recruit centre, all eager to show their mettle.

The scale began in the Second Form, composed entirely of first and second termers, ticking off the days as they adjusted to the pangs of homesickness. One looked for no trouble at all with these. All that was necessary was to slip into the role of jovial uncle, or brother separated by a wide age gap, and jolly them along, spicing the lesson with a few old chestnuts and injecting the spice of romance into pages of the textbooks where all the tedious milestones of British history were marked in heavy, marginal print, a row of cromlechs tracing a road across a waterless desert.

In the Lower, Middle and Upper Third sights had to be

adjusted. Here were the thirteen- and fourteen-year-olds, who had played themselves in and were now in the process of separating into four streams, streams that he came to think of as the anxious-to-learners, the occasional-triers, the professional time-passers and the practical jokers, bent on making a reputation for themselves.

It was in the Fourth Forms that trouble really began. The Fourth Forms were the school watershed, boys of fifteen and above, with two or three years of rough and tumble behind them and no immediate responsibilities ahead, a majority of skrimshankers who reminded him of the crafty, time-serving men, whose experience earned them stripes one day that were taken away the next. And of the three Fourth Forms the Lower Fourth was the toughest, perhaps because the Cambridge examinations would be that much nearer after removes to the Middle and Upper Fourth were achieved, and pressures were applied by parents reacting to end-of-term reports.

At all events, his first crisis came on his second morning at Bamfylde, when he introduced himself to some thirty blank-faced fifteen-year-olds in Big School, used as a formroom for the Lower Fourth during the day and as a communal prep room for the whole of the Middle School in the evenings.

It was a difficult room to overlook. The space between the rostrum and the first row of desks was unusually wide, so that he had a sense of being detached from the class in a way that did not happen elsewhere. The ceiling was high and arched and the three Gothic windows gave a clear view of the forecourt and east drive, an open invitation to idlers to concentrate on comings and goings out there rather than on the blackboard or the rostrum.

Boyer, a well-grown, rather saturnine boy with dark hair and high cheekbones, occupied a desk in the back row and even before the incident David marked him down as a jester. He had humorous, heavy-lidded eyes, grey, watchful and mocking. From the moment of making his first appearance, however, David was struck by the unusual passivity of the class. They sat very sedately, attentively awaiting his opening gambits, so that he was well launched on a survey of Elizabeth's foreign policy when there was a sudden stir at the back of the room. A glance, centring on Boyer, warned him he was in trouble, serious trouble if he let it get out of hand, for Boyer had turned very pale, blinking his humorous eyes rapidly as his limbs twitched and jerked, setting all the ink-pots in the communal desk leaping in their sockets. Before David could make even the briefest assessment of the situation the mouth began to twitch in sympathy so that one had the distinct impression that Boyer was in the grip of some form of palpitation or spasm that would bring him, in a matter of seconds, to a point of prostration. David stood up and made a single step towards the edge of the rostrum but at once a forest of hands shot up and reassuring advice was shouted at him from all directions.

"It's all right, sir!"

"Don't worry, sir!"

"Only one of Boyer's fits, sir . . .!"

"Shall I take him to Matron, sir?" And then, calmly stated above the chorus by Dobson, Boyer's right-hand neighbour, "It happens about once a week, sir! Fresh air always brings him round, sir. Shall I open the window and loosen his collar, sir?"

It was Dobson's unceremonious handling of the boy that alerted him for, as he bent over Boyer to loosen his tie, he overplayed his hand by tightening it. Boyer, choking on the knot, came to for a fleeting second, long enough to push his outstretched hand into Dobson's face with such force that Dobson reeled across the aisle until stopped by the water pipes. At the same time concern seemed to ebb from the boys crowding round and some of them began to titter, establishing beyond doubt that Boyer's performance was very much appreciated.

He took a chance then. He had nothing but instinct to tell him that Boyer's seizure was a well-rehearsed trick on the part of the Lower Fourth to relieve the tedium of an hour devoted to De Silva, Walsingham and the Dutch. He roared, at the top of his voice, "*Silence! Places!*" and the command at least had the effect of dispersing the crowd about Boyer's desk, giving him his first real chance to weigh the probabilities. Then Dobson rallied but again, a mere amateur alongside Boyer, he overplayed, saying, in an aggrieved voice, "I was only trying to *help, sir* . . .!" and that did it. Colour returned to Boyer's face and he sat upright, blinking and looking confused, a traveller who has awakened in a train to discover he has passed his station. And in a sense he had for David descending from the rostrum, and moving down the centre aisle, scented victory in the hush that fell in the class as he said, quietly but menacingly, "Stand *up*, Boyer! You too, Dobson!", and both boys raised themselves, looking, David thought, surprised and vaguely apprehensive. He said, in the same level tone, "*Quite* a performance! But it needs working on, Boyer! You're not bad but your partner is a terrible ham," and the astonished laugh, heavier and more sustained than the obligatory response to a master's quip, set the seal on his triumph. He paused then, savouring it and wondering if either Boyer or Dobson would have the nerve to carry the bluff a stage further. When they did not he said, mildly, "It's only fair to warn you I'm familiar with all forms of hysteria. In fact, I'm an expert, having spent the last seven months in shell-shock wards."

It was well below the belt. He was aware of that but he didn't care. It was a crossroads in his life, and victory was essential. In the uneasy silence that followed he weighed his words carefully, finally opting for a middle course, halfway between outrage and appeal, but choosing irony as the weapon best suited to the occasion.

"Well, now," he said, "Boyer being happily restored to full health, suppose I begin by being frank? This is my second day here but I'll add to that. It's also my second day in the teaching profession — teaching in school, that is, for I've been engaged, among other things, in teaching recruits how to deal with the Opposition. Think about that, because the Opposition, from here on, is *you*. Right, sit down, both of you, and let's have a show of hands. How many of you were in on Boyer's little relapse?"

Four hands were raised. Then eight and finally two more, near the front. Their readiness to admit complicity touched him. He said, easily, "Well, that's honest at all events. Boyer took the risks alone, so I don't really see why he should be expected to carry all the bacon home. Everyone concerned, including Boyer and his male nurse, can copy out the chapter we were doing and bring it to me at morning break tomorrow. You deserve far worse, of course, but they tell me every dog is allowed one bite."

The murmur told him all he wanted to know but Boyer still had a surprise for him. He stood up again, red in the face but resolute. "My . . . er . . . apologies, sir . . . It was only . . . a . . . well . . . sir . . . a . . ."

"A tryout?"

"Well, yes, sir. None of us knew, sir. About the hospital, I mean."

"No reason why you should." He lowered himself on the edge of the desk for a moment. At any minute he knew that his hands would begin to shake and the prospect terrified him. He said, carefully, "You've no exams this term, have you?" and Youings, a studious-looking boy in the front row, said, "No, sir, not this term," and made it sound as if he regretted it.

"Has anyone here ever tried teaching you more up-to-date history? The basic causes of the present war, for instance?"

"A little, sir," from Youings, who continued, "Germany's commercial jealousy, and need for overseas markets, sir?" but then, to his surprise, Dobson's hand shot up and he said, in response to a nod, "Kaiser Bill's trying to rule the world, isn't he, sir?"

"According to the *Daily Mail* he is. Any other ideas?"

In their collective concentration he sensed a desperate eagerness to appease. Letherett, a red-headed boy, reminded the class of the assassination of the Austrian Archduke at Sarajevo. Gibson seemed to think it was all a bid on the part of Germany for naval supremacy. Hoxton was more subtle, stating categorically that Germany had gone to war in the belief that Britain would stand aside and let her occupy France. They were still having their say when the bell went and they seemed genuinely interested in his assessments of their answers. He said, by way of valediction, "We'll continue the inquest on Friday if my reading of the time-table is correct. Class dismissed," and he gathered up his books and left without a backward glance.

* * *

It was different again with the Classical Fifth but perhaps not so different from his point of view, for here again he deliberately pushed himself out on a limb.

The Classical Fifth were beyond the skylarking stage. Some of them, a sizeable minority he would say, were genuinely interested in the subject, and he was luckier here, for they were preparing for summer exam questions on the late nineteenth century, as far as the death of Queen Victoria.

It was easy to introduce them to the same theme, and be sure of their attention. He took the same line, stating the basic causes of the war and inviting questions. Foster Major's question gave him his cue; Foster Major, six feet tall, and already sprouting golden hairs on his upper lip. He asked, eagerly, "How much longer will it take us to beat the Hun, sir?"

"We can't beat him now, Foster!"

The murmur that greeted this heresy dismayed him so he added, quickly, "Not in the real sense, not in the way we might have done if the Gallipoli show had been a success." He waited for that to sink in, then said, "Now we've no alternative but to crush him and don't fool yourselves into believing that that is a final answer. It'll buy us time but that's about all. Jerry is bled white, but then, so are we. I don't know what you fellows think of the Americans but I'll tell you what the chaps think of them over there. Our one chance of avoiding a stalemate."

They digested this. He could sense incredulity doing battle with other, less complicated reactions. Indignation, possibly, something that ran counter to everything they had been told over the years by men fighting the war from Fleet Street. Finally Gosse, a languid, smartly dressed boy, whose heavy horn-rimmed spectacles gave him a slightly aesthetic look, raised his hand. "Are you saying, sir, that we couldn't beat the Hun without the Yanks—without the Americans, sir?"

"I'm saying it would take us another two to three years, and that's only another way of saying there wouldn't be a victory. The object of war, as the men over there see it, is to preserve our way of life. That's what they've been told and that's what they believe, those of them that still believe in anything except each other. In three years there would be nothing worth preserving. One other thing, Gosse. Over there nobody uses the term 'Hun' any more. I stopped using it at a place called St. Quentin. Two Germans carried me in a blanket across four hundred yards of open ground under a box barrage. If they hadn't I wouldn't be here arguing the toss with you."

But Gosse, a diehard if ever there was one, stuck to his point.

"I take it they were prisoners, sir?"

"Yes, they were. But shell-splinters aren't particular where they find a billet. They risked their lives to save mine."

"But in 1914 they burned Louvain, sir."

"Yes, they did. But I like to think they've learned since then. We've all learned something, or should have. If we haven't, getting on for a hundred chaps who occupied those desks of yours a few years ago died in a circus, not a war."

He hadn't meant to say as much as this but later he was glad. For two reasons, separated by a few hours. In the first place, when the bell sounded marking the end of morning classes, they crowded round him, asking all kinds of questions, a few baffled and even hostile, but every one of them prompted by a burning curiosity. Then, as dusk was setting in, and he was closeted in what Herries called Mount Olympus—the ground-floor lavatory in the head's house with its opaque window opening on to the covered part of the quad—he overheard Gosse and two other Fifth Formers discussing him. Dispassionately, as though they already accepted him as a queer fish. He made haste to get out then but before he could escape he heard one boy say, "All *right*, he's a Bolshie. But what he says makes sense to me, Starchy!"

He was getting to grips with the Bamfylde obsession for nicknames. There were two Gosse boys at the school. The elder, a beefy extrovert, was called 'Archibald', so it followed that he should be labelled 'Archy' and his elegant brother 'Starchy'. Starchy Gosse was a pedant but fair-minded, it seemed, for he said, mildly, "It depends on how long he's been out there," and the third boy asked, "Why Starchy?"

"They say it gets a man down in the end. That chap talks just like my Uncle Edward. He was invalided out two years ago, but my governor has stopped inviting him over. Seems to think he's . . . well, almost pro-Hun . . . pro-Jerry. I don't think he is. I mean, how the hell could he be, with one eye and one leg gone?"

David was sweating when he reached the stairs but in the privacy of his rooftop room, lent to him until he took up his quarters in Havelock's House at the start of the summer term, he found he was able to take a more encouraging view of the conversation. At least Gosse had begun to think out-side his prejudices. And at least doubt had begun to cloud the Classical Fifth's conventional picture of the war, as drawn for them by Northcliffe and Bottomley. And also, as a bonus, Starchy had corrected himself when using the word 'Hun'. Did it matter a damn if they thought of him as a Bolshie?

*   *   *

The Sixth Forms had to be handled very differently. In a way he equated them with the very youngest boys in the school, for they were exceptionally vulnerable at seventeen-plus. If the war dragged on for a few months, some of them would be out there and they were all too aware of it. The Rupert Brooke approach—'Breast expanding to the ball'—spent itself long ago, and disillusionment was general among all but the fanatics and armchair strategists. Sometimes it seemed to him that the foul blight had already touched these youngsters, so that he saw them stripped of their high spirits, leading some forlorn attack on a German sector, defended by heavy machine-guns and belching mortar fire. They pressed him shyly for technical details, extensions of questions posed in the drill books of the Officers' Training Corps that paraded twice a week in the plantation and on the hillsides beyond. He humoured them, feeling his age here more than in any other part of the school. The gap between him and the eldest of them was no more than four years but it might have been fifty.

And then, towards the end of term, a week or two after Ludendorff's shattering breakthrough on Gough's Fifth Army front, with the appalling prospect of Paris falling, and the British being flung back on the Channel ports, there was another incident that left its mark on him yet encouraged him to see his presence here as something of real value.

Algy Herries told him at breakfast that young Briarley's father, a captain in the Rifle Brigade, had been killed on the Lys, and the boy had been told the news by Ellie, who usually took it upon herself to perform these melancholy chores. "The poor little toad is sunning himself out front now," Herries said, "Suppose you go and have a chat with him?"

"What could I say that Mrs. Herries hasn't already said?" David asked, and Herries said, airily, "Oh, I don't know . . . something about all the chaps who have gone on ahead, maybe. And perhaps what it's all in aid of," and at this David guessed Herries had heard, through the Bamfylde grapevine, of his 'Bolshie' chats with the Fourth and Fifth Forms, but was giving no clue as to whether he approved or disapproved.

He went out into the forecourt where Briarley sat on a seat under the huge cedar that spread itself across the head-master's lawn. The boy looked stunned but more or less in control of himself. He sat very still, his hands on his knees, staring down across a field of rough pasture, part of which had been dug over for potatoes. Beyond the violet skyline granite outcrops of the Exmoor plateau winked and glistened in the pale sunshine, but nothing moved out there. The spring landscape looked as lonely and desolate as Briarley.

He sat down beside the boy, saying nothing for a moment, but then he saw Briarley's lip quiver and lifted his arm, resting it gently on the boy's shoulder. He said, at length, "Was he a professional, Briarley?" and when Briarley nodded, "We couldn't have held out this long without them, lad. They taught us everything we knew in the early days," and then, when the boy made no reply, "Do you care to tell me about him? I've served in the Lys sector twice. Maybe we met, spoke to one another."

He could not be sure whether his presence brought any real comfort but it must have eased Briarley's inner tensions to some extent for presently he said, "I didn't see a great deal of him, sir. When I was a kid he was mostly in India or Ireland. He came here once, on leave. Last autumn, it was. We . . . we sat here for a bit, waiting for the school boneshaker to take him to the station."

"Did he talk about the war, Briarley?"

"No, sir, not really. He only . . ."

"Well?"

"He said if anything did happen, and he was crocked and laid up for a time, I was to be sure and do all I could to look after the mater while he was away."

"Are you an only child, Briarley?"

"No, sir. I'm the only boy. I've got three sisters, one older, the others just kids."

"Well, then, you've got a job ahead of you. Your mother is going to need you badly. That's something to keep in mind, isn't it?"

"Yes, sir. I suppose so, but . . ."

He began to cry silently and with a curious dignity, so that David automatically tightened his grip on the slight shoulders. There was no point in saying anything more. They sat there for what seemed to David a long time and then, with a gulp or two, Briarley got up, "I'd better start packing, sir. Algy . . . I mean the headmaster said I was to go home today, ahead of the others. Matron's getting my trunk down from the covered playground . . ." And then, in what David thought of as an oddly impersonal tone, "The telegram said 'Killed in action', sir. What exactly—well, does that always mean what it says?"

"If it hadn't been that way it would have said 'Died of wounds', and there's a difference."

"Thank you, sir." He was a plucky kid and had himself in hand again. He nodded briefly and walked back towards the head's house. David would have liked to have followed him, letting himself be caught up in the swirl of end-of-term junketings, but he could not trust himself to move. His hands were shaking again and his head was tormented by the persistent buzzing that always seemed to assail him these days in moments of stress. He said, explosively, "God damn everybody! Where's the sense in it . . . ? Where's the bloody sense, for Christ's sake?" And then, like Briarley, he was granted the relief of tears.

II

There were plenty of moments during that period of initiation when he was able, to his own surprise, to put the war out of mind and find handholds that promised hope of a climb back to objectivity. Occasionally it was in class, when he was interested in some particular aspect of the syllabus, but more often it was in the common room, rubbing shoulders with the assortment of eccentrics that the arch-eccentric Herries had assembled round him to tide him through the war.

They were not a very likeable bunch but one had, David assumed, to make allowances. The older men were petrified in the Victorian mould, some of them so deeply rutted that they appeared to regard the war as a tedious and irrelevant interruption to their careers or well-earned retirement. Of the younger bunch, the C.3 men were almost pitiable, feeling themselves terribly handicapped as civilians in authority over four hundred boys, almost all of whom had fathers, brothers and uncles at the front. There was one among this latter group who was teetering on the edge of a nervous breakdown, Meredith, a twenty-five-year-old diabetic, with a sallow complexion and huge defenceless eyes. Meredith's classes, David learned, usually ended in a riot, and he was said to stand on the rostrum and let the tide of ribaldry sweep over him, bleating, "I *say* there . . . I *say*, you fellows . . .!" Beyond that he would make no protest. Meredith had a curious sideways-sloping gait, moving over the ground with long strides, one shoulder raised an inch higher than the other. The boys had taken to mimicking him and some of them did it rather well, occasionally, it was alleged, lurching up to the blackboard in his actual presence and taking over, while Meredith stood helplessly, whimpering, "I *say* . . . I *say*, you fellows . . .!" Herries had done what he could to help and even advised Meredith to take a cane into class, but when the poor devil followed this advice even worse chaos resulted. Boyer and his ilk, pretending to be terrified of Meredith's ineffectual swipes, fled in all directions. When cornered they fell on their knees, shrieking for mercy.

The older masters showed no sympathy at all with the poor chap and frequently complained of the uproar resulting from his classes. Carter, the only younger master apart from David who had been in uniform, was the most persistent common-room nag, and David soon conceived an intense dislike for the man, whose conceit amounted to arrogance.

Carter was a stocky, rather florid man, with smooth red hair that he kept oiled so that it gleamed like wet rust. He had a long inquisitive nose, rimless glasses and no eyelashes to speak of. On the strength of six months' service as a Territorial officer, at a camp in Northumberland, he claimed David as a war comrade, explaining in great detail how a knee injury, received in a prewar football game, had been responsible for his discharge in 1915.

"Let me down with a bump, old man," he said, during one of his interminable reminiscences, that made David think of himself as a newly joined officer buttonholed by a patronising major. "Damn thing gave out the week my draft was due to leave for France. Most of them went west at Loos, of course. Damned awful show, Loos. Badly bungled, I gather."

David murmured that it was, and that he had seen some fighting in the area, but Carter was not interested in positive experience, preferring to talk of his triumphs on the drill ground outside Newcastle in the early days of Kitchener's army. He was still very much the martinet, with a small army of his own, the school O.T.C., and was extremely put out when David politely refused to join the Corps.

"Damn it, why not, old man? We could use a chap like you, someone with trench experience. I daresay you could teach us a few wrinkles if you cared to, and the top brass regard the O.T.C. as the nursery of subalterns, don't they?"

"If they do then God help the lot of us," said David, the Welsh lilt edging back into his voice as it often did under stress. "The average life of those kids out there is three weeks. Good God, man, they don't even have time to learn when to duck!" and at once regretted his testiness. He need not have bothered. Carter was exceptionally thick-skinned and said blandly, "Well, that's war, old chap. Can't win a war without losing a few. However, I'll not take no for an answer. The head tells me you're still convalescent. We'll talk about it again later, eh?"

He drifted off, unaware that the convalescent was having the greatest difficulty in restraining himself from committing assault upon his person, but the moment he was out of ear-shot Howarth, the senior English master, said, "Ignore the poopstick. Most of us do, whenever we can," and he at once felt cheered, for he was by no means sure, at this stage, whether Herries would expect him to take part in O.T.C. activities. He said, cautiously, "Is that true about his knee?" and Howarth, reluctantly laying aside his *Times*, said that everybody at Bamfylde took that knee on trust, as the medical board must have done, Carter being but thirty-one years old. He added, however, "The devil of it is it gives him the edge on all the civilians about here and being Carter he makes the utmost of it. Maybe somebody was lucky he was crocked on the football field. Shouldn't care to have him lead me into action, would you?"

"No, by God, I wouldn't," David said, and at once saw the testy, taciturn Howarth in a new light. Up to then he had been very wary of the man, a notable disciplinarian, with the reputation for possessing a bitter tongue. No one at Bamfylde, save Herries himself, had escaped Howarth's sarcasm, but he was recognised as a first-class teacher who had the respect, if not the affection, of the boys, even the wild ones in the Lower Fourth. When the other masters had drawn their dishwater coffee from the tarnished urn and moved off, David said, "You've been here a good many years, Mr. Howarth. How would you say it compares with other schools, schools of the same standing?" and Howarth said, for once without irony, "I can tell you that. It compares extremely well under Herries. It'll never be a Harrow, a Clifton or a Rugby. That chance passed us by when our numbers dropped in Bull's day. But I think of it as a first-class second-rater. Or could be, when the wartime chaff is blown away, and the Governors spend some money on the fabric." He seemed to reflect a moment. "I stayed when I might have moved on and I've had my chances, especially in the last few years, when my age group has had it all their own way. But if you asked me why I don't think I could give you a specific answer. Maybe it's because I like and respect Herries. He's an original."

"You don't look for originality in this profession, do you?"

"You do here," Howarth said shortly, and abruptly terminated the conversation by picking up his *Times*, leaving David with the impression that Howarth was someone on whom it might be wiser to reserve judgment. He was right about Bamfylde as regards originality, however, as David soon discovered when he became better acquainted with the older men on the staff.

There was Cordwainer. There was Acton. And there was Gibbs, respectively known as 'Judy', 'Bouncer' and 'Rapper'. The Sixth called the trio 'The Magi', for each, in his different way, was a man of distinction. Judy Cordwainer taught geography as his main subject, and elementary mathematics to the juniors, but he did many other things. He played the organ at Stonecross Church, where the school worshipped on Sundays, marked out the cricket and football pitches with fanatical precision, presided over the school stationery cupboard and even taught woodwork. Judy came of the generation of school-teachers who practised before the age of specialisation and could turn hand and brain to anything once he was persuaded Bamfylde had need of his services. A tall, austere man, with cadaverous features, he was without a sense of humour, but his unswerving loyalty to boys and colleagues more than made up for this and, over the years, he had acquired a gratuitous popularity. Wags were fond of explaining how he came by his nickname, back in the nineties, when he had been housemaster of Outram's, a post he had relinquished in favour of Carter on his official retirement. It appeared that Outram's was cock-house that particular year and were expected to win the house cup for rugby, but their final game against Havelock's showed a lamentable lack of form. Cordwainer, disgusted by their poor performance, trotted up and down the touchline shouting encouragement to their rivals, who finally won both match and trophy. Cordwainer's own fifteen were so outraged by this treachery that they styled him Judas, softened, over the years, to Judy.

A standard entertainment at Bamfylde was to crowd round the stationery cupboard in the Remove in order to witness Judy issue replacements. He would refuse to renew an exercise book unless he was satisfied that every page of an old one was covered with scrawl, and would sharpen an inch of pencil and uncross Waverley nibs when boys presented evidence of spent equipment. He had a high-pitched, honking voice, and despite his age could still subdue a classroom, hurling a huge bunch of keys at inattentive pupils and sometimes hitting the hot water pipes in a way that sent an echoing clang through all the classrooms of Lower School. He had a passion for neatness and precision. Later on David saw him award marks to Third Formers with wrong answers, rejecting correctly answered exercises that were decorated with blots. Cordwainer saw Bamfylde as a kind of rural Athens, and probably thought of it as the centre of the cultural universe. Being as bald as a tonsured monk (and looking like one in his voluminous gown) he would wear his tweed cap in class on cold mornings and stand honking there, a perfect prototype of the old-style dominee, whose methods were unchanged since he came down from Cambridge in the early seventies. Indeed, a parody of Judy Cordwainer, one of the standard turns among the juniors who could exactly reproduce his honking voice, usually began with one or other of his favourite precepts—"I'll have *method* before speed, d'ye hear?" or "Oh . . . *prince* of fools! Take it away, slovenly numbskull!"

By contrast, Bouncer Acton was a hearty, excessively

amiable man, an ordained priest who ministered to a small parish north of the school, where he occupied a rectory used as a spill-over for new boys. Everyone liked Bouncer, who taught divinity throughout the school, and Latin to the juniors, but everyone took shameless advantage of his slight deafness and near-sightedness, and the fact that he preferred to look over rather than through the steel-rimmed spectacles perched on his pudgy little nose. It was said that Bouncer had donned those useless spectacles while taking part in a charade as a boy, and had subsequently forgotten them, leaving them perched there even when he went to bed. The bolder boys were fond of asking Bouncer earnestly phrased questions, concerning passages in the Bible relating to Lot's incest, circumcision, concubines, how much the elders saw of Susannah, and the Virgin birth, but he would always answer straightforwardly, seldom suspecting he was being hoaxed. On occasion, however, he could be savage. His standard punishment, for the few misdemeanours he detected, was a volley of four penal marks and this meant one hour's drill on Saturdays. As four was the limit allowed, and any penal marks in excess earned the delinquent a thrashing, this had the effect of keeping skylarkers in purdah for the remainder of the week. The wags were equally expert at mimicking Bouncer, who had pendulous cheeks that quivered when he bobbed up and down, the trick that had won him his nickname.

Rapper Gibbs was different again, a wizened insignificant-looking man, who taught music and accompanied the popular choral and operatic societies that Herries had founded on becoming headmaster. Rapper's soubriquet stemmed from the short pointer he used on the knuckles of blundering amateur pianists, but despite his asperity he was an excellent tutor, and music, David discovered, played a prominent part in the cultural activities of the community.

There were some two dozen masters on the staff in the spring of 1918. Apart from outstanding characters, like Judy, Bouncer, Rapper and the sarcastic, withdrawn Howarth, there were several other oddities, some of whom David did not get to know until the following term. Ferguson, for instance, a volcano of a man who taught French, and would never utter a word of English during a class, ignoring boys who addressed him in their own tongue. His habit of prancing up and down the classroom, using his gown like a sail, had earned him the nickname of 'Bat'; Barnaby was an amiable, erudite man who taught Latin in Senior School, and was said to be inordinately fond of porridge, even the glutinous concoction ladled out in Hall every morning throughout the school year. There was the motherly Mrs. Parminter, who presided over the Second Form, and was so formidably corseted that her substantial bust projected like the flying buttress of a Gothic town hall. She was known, on this account, as 'Ma Fender', but the smaller boys, particularly those newly removed from home, were glad of her comfort and sympathy. There was only one other woman on the staff, Mrs Gorman, the elderly Matron, who was inflexible and matter-of-fact with patients and malingerers alike. No one had coined a nickname for her until a returning Old Boy, happening to seek her out for relief of some minor ailment, emerged with a slip of paper marked 'M & D', that meant, so he told his audience, 'Medicine and Duty', thus establishing a legend that Mrs. Gorman had served in the R.A.M.C. in the Boer War. After that the boys referred to her as 'Kruger'.

They were, David decided, a very colourful lot, but apart from Herries himself he was unable, during those first weeks, to strike up a friendship with any one of them. It was as though he had joined a band of castaways on a desert island, the lone survivor of a subsequent wreck, and at first he was inclined to view his isolation as the inevitable result of his own mental confusion. In the end he took his problem to Herries.

"In a sense you *are* an outsider, my dear chap," he said, "and that's the reason I grabbed you the moment you showed up. You're the bridge, don't you see? A passage over a generation gap, and it isn't the conventional generation gap we all have to cross if we know our business properly. Your gap, caused by the war, is semi-permanent. It might take twenty years to close."

"But some of the chaps on the staff are only a year or so older than I am," David argued. "There's the C.3 men, and Carter."

"It's not a matter of years, but of experience, don't you see? What are our casualties to date? Not far short of three million, I'd say, and a third of them dead at eighteen-plus. No one who hasn't been out can imagine what it's like. Mentally a man like you must have aged about a year every month, and that makes you immeasurably senior to theorists like me, and faithful old buffers like Cordwainer, Acton and Gibbs. *Someone* has to tackle the job of nudging all those young rascals over the threshold into what I sincerely hope will be an entirely new world. *We* can't do it because we're even more adrift than they are and haven't a compass reading between us. In a year or so I daresay we can find you some help. Hang it all, everyone in his early twenties can't be dead or maimed or gassed. In the meantime you're on your own, lad."

He thought about this during his long tramps across the moors and his moochings around the silent and deserted buildings during the Easter holidays, when most of the staff and all the boys were gone save a dozen who lived in the head's house while their parents were abroad. It was a sombre thought but it represented the challenge that he, and Herries, and the Osborne neurologist thought of as therapy, and with the slow return of vitality, and a surer grip on his nerves, he began to respond to it in a way that revived his self-confidence.

The news from the front was bad but his infantryman's eye had taught him to read between the lines of press reports so that, alone among everyone he met in this backwater, he was able to assess the problems of the German vanguard, who had far outrun their supplies in the surging advance that began on March 21st. Right now they were crossing the old battlefields of fifteen, 'sixteen and 'seventeen, devastated country where the difficulties of the victors would be more formidable than those of divisions falling back on base areas. Eventually, he supposed, there would be a counter-attack, spearheaded by the Americans, so that on the whole he was optimistic of the eventual outcome.

By the last day of April, when the school reassembled, he was scanning the newspapers for signs of a large-scale holding operation and found his opinion eagerly solicited by boys whose fathers and brothers had been caught up in the spring débâcle.

"Will the Yanks attack, sir?"

"Is our own show under way, sir?"

"Do you suppose Jerry has shot his bolt, sir?"

It was curious, he thought, that even the fourteen-year-olds were more instinctively aware of what was at stake out there than men thirty, forty or even fifty years their senior. In a way, in a perverse way, it might even be hopeful.

CHAPTER THREE

I

He was finding his way about, familiarising himself with the great, sprawling barn of a place that straggled halfway up the rise behind the grey-stone buildings of the original Bamfylde, built of imported materials that always seemed at odds with the honey-coloured local stone used for the extensions.

There were really two schools here, the tall squarish pile that reared itself four sides of the quad (and even after seventy years of Exmoor weathering, still looked like a baroque folly) and the utilitarian additions added over the years, that had already adapted themselves to the green-brown hillside, a straggle of farm buildings, and unfenced pastures bounded by the sports fields in the south and west, and plantation windbreak to the east, and the crest of the moor to the north. Herries and Howarth were right about the decaying fabric. It had needed extensive renovation long before the war began. Now it was beginning to look seedy, scarred and very shabby.

Most of the classrooms, together with Big School, and the headmaster's house that occupied the whole of the south side of the quad, were housed in the older block. Big Hall, the kitchens and all but one of the dormitories, were in the newer block. Long, stone-flagged passages connected these quarters with the quad. Branching from it, one floor up, was a wainscoted passage known as the Rogues' Gallery. Here, in a sombre row, hung portraits of Bamfylde's five headmasters, including a younger, cherubic-looking Herries. Opposite them, posed in wide-eyed, dutiful groups, were football and cricket teams, reaching back to the earliest days of the school when nobody wore special clothing for games and everyone played cricket and football in workaday boots and shirt-sleeves. There was a veritable warren of music rooms, laundry rooms, a boothole and a stray classroom or two about here, together with a school museum and, on the floor above, a range of attics used as storerooms. There was also a garret where, once a fortnight, the barber from Challacombe, the nearest market town, plied his clippers. One of Algy Herries' aversions was overlong hair and the boys, from the Fifth downwards, were shorn at frequent intervals. For a day or so after the appearance of Bastin, the barber, known and reviled as 'Sweeney' by the boys, everyone on the premises (the Sixth had won an exemption charter) went about with a whitish skull and Bastin was seen to drive away with a sack of clippings. The boys swore that he used them to make hairshirts that he sold to monks, but David later discovered that a condition of his contract was to dispose of his debris after a mass haircut, the school being desperately short of domestic staff.

Apart from the headmaster's house, which was spacious and comfortably furnished, and some of the quarters occupied by living-in masters, the premises were bleak and daunting to a newcomer. When he left the temporary refuge of the O.B.A. President's room, David was given a sitting-room and tiny bedroom in Havelock's House, ruled by Ferguson, the French master. Mrs. Ferguson was a French-woman and reminded David of the black-draped madames he had seen counting their takings in estaminets behind the lines. The Fergusons were a staid, methodical couple, who left him to his own devices in his limited free time, and he grew to like his little sitting-room that looked south over a stretch of moor dotted with birchwoods and the rhodo-dendron forest he had noted on his first walk from the station.

The aspect of the moor changed dramatically during his

first few weeks up here. When he had arrived, in early March, the countryside had a wind-swept, breathless look, as though its hardihood had been taxed to the limit by winter gales and frosts, but even before the summer term opened, spring had enlarged its hold. All the beeches and elms in the two drives began to sprout new leaves, a sheen of bright green varying the mottled pattern of gold and russet, and a rash of primroses appeared in the breast-high banks, relieved every few yards by great plumes of cow-parsley and a scatter of scarlet campion. Soon, in the folds under the copses, where the little river Brent ran to join the Bray or the Barle (it seemed undecided which) acres of bluebells dusted the margins, like early morning mist masking the shallow valley. The sky patterns changed minute by minute, now streaked and dappled with bluish trailers, now a jumble of plumped-up pillows, gashed by gusts of wind that came soughing down from the upper moor. This high land stretched away into the far distance, a series of brown and grey ridges, broken here and there by the blur of woods where pockets of ash, sycamore, thorn and elderberry had found some kind of refuge from the north-easterlies and south-westerlies that Herries said took turn and turn about from October to May.

The air and its landscape improved his health, soothing his ragged nerves and inducing a state of suspended dreaminess when he was not occupied in class, or with games, or dormitory supervision. Slowly, week by week, the Western Front began to recede, an old wound he was learning to live with, and sometimes the war seemed so remote that it might have been fought by Wellington or Marlborough. He was helped in this by his growing rapport with the boys.

He had his favourites or, if not favourites, then his star-performers, whom he saw as he had once seen the section leaders of his platoon. There was a star-performer in every group and round him were gathered his acolytes. The mystique of leadership was as obvious here as in the trenches and he found he could soon spot the rankers marked down for a stripe. Boyer, of the Lower Fourth, was such a one, with Dobson as his runner-up. Blades, in the Upper Third, was another, a handsome boy who took the leadership of his group for granted and was said by Howarth to have an original mind. "Might even write some good verse when he matures," Howarth said, and then, as though unwilling to forgo the characteristic touch of acidity, "Poor devil!" Below Blades, in the Remove, was Bickford, a lumbering fourteen-year-old, lazy as a mastiff in the sun and attended, wherever he went, by his two henchmen, Ribby, a farmer's son, and Ford, whose father was said to be a bookmaker. Bickford, although indolent, was a bit of a bully, much feared by the urchins of the Lower Third and Second Form, over whom he held sway, a slothful, medieval despot, who could be mollified by tribute or subservience. The sort of boy, David thought, who needed watching, although his grin was infectious and he could sometimes exhibit a certain inventiveness. David discovered this one day when Bickford made use of a warped floorboard to set the stationery cupboard rocking without apparent agency, declaring that the manifestation was proof of the existence of the Remove ghost, a failed master of Bull's era who had, so the story ran, swallowed salts of lemon and been buried in Stonecross churchyard with a suicide's gravestone placed at a different angle from all the other monuments.

He grew to like some of the older boys in the Sixth, most of whom would be leaving to join one or other of the Services at the end of summer term. Cooper, Fosdyke and Scrubbs-Norton were typical of this cadre, boys who had come to Bamfylde in the last year of peace, and were now prefects and far better at keeping order than some of the younger masters. Their eagerness to get into uniform touched David as nothing else was able to. He already saw them in their Sam Brownes and British warms, seeking an opportunity to prove themselves as men, and while he was often tempted to introduce them to the stark realities out there, he never did. It would have been like telling five-year-olds that Father Christmas was a myth. He did get as far as accepting their shy invitations to take cocoa with them in their studies after prep, and would sit there discussing the war news with them, news that came to Bamfylde a day late in a bundle of papers from Challacombe. Luckily it was getting progressively more cheerful, with the successful British counter-attack at Villers Bretonneux, a unified Allied command and, in the first days of July, the beginning of the Le Hamel offensive. Farther south, in the Chemin des Dames area, the French were still taking a hammering and there were some spectacular German advances but these, David assured them, would soon peter out, as all offensives did in the nonstop slogging match. More and more Americans were landing in France, and the general pattern of the summer fighting was becoming clearer every day. "I think Ludendorff may have shot his bolt by the time you get back here in September," he said, cautiously, but then Cooper reminded him that most of the Sixth would not be returning for the autumn term, and all he could do was offer up a prayer that somehow these babies would be kept in training bases until the promised all-fronts counter-attack was launched.

The climax came, for David Powlett-Jones, on the eleventh day of August, just before he set off on his belated visit to his mother at Pontnewydd. Screaming headlines announced the breaching of the Hindenburg Line and unheard-of advances by the British in most of their sectors, places where, only a year ago, the gain of a few hundred yards of quagmire was won at the cost of a hundred thousand casualties.

He took Northcliffe's journal up to Herries' thinking post

and read it very carefully, his heart-beats quickening when he came upon the familiar name of some devastated village where no building was more than a foot high, and the soil was rich with the bones of the dead of earlier battles. There could be no doubt about it now, surely? Cooper, Fosdyke and Scrubbs-Norton were reprieved. They would take their place in some office or factory, or perhaps spend a pleasant spell at one of the universities, after which, no doubt, they would marry some fluffy girl and have children of their own, earmarked for Bamfylde if they were boys.

He toyed with the fancy for a spell, visualising a subdued thirteen-year-old young Cooper, or a young Fosdyke, who would be coming here halfway through the nineteen-thirties, and the prospect must have caused him to smile, for suddenly he heard Herries' chirpy voice say, "Good news, P.J.? My stars, it would have to be to fool me! I've been inflated and deflated so many times by that rag that I've stopped reading it, apart from casualty lists."

David said, "It's real enough this time. We've broken the Hindenburg Line. I'd stopped believing that was possible. It'll be open warfare from here on and that's something positive."

"Was that worth grinning at?"

"In a way, sir." He could always talk uninhibitedly to Herries. "As a matter of fact, I was smiling at the prospect of Cooper's boy sitting under Mrs. Parminter in the Second in a dozen years or so," and he smiled again when Herries' tufted eyebrows shot up. "Pure speculation on my part, I'm afraid. What I mean is, the chances are that Cooper will live long enough to marry and have children. If he does he'd want to send his boys here, wouldn't he?"

"They all do," Herries said. "Without them we should wither, I'm afraid." He sat down on the shaft of the horse-roller, parked up here in obedience to his decree every time the roller-gangs finished a stint on the cricket pitch. "Haven't seen so much of you lately. Settling in?"

"I think so, sir. What do you think?"

"You'll do. You've frightened one or two of the old stagers, I'm told. Oh, don't let that bother you. It never did me. If you can't smuggle your own convictions into the curriculum you might as well go away somewhere, dig a hole and live in it." He lit his short pipe and puffed contentedly for a while. Then, cocking one eyebrow, "How do *we* look to you?"

"I've been very happy here, sir."

"I didn't mean that. How do we seem to be trundling along to someone from outside?"

David hesitated. It seemed a propitious time to make a point he was very eager to make.

"I can only answer that from an academic standpoint, Headmaster."

"Go ahead."

"It's the text-books I've inherited. Most of them were printed about the time of Victoria's first Jubilee. How much say does an unqualified man get in the choice of texts?"

"Depends on the man. You? I wouldn't pull on the bit unless I thought you were rushing your fences. You're a bit inclined to. Not that that's unusual in a chap your age. What kind of history were you taught as a boy?"

"Strings of dates and battles. The Treaty of Troyes and the War of Jenkins' Ear."

"Ah, that fellow Jenkins. I always thought that was a bit of liberty, passing his ear around Parliament like the plate at church. Still, it worked. They had their war, didn't they?"

It was always difficult to decide whether or not there was a coded message in Herries' puckish good-humoured talk and this time David decided to put it to the test. "I think we should have different text-books for different ages," he said.

"The subject needs to be introduced with colour—Alfred's cakes, Bruce's spider and so on, but it ought to progress from there without getting dull."

"What's your prescription?"

"To catch the interest in Lower School with the legends, move on to a more solid diet in Middle School, and then use half the periods for free discussion in the Fifth and Sixth. Especially the Fifth, when they're coming up to School Certificate and Matric. Discussion promotes original thought, doesn't it? And I believe most examiners like originality, even when it reads like heresy."

"Something in that. Maybe you'd like to work out a syllabus for next term. After all, you'll have more latitude then. I'll get someone else to take the Lower School in English. It won't be Howarth, of course. He likes his subject too much to reach down. Maybe one of the new chaps, there are a couple coming. Why the frown, P.J.?"

"If it's all the same to you, sir, I'd like to continue English with the Second and Third. I know I'll have to start reading for my own degree, but I can manage. The fact is . . . well, it might sound absurd, but those extra periods have helped. Helped me, I mean. In rediscovering Gray, Cowper, Tennyson and Goldsmith, and those excerpts from some of my old favourites, like *Silas Marner* and *Westward Ho!*. The mugging up enabled me to get things into a better focus."

"Well," Herries said slowly, "that sounds encouraging. If Gray's 'Elegy' still has relevance to you after all you experienced out there, then the sooner the young come to it the better." He relit his pipe and over the flaring match David saw he was smiling. He went on, "The jungle drum tells me you occasionally feed them something more up-to-date than Mr. Gray. Is it true you read the Sixth a poem by that chap Sassoon?"

"Yes, it's true. They're going out there, some of them. It

seemed to me that someone ought to do something to counter-act all the rubbish these chaps print," and he indicated the newspaper he had laid aside.

"What was it, exactly?"

"It was a poem called 'Memorial Tablet', that Sassoon published this year. I've got a copy of his later poems. Some of them are strong stuff but they have more relevance to what's actually occurring in Flanders than all the leading articles I've read on the war. I . . . er . . . I could lend you a copy, Headmaster."

"I'd be obliged," Herries said, without irony. "I like to keep up to date. Well, then, my compliments to your mother, and we'll expect you back a day or so before term begins."

"Yes, sir. Thank you."

They got up by mutual consent and went down the slope towards the nearest of the outbuildings, but when they drew level with the fives court Herries said, "I suppose you're aware of your nickname by now?" and David, suspecting it would be 'Bolshie', said he had certain suspicions but had thought it best not to pursue them.

"Oh, it's an amiable one," Herries said, "not like some of them. It stems from your . . . consultative methods in class." He stopped, taking his pipe from his mouth and extending his hand. "Well, goodbye, 'Pow-wow'. Have a good holiday!" and he wandered off towards the piggeries. David remained standing by the fives court for a moment, thinking, "I've had my share of luck, God knows, but running across him beats anything that happened to me."

He had a curious afterthought then, concerned with a squat, bowlegged, round-shouldered man, who had died underground in the summer of 1913, a man who, even then, had had unwavering faith in him and had never been dif-fident about showing it. It was as though his father, feeling the darkness pressing in, had called for help on his behalf, and Herries, walking his rounds on this high plateau, had heard him across the width of the Bristol Channel.

II

Just over a year had passed since he had visited the Valley on leave, a month or so before the Brandenburgers' mortar shell had blasted him out of the war. It seemed narrower and shabbier, a place of steep, huddled streets, fortress-like chapels, rundown corner shops with nothing much to sell, and the familiar tip overshadowing them all. The corporate spirit of the Valley, that had been its sturdiest plant ever since he was a boy, seemed also to have withered, translating itself into bitterness, a different kind of bitterness from that of front-line men, for it lacked the inevitable sardonic humour. There was no jingo stridency here, only a glowering sense of exploitation by politicians, by mine owners, by royalty leeches, by war profiteers. For the vicarious prosperity that had come to other industrial areas seemed to have by-passed the coalfields. No one was encouraged to forsake the industry and enlist, or join in the scramble for high wages in the munitions factories. Instead they were expected, almost compelled, to go on dragging coal from the hillsides at twice the speed and without comparable rises in rates. There was an undertone of militancy and strikes, of demands to put the industry on a new and realistic basis, a war that had little to do with the war of the headlines. He sensed what was happening even before he talked to his brothers-in-law, both miners, and although this world was almost lost to him now, fenced off by an education that none of these men had had, and experiences at the Front they had been spared, he still thought as a miner's son and could identify with their grievances and fear for their future when the need for coal was not so desperate and their bargaining power had been removed.

For the first time he heard men of his own race openly champion the Russian Revolution, and Trotsky's separate peace at Brest-Litovsk, an act that many Welshmen in the line had regarded as a betrayal, but which miners here saw as a portent of enormous social significance. Ewart Griffiths, married to his elder sister Gwynneth, was the first to put this into words when he said, "There's a rumour we're going to be asked to dig coal and help turn the Bolshies out but I'm telling you, man, they'll get no bloody help from us down yer! Time we started our own bloody revolution, Davyboy."

His mother, miraculously, was untouched by bitterness. The tragedies of her life did not show in her round, smooth, unmistakably Welsh face, with its pink and white bloom, still there after sixty years in the valleys, and forty-odd years of making twopence do the work of a shilling. She still kept the little terrace house spotlessly clean, still spoiled her five grandchildren, still cooked an appetising meal from the cheapest ingredients, and glowed when he told her he was now teaching in a school of four hundred boys, a place she would surely think of as a Gentleman's College. To her this was a far greater achievement than surviving three years on the Western Front, scholarship representing maturity, warfare being a little boy's scuffle in the street outside. "Been that proud of you, Dadda would," she said, when he told her his post had been made permanent. "There's a wonder it is! That Dadda should know it all those years ago, and your brothers Hughie and Bryn too, for you were the only real bookworm of the litter. Are they feeding you well down there, boy? You could do with more flesh on your bones, but maybe that's on account of all those hospital slops they gave you when you were hurt in the fighting."

He reassured her as to his health, but as he did so a thought struck him. He said, "God knows, you've earned a rest, Mam. Why don't you pack your things and come back to Devon with me? It's beautiful country down there—like Wales in Grandfather's time—and we could rent half a cottage from old Mrs. Bastin, the wife of our lampman. He's got a splendid garden, chock full of vegetables. You'd like it down there." But she said, sadly, "Nice to be asked it is, Davy, but my place is here, so long as I can give Gwynneth and Megan a hand with the children. Besides . . ." and she glanced through the gap between the freshly-laundered curtains of the tiny kitchen, contemplating a view of her lean-to shed and the uniform backs of the houses in Alma Street, "whatever would I do with myself in a strange place among strange folk? I was born yer, and I'll die yer among my own people. It's different with you. You've moved on, as Dadda said you would."

He left it at that, but soon the stale, claustrophobic atmosphere of the little town began to oppress him so that he thought longingly of the miles of moorland he could see from his dormer window in Havelock's House. In the last week of August, when the newspapers were trumpeting the British advance on the Ancre and the capture of Bapaume, he slipped away, promising to return for Christmas. Late the same evening, he caught the Challacombe train for Taunton and got out at Bamfylde Bridge Halt, revelling in the two-mile tramp up the twisting roads to the sportsfield gate, still lacking a hinge and leaning outwards.

Dusk was settling in the highest folds of the moor and the scent of honeysuckle and thyme came to him, together with the pungent whiff of grass clippings where old Tapscott, the one groundsman remaining to them, had been scything the grass on what would be the scene of the autumn house matches. The school buildings, from this angle, were silhouetted against a tangerine sky, where the sun was sliding down behind the sentinel beeches of the west drive. He thought, "It's the damnedest thing . . . I've been here six months but it's already more home to me than Potnewydd. Can't imagine being anywhere else ..." and vaulting the crippled gate he moved up towards the southern fringe of the Planty, as the boys always referred to it, then down past the cricket pavilion and swimming pool to Herries's thinking post and a blur of light showing in the headmaster's house. "It's a niche," he told himself, "and damned if I don't cling to it as long as I can!" It struck him, passing the Gothic arch into the empty quad, that niches, like most other things, were likely to be in short supply for ex-servicemen in the years ahead.

III

The world of school enfolded him. By half-term even the mounting relief that the war was nearly over was muted by the immediacy of Bamfylde's problems, by the trivia of existence within the periphery of his work and personal encounters. When Bulgaria sued for peace, in early October, he was very elated, but only for an hour or so. Beatty, the games coach (who also acted as assistant bursar) had persuaded him to replace Wilton, the running captain, as chief whipper-in for the fortnightly cross-country events and this was no sinecure for a man eight months out of hospital. Bamfylde took its runs seriously and in rough country like Exmoor, the post of whipper-in was equivalent to a rear-guard command. Small boys, lagging a long way behind, and unfamiliar with the country, had been known to get lost. The job of whipper-in was to co-ordinate the efforts of the prefects who were not running colours and keep the laggards closed up over a five-mile course.

And then, on his very first run-in, Archer the Third had to go missing when call-over was held in the quad and the boys were about to disperse for high tea.

It was almost dark then and inclined to be foggy. With

storm lanterns and a band of volunteers he headed back
beyond Stonecross, where Archer the Third was found
snivelling in a gully, nursing a twisted ankle and the fear of
death from exposure. They carried him home sedan-chair
fashion and when he sat down to his pea-soup David was in
worse state than Archer, and so stiff that he had to haul
himself up to the staff bathroom and soak in soda. He had
forgotten all about Bulgaria.

It was easy to see how ageing men like Cordwainer and
Acton had become so barnacled, tending, as the seasons
passed, to identify the universe with Bamfylde and Bamfylde's concerns. Decisions like the date of speech-day, which
pitch should be used for the house semi-finals and crises like
the influenza epidemic that filled the sanatorium in ten days,
or the near-mutiny of the O.T.C. over threadbare puttees that
kept unrolling during manoeuvres, had a way of enlarging
themselves into events of tremendous importance. Who was
the locker-pilferer in Outram's? Was he boy or domestic?
Who was covering for Howarth, himself down with flu?
What could be done to stem the overflow of the brook that
flushed the latrines, inevitably known as the Bog?

Surprisingly, it was Algy Herries who restored to him his
sense of proportion once a week when he announced, often
with tears in his eyes, the death of yet another Old Bamfeldian in action, and spoke a few words about the boy's years
at the school. It was a sombre, almost masochistic duty he
inflicted upon himself but David, who was beginning to get
the full measure of the man, understood why he performed
this weekly penance. He would see it as an obligation, to
speak aloud, possibly for the last time, the name of a youngster, or perhaps someone who was not so young, whose
shouts had once been heard on the pitches beyond the pointed
windows of Big School, a person who had taken away with
him some tiny part of the ethos of the school, planted in his

mind and muscle during his time here. It was on these occasions that David would get a glimpse of that multitude of khaki-clad figures who had disappeared in the slime of Passchendaele, or fallen on the chalky wilderness of the Somme. For casualties, despite the Allied surging advances almost as far as the battlefields of August, 1914, were still trickling in, four in August, three in September, two more in October, one of them Bristow Major, who had been head prefect the term before David joined the staff and whose younger brother, Bummy Bristow, was still in the Upper Fifth.

But then, like a thunderclap, it ended. Word came over the telephone—from Second Lieutenant Cooper, of all people, now training as a demolition expert in London—that he had it on the best authority (an uncle in Fleet Street) that a cease-fire was to be declared at eleven a.m. the following day, and although no newspapers confirming this stupendous news could be expected until late afternoon, Algy took a chance and announced a school holiday, with leave to go into Challacombe, if transport could be arranged. Local boys disappeared but a majority stayed on, pooling their pocket-money to empty the tuckshop, and Ellie Herries was set to work with other masters' wives to perform a prodigy of baking for a communal supper and sing-song in Big Hall instead of the usual prep.

The immediate effect upon David was to increase his popularity as the one member of the staff who had fought at First Ypres, Loos and Neuve Chapelle, and who was regarded, somewhat to his embarrassment, as the ultimate authority on all things martial. He was cheered when he made his way up to the dais, luckily a little in advance of the other masters save Bouncer, who was there to say grace, and found himself blushing, for although he felt an immense sense of gratitude he could feel no personal achievement in survival when nearly a hundred Old Boys had died.

He kept his gaze on the floor until Bouncer had subsided, but there was worse to come. When the school orchestra had assembled and the singing began, they chose numbers that the troops had sung so repetitiously down all the roads of Picardy and Artois, 'Tipperary', 'Who's Your Lady Friend?', 'Long, Long Trail' and the like. To someone who had heard these choruses sung in that setting it was unbearable and soon, but inconspicuously, he escaped, slipping out through the sculleries to the cinder path leading to the piggeries. And here, unashamedly, he wept, blundering through trailers of mist until he found the path to Herries's thinking post, and pausing there, gulping down the dank, night air but still within earshot of the uproar in the Hall. He thought, desperately, "For Christ's sake ... what is there to sing about ...? Why does it have to be a celebration when it ought to be a wake?"

He lit a cigarette, inhaling deeply, and he was still there when he saw a match flare down by the fives court. Feeling the need to communicate, he made his way down, certain that he would discover that Algy Herries had excused himself under similar pressures.

It was not Algy, however, but that dry old stick Howarth, the English master who had once advised him to ignore Carter's appeal to join the O.T.C., still the basis of a feud between them. Howarth's pince-nez flashed in the glow of his Gold Flake. He smoked, they said, forty to fifty a day and this was not his only vice. Rumour had it that he also accounted for three bottles of gin each week in his cosy rooms at Nicolson's, where he was housemaster.

He said, greeting David, "Saw you slink off and decided to take the same route. Obliged to you for the hint." And then, in the friendliest tone he had so far employed, "I imagine you've even less stomach for it than a slacker like me, P.J. But I'm human, after all. Bristow Senior was one of the brightest boys I've ever taught. He wrote to me several times from France. Said he was going into publishing with his step-father and would have made a success of it, I daresay. But he had to die, at eighteen. For what? Can you tell me?"

"Not yet. I might, in a decade or so."

"You're another of the millennium boys, then?"

"Not necessarily. But something hopeful must emerge from it. If it doesn't it'll be our fault—yours, mine and Algy's. Even the fault of the old stagers, so long as they stay on the job!"

"The devil of it is," Howarth said, "I never did go along with all this hang-the-Kaiser balderdash. I've never been able to hate the Germans. Have you discovered Heine yet?"

"I'm afraid not."

"Try him, sometime. He's got a trick of suiting all kinds of moods. Tonight's for instance—'*Enfant Perdu*', Houghton's translation—

> *But war and justice have far different laws,*
> *And worthless acts are often done quite well;*
> *The rascal's shots were better than his cause,*
> *And I was hit—and hit again, and fell*

—appropriate, wouldn't you say?"

"It's appropriate to the whole generation."

Howarth said nothing and, more from a need to divert his own gloomy thoughts than his companion's, David added, "Didn't Heine write a lot about love?"

"Yes, he did.

> *The old dream comes again to me;*
> *With May-night stars above,*
> *We two sat under the Linden tree*
> *And swore eternal love.*
> *Again and again we plighted troth . . .*

Here, what the devil has got into me?" and Howarth hurled his cigarette across the gravel, as though its trail of sparks would purge him of sentimentality.

"Has Heine personal significance for you?"

"He did have, a long time ago."

"Were you ever married?"

"No." There was a pause. In the darkness David could sense Howarth doing battle with himself, trying to break through the home-baked crust of reserve that he wore like a breastplate wherever he went. Finally he said, "I was to have been, when I was about your age. But she made the right decision. She married a stockbroker. It wasn't the financial aspect,"—he said this almost defensively—"she just couldn't see herself as a schoolmaster's wife, and I don't blame her when I look at some of the old birds roosting about here. Besides, this is a job for a bachelor if you mean to make a go of it. Miserable pay, no real prospects unless you strike lucky, and a fresh family every four to five years. What woman in her senses would take that on?" He stood up, lighting another cigarette. "What the devil are we doing, sitting here in the fog and talking drivel? Come up to my rooms and let's do our celebrating in the warm," and without waiting for David's assent he stalked off, leading the way through the quadrangle arch and up the steep flight of slate steps to his quarters.

That was the beginning of his tacit alliance with Howarth and he was to be grateful for it, for Howarth, by far the prickliest pear of the common room, was a counterpoise to Carter and one or two of the older men who had already begun to identify him as a radical. He had a conviction that this was not so much on account of his discussions with senior boys on the war, or his championship of a poet like Siegfried Sassoon, who had bravely challenged the establishment the previous year, but because they saw him as a someone better qualified than they were to communicate with a generation that had moved into adolescence in the last four years. Howarth, for his part, recognised and accepted this, as indeed did Herries himself. Their patronage probably encouraged men like Carter to think of him as an interloper currying special privileges on the strength of his war record.

Three other shifts in the pattern of his life at Bamfylde occurred before the anniversary of his arrival came round. One was distressing, one reassuring. The third was a compromise, made with the object of closing the breach between him and the commandant of the Officers' Training Corps.

The compromise was proposed by Algy Herries, an admitted past master at reconciling extreme points of view. Hearing of David's uncompromising refusal to take part in military exercises, he buttonholed him outside the tuckshop between periods one December morning and said, gaily, "You're a Welshman, Powlett-Jones, and all the Welsh are musical. How do you fancy yourself as a bandmaster?"

"A bandmaster, Headmaster? You mean a stand-in for Pym, as orchestra leader?"

"No, dear boy. As the organiser of a drum and fife band for the Corps. We've had a legacy. A consignment of instruments from an Old Boy, name of Cherriton. Before my time, but it seems he was a local Volunteer enthusiast up in Yorkshire, before the Volunteers were merged into the Territorials. They had a band and Cherriton stipulated in his will that the instruments should be sent on to us. They arrived yesterday, half a cartload of them. Do you play an instrument?"

His relationship with Herries was sufficiently relaxed to encourage him to slip back into the familiar idiom and he replied, smiling, "Play the piano by ear, I do Mister Herries. Blew the cornet too, as a boy in Chap-pel now," and Herries responded, "You see, I have second sight. We're not hoping to qualify for tattoo status, at the Tidworth annual camps. All Carter wants is something to jolly the company along on route marches." He glanced shrewdly at David under his tufted brows. "You and Carter don't hit it off, do you?"

"I wouldn't say that. He seems to resent my not taking an active part in the Corps but frankly, sir, I've had a bellyful of bullshine and brass. Did Carter actually propose me for bandmaster?"

"No, he didn't. As a matter of fact he doesn't yet know we've got the instruments, but he's put in several requests to the Governors for a band allocation over the years. It's my idea. I'm not putting any pressure on you to join the Corps. It's run on a purely voluntary basis, even for the boys, and this job is unofficial. You wouldn't have to appear in uniform, or even turn up on parade. Just supervise the practices."

It was as close to an order as Algy Herries ever issued concerning extra-scholastic pursuits. Put like this David did not see how he could refuse without seeming churlish, so he said, "I'll take a crack at it, until somebody more qualified turns up," and Herries said, "Splendid! I'll get that tip over the armoury cleared out and you can use it as a bandroom. I'll also post a notice, announcing auditions."

Before the last day of term David had mustered a band and Herries was correct in his assumption that this would reestablish a working relationship with Carter. It was impossible to like the man. He was too sure of himself and inclined to be testy if his prejudices were challenged, but he saw a band as something likely to enhance the prestige of his beloved Corps. Luckily he was tone deaf and unlikely on this account to challenge the dispositions of any bandmaster.

There were those whose steps led them past the bandroom in the early days of the Lent term who would have regarded tone deafness as a boon. Of the sixteen boys selected only three were familiar with instruments, that included four bugles, as well as six fifes, a bass drum, two sidedrums, two kettledrums, and a pair of cymbals. A seventeenth volunteer, Boyer, was chosen for drum major on account of his stature, imposing for a boy of sixteen.

From the first session David enjoyed the extra chore thrust upon him and arranged rehearsals three times a week, fitting them in between tea and prep and sometimes consulting Rapper Gibbs on technical points. Rapper advised him to discard the bugles but the embryo buglers made such an outcry that David improvised fanfares at stipulated intervals, wedging them into tortured renderings of 'The British Grenadiers' and some of Sousa's marches.

The Corps band was soon an institution and a great joke for those unconnected with it. The bandsmen did not mind, aware that there were a dozen volunteers waiting to take advantage of one resignation, as was proved when fourteen sent in their names after the inexpert cymbalist had clipped a piece from his thumb. David gave the job to Briarley, the boy he had tried to console the day news came that his father was lost on the Lys. He had kept his eyes on Briarley, noticing that the boy was slow to shake off his depression and inclined to walk alone, daydreaming on an old log up at the Planty, or on the seat under the fives court where every Bamfeldian seemed to drift when he was in the dumps. The cymbals did the trick. After a rehearsal or two Briarley became an ornament of the band, whirling the polished discs in a way that spilled sunlight over them like a gyrating halo. Boyer made a spectacular drum-major in his pipe-clayed collarette and spent hours in a secluded corner of the rugby field, practising his extravagant flourishes, including one that sent the staff spinning twenty feet into the air. The fife players soon learned to read notes marked out on cards by Rapper, who was unaware that he was thus identified with a group known, at first, as 'The Boys' Brigade', then as 'The Cacophoneers' but finally, through the agency of Barnaby, the classics master, as 'The Orpheans'.

Barnaby was a good jester, but he liked to send his jokes out to work. It happened that he was presiding over a con-strue in the Lower Third, who occupied the nearest class-room to the bandroom, on a day when the band had been granted a free period to rehearse for the drill competition. Intermittent snatches of 'The British Grenadiers', graced by the shrill blasts on the bugles, reached the juniors and Barnaby ignored the chortles until he happened upon a passage from Horace and invited Taylor, the most promising Latinist in the class, to try a free translation. Taylor began, " 'Dapibus supremi—Gratat estudo Jovis . . .'—'The lyre is welcome—at the feasts of supreme Jupiter . . .' " The general titter was enlarged into a gale of laughter as Barnaby slammed the window, saying, "We are not feasting, gentle-men. And Orpheus, alas, has lost his touch!"

The band provided everybody with light relief during a season of hard frost that reduced football to a minimum but somehow persuaded the diligent Carter that he was training a company of Alpine troops. The band, all members of the Corps, slogged ahead wherever the rank and file went but were relieved of the necessity of humping kit and rifle, a privilege won for them by David. Thus, in a curious way, they formed a nucleus of boys who were disposed to champion unorthodox views on tradition and soon, without in the least wishing it, he found that he was regarded as the standard-bearer of dissenters.

Some of the boys in Middle School, David noticed, had reduced cribbing to a fine art. Everyone in the common room knew it went on, and punished it on the rare occasions when a culprit was caught, but they seemed to draw no distinction in cribbing during examinations for removes, and cribbing during Lent term examinations, when undeserved prizes sometimes went to accomplished practitioners of the art.

By keeping his eyes and ears open, yet without identifying specific culprits, David became familiar with methods employed during his own periods and those of the short-sighted 'Bouncer'. There was the time-honoured blotting paper memoranda, the strategic positioning (with or without complicity) of the more advanced boys during tests, the cautious raising of a sheaf of notes through the cracked lid of a desk, and the more sophisticated method of attaching notes to a shred of elastic fastened to the shirt cuff. He had still not succeeded in catching anyone, but by the end of term he could have assembled a black museum of cribbing apparatus. What dismayed him was the startling result of an examination paper set for the history prize in that citadel of the work-shy, the Lower Fourth. Youings, by far the best scholar in the class, was placed seventh, whereas the position of some of the leading six could only have meant cribbing on an organised scale.

He let the result pass without comment, however, until he had had a chat with Youings on the questions set, and satisfied himself that the boy had answered all but one correctly. Then, after the list had been pinned to the school notice board, he fired a range-finder at the class, announcing that "the standard of work exhibited in the examination was encouragingly high, so high, in fact, as to pass the limits of credibility". He let this sink in for a minute before adding, "I'm not actually accusing anyone in the first six of—shall we say—jogging their memory a little, or pulling themselves up by their bootstraps. Why should I? I didn't catch them at it, any more than I can explain poor performances on the part of those same experts in the weekly tests. Perhaps the questions were happily chosen. Perhaps some of you may have done some . . . er . . . late mugging-up," and at this the class relaxed and there was a subdued chuckle.

He did not react to it, as he generally did, for chuckles were by no means unknown during his periods. Instead he stepped down off the rostrum and sauntered up the central aisle, pausing beside Dobson, who had been placed fourteenth in test averages but who had scored ninety-six out of a possible hundred in the exam and qualified for the form prize. The chuckle died before it had properly begun and Dobson, flushing a little, avoided his eye. He went on, keeping his tone level and jocular, "There's something of a moral problem here, however. This particular exam wasn't for a place in form, or a comment on the reports you'll take home at the end of term. It wasn't for outside examiners either. It was for a specific gain, a prize with the prizewinner's name on the flyleaf, and there's a difference. To my mind at any rate. Think about it."

The bell sounded then and he left abruptly, wondering if he had made a fool of himself and feeling somehow that he had. It bothered him so much that he finally took the problem to Howarth, giving it as his opinion that Youings was the only boy in the first seven who had written an honest paper, and recounting as much as he recalled of his sermon. "Was that the right way of going about it?" he asked. "I mean, having failed to spot anyone cribbing, wouldn't I have been wiser to keep my mouth shut?" and Howarth replied surprisingly, "You know a damned sight better than that. As to whether your pi-jaw did any good I can check on that tomorrow."

"How, without actually accusing anyone?"

"Oh, by means unknown to the beginner, old man," and he left it at that.

He was as good as his word. Just before prep bell the following evening Howarth accosted him as he was reading the exam lists of the Lower Fifth on the quad notice board.

"Thought you might care to know you scored a bull's-eye with the Lower Fourth yesterday. They've had a public soul-searching and that half-bind ass Acton has been reaping your harvest. You see those Lower Fourth Divinity prize-list results? They represent today's sitting, and the reverend gentleman has assured me they are a very accurate reflection of his preliminary tests."

"How can either of you be sure of that?"

"How? For God's sake, man, don't you know me well enough yet to realise I haven't taken a damned thing on trust since I left kindergarten? I asked Acton to play a little game with me. He wrote down his forecast of the first ten in the exam today and here it is. Compare the two lists and draw your own conclusions." David took the list and held it alongside the list on the board. It was almost identical. He said, wonderingly. "Does that mean those young devils have decided to stop cribbing?"

"Only when there's a prize at the end of it, I'm afraid, and you have Boyer to thank for the mass conversion. Don't ask me how I know that either. When you've been at this job as long as I have you develop a sixth sense in these matters. However, you appear to be developing satisfactory techniques of your own," and with that he drifted away, the inevitable between-periods Gold Flake stuck between his lips.

As it happened, David had to wait until prize-giving for confirmation. Dobson, to the accompaniment of ironic Middle School cheers, marched up and collected his history prize, a leather-bound copy of Prescott's *Conquest of Peru*, and David glowered as he shook hands with Countess Hopgood, the guest of honour. His resentment was premature. A day later a puzzled Youings hung about after second bell and seemed to want a word with him. When everyone had left Big School, he laid the copy of *Conquest of Peru* on the desk, open at the presentation page. Dobson's name had been blocked out and above it, in anonymous script, was the legend, '*Presented to Edward Youings, in appreciation of his unfailing assistance in history periods. By his grateful comrades in the Lower Fourth!*'

Youings said, "Is it . . . er . . . some kind of practical joke, sir? I mean, should I keep it? I found it in my desk this morning."

"It's not a joke, Youings," David said, "more of a peace-offering. The kind an errant husband brings home in the form of flowers when he's been out on the beer."

"Sir?" Youings, like many academics, was not very quick on the uptake.

"Keep it," he said, "it's yours anyway," and went in to lunch with a sense of elation and a sharp awareness of Howarth's sagacity.

He extracted no elation from another episode that occurred on the last Sunday of the Lent term but once again it taught him something.

He was in the library returning books when he happened to glance through the window that gave on the quad. A group of boys were skylarking under the Founder's statue and prominent among them was 'Bull' Bickford, and his two henchmen, Rigby and Ford, all three engaged in forcing the head of a struggling Second Former into the fountain that ran around the plinth. To further the work Bickford was methodically rooting at the victim's buttocks. David, through the open window, bawled, "Stop that, Bickford, and come up here! You too, Rigby—Ford. Look sharp about it!"

The Second Former, unaware of the source of his reprieve, scuttled away as his tormentors slouched across the quad and up the steps to the library. Presently they appeared dishevelled, but not particularly apprehensive.

"What was that about, Bickford?"

"Oh, really nothing, sir. We were only teaching Skidmore how to make his bow. It's the last Sunday of all, you see, and Skidmore's a first-termer. He's a bit bucky, sir, and we gave him the chance of doing it on his own. When he wouldn't we had to make him."

"Make him half-drown himself?"

"Yes, sir, just as it says—'Last day but five, new kids take a dive.' Maybe you don't know how it goes, sir?"

David knew how it went. It was part of a string of doggerel devised, over the years, as an initiation rite for new boys. When Sundays fell on certain days, measured in relation to the days left in the term, rhyming couplets decreed that they perform certain idiotic procedures. One or two came to mind—'Last Sunday but six, new kids pick up sticks', 'Last Sunday but two, new kids feel my shoe', and so on. Towards the end of term, with only a few days to run, the nonsense proliferated, for the programme of work and games began to run down, and boys like Bickford had time on their hands to flush victims from the limited security of the Bog, and subject them to the rough and ready dictates of the tradition. There was no real harm in it, he supposed, except when they picked on a very sensitive boy, or when the ritual made a sadistic appeal to a natural despot like Bickford. He said, "Well, I don't give a fig for that kind of tradition. It's no more than a flimsy excuse for bullying. The next time I see you rough-housing a new boy I'll devise some doggerel of my own and you'll be at the receiving end of it. Is that clear?"

"Yes, sir," from all three, but he knew what they were thinking—"Who the hell is he to stick his nose in? He's only a third-termer himself!" The devil of it was that all the rest of the staff, even Herries himself, tolerated this kind of thing, so long as it was kept within limits, but who could say where those limits ran? He wondered briefly what made him so squeamish about it. Was it the orgy of bloodletting he had witnessed in Flanders, or the thought that there was already too much gratuitous cruelty in the world?

He went off in search of Skidmore, finding him, as he had half-expected, barricaded in a cubicle in the Bog, the one relatively safe retreat throughout a 'last day but five', or a 'last Sunday but six'. He called, "Come on out, Skidmore, I want a word with you," and Skidmore emerged, a pallid little wretch, with a crumpled Eton collar a size too large for him and a tear-streaked face. He said, "All right, it's nothing to worry about. I only wanted to know why you stood out against Bickford. Wouldn't it have been easier to make your bow to the Founder? All the other new boys have," but Skidmore replied, "No, sir, it's an image."

"An image? What's an image?"

"That statue. You don't bow to images. It's in the Bible, sir."

He was taken aback. It seemed astounding that, in this day and age, a child like Skidmore should be animated by the spirit of Christian martyrs facing circus lions. He said, wonderingly, "Is *that* why you preferred to be rooted? You're not pulling my leg?" and Skidmore assured him gravely that he was not, and that there was a hymn they sang in chapel that ran, 'the heathen in his blindness, bows down to wood and stone'. He thought, dolefully, "Good God, when do you stop learning about boys . . .?" and just stopped himself laughing.

"What's your father, Skidmore?"

"A minister, sir."

"Really? What denomination?"

"Wesleyan Methodist, sir."

"Will you tell him about this when you get home?"

"No, sir."

"You'd see that as sneaking?"

"Wouldn't it be, sir?"

Like himself, Skidmore was learning. You made your point, where you could, but you didn't brag about it.

"All right, Skidmore. Run along and keep out of Bickford's way if you can," but then, as the boy turned to go, "How are you liking it here? In spite of today's business?", and Skidmore said, "Well . . . all right, sir. I daresay I'll get used to it by next term."

"Me too," said David, grinning, and turned away from the boy's surprised look.

PART TWO

CATALYST IN A BERET

CHAPTER ONE

I

The hat plummeted down out of nowhere, brushing his nose and pitching at his feet where it settled like a grey bird making a clumsy landing on the shingle. It was an altogether unremarkable hat, not a beret exactly, and not quite a tam o' shanter, but something in between, slightly larger than the hats French peasants had worn in the fields behind the line and with a tassel like a stalk.

Seconds passed before he realised the hat must have an owner and then glanced up, to discover he had been on the point of walking under the pier when the beret fell. A girl was looking down at him from a height of about twenty feet and the moment he saw her she began to wave, pointing to her head, then down at her beret. He smiled and picked it up, joining her in her dumb show by pointing to himself and then the pier, whereupon she nodded eagerly and put her hand to her mouth, masking a laugh. It was a trick the Second Form practised whenever he made one of his small jokes.

He climbed the shingle bank and vaulted the iron rail on to the promenade, moving along to the turnstile and paying his twopence to pass the barrier. The girl was awaiting him on the far side and he noticed now that she was less sure of herself and looked, indeed, a little shamefaced, again like one of the Second Form caught out in a piece of mischief. But then he noticed something else. She was a very pretty girl, with dark brown hair parted in the middle. She had large brown eyes with long, curling lashes, and small hands and feet that seemed no larger than a child's the way she was standing, feet close together, hands drooping and half-hidden in the folds of a tartan skirt. He said, diffidently, "It is yours, I suppose?", and she replied, breathlessly, "Yes . . . thank you very much . . . it was a silly thing to do! I was leaning out too far and I grabbed but missed. I say . . ." as she took the hat and began fumbling in her little handbag, "I owe you twopence!" but at that he laughed and she did too as he said, "It isn't every day of the week a girl throws her cap at me." And then, for want of an idea as to how the conversation could be prolonged, he looked over her shoulder and saw the word 'Teas' on the shore side of the pier pavilion. "Couldn't we have some tea? Or coffee? Are you with any-one?"

She smiled, implying that she was more expert at this game than he was. "No, I'm not 'with anybody', and I'd love some coffee. I was just going in for some. They make good coffee here. For a pier pavilion, that is," and they walked along the echoing planks to a café that was almost empty. "Here," she said, "my favourite table. You can see the sea," and indicated a table looking over the western section of the bay.

He was so disarmed by her assurance that he forgot his manners and sat down without waiting for her. She said, trying to coax him out of his shyness, "What a nice thing to happen on the first day of the holiday. Yes, I know, you'll be wondering why I said this was my favourite table. I've been here four years running, you see. My sister and brother-in-law live here. He's a dairyman, and I come up on my unpaid week each spring. The paid week, in September, I'm expected to spend at home, and that isn't nearly so much fun. My name is Marwood, Elizabeth Marwood. What's yours?"

"Powlett-Jones," he said. "David," and was surprised when she brought her hands together, like a child expressing glee. "Why, that's better still she cried!". "David is my favourite boy's name. It used to be Paul, until I had a fresh look at the Acts. Then I had second thoughts. Paul was a kill-joy, don't you think? But David was a proper old rake and much more human, if you see what I mean."

There was absolutely no resisting her. She had the charm and ebullience of a pretty child of about eight, reared by a pair of indulgent parents, and yet this assumption was not supported by her clothes. They were obviously off-the-peg clothes, chosen by someone who had to watch pennies. The tartan skirt, ending halfway up the calf, was all the rage that year, and the white silk blouse was almost certainly run-up by a home-plied needle. Hers or her mother's, he wondered? Shoes and handbag were of cheap imitation leather, and the heart-shaped cameo brooch at her breast was what his mother would have called a 'gee-gaw'. She had strong views about gee-gaws, dismissing them as an indication of extra-vagance in a woman.

A waitress arrived with a pot of coffee and Elizabeth poured, after asking him if he liked it black or white, and this surprised him a little. It was not until he became a member of the mess, in 1917, that he had known the difference or, indeed, so much as the taste of coffee. In Pontnewydd every-body drank tea.

He had an opportunity to look at her closely while she was pouring, deciding that she was one of the prettiest girls he had ever seen, although his experience was limited. Up to the out-break of war he had been too busy with his studies to join his elder brothers in skirmishes at choir practice, and Eisteddfod rehearsal that led, in most cases, to walking out, and a wed-ding at one of the innumerable chapels. Then, during his years in the army, he had rarely seen a woman, except the hard-faced daughters of estaminet madames, or nurses of all ages, who had no time to spare for skylarking with wards full of the wreckage swept from one battlefield or another. And, on top of that, with most of his youth spent, he had chosen to live in another male preserve, so that he was not surprised to find himself tongue-tied in the presence of an attractive, talkative girl. Her friendliness, however, encouraged him to make an effort, and he said, "You pour like an expert. Do you work in a restaurant or hotel?" and she said he was getting warm, for she worked in 'a sort of hotel'.

"An orphanage?"

"A hospital, in Swansea."

She did not fit his idea of a nurse. Most of the older nurses, he recalled, had been martinets, sharp with their tongues, bossy and always in a hurry, and now that he thought about it they had all seemed mature, whereas she was hardly more than a girl, no more than nineteen, he would say. He wondered about her involvement in the war, for he had learned to tell at a glance those who had been scarred by the bloody business. Usually it showed in the faces of the young and middle-aged but there was no hint of it here. She was fresh, eager, unspoiled, chock-full of vitality.

He heard her say, "A penny for them?" and hastily he refocused his mind. "Eh? I'm sorry . . . I was wondering . . . you being a nurse, I mean. Did you nurse soldiers?"

"No, worse luck," she said, "the staff nurses always hogged the men's wards. I was still a probationer while the war was on, and was fobbed off with the pensioners. The matron never encouraged probationers to nurse younger men. She seemed to think it might make them sit up and take notice too quickly!"

He laughed, responding gratefully to her sparkle. She said, "Were you in the army? You were, weren't you? I can tell, somehow. All the men who were in the trenches have that same look, as though . . ." but she checked herself, stirring her coffee so vigorously that it slopped into the saucer.

"What were you going to say?"

"It doesn't matter. Men who were out there don't want to talk about it."

She was not only pretty and forthcoming, he decided, but discerning for a youngster of her age. He said, "That's so, but I've been far luckier than most. Not only coming through more or less intact, but having something to take my mind off it when I was discharged."

"When was that?"

"Over a year ago. I got a Blighty, in the autumn of 1917, and started teaching as soon as I was boarded. It's amazing how it helped. The war already seems something that happened when I was a kid."

"Well, don't make it sound as if you were in your dotage," she said cheerfully. "How old are you, Mr. Powlett-Jones?"

"Twenty-two. And you?"

She blushed and then threw her head up smiling. He noticed her white, even teeth, and her elfin prettiness touched him again, so that he was aware of the sense of renewal he derived from the juniors at Bamfylde. "I'm nineteen today," she said, and for some reason the news disposed of the last of his reserve.

"You are? Well, we can't celebrate on coffee. Wouldn't you like an ice or something?"

"No, thank you," she said, laughing, "but if you're free and on your own we might . . . well, we could have lunch. Not here. I know a café in the town where the food isn't at all bad,", but then her irrepressible high spirits hitched on a small snag of modesty and she said, "I say, this is awful! I'm absolutely throwing myself at you. First the beret, then asking myself out to lunch. For all I know you've got a girl somewhere. You might even be married!"

"I'd be lucky where I work. There are four hundred boys, twenty-odd masters, most of them bald and grey, and two women. One is like your matron, the other a middle-aged widow. How's that for credentials?"

"Couldn't be better. Tell me about it. Is it a boarding school, one of those famous ones? And what do you teach? No, let me guess." She put a finger in her mouth. "French or Latin, isn't it?"

"You're not much good at guessing, Miss Marwood. History. And a little English to the juniors."

"You don't look like a schoolmaster."

"I'm very glad to hear it, especially from someone nineteen today. All right, I'll tell you about it if you like, but let's go out along the prom so far as Rhos. Then we'll have lunch, as you suggest, and after that ... well, I was thinking of taking one of those afternoon charabanc trips to Conway Castle. I haven't been there since I was a kid. You'd be very welcome if you'd like to come along, but I'll almost certainly bore you if you do. Edward the First is one of my favourites. And me a good Welshman! How's that for heresy?"

That was how it began, effortlessly and casually, yet the most exciting thing that had ever happened to him, beginning with the drop of a beret from the head of a saucy girl, leaning over the rail of the pier at Colwyn Bay and ending in an involvement that was to shape the course of his life as surely and permanently as his arrival at Bamfylde, when he was still in a state of shock and nervous and physical exhaustion. Bamfylde had been a kind of staircase that he was obliged to ascend falteringly, grabbing at handholds and footholds represented by individuals like Algy Herries and Howarth, and by experiences like the first confrontation with the Lower Fourth and his attempt to console Briarley. Elizabeth Marwood offered herself as a smooth, level stretch, one he could pass without stress of any kind, someone who, in herself, was the very essence of hope, sanity, sweetness and

promise, someone of his own generation who was able to
convince him that, despite all that had happened out there
under the growling bombardments, innocence survived, and
was already throwing up new, green shoots. He sensed this
much that first day and within a week he was gloriously
certain of it. But by then, of course, he was hopelessly in love.

II

He never forgot the smallest particular of their first day together, their encounter on the pier, the walk along the promenade, lunch at a café called The Lantern, the chara trip to
Conway and the almost comic deference she had shown him
when he linked the valerian-sown ruins with events that had
occurred there. And after that there was the visit to the
churchyard to see the seven-spiked grave, featured in Words-
worth's poem, the row up the river, tea at a cottage on the
quay next door to the Smallest House in the World, and then
back to Colwyn Bay to meet her dairyman brother-in-law,
Griff, and her sister Esther, who welcomed him into their
flat over the shop as though he had been an old friend they
had unexpectedly re-encountered.

But even that was not the end of it. In the evening he took
Elizabeth to a variety concert in the pier pavilion and afterwards, when he saw her home, he kissed her at the gate. A
very shy, restrained kiss it was, his first since party days in the
Valley, a thousand years ago. Yet it did something to him,
reviving, deep within him, a sense of being and existing, that
snapped the final cord attaching him to the dried-out husk of
a man he had been in the rejuvenating months at Osborne, a
restoration of youth that he had come to accept as dead and
buried, along with his generation, a quickening of ambition
passing into his bloodstream like a powerful stimulant. It was
too vitalising a mood to waste in sleep, so, instead of returning
to the Y.M.C.A. where he was staying, he went back to the

pierhead and leaned on the rail, looking out across the whispering bay and watching a sliver of moon ride the piled-up masses of blue-black clouds. He caught himself murmuring her name, catching and savouring its six syllables, and on its utterance the memory of her soft, eager lips returned to him, the final bonus of what he saw as the most exhilarating day of his life. He remained there a long time until he recalled he had no key and there was no night porter at the hotel. Then he moved on, smiling at the prospect of rousing the hotel at one in the morning but not caring a damn for he saw himself then as a wandering drunk who, against all probability, had found his way home.

In the morning, the moment the shops were open, he went out to buy her a birthday gift and ended by buying three, an early nineteenth-century print of Conway Castle, a small bottle of perfume and a great bunch of narcissi, daffodils and tulips, taking them down to the pierhead where they met by appointment, not caring whether she thought him naïve. She was overwhelmed, and when his parcels had been opened, and the bouquet laid aside, she threw her arms round his neck and kissed him, exclaiming, "You know just how to impress, don't you, David? I believe you've had hundreds of girls and years of experience," but he said, shaking his head, "I've had far less experience than you—or rather, you couldn't have had less. I wanted to pay you back for that wonderful day we had yesterday. Where would you like to go today?"

"Somewhere less expensive," she said, laughing. "A walk up to Blackberry mountain, where you can't spend any more money."

"Oh, to blazes with that. I haven't touched my gratuity yet, and there's absolutely no way of spending money at school. The nearest real shop is at Challacombe, miles away. Why don't we book a round trip and explore all the castles?

Unless you're fed up with conducted tours, that is. I've never seen Harlech and Beaumaris, although I've been to Caernarvon, and along the Straits as far as Telford's bridge."

"I'll go if you let me pay my share. That all-day tour is ten-and-six."

"I don't care if it's ten guineas. I came up here to enjoy myself and I don't fancy doing it alone any more. When are you due back at the hospital?"

"Sunday," she said. "What an awful thought. You've got a month, haven't you?"

"Not really," he said. "I've got to put in the last fortnight swotting for a degree. I should have done it last year but there was so much to learn about the job and, anyway, I wasn't really fit then."

"You are now, though?"

"Never felt better in my life. Partly Exmoor air but mostly you."

It surprised him that he could talk to a girl this way, easily and naturally, as he was learning to communicate with the Sixth, and some of his favourites, like Boyer and Briarley. But then, he supposed, she was easy to get to know, having none of the artfulness his memory associated with girls that the newspapers were beginning to call 'Flappers' for some curious reason. She laughed easily, said the first thing that came into her head, and flattered him a little by listening very carefully to everything he had to say about the castles, the men who built them, and the men who garrisoned them before they were made obsolete by gunpowder.

"My stars!" she exclaimed, when he told her about the Roman invasion of Mona, and the last stand of the Druids in Anglesey, "Where on earth do you *put* it all, David? I mean, you don't have to look it up! You hardly glanced at that guide we bought," and he replied, chuckling, "You'd be astonished how much I have to mug up when I'm taking the Upper

School in a period I'm not familiar with. It never does to let them see you at it, of course. They have to be bluffed. Like you."

"But you must have read a tremendous amount, in spite of all those years in the war when reading couldn't have been easy. Don't you ever want to write?"

Unconsciously she had touched on an ambition dormant in him since he was a child, something unfulfilled in his personal awareness that had surfaced from time to time in the years leading up to the summer of 1914, and again, but infrequently, in rest periods behind the lines, when he was looking for an escape from ennui.

"It's odd you should ask me that. No one else ever has. It's something I've often felt I could do, within limits."

"What kind of limits?"

"I don't think I could write fiction or verse. Maybe I could have, if things had been different, but any creative impulses I might have had were shelled out of me long ago."

"But soldiers did write poems, didn't they? I remember one of our staff-nurses was engaged to a boy who sent poems to her. Poems about the war, I mean."

"Yes, some of them did, and marvellous poems they were too. Sassoon and Owen and Rosenberg were three, and I've already introduced their work to the seniors. But they were articulate. With me it was always as if I was experiencing it secondhand. Maybe that's why I survived. Owen and Rosenberg didn't."

She must have noticed the change in his tone and expression for she said, quickly, "I'm sorry, David. I didn't mean to make you remember," but he said, taking her hand, "I don't mind talking about it to you. In a way it helps. It's not good, keeping it bottled up, the way I have to with the boys. They always seem so terribly young to me. Babies almost."

"But I don't?"

"No, and that's curious too, for you're only a year older than Simmonds, our head boy. Can you explain that?"

"The job, maybe. A nurse, even a pro', is always in charge. She's mobile and her patients aren't. It makes us seem bossy."

She would be a wonderful person to have around in the common room at Bamfylde, he thought, poised to puncture all those balloons of complacency and pomposity. He said, thankfully. "No man in his senses would mind being bossed by you, Elizabeth," and kissed the top of her head, but she was not to be dismissed in this way and said, "Save that, Davy, and go on with what you were saying. If you did write *what* would you write. Would it be plays?"

"Good Lord, no. Plays require a very special technique, and most playwrights serve an apprenticeship as actors. I'd write historical biography, but in a different way from academics. Most studies of the past are written by professional scholars, and dry as dust unless you've done your homework on the background. The ordinary reader has got to see historical characters as flesh and blood."

"But how would you discover human touches after all this time?"

"I suppose by putting two and two together. Fashions and attitudes change every generation but people don't."

She seemed to ponder this. Finally she said, "I think you'd do it splendidly, David. Who would you like to write *about*?"

For possibly the first time in his life he gave his potential subject matter serious consideration. "Well, now that you raise the question, the royal tigress for one."

"Who on earth was she? Boadicea?"

"Someone much nearer our own time. Margaret of Anjou, the French wife of Henry VI."

"Never heard of her. Tell me about her."

He gave her a potted history of Margaret of Anjou, as the charabanc bounced along the road from Caernarvon to

Menai Bridge, then round the tortuous coast road to Beaumaris. She listened attentively and it reminded him that he was becoming as didactic as old Judy Cordwainer and he broke off, saying, "Look here, that's enough of that. I'm beginning to talk like a schoolmaster off duty and that's a sobering thought."

"Why? After all, you are one."

"I don't care to be recognised as one wherever I go. You'd see what I mean if you met some of the codgers in our common room," and that, he thought dolefully, was unlikely.

But was it? For a moment his imagination conjured with the wholly delightful prospect of absorbing her into the Bamfylde scene, so that he saw her, fleetingly, as someone always on hand to encourage and sustain him. But then common sense caught up with him as he thought, "What the hell have I got to offer a girl like her? Two hundred a year, Mam to help out, and a life removed from everyone but boys and old trouts, who would tut-tut at the powder she dabs on her nose!" and he recalled the opinion expressed by Howarth under the fives court on Armistice Night, concerning the unwisdom of trying to combine marriage with a job requiring so much dedication and monastic seclusion.

The fancy remained, however, and unconsciously she kept it glowing, particularly when they said good night after tea and bread and cheese at her brother-in-law's. She came out with him into the backway that ran behind the shop and it seemed to him that she was just as reluctant as he to bring another gloriously fulfilled day to a close. When he kissed her, as gently as he had the previous night, she said, with her delightful lack of inhibition, "Here, let me show you! I won't break, Davy!" and threw her arms round his neck, kissing him in a way he had never been kissed and leaving him breathless with gratification but also a trifle dismayed at such irrefutable evidence of a far wider experience than he possessed. He said, still holding her close, "Have you had lots of boy friends? You must have, a girl as pretty as you."

"I've had my share," she admitted gaily, "but never one the least like you, Davy."

"How am I supposed to regard that?"

"As a compliment, of course. No, I *mean* that! Most men don't need much encouragement, I can tell you."

"But I do?"

"Yes, but you don't have to apologise for it. All the boys I've known would have taken full advantage of the way I threw myself at you and I can't say as I'd blame them. By now I would have been fighting them off."

"I'd back you to take care of yourself, Elizabeth. You seem to me to be pretty well equipped to stand on your own feet in all kinds of ways."

"Not that way always." She was silent a moment. Then she went on, "Two or three of the boys who took me out the first year I was nursing tried it on, and made me feel a bit of a prude for holding out. There was always the chance of the war going on indefinitely, and them being sucked back into it. I don't think it was squeamishness on my part. It was a thought, in the back of my mind, of bringing a poor little beggar into the world whom nobody wanted, who would probably end up in an orphanage. So there you are, Davy. I'm still a virgin. Like you."

Her perception diminished him a little and she was quick to sense as much. "What's wrong with that? You're not the kind of person who would go looking for a prostitute. You're too fastidious for one thing. I daresay that's what kept you clear of the brothels out there."

"Good God! You know about that kind of thing?"

"David," she said, chuckling, "use your head, lad. I've been nursing for two years!"

"But not servicemen."

"What do you think nurses talk about in their free time? Crocheting?"

He laughed. "You're a very surprising person, Elizabeth. What old Algy Herries, my headmaster, would call 'A bit of a card'. Same time tomorrow?"

"Yes, *please*!"

He kissed her again, but as the week sped by he began to be aware of a sense of desperation that was not moderated by her promise to write once a week, 'no matter how rushed we are'. Her train to Chester, where she was catching her connection to Swansea, left at midday on Sunday, and his spirits were at low ebb as he accompanied her to the station. It was no good telling himself he was exaggerating the terrible need he had for her gaiety and warmth, that something positive might develop from their correspondence, that they had made tentative arrangements to meet in London where her parents lived when she took her paid holiday next September. September was a long way off, and all kinds of things could happen before then. She might get bored writing. She might meet someone far more eligible in that hospital, probably crammed with young men with gratuities to spend, and four years' lost youth to make up.

They hung about waiting for the whistle to blow and when it did the blast hit him in the belly like the signal for an attack. The train began to move and he watched it slide away with a terrible finality, carrying with it all his hopes and certainties. It had moved about ten yards when he responded to an irresistible urge to stop it and sprinted along the platform until he was level with her comparment where she stood framed in the window. "Stand away!" he shouted, clutching the brass handle, "Coming with you!" and at that the guard, lower down the platform, roared his disapproval. A second later the heavy door was swinging free and he was inside the carriage on his hands and knees, and she had reached over him and slammed it and they were alone, Elizabeth looking at him with a stunned expression as he scrambled up, dusting himself.

"What on earth—Davy—you've no luggage..." and then she threw back her head and laughed and he caught her in his arms, so that they lost their balance and collapsed as the train gathered speed.

"To hell with luggage," he said, "I'll catch a train back from Chester, pick up my stuff and go on home to Bamfylde. It won't be any fun here without you. Besides, there's something I've got to know, and it can't wait on letters. Will you marry me, Beth? I'm very much in love with you, and if you wouldn't mind being the only wife under forty at a school miles from anywhere..."

He got no further. She caught his arm, pressing his hand fervently against her breast, crying, "Why, of course I'll marry you! Just as soon as you like. And as for living on the moors in Devon, with all those boys and funny characters you've told me about, I can't think of anything nicer! I'll tell you something else too. I'm jolly glad you didn't propose to me solemnly, by letter. This is much more romantic, the first really romantic thing that's ever happened to me. There!" and she kissed him, first on the ear, then on both cheeks and finally on the mouth, so enthusiastically that a smudge of dust, gathered in his headlong fall into the compartment, transferred itself from his forehead to hers.

III

They had planned to be married in August, a week or so after the school broke up, and he had had a chance to make the half-ruinous cottage in Stonecross Bottom habitable after sub-leasing it from Farmer Brewer, the taciturn tenant, for fifty pounds a year. "A typical peasant-robbery", old Howarth called it, especially as neither landlord nor chief tenant was prepared to contribute a penny-piece towards rethatching, reflooring and generally renovating the place. It was not the outlay of capital that bothered him, however, but the shortage of skilled labour during that first, brilliant summer of the peace, when the sun shone from early morning until late evening, as though trying to make amends for the unremitting drizzle of successive Flanders summers.

Nobody recalled a summer as hot and dry as this, not even the long period of unbroken sunshine that preceded the outbreak of the war in 1914. The streams went dry and the grass withered. Cow-parsley, heavy with white dust, drooped in the hedges, and a special meeting of the Governors had to be called to do something about the drainage system. Everyone turned as brown as a longshoreman and the cricket pitches were bumpy and sun-slippery. "A damned menace to batsmen," Carter, himself an enthusiastic cricketer, declared after Simmonds, the head boy, had returned to the pavilion with a bump over his eye that would not have disgraced a prize-fighter. But for all the drought, and the euphoria the long sunny days produced in class, Bamfylde revelled in the heat, and Sports Day, the first dry Sports Day since 1914, according to Herries, was a tremendous success. So many of the parents seemed to have acquired expensive-looking motors that the sports field looked like Lords, as scores of fashionably dressed mothers and pretty sisters nibbled their ices, and God alone knew how many war profiteers sat around smoking cigars and practising refined vowel sounds. All this from the sardonic Howarth, who stood throughout the afternoon at the finishing line, with stop-watch in his hand, and inevitable Gold Flake in his mouth. There were plenty of Old Boys, too, some of them, including Cooper and Fosdyke, in khaki, and a few others on crutches.

"There's a whiff of national recovery about," Algy Herries remarked, watching Cooper win the Old Boys' 880-yards at a canter. "Something tells me we're getting back on course and, if *we* are, here in the wilderness, then everyone else must be, my friend. We've got a healthy waiting-list already, and when the post-war crop of babies grow up—a majority of them boys, please God—we'll have to tackle the Governors about the new wing behind Outram's. I doubt if I'll be here to see it full, P.J., but you will since, you've burned your boats by taking a wife! She's a fetching gel, I hope. We could do with a little uplift in that direction, although Irvine seems to be setting a spanking pace."

Irvine was the first of the reinforcements Herries had promised him, a genial, bullheaded, heavy-shouldered young man, almost exactly his own age, who arrived via a shortened ex-subaltern's course to teach geography to all but the Second and Third Forms, where Judy Cordwainer still campaigned for neatness in preference to speed and accuracy.

David soon made a friend of Irvine, despite the fact that he was a breezy extrovert, with limited imagination. Alone among the staff Irvine had an active service record, a year and a half spent in Palestine, where he received a foot injury severe enough to get him shipped home and discharged a year before the Armistice. The wound had healed satisfactorily but one of his great toes had been amputated, leaving him with a curious, bobbing walk, as though, at any moment, he would over-balance and turn a neat somersault. He had a good Army and Varsity sports record, despite his slight disability, and promised to prove very useful when the rugby season began. In the meantime, before even settling in, he produced a blonde wife, a pretty, talkative girl with a pink and white complexion, violet eyes and a quick smile, who was no sooner introduced to the Saturday night dancing class than the senior boys were queuing for foxtrots and one-steps.

Phyllis Irvine's tremendous popularity among the boys

was a source of uproarious amusement to Irvine, a cheerful fellow who would laugh his head off recounting the circumstances under which he lost his toe. "Damnedest thing you ever saw," he said, telling the story to David over a gin and lime, in the tiny sitting-room at Havelock's. "We were lobbing five-nines from lorry to battery in a chain, and I happened to sneeze just as I laid hold of one of 'em. I dropped it, and didn't feel a thing until I came to after the anaesthetic, and saw my foot slung up to a gantry, swathed in bloody great bandages. Then I knew about it all right, and reckoned myself damned lucky it was one of ours and not one of theirs. Slice of plum cake really, since I missed the draft when we were pulled out and went in at St. Quentin, just in time for the Big Push. My battery was wiped out on March 21st. Jerry went through it like a dose of salts. Chum of mine defused my five-nine and sent me the case before he went west, poor devil. Phyl and I intend to use it for an umbrella stand."

That was Irvine, whom the war seemed to have touched very lightly, but he was honest enough to draw a sharp distinction between his eighteen months in the Near East, and David's three years on the Western Front. "Damned if I know how any of you chaps stuck it out without going loco, old man. Bloody shambles, they tell me. Don't wonder you holed up here the moment you got the chance, but I had second thoughts myself when I climbed aboard the old buggy down at the station. Reminds me a bit of Sinai—with vegetation, of course. I'm a bit worried about Phyl sticking it out in winter. Everyone except you and Carter are practically superannuated, aren't they?"

"You'll get used to it after a term or two," David said, "and if I was you I wouldn't be in too much of a hurry to move on. You might get a better social life but you won't find a more easy-going head and even some of the old stagers grow on you after a bit."

"Well, maybe you're right, but Phyl says she'll be relieved when your missus arrives. She says it's a bit like going back to school herself, with old Mother Kruger searching her desk for lipstick and letters from boys. The kids themselves seem a decent lot, taken all round. Is that your experience?"

David admitted that it was, adding that every time he moved among the seniors he had to remind himself that they were not so much sausage meat, queuing for Haig's mincing-machine.

By now, however, he was adjusting to all grades, enjoying teaching in a way he would not have thought possible a year ago. He had his own methods with the syllabus and had already introduced a range of new text-books.

His formula for teaching history seemed to produce good results, simple stuff up to Middle School, with the emphasis on personalities rather than text-book landmarks, and from then on any amount of free discussion on topics likely to crop up in the question papers of the junior and senior Cambridge exams. In the Second and Third Forms he instituted a question-and-answer system of oral tests, taught him by Howarth, who did not trust written work. "Like to find out on the spot how much has sunk in before I waste too much breath," he said. "When I'm sure I concentrate on the odd plant or two, where a modest crop can be expected. Damned waste of time marking all those bloody little test-papers, half of them cribbed. Nobody can hide ignorance at an oral round. Line the little beggars up, number 'em off, and throw spot questions at them. Give 'em three seconds before they pass and the first boy who comes up with the answer moves up to where it all started. Let 'em try and play fast and loose with that box of tricks."

It worked, as David soon discovered, but so did an innovation of his own that he employed not only in the Second and Third Forms but also in Middle School, and just occasionally in the Fifth. This was to capture the attention of the class by a whiff of scandal, or a bizarre episode that the academics would have dismissed as trivial or apocryphal.

His first real success was with the story of Owen Tudor's siege of the widow of Henry V, giving him licence to draw a lively picture not only of court life as it was lived in the mid-fifteenth century, but also of Newgate, and the administration of justice. He scored again in the blood-and-thunder-loving Third Form with a blow-by-blow description of Colonel Blood's attempt to steal the Crown jewels, an incident that led him to a general assessment of Charles II's character and policies. He sometimes started a class on a new period by plunging straight into an account of a particularly colourful incident, usually one with cliff-hanger aspects, like the flight of the Young Pretender after Culloden. All the time, with whatever period he was dealing, and whatever the age and standard of his audience, he strove to make history come alive, and would compare statesmen of the Tudor and Stuart periods with men like Lloyd George, whose antics featured in the daily headlines.

Sometimes, if he was lucky, or dealing with one of his favourite eras or characters, the lesson would fly, and both he and his class would be surprised by the five-minute bell, warning them that it was time to put away books and forage in their desks for the next period, or disperse to the dining-room.

For the rest, he was pretty well extended supervising sports, performing roster duties in the dining hall and dormitories, and helping out with activities connected with the Old Boys' Association, of which Cordwainer had been secretary for twenty-five years.

It was in this area that he began to perceive hidden qualities in the meticulous, unsmiling Judy, among them a fanatical loyalty to the school, that showed itself in endless letter-

writing and formidable documentation. Judy had a phenomenal memory. He could tell you the age, occupation and
address of every paid-up member—and there were many
hundreds of them—but Judy's approach to Old Boys was
never moderated by the passage of time. He still addressed
distinguished members of the Governing Board (or such of
them who had been boys at Bamfylde) as though they were
thirteen-year-olds, presenting a botched exercise, whereas
the Old Boys, for their part, treated him with tolerant amusement, and never resented his honking dismissal of what he
sometimes denounced as a slovenly approach to problems of
patronage and administration. Even when suggestions were
put forward by Sir John Riscoe, who had been responsible for
all troop movements in the northern command during the
war, or Brigadier Cooper, who had been on the staff of
General Plumer throughout the battle for Passchendaele
Ridge, he would still honk them down if they trespassed on
his preserves, and David would not have been surprised to
learn he had hurled his keys at them into the bargain.

David also accepted the chairmanship of the Sixth Form
'Owl' Society, a group that specialised in debates on current
topics, and played an important part in the social and
cultural functions of the school, but all this was only his outward, visible life. Beneath it was a pulsating glow centred on
Beth Marwood, and stimulated by her letters, helter-skelter
outpourings of hospital gossip, preparations for their August
wedding, and quaintly expressed endearments. Sometimes,
musing over her letters for the fourth of fifth time, he would
see her again as a lively, lovable child, living in constant
anticipation of a stupendous treat.

In her actual presence he had never been conscious of his
relative maturity, of the small gap in years, only the great
gulf of experience brought about by his experiences in
Flanders. But when he read her letters, or studied her photo-

graph in nurse's uniform that stood on his bedside table, he
began to see her in the context of boys about two-thirds of the
way up the school, colts bursting with animal high spirits
almost ready for the responsibilities thrust upon them by
Algy Herries (a great advocate of the prefectorial system) the
moment they reached the Sixth.

He wondered about her a great deal. What she would
make of life in this remote but surging community; how his
dour old mother would view her; whether she would make
allowances for the terrible ageing process, forced upon every
member of his generation who had survived the trenches but,
above all, how they would adjust to one another as lovers.
For here, he suspected, she would be far more knowledge-
able than he was.

He became so apprehensive about this that he ultimately
confided in Willoughby, the ex-R.A.M.C. doctor in his mid-
fifties, who lived at Stoke Steps, the nearest village to Bamfylde, and was regarded as the school doctor.

Willoughby was a brusque, hardworking man, with a
severely practical approach to his patients, and a sharp eye
for malingerers. David would have thought of him as a
typical ex-army doctor had not Howarth, whose standards
were impossibly high, spoken of him as a man thoroughly up
to his job. He made an appointment with Willoughby on the
excuse of a general check-up demanded by an insurance
company but when the doctor pronounced him one hundred
per cent fit, he raised the subject uppermost in his mind. To
his relief Willoughby shed his brusqueness and became
almost sympathetic.

"Don't think your misgivings are singular," he said.
"Quite the contrary. 'Veldt-starvation', we used to call it in
South Africa—any number of men came to me after we had
rounded up the last of De Wet's commandos over there.
Same thing cropped up in P.O.W. camps this time. Fellows

seemed to think they'd lost all interest, and capability into the bargain!" He smiled, as though recalling something out of his own youth. "I've known men ask for aphrodisiacs, along with their demobilisation kit, but it's all poppycock. The fact is, most males adjust to deprivation after a time. Damned good job they do, or every single one of you chaps would have come home with a roaring dose, and passed it on to the first decent woman he met. But why should you worry, seeing you've found yourself a filly you fancy? That speaks for itself, doesn't it? I hear you didn't take long to make up your mind about the girl."

"No, I didn't," David told him, "and Beth being a trained nurse ought to help, but . . . well, the fact is, before running into her I never had the slightest inclination to go out and find myself a woman. Isn't that unusual, a virgin at twenty-three?"

"Not in your case, old chap. Nonconformist upbringing, for one thing, and I've met plenty of Nonconformists who regard sex as the ultimate sin. Sensitive nature too, I daresay, but above all, pitchforked into that bloody holocaust, before your eighteenth birthday. The wonder is you can bring yourself to discuss it with a stranger. Oh, I could use a lot of long words, and sound off like a medical dictionary, but it isn't in the least necessary in your case. You're fit now. You've got the moor and that place up there to thank for that, and you've had the luck to meet a girl who revived your natural instincts. My advice to you, old man, is to let well alone and give those instincts free rein. And for God's sake, don't go into a solemn conclave with the poor girl when you're supposed to be enjoying your honeymoon. Don't plough through any of these well-meaning tracts my fellow witch-doctors are always bringing out, either. The world's been going a long time, and the population is still rising, despite our attempts to kill one another off for the sheer hell of it! Do you want children?"

"I don't think I've thought about it."

"Well, don't. If they come, they come. When they like rather than when you like. At all events, that's my experience. Family planning, my good right foot!" His face clouded for a moment. "Had two myself. Boy and a girl. The boy was killed at Vimy. Fine young chap. Made up his mind to go for surgery, like his grandfather, but a Jerry hand-grenade put paid to that. Daughter's married to a chap about your age. He came out of it with a bad whiff of gas and they're living in Scotland. He had to take a forestry job, although he was trained as an accountant. Six months in an office would kill him. Told him so and he took my tip. Got a photograph of your fiancée?"

David showed him a snap of Elizabeth, taken with her Brownie camera on the walls of Caernarvon Castle and Willoughby studied it, objectively. "Looks a bonnie lass," he said. "Should be very good for you." And then, incuriously, "How are you liking it up there?"

"I like it fine, mostly because Herries knows what he's about."

"Aye, he does. But he's had his troubles, converting the traditionalists to his peculiar style of government. Well, proof of the pudding, they say. He's getting results, and it was Dotheboys Hall when I remember it, in Wesker's time. Couldn't stand the man, neither could the boys. Here, what the devil am I doing gossiping to you? I've got a baby due over at Barrowhead Farm," and he grabbed his bag and hat and hurried out to a high-slung gig that his man had brought round from the stable. "I'll trade this in for a car as soon as they improve the roads about here," he called from the driving seat, and cracking his whip went off at a spanking trot, leaving David with the impression that Howarth was an excellent judge of character.

And suddenly it was here, the end of term with no time for

any more private misgivings. Shouted good wishes from departing boys—"Have a good hols, sir!" "Make the most of it, sir!" and a daring parting shot from the irrepressible Boyer, who had got to hear of the approaching wedding, "Don't be good, be careful, sir!"

Watching Carter's spick and span Corps march off behind his band, to entrain for its annual camp at Tidworth, he thought, "Hanged if I don't belong here, almost as much as Herries and the old fogies. And me what Bull Bickford would dismiss as 'only a fourth-termer'." Suddenly he made up his mind to ask Howarth to be his best man and Howarth surprised him by being the slightest bit flattered. "You really want an old shellback like me? I haven't worn striped pants in twenty years, man."

"It's not going to be a dressy occasion. I persuaded Beth and her father to save money on the ceremony. There's only one bridesmaid, and about twenty of us at the reception. No one from my side, except my mother and younger sister. Almost everyone else I knew is either dead, or can't afford a trip to town."

"Very well, then, but I hope your wife won't judge Bamfylde on your best man. She'll get the impression she's being sold into bondage. You're sure an ordinary suit will do?"

"Of course it will, it'll be a very simple affair."

But it wasn't as simple as all that. Waiting in the front pew of the little church at Elmer's End, where Beth's father had a clerical job with the South Eastern and Chatham Railway, David was surprised to see twenty to thirty onlookers file in, sober-looking, blue-suited men, for the most part, with hearty, shapeless wives, who he guessed were railway colleagues of Mr. Marwood, but also three youngsters in their teens, whom he recognised as Beth's younger sisters. The sight of them interested him, for he had forgotten he was acquiring a string of in-laws as well as a wife. But then a duty-conscious Howarth nudged him and he stopped looking over his shoulder, and sat waiting for the minutes to tick by, more diminished than at any time in his life, including the occasion he had first appeared in the mess on arrival from the commissioning course. His collar was fiendishly tight and his mouth and throat were parched. The organ began to play, and everybody stood up, himself in response to another nudge by Howarth, and suddenly there was Beth on the arm of her dapper little father, a cool, utterly composed vision in billowing white but with a very reassuring half-smile lighting up her brown eyes as he took his place.

CHAPTER TWO

I

Whenever he recalled that day he could never reconstruct it
in ordered sequence. It had that much in common with the
early days of his spell in hospital, a series of fitful flashes,
mostly unrelated, involving not so much himself as those
about him. Beth's clear, almost defiant responses; his own
nervous fumble with the ring, causing the rigid expression of
Howarth to relax; the eager faces of Beth's three sisters,
Margery, Beulah and Anne, as they left the church; the
shower of confetti, a handful of which hit Howarth, inducing
such a stare of outrage that David laughed out loud just as the
photographer snapped them all in the porch.

And back at the semi-detached of his new father-in-law,
with Beth's stepmother (who embarrassed him because she
somehow conveyed the impression that Beth had captured an
Oxford professor) piping her eye during the speeches. The
latter were brief and banal including his own, but there was
one exception. Howarth, charged with proposing the health
of the bridesmaid, used the opportunity to deliver a blush-
making account of the groom's war service, and his arrival
in Bamfylde where, Howarth declared, " . . . he is surprising
everybody, because he is that rare phenomenon, a schoolteacher more anxious to learn than to teach". The company
were inclined to accept this as a joke and began to laugh, but
Howarth silenced them with one of his bleak stares, that must
have killed ten thousand laughs over the past thirty years. "I
don't say that in any spirit of levity," he went on, rubbing it
in, and ignoring David's agonised look, "but on the strength
of a close acquaintanceship of eighteen months. On behalf of

Bamfylde School I welcome Mrs. Powlett-Jones" (it seemed odd to hear Howarth refer to Beth as that), "because new blood is badly needed in all our institutions nowadays, and none more so than in educational establishments. I should know. I've gone a distinguished shade of grey in the service."

It was permissible to laugh at that and Howarth implied as much by giving one of his rare, wintry smiles. They applauded enthusiastically and David got the impression that all those dour old railwaymen and their wives, and all the in-laws he hardly knew, and even his glum-faced mother toying with a glass of untasted port wine, wished them well—partly no doubt, on Beth's account for she looked breathtakingly pretty—but also, in some devious way, because of old Howarth, and the way he had spoken up for a groom few of those present had heard of a week or so ago.

He would have been worried about leaving his mother in town for the night but Esther, Beth's elder sister, the one married to the Colwyn Bay dairyman, promised to look after the old lady. So the couple were given a rousing send-off at about three-thirty, and set out for Waterloo in a beribboned taxi, arriving just in time to catch the four-twenty for Portsmouth, en route for Shanklin, Isle of Wight.

* * *

The ability to think coherently returned to him when they were sitting facing one another over tea in the restaurant car, but a crippling shyness now seemed to have overtaken her as well as him. Their conversational exchanges had a hollow ring and neither one of them, it seemed, could think of anything worth saying. He continued to fight against it and, so it appeared, did she, but presently she excused herself abruptly on the grounds of disposing of confetti that she declared was still clogging her hair, although he could not

see any from where he sat. After a few minutes he paid for
the tea and went back to their compartment, expecting to
find her there, but it was empty. She had been back, however,
for her big attaché case had been opened and closed hurriedly
leaving the shoulder strap of a slip showing. A long time
seemed to pass before she emerged looking, he thought, not
merely distrait but tense.

He began to panic a little then, casting about for some
phrase that might help to put her at ease, for the tight-lipped
girl in the opposite corner, in her smart little two-piece, tan
gloves, and blue straw hat, was a stranger to him and from
the nineteen-year-old in whose company he had explored
Welsh castles, and equally so from the confident bride who
had smiled a welcome at him at the altar. He told himself,
"It's reaction, I suppose. It's caught up with her and she's
regretting it already! Why the devil was I in such a hurry?
We should have waited and got to know one another properly
in this hols, and over Christmas, then arranged a wedding in
the spring . . ." But suddenly he saw, from her hardening
expression, that she was on the point of saying something
important and anticipated her, saying eagerly, "What *is* it,
Beth? Tell me what you're scared of? It can't be me because . . ."

She relaxed somewhat and he smiled as she said, "Because
you're scared enough for both of us? No, Davy, it's not that.
Nothing to do with you, really. It's just . . ." and to his dismay
her face turned scarlet, and her teeth clamped down on her
lip.

"Tell me."

"I . . . I can't tell you, Davy."

"But you must. You were so sure of yourself at the church,
far more so than me."

She said, desperately, "All *right*, then. If it stops you
thinking I'm scared of being married, and that I regret any-

thing . . ." He did not recall anyone ever looking so embarrassed but she pressed on: "You've . . . you've got sisters, thank God. You grew up in a little house just like ours . . ."

"What on earth has that got to do with it?"

"Everything, Davy. You see . . . well, something, awful has happened—oh, no, nothing so out of the ordinary, just—just horribly embarrassing and very annoying, particularly now. That's why I dashed off. *Now* . . . of all times! Maybe it's the excitement, maybe I miscalculated . . . I don't know . . ."

Suddenly, and with a tremendous surge of relief, he understood what she was trying to say and what had caused her plunge from serenity to near-panic. And then, on the heels of relief, came a sense of the ridiculous, so that without pausing to think whether or not it would add to her embarrassment, he shouted with laughter, dived across the compartment and threw his arms about her.

She looked momentarily bewildered but then, with urgency, "Pull the blinds!"

"The blinds? But won't it be obvious to anyone passing down the corridor?"

"I don't care about that! Pull them."

He did as she asked and while his back was turned he heard her giggle and then laugh outright. Her laughter was the most welcome sound he had ever heard and it encouraged him to laugh again.

"I feel such a fool," she said, presently. "I mean, any girl getting married *thinks* of that . . . if she's got any sense, that is. I know I did, but there it is, and it's really nothing to laugh at, is it?"

But it was, because the fact that they could laugh, and that she could blurt it out in that way, seemed to him of the greatest significance. It meant that they were in accord, to a degree that not so many newly-weds could be, and he saw it all as a tremendously encouraging portent for the future.

He said, "Well, *I* think it's damned funny. And so do you really. I suppose, in some circumstances, a bride might be relieved," but she said, quickly, "Not since Victoria's reign, and even then the groom would be entitled to feel diddled," and they both laughed again, and were still laughing when the ticket-collector looked in to clip their tickets and said, as David pocketed them, "Sorry, sir . . . madam . . . got to be done. But the best of luck and I'll lock you in if you like?" and Beth said, when they had declined his offer and he had pottered off, "Now *what* a considerate man! That's just the kind of thing you would have said if you had been a railway guard clipping honeymooners' tickets! There, that's for being so understanding!" and she kissed him in that special way of hers, absentmindedly at first but then, on second thoughts as it were, enlarging the kiss and afterwards dabbing his mouth to remove a smear of lipstick.

It set the tone for the fortnight that followed, a time of laughter, discovery and great tenderness, so that as he lay awake listening to her regular breathing, and sometimes reaching out to touch the dark hair spread on the pillow, he thought, "Time was when I had to get by on nothing but comradeship . . . comradeship of poor devils in the same boat, and it was enough when every minute might be your last . . . but now . . . well, she stands for hope, in the way kids like Boyer and Skidmore and Briarley do, and between 'em I daresay they can teach the left-overs to start out all over again . . ."

This notion of fusion, between Beth and his boys, enlarged itself in other ways during the honeymoon. It enabled him to see resurrection in others about him, at the little private hotel where they were staying, especially in the ebullience of a middle-aged Cockney with an empty sleeve and the placidity of his fat, amiable wife, and their tribe of children. "Two nippers the results o' two leaves from the front," the man told him, after a brief exercise in telepathy that was the language of all who had served time in hell. It was there also in the brassy summer sunshine, when it seemed that all the rain in the world had been absorbed into the Flanders sponge and there was none left in the sky; in the shouts of children, splashing in the shallows down at the beach; in the cheerful, vulgar postcards on the revolving display stand of a stationer's near their hotel, three of which he sent to Herries, Howarth and Judy Cordwainer, and a fourth (inscribed '*Giving my instincts full rein—damned good prescription!*') to Willoughby. But, above all, he looked for and found it in Beth, who came to him gaily and gladly, who seemed to understand better than he did what was needed to erase the past, for she said, unexpectedly, "I hope I have a child right away, Davy. For both our sakes. For me because I'd like to be young enough to enjoy watching children grow up. For you because I think you'd see a son of your own as some kind of answer to what you and all those others had to put up with all those years. I mean, you'd be even more determined to make certain nothing like it ever happened again."

It was very perceptive of her, he thought, to say a thing like that, but then her perception, revealed by her intuitive grasp of the male ego, was one of her most surprising characteristics, as he discovered within a week or two of their return to Bamfylde, and the opening of the new term bringing a clutch of new boys fresh from home and prep school. They needed a little mothering, she said, when she proposed the first of her new boys' tea-parties at the cottage.

At first he was inclined to think that she was overdoing it a little. Mrs. Ferguson, who had been a housemaster's wife for years, never gave tea-parties, not even for the prefects of Havelock's, and he suspected that some of the other wives of senior masters would click their teeth over the innovation.

But she soon infected him with enthusiasm for the idea. Seven crop-eared newcomers showed up that warm September afternoon, to scoff tea and chudleys—a Devon dainty, dripping with strawberry jam and yellow cream—on their tiny lawn, where tea was spread under their one tree, a wind-blown horse-chestnut that had weathered fifty Exmoor winters in the relative shelter of the Coombe.

The party, a little slow at first, was an unqualified success. Once their shyness had worn off the boys opened up to her, as they would to a cheerful elder sister, and he was very amused when Graves-Jones, the most forward of them, gave her a Prussian heel-click when he shook hands and thanked her gravely.

She said, when they had taken themselves off, "Well, did I strike the right note? I don't want them thinking all of us are as old as God and twice as high and mighty!" and he said, kissing her, "You were marvellous! I believe that saucy little devil Graves-Jones is hopelessly infatuated. He was looking at you over his last chudley as though you were Mary Pickford in the flesh."

"Very proper," she said, "for it's time someone did something to offset the monastic seclusion of this institution. The poor little beggars don't get a glimpse of a bit of fluff from the moment they board the train at the nearest junction, until they get back there the first day of the holidays. You can't count Matron, and that nice Mrs. Parminter. One's a dragon and the other treats them all as though they were still in the nursery."

"I'm not sure we should expect them to speculate on bits of fluff at thirteen," he said, but she replied, sharply for her, "Why ever not? They're just coming up to the age when the sex taboos are so impossibly complex that they have to be translated into dirty jokes. That's one of the mistakes about places like this. Oh, it's unavoidable, I see that well enough, but if they've got to have fantasies—and all the normal ones always will—then let them be romantic ones. I was madly in love with the All Angels choirmaster at their age."

"What was he like?"

"Like Lewis Carroll in temperament, but a little more positive. Much given to patting and pinching. He tried hard to get the vicar and churchwardens to include girls in the choir, and even designed fetching little caps for them, but they warned him off, poor little man."

That was the way of her, from the very first. Unafraid, relaxed, perfectly at ease with the establishment, but never worrying overmuch about saying or doing the wrong thing in a world where, despite all Algy Herries' innovations, tradition still rose about them like a wall patrolled by an older generation suspicious of post-war freedoms and assuming that the Edwardian *status quo* had been restored by the armistice.

She got along very well with Herries, who at once enrolled both Beth and Phyl Irvine in his operatic society, allotting them principal roles in the forthcoming production of *The Mikado* as Yum-Yum and Pitti-Sing respectively. Rehearsals in Big Hall, with Herries himself as Ko-Ko, and old Rapper Gibbs at the piano, gave her an opportunity to mix with the boys from all grades, and she formed very definite conclusions about some of them, but did not necessarily confide her conclusions to him, or not yet.

Secretly she was hard at work sorting them into their various type-categories and the exercise afforded her a good deal of amusement. There was the dashing type, like the young heel-clicking Graves-Jones, and his well-grown proto-types, like Boyer, Dobson and Letherett, now wearing double-breasted lounge suits and narrow collars after moving up to Senior School. None of these were the least shy in her presence, but all treated her with exaggerated courtesy, as if they were rehearsing an approach to the flappers they would partner at dances in a year or so, and embrace if they could prevail on them to step outside.

Then there was the blushing, gawky type, mostly in the Sixth, almost fully adult now but having a hard time of it adjusting to the presence of two pretty girls in their midst, and not in the least sure how to approach them without seeming presumptuous. Bristow, who had followed his dead brother as head prefect and captain of the First Fifteen, was such a one. Invariably he began to stammer when he played Nanky-Poo to her Yum-Yum, so that she had to cast about for a means of putting him at ease and found one by getting him to tell her about his trainee manager's post in a rubber plantation he intended to take on leaving at the end of the summer term. And here and there she came across the arty type, like Archer the Second, who played the violin well, and Blades who, at fifteen, wrote poetry, and the brash beefy extrovert types like Rigby and Bickford, who needed slapping down, she thought, before they grew too big for their boots. There was yet another type that interested her and even puzzled her a little, the boy who walked alone, not as a romantic, like the musician Archer, or the poet Blades, but dourly, as if they were repelled by the gregariousness of school life. Briarley, whom David had told her about, was such a one, and she entirely approved David's efforts to develop the slender bridge between them, begun the day the news came that Briarley's father had been killed in France.

There were one or two others she felt very sorry for and mentioned to David, but tentatively, for it seemed to her easy, in this male world, to jump to facile conclusions. Young Skidmore, the idol-hater, was one of them, for David was right about him, in that he did seem hell-bent on martyrdom. Whatmore was another, whose parents had just been divorced, imposing all the stresses that would bring to a thirteen-year-old. She said, learning that Whatmore was taking it badly, "I've nothing against divorce if a marriage is intolerable to man and wife but why the hell can't they pretend to rub along until their children are old enough to acquire a little philosophy? I think I would even if I hated the sight of you, Davy!" and as always, when she showed storming indignation over something, she made him laugh.

All kinds of boys. Fat ones, thin ones, handsome ones, homely ones. Boys with plausible excuses, boys with lame ones, boys who never bothered to offer an excuse. Boys who excelled in class but were weeds on the playing field, amiable oaks who were lions on the field and played games inside their heads through four periods in succession. Integrated boys, like Nipper Shawe, the school bell-ringer, high-principled boys like Skidmore. Intelligent extroverts, with a bubbling sense of humour like Boyer, and boys who were having a very hard time of it, like little Whatmore. One would never have thought it possible to find so many varieties in one school and there were still others waiting to present themselves as term followed term. It was very exhilarating, however, to have so many male eyes on one at church and school concerts, and to have five eighteen-year-olds competing with one another at the Owl Debating Society to bring one cup of watery coffee during an interval in the motion, 'That we support Home Rule for Ireland!' Occasionally she heard something she was not meant to hear but when that happened she was unrepentant. In a world where women were outnumbered a hundred to one, a chance to eavesdrop was a bonus.

The cottage hedge adjoined the long stone wall of Ricketts' Farm, where the boys flocked between the end of afternoon school and high tea to buy hot pasties and apple tarts, baked by old Mrs Ricketts, universally known as Ma Midden, on account of the permanent slush pools in her yard. Towards dusk one October evening Beth was in the roadside corner of the garden, screened by the overgrown hedge, planting a rowan tree in a cleared patch of ground when she heard the cheerful voices of Boyer, Dobson and Letherett approaching the farm gate.

She had not lit the oil-lamps and they must have judged the cottage empty, for Dobson said, "Old Pow-Wow's a lucky dog and no mistake. His wife isn't the kind of lulu you'd expect to bury herself alive in a dump like this. After all, she's not twenty yet, and with her face and figure she could have married ackers, couldn't she?" She only just stopped herself exclaiming at the implied slight on David overshadowing Dobson's compliment, but curiosity won and she remained bent over her spade as Letherett said, "Betsy's a corker and no mistake. I'd sooner go to bed with her than you, old sport. But don't get the idea she isn't stuck on him. Anyone could spot that a mile off." And then, mercifully before they passed out of earshot, she heard Boyer say, "And why the hell not? Pow-Wow's a damned good sort, and more on top of his job than any of them, bar the Old Man, and Howarth maybe. Jolly good luck to 'em, I say. Tumbler's blonde is easy on the eye, but a bit of a nag, I'd say . . ." and then Mrs. Ricketts' gate clicked and she heard them bawling for Ma Midden, and scampered back to the house to compose herself before Davy got home.

She didn't know quite what to make of that conversation, even though she was already sufficiently familiar with school slang to translate it without much difficulty. 'Ackers' meant money, a Birmingham word that had strayed into the Bamfylde glossary, and Davy's nickname, of course, was acknowledged by all. 'Corker' signified sex-appeal, and Herries was 'the Old Man' to everyone who did not use 'Algy', whereas Irvine had acquired the soubriquet of 'Tumbler' on account of his bobbing gait. She was a little shocked by the trio's genial contemplation of her as a bedmate, but decided adolescent boys talked the same language as hospital proba- tioners, particularly here, where women were in such short supply. What intrigued her far more, however, was Boyer's championship of Davy, and his emphatic blessing on their marriage. It meant that Boyer at least, and perhaps most of the senior boys, had considered marriage, and her particular marriage, in the abstract and that, she supposed, was evidence that it was regarded as a success. She thought of it as such, of course, and so, she was sure, did Davy, but they were prejudiced. It was something else to have it blessed by a boy of sixteen, and she would have liked to have told Davy about it but knew, instinctively, that this wouldn't do at all. Instead she lit the lamps and gave the Irish stew a vigorous stir as it simmered on the old iron stove. 'A dump' Dobson had called the cottage, but to her it was very far from that. It was a home already, a cosier and more rewarding home than she had ever hoped to possess, notwithstanding Dobson's optimistic assessment of her chances in the marriage market. Dobson was in error anyway. Men of marriageable age were scarce, with a million dead and two million maimed and incapacitated and men of Davy's temperament were scarcer still. She had made up her mind as to that months ago.

He would have been surprised to have learned the real reason prompting her display of demonstrative affection the moment he loomed out of the dusk, and its sequel initiated by her the moment they turned out the lamp and climbed into bed. Up to his job, was he? Well, she was up to hers too, she hoped, and in the moment before she slept she raised his hand to her breast and held it there, thinking, "Dear God, how lucky I was to lean over that pier-rail that time and fish Davy up from the beach . . . !" and the random quality of life made her shiver a little, so that she tucked herself into him, as though fearing he might be snatched away and swallowed up with the rest of his generation, with all the boys she had flirted with in the middle years of the war, boys who had been there one day and photographs on their mothers' mantel-shelves the next.

II

Her luck was set fair. She was granted her honeymoon wish. By late October she was so sure that she was carrying his child that a call on Dr. Willoughby for confirmation was a formality. She was amused by Davy's fussy concern, how-ever, and even more by his immediate association of preg-nancy with her forthcoming appearance in the star role of *The Mikado*.

"Good Lord!" he said, when she told him Willoughby had confirmed her hopes, "that'll put Algy Herries in a frightful fix! Who can he get to replace you at this stage?" and she said, through her laughter, "Why should he get anyone? I'll be less than four months on. Do you imagine I'm spending the next six months in a wheel-chair?"

"I wasn't thinking of that, Beth. Just the . . . well . . . the look of the thing. I mean, won't you feel damned silly, stand-ing up there singing to an audience of four hundred boys in those circumstances?"

"Not in the least," she said, "for I shan't show much. At least, I hope not, and even if I did why should I be embar-rassed? Good heavens, Davy, it's not as though the youngest of them doesn't know the facts of life. I'll wager some of them know more than me," and she remembered the con-versation heard through the hedge.

"Well," he said, doubtfully, "if you don't care I don't see why I should. Look, do you mind if I tell Ellie? I'm sure she'll be delighted. The great sorrow of her life is that she and the Old Man never had any kids and I'd like her to stand god-mother."

"Tell whoever you like," she told him gaily. "I'm already feeling insufferably smug about it, especially as Phyl Irvine's no-go turned out to be a false alarm." And then, squeezing his arm, "We haven't wasted much time, have we?"

"Who would, with you around?" he said, and although he said it as a joke she had a serene impression that he meant it.

As it turned out she was over-optimistic concerning the risks of a public display. In the straight, loose-fitting frocks of the current fashion it didn't show at all but it was a different matter when she came to tie the tight kimono sash of Yum-Yum, in the attic dressing-room she shared with Phyl Irvine at the top of the head's house. Inspecting her, Phyl succumbed to a fit of the giggles.

"I must say you look a very enterprising little maid from a ladies' seminary in that outfit," but Beth said, "It's all over the school by now anyway. Things like that are relayed by the jungle drums. I expect poor Driscoe will be more embarrassed than either of us."

Driscoe, a fourteen-year-old with an excellent treble voice, was the third member of the trio, but if he did notice he didn't give himself away and the number went off very merrily, as indeed did the whole show, playing three nights to packed houses, that included several carloads of visiting parents. Algy Herries declared that it was the best opera yet, and booked Beth and Phyl a year in advance for *H.M.S. Pinafore*.

The predictability of a place like Bamfylde struck both David and Beth that winter and each of them pondered it in different ways. David saw it as a kind of sheet anchor, something to be prized in a world that he had come to accept, up to the time of his coming here, as disintegrating in volleys of thunder and deadly flashes of lightning, a place where one could be sure of nothing. She saw it, and welcomed it, in a more subdued light, part of a pleasant rhythm that was at one with her new life and the child in her womb. It was a reversion to sanity, where people were born, passed through infancy to childhood and adolescence, and then out into the world beyond Bamfylde to earn their bread. David she saw as a conscientious overseer, poised by the conveyor belt, adding a touch here and there as the products trundled by.

She enjoyed her first term immensely, with its nonstop hilarity and avalanche of tiny events, but to David's astonishment she also enjoyed the silence of the place when all the boys and most of the staff had departed, and those few remaining drew closer together, the rump of an enormous family getting its second wind after a long, rackety party.

It was then, when the north-easterlies came flailing over the moor bringing flurries of snow, and plateau temperatures dropped below zero, that she began to think of his immediate future and made an important decision on his behalf. He said one night, when they were sitting drowsily by a big log fire in the open hearth, "Look here, Beth, this won't do at all. I shall have to use this break to set about doing something practical about my degree. Damn it, I'm the only man on the staff without one. I can't expect Algy to regard me as a permanent wartime stop-gap. There's always so much happening term time. Would you mind much if I spent the afternoon up at the school, cramming?"

She said, "Why up at school? Why not here, over in the window alcove? We could get a desk and put some shelves up between the window and chimney breast. I wouldn't get under your feet, would I?"

"No," he said, "not in that sense, but I daresay you'd distract a man from the Reform Bills and Henry VIII's foreign policy from time to time. So far I've lived almost wholly in the past, even during my first year here. I don't mean the recent past, the war and all the bloody misery chaps went through over there, but the distant past, particularly the Middle Ages. But not any longer, or not in the way I did. It's the present that counts, and the future. I even find myself getting damned impatient with text-books that stop at Gladstone's first Government and the Corn Laws. I want the kids to concern themselves more with their own times, with living history."

"I've heard you say more than once history is all of a piece."

"So it is, if it's taught properly. But the exam syllabuses don't even acknowledge the twentieth century. There wasn't a single damned question on it in last summer's Cambridge senior papers."

"I daresay all those old buffers who set them regard what happened between 1914 and 1918 as another Crimea. They'll get around to it in time."

"But that's the point," he said, "there isn't time, at least, not if we waste it, the way those bloody politicians did at Versailles last summer. That treaty is an absolute shambles. Jerry was saddled with the entire responsibility for the war, and any chance of a just peace was lost in a sordid haggle for territory and reparations. There must be some way of putting that over."

"In a text-book, you mean?"

"No, but in a book written in language an intelligent seventeen-year-old could follow without yawning."

She had a mild inspiration then, arising out of one of the first conversations they had had when he introduced her to Margaret of Anjou. She said, "If you feel it that deeply you're the person to write it, Davy. Start tomorrow!", and he replied, looking at her with his head on one side, "*Me?* Oh, go easy, Beth. It's a job for a political journalist, based on London, with access to state papers and inside contacts."

"Why is it? You went through the war and you were born and raised in a Welsh valley, where your father and two brothers died for somebody's greed. I think you've got better qualifications than any journalist or academic. Besides, you're a born teacher. Anyone spending a day in your company would concede that."

He lounged over and sat on the hearthrug, leaning his weight against her knees. "Get along with you, you think I'm capable of anything, Beth."

"So you are. And I'm not the only one."

"Who else, apart from Mam, over at Pontnewydd?"

"The head, and Howarth. Both of them are much older than you but that doesn't stop them looking to you for a lead sometimes."

"A lead? In what cause, for God's sake?"

"Against the diehards, the people who think the clock was put back four years the day the war ended. But not only them. They're no problem really because they'll soon die off. It's the group around Carter I mean, people who escaped the war but are already looking on the job in an entirely different way from you or Algy, or even dear old stick-in-the-muds like Cordwainer. This place seems united enough on the surface but it isn't really, you know. Different people are trying to steer it different ways. You believe in real education, in letting boys develop their individuality, but Carter and some of the others don't. They're only interested in exam results. There's a conflict here. Even I can see that, after four months. In fact, I can probably see it more clearly than you because I'm outside, looking in on all but the frolics."

It struck him that she was extraordinarily bright for a girl not yet twenty. Sometimes it puzzled him a little. Where did her perception and natural intelligence come from? Not from her stolid old father, certainly, and a couple of years as a hospital probationer wouldn't account for it. He said, unconsciously expressing his line of thought, "How old were you when your mother died, Beth?"

"Seven. Why?"

"Remember much about her?"

"Not a lot. I remember she wore the trousers in our house. Father was quite helpless when she died. Esther and I didn't blame him marrying the first eligible woman who caught his eye, and Nell and I have always got along. She was a good stepmother, as stepmothers go. Why, what are you driving at?"

"You. Your way of looking at things, and seeing more than the average person would see. I think your mother must have been quite a person. How about your grandparents on her side?"

"He was a Methodist minister, and gran was a school teacher in one of the first elementary schools, but I don't remember either of them clearly. Longevity isn't a strong suit in the McLeods."

He had forgotten she had Scots ancestry and this might account for all manner of things. Her earnestness, for instance, her forthrightness and preoccupation with abstract ideas, watered down by the Cockney strain on her father's side, and a Cockney upbringing that would develop a latent sense of humour. Her directness flashed out again now as she said, "You're side tracking. It's a weakness of antiquarians and you're particularly prone to it. We're talking about *you*, Davy, not my family tree. Didn't I hear Algy or Howarth say something about you doing a thesis for your degree?"

"Not for my B.A. I'd have to get that first and turn in a thesis for Master of Arts."

"Right. We'll take it from there. I'll get that corner fixed up as a study as soon as the snow lets up. You start swotting for your B.A. and you've already got a theme for your thesis —'The Gadarene Rush' or 'How-we-got-into-the-pickle-in-the-First-Place'. I'll keep you at it. I want to be a helpmate, not just a bedmate and a brood mare. Pull me up and rake those ashes down."

They left it there for the time being but she held to her purpose and the new year saw him installed in his inglenook, where he could get the benefit of the fire in a room of persistent draughts. It took him a little time to get used to working there, with her rustling about in the background, unconsciously diverting him by her over-solicitous efforts to do everything quietly so that he said, chuckling, "You don't have to walk on tiptoe and practise controlled breathing. My first two terms I taught a class adjoining that poor devil Meredith, before he got his marching orders. It was like teaching in the crater of a volcano."

After that she relaxed and he was able to lose himself in study and analysis, working steadily until the little French clock her stepmother had given them chimed nine thirty, when she came in with the cocoa and the bread and cheese.

But then, in the third week of January, Bamfylde erupted again, and what old Howarth called the 'tight-rope term' began, meaning the cold, blustery period between late January and mid-March, when inches of rain could fall in twenty-four hours, and the school was often shrouded in seeping mist. Sometimes the weather was so vile that the football field became a quagmire and matches had to be cancelled, but the runs went on. Nobody minded getting plastered with black Exmoor mud if it meant an afternoon's change of scene.

By that time, of course, Beth, in her own phrase, was beginning to look more and more like a penguin, and kept to the house, fearing a fall and disastrous consequences. But she remained very cheerful and knitted, he thought, enough tiny garments to supply a city orphanage, an occupation that seemed to bring a repose that by-passed him. For, towards the end of term, his mind was switched from her, and the winter discomforts of the cottage, by a confrontation that he was reluctant to confide in her. It was another and more serious clash with the Carter faction, highlighting her feeling that Bamfylde was indeed being pulled in opposing directions.

III

It was a deeper quarrel than the initial one, arising from his refusal to join the Corps, and left him with a sense of unease that augured badly for the future. It became known, in Bamfylde history, as 'The War Memorial Spuddle', 'spuddle' being a local word signifiying a dispute between two rival parties.

It began on a relatively civilised level but quickly deteriorated into a sour, ding-dong battle, with himself and Howarth ranged on one side, Carter and the traditionalists on the other, and Algy Herries poised in a position of uncomfortable neutrality.

The controversy stemmed from the offer of Alderman Blunt, of Challacombe, to donate five hundred pounds for the setting up of a memorial to Bamfylde's war dead, an offer that was accepted by the Governors without prior conditions. Blunt was a local war profiteer, a timber merchant who, as Howarth put it, had been a two penny-ha'penny supplier of builders' materials before August, 1914, but had burgeoned, in a matter of six years, into a magnate, with a yard, a country house set in a forty-acre country estate, an enormous Rolls-Royce, and a grand manner, far more impressive than that of old Hopgood, head of the Bamfylde landowning family with roots in the Middle Ages. Carter had spent a great deal of time and patience cultivating Blunt, and enlisting him as a patron of the school. He was therefore inclined to take upon himself the credit of finding the finance for a splendid memorial to the Old Boys and in making the gesture public somehow implied that he, personally, was giving the money.

Ordinarily it would have been a matter for the headmaster and Governors alone, but a special committee had been set up to consider the provision of a memorial, and both Carter and David had been co-opted on to it, the one representing the housemasters, the other the Old Boys' Association.

At its first meeting the committee were asked to consider three designs submitted by Blunt's tame architect. They were conventional monuments, a plain stone cross, to be erected at the head of the east drive, a bronze statue of an infantry-man in battle order, and a more pretentious design featuring an angel poised on a globe representing the embattled world. David, already nursing a profound prejudice against the rash of memorials sweeping the country, spoke out against all of them.

"As an ex-serviceman," he said, "I'm qualified to express an opinion on this. These things are meaningless. If five hundred pounds is going to be spent on a memorial to the dead why can't we spend it on something practical?"

"Such as what?" demanded Carter, sharply.

David was ready for this. "A gymnasium to replace the old covered playground. The installation of modern cooking equipment in the kitchen. Even a dynamo down by the piggeries, to provide us with our own electricity."

Algy Herries seemed impressed by the alternatives. "What do you say to that, Carter? Seems worth considering, doesn't it?"

"With respect, no, Headmaster," Carter said, "because it's out of step with the sentiment behind the gift. Mr. Blunt wouldn't favour it, I'm quite sure of that."

"You could consult him on the matter," David suggested, and Carter, seeing the head undecided, said he would do this, but was obviously delighted to inform the next meeting of the committee that his forecast had been correct.

Alderman Blunt, he reported, had now expressed a preference for the stone cross, inscribed with the eighty-odd names.

"Well, that's that," Herries said, philosophically, but David, nettled, said one aspect had been overlooked. "I think we should get the views of Old Boys before we accept," he said. "Nearly a hundred fell but six times that number served and survived. I propose we put it to the O.B.A. general meeting at Whitsun and get their views."

At this point old Bouncer, representing the church, rose to his feet and surveyed the meeting benignly under his useless spectacles. "Offer might be withdrawn by then," he said. "Settle for the bird in hand. That's my notion. Eh, eh, Carter?"

"My sentiments exactly," Carter said, "We don't want to give Mr. Blunt the idea we're looking a gift horse in the mouth. I'll move an amendment that we accept the money now and get the work in hand right away."

The amendment was put and carried, four votes to one, Herries as chairman, abstaining, and that should have been that, and would have been had David accepted his defeat gracefully. He would not, however, and sought the advice of Howarth, who said, sourly, "Since you seem determined to put a spoke in Carter's wheel, I'll give you some free advice, P.J. Can't stand the little squirt. Never could, although, for my part, I don't care a damn whether a gift from a man of Blunt's reputation is a stone cross or a supply of gold inkwells. His money's tainted and I wouldn't want it to feed starving children. The fellow's a frightful bounder!" and in a few acid phrases he outlined, for David's edification, Blunt's spectacular rise in the world. "Your best bet is to contact the Old Boys personally. Get out a circular letter on the duplicator, and ask for replies within the week. Then, if a majority support your view, throw the statistics at them." And this is what David did, sending out more than four hundred and fifty letters, and enclosing stamped addressed envelopes.

The response was gratifying. Within a week he received nearly four hundred replies. Eighty-seven per cent of them backed his proposal, favouring a memorial of some practical value to the school.

Armed with his figures he asked Herries to call a special meeting of the sub-committee and made his circular public, but Carter, forewarned, produced an ace from his sleeve in the person of Blunt himself, a florid, ponderous man, who struck David as a truculent peasant using his unexpected wealth to whip the shoulders of all the locals who remembered his hand-to-mouth days. Faced with the result of the postal poll Blunt said, without preamble, that when he proposed a memorial he meant a memorial, not an addition to the school that would lose its identity as soon as it was built or installed. There was nothing David could do but back down and if Carter had left it there the whole thing would have been forgotten by the time the cross was unveiled at the dedication service Herries had planned.

That was not Carter's way, however. Determined to savour his triumph he buttonholed David in the quad on the first day of the summer term, and said, with counterfeit affability, "Word in your ear, Powlett-Jones, and I hope you'll take it the way it's meant. You're comparatively new here, so you can't be expected to know how to handle the locals like Blunt. It so happens I do, not because I've spent ten years of my life here—aside from that spell in the army, of course—but because I'm West Country born. I know these chaps, believe me. Played the right way they can be damned useful to us. Blunt is rolling in money, and he loves kudos like a cat loves cream. Fine, let's humour him. Let's get all we can out of him. He'll end by endowing us handsomely if he's left to me."

"You want his kind of money that much?"

"Why the devil not? It's as good as anyone else's money, isn't it?"

"No, it isn't," David growled, "it's come from soaking the Government when they had no alternative but to pay anything men like Blunt had the nerve to demand. I hate the bastards who sat tight and made fortunes in the war. I've got a hell of a sight more time for the conscientious objectors."

Carter blinked at him. His eyes, David noticed for the first time, were angry, ferrety eyes, red-rimmed, as though to match his rust-coloured hair. Suddenly, inexplicably if he had been able to contemplate it in a rational mood, David discovered that he hated him.

"That's a high moral tone to take at your age," Carter said, in the voice he used to subdue mutinous spirits of the Fifth. "Why not go down to Blunt's bank and ask the manager if you can sniff his pennies one by one? Just in order to satisfy yourself none of them are tainted?"

"I don't have to, I know they are. I slept in barrack huts men like Blunt provided. They were built of unseasoned timber that worked out at about five bob a foot. The men who inhabited those rabbit-hutches—when they were lucky, that is—were getting a shilling a day, for keeping Blunt and his like from being walked over by Prussian jackboots. To hell with Blunt and everybody like Blunt! I feel like spitting every time I pass his bloody memorial, and you can tell him so if you care to!"

"But I don't, old man," Carter said, easily, "I've better manners," and drifted off, clearly quite unruffled.

It soon got around, as everything of that kind always did in a place like Bamfylde. A garbled version too, as David realised when Howarth drawled, "Hear you're likely to be running short on saliva as soon as that shroud comes off the war memorial, Powlett-Jones. Not wise, I think, to empty your chamber at a tyke like Carter. Better to leave a shot or two in reserve. You'll have more trouble with him, so take a tip from a veteran common room skirmisher like myself."

"How the hell *is* one to handle a man like Carter?" asked David, thoroughly exasperated. "He knows it all, doesn't he?"

"He doesn't know me," Howarth said, "and that's encouraged him to keep out of my way for years. In a place like this you don't fight with drawn swords, my boy. You find a nice little spot behind a chimney pot and snipe. Imagine me telling you about sniping! However, you're not a fool and you'll learn. Providing you stay long enough, that is."

It was odd how persistently his defeat at the hands of Carter nagged at him, and it wasn't long before Beth dragged it out in the open, demanding to hear the full story. She said, when he declared that he intended looking for a new situation the moment he had taken his degree, "That's silly, Davy, and if you think about it you'll see it is. There'll be a Carter in every school, and if you mean to stay in the profession you'd better face the fact. Howarth's right. It's your tactics that are amateur. You never want to give the Carters of this world an opening. I wish you'd told me about this before."

"Do you think I wanted to worry you at a time like this?"

"Pooh," she said, "a time like what? Life has to go on, doesn't it? But, in any case, I've news that should take your mind off Carter and Mr. Blunt for a spell. Doc Willoughby was here this afternoon and brought a friend of his. A gynaecologist from Bristol."

His jaw dropped and he looked so dismayed that she yelped

with laughter. "Oh, David, don't keel over! It's not that bad; at least, *I* don't think it is. Tell me, are there any twins in your family?"

"*Twins!* Good God . . . are you sure? . . . Is Willoughby and that Bristol chap?"

"More or less, I think, but doing well so they tell me. No wonder I was such a size. I was beginning to think of discarding the name 'David' for 'Goliath'. Now it'll have to be David and Jonathan."

He said, wonderingly. "You . . . you don't *mind*? You're not scared?"

"Not in the least. No, honestly I'm not, I'm . . . well . . . rather excited if anything. But Willoughby says I can't have the baby—babies—here, as planned, with Nurse Arscott standing by. I'll have to go into a Challacombe nursing home a few days in advance. Can we afford it? It'll cost about eight guineas a week, they say."

"Good Lord, of course we can afford it if it's necessary. But are you sure it doesn't entail complications? I mean, why did he bring that chap here in the first place?"

"Just to make sure," Beth said, but nothing would do but that he should go hurrying over to the village the minute prep was over, to pursue his own line of enquiry. Willoughby satisfied him, or at least moderated his anxiety, assuring him that Beth was a good, healthy girl and unlikely to run into trouble. "At the least hint of it I'd plump for a Caesarian," he said, "but I don't advise it. Go on home, and let her calm you down, old man."

And David went, walking ruefully across the little strip of moor that gave access to the junior pitches and then, through a gap in the hedge, down the road to the cottage. As he passed the angle of the buildings housing the prefects' studies, however, his ear caught the lilting whine of Carrington's portable gramophone, playing one of his favourite jazz numbers. Part

of the refrain, sung in a high nasal tone, came to him in the
fading light.

> *Yes, I'm goin',*
> *Yes, I'm goin',*
> *And soon I'll be hallo-ing*
> *To that coal-black Mammy o' mine . . .*

It soothed his nerves somehow, so that he grinned, remembering that Carrington was jazz mad, and played the saxo-
phone at school dances, familiarising everybody with the
latest wave of song-hits from the U.S.A. He thought, "Two
of them, eh? Well, if they're boys, and she swears they are,
I'll have two Carringtons here about seventeen years from
now. I wonder what they'll be playing then?"

He looked back over his shoulder as he vaulted the lane
gate at the corner of the cricket field, seeing a violet glow
moving like a slowly drawn curtain across the last rays of the
sun. In the uncertain light the huddle of buildings no longer
seemed incongruous up there on the lower edge of the
plateau and he thought, glancing back at them, "Well, that's
home, all right, and I'm damned if I let a twirp like Carter
turn me out of it," and he went down the incline to Stonecross thinking of Blunt and his war memorial as very small
beer indeed.

CHAPTER THREE

I

He was down at the long-jump pit when little Stratton-Forbes brought him the news. Stratton-Forbes of all people. The smallest boy in the school, with round, cherubic face and snub nose supporting professorial, steel-framed spectacles, for Stratton-Forbes had a squint they were trying to correct— "Before it grows on me," as he had remarked, quite innocently, to would-be tormentors, completely disarming them.

Sports Day was upon them again by then and some of the junior events were scheduled to be run off in advance. Irvine, who had appropriated to himself the role of sportsmaster, asked David's help in measuring the cinder track leading to the pit, but Irvine was not the only one at work on the jump. Carrington, the Sixth Form jazz enthusiast was there, and with him two or three other seniors engaged in spreading the cinders, when a breathless Stratton-Forbes appeared and shrieked, at the top of his voice, "Please-sir-message-from-the-Head-sir! Head-said-to-say-two-girls-sir-both-doing-well-sir!"

The entire group, David excepted, exploded with laughter and Stratton-Forbes blinked, wondering what was so funny, so that the incident passed straightaway into Bamfylde legend and Barnaby, that master-coiner of nicknames, bestowed upon Stratton-Forbes the title of 'Annunciator', soon shortened to 'Nun'. Years were to pass before Stratton-Forbes, a very serious-minded boy, fully understood how he came by his soubriquet.

But David did not hear about this until much later. The annunciation projected him through the beech hedge behind the jump-pit, up the east drive and across the threshold of the head's house in twelve seconds flat. Carrington, seeing him go, afterwards declared that Pow-Wow had beaten the world's sprint record, without even trying.

Algy Herries was standing beside the telephone in the hall, the receiver in his hand, a beaming smile on his face, so that David had no need to seek corroboration before grabbing the phone and bellowing, "Powlett-Jones here! That you, Doc? Is she all right?" and Willoughby assured him that she was as right as rain, except that the lady seemed a little put out they were girls, but had come to terms with her poor showing as a sex-determinator as soon as she was shown the twins. "She's tired, naturally," he went on, "but who wouldn't be? The first little monster turns the scale to six three, her sister at just under the six mark. Faultless performance. Congratulations, old man. Will you put me back to the head?"

"Hold on a minute . . . when can I see her . . . them . . .? Some time tomorrow, first thing? I can get Irvine to cover my periods. To hell with his hurdle course!" and at that both Herries and Willoughby laughed, and the doctor said, "Why not this evening? Say around seven. She's asleep now but they'll wake her for supper," and David turned to Herries, who nodded, and said, thankfully, "Seven sharp then. Thanks, Doc. I'll get there somehow."

"All in a day's drudgery," Willoughby said and had his word with the head, leaving David standing to one side and feeling extraordinarily foolish. He said, when Herries hooked up the phone, "Er . . . thank you for sending Stratton-Forbes, sir . . ."

"He got it right, then?"

"Word perfect. A little too perfect. He blurted it out in front of everyone. Shall we go in and tell Mrs. Herries?"

But there was no need. Ellie, concealed in the archway at

the entrance to the study passage, had been present all the time and now came forward.

"Congratulations, dear boy. It's splendid, isn't it, Algy? The first Bamfylde twins I can remember."

"The first ever," Herries said, "but it would have been better if Powlett-Jones had had a house, and the brats had been born on the premises. Wonderful headline there. 'Girl twins born in boys' school'," and he chuckled, as he usually did at his own jokes.

"Don't tease the poor boy," Ellie said, "try and be serious for a moment, do! What will you christen them? Was it fixed in advance?"

"No, it wasn't, Mrs. Herries, for Beth would have it they were boys. They were going to be David and Jonathan, but now . . . well . . . have you any ideas?"

"*I* have," Herries said, unexpectedly. "Have you seen yesterday's papers? They're canonising Joan of Arc today. There was a lot about it in yesterday's *Times*. Your subject's history. Won't Joan do for one of them? I've always liked the name myself."

"I'll certainly put it up to Beth. Joan. Yes, I rather like 'Joan' myself."

"And how about the other?" asked Ellie. "Joan of Arc was unique, wasn't she? You could choose another saint of course . . . Ursula, Veronica, Mary . . . they're all nice names," but Herries cut in, impatiently, saying, "Pish, my dear! You're missing the point. People will never see Joan of Arc as a saint, no matter how much Rome puts out about the poor girl. She'll always be associated with simple heroics. What we need now is another heroine. An English one, for preference. Any ideas, P.J.?"

It seemed absurd to be standing here in the tiled hall, discussing his children's given names with Herries and his wife. Absurd but very cosy and reassuring, almost as if the rubicund, white-maned old chap had really assumed the personality of that earnest bowlegged miner, who had gone into the lower workings of the Pontnewydd pit one summer morning and never been seen again. And thinking this David felt an impulse to humour Herries at all costs and said, "How about 'Grace'? Grace Darling, of course! Or 'Emily', after the suffragette, Emily Davison, who comes from the same part of the world?"

"I'll plump for Grace, if you don't mind," Herries said, "We've had about all we can stand from the suffragettes."

" 'Grace' will do very nicely," said Ellie, "but for heaven's sake don't let him bully you into using those names if your wife doesn't care for them. He's always been very silly about names, and that's nonsense, of course. He's never liked my sister Maud, simply because he had a nagging aunt of the same name. But here, what am I thinking of? We should be drinking your health, shouldn't we? Wetting the baby's head, isn't that what it's called?" and she led them into the drawing-room where Algy unearthed a fine pale sherry that he kept for himself and a few chosen friends. "I never waste this on parents," he said. "Sweet does for them. For the Governors, too, except one or two Old Boys, sharp enough to hang about until the others have gone."

They drank to him and then to Beth and the twins, and by four o'clock that afternoon, having skipped his last period, he was halfway to Challacombe by the lower road, the longer but faster route on account of its surface and gradients.

It was years since he had sat a motorcycle. The last, he recalled was a Brough Superior he rode in the Salient while doing a spell of despatch-carrying. This one chugged along at an uncertain twenty-five miles per hour, giving him time to bask in his own serenity, that merged with the flowering May countryside and made him want to express his glee in song. And soon he did, keeping time with the stuttering beats of the Douglas engine, crooning snatches of 'Coal Black Mammy', Carrington's favourite dance-tune,

> *Not a cent, not a cent,*
> *And my clothes are only lent . . .*
> *But I know she'll think I'm just fine . . .*

His high spirits expressed itself in other ways, in cheery waves at farmhands he passed, and in squeezing the bulb horn at every bend in the road, and in this way, with two hours to spare, he chut-chutted into Challacombe and stopped outside Gorman's the florists, to buy an enormous bunch of flowers, remembering as he did that huge bouquet he had bought her the day after her nineteenth birthday.

*   *   *

She looked prettier and more radiant than he ever recalled, with colour in her cheeks and a triumphant sparkle in her brown eyes. Clearly she was tremendously pleased with herself and said, when he kissed her with the restraint he had shown that first time outside her sister's dairy, "Oh, come *on*, Davy! Don't travel backwards! You can do better than that, can't you?" and she kissed him, with no nonsense about it, and said she was quite reconciled to the girls because they were unbelievably pretty—"Far prettier than I ever was, and prettier than Esther was as a baby and she was the flower of the flock, so Father says. You can't actually see them but you can nip into the corridor and peep through that glass-panelled door. The staff nurse there is a frightful dragon. You'd think she'd given birth, and I'd tidied up afterwards!" and as much to humour her as satisfy his own curiosity he slipped out and glanced through the glass panel of a door marked 'Maternity', and was rather taken aback by what he saw, a row of half a dozen cots, each, presumably, containing a baby, although he couldn't be sure because some of the canopies were raised.

He was still craning his neck there, trying to identify his own children, when a pleasant voice at his elbow said, "Mr. Powlett-Jones, I presume?" and he turned, blushing, to confront a slim, blonde woman wearing a red-lined cloak of matron.

"Yes," he said, "I'm Mrs. Powlett-Jones's husband. I was trying . . . er . . . er which two *are* mine, exactly?" and the matron smiled and edged him over the threshold, saying, "Just a peep. They're sleeping and, anyway, you mustn't stay long. We don't usually allow visitors the same day but Dr. Willoughby said you were rather special. Are you, Mr. Powlett-Jones?"

"Every father of twin girls is special," he said, quickly getting the measure of her, in the manner boys like Boyer and Dobson had taught him. "These two?" and when she nodded, "Well, Beth's right! They are pretty, the pair of them, but I suppose all the fathers say that, don't they?"

"No," she said, "mostly they stammer and goggle, and don't say anything intelligible. I suppose you don't because you're accustomed to infants."

"Not this age, and certainly not this sex," he said, taking a sudden liking to her. Then a door at the far end of the little ward banged open and a buxom nurse cruised in like a Whippet Tank, and sensing her extreme indignation both he and the matron made a strategic withdrawal to the passage where she went about her business. He returned to Beth's room, announcing that he had not only seen Joan and Grace but compromised the matron in the eyes of her underling.

"You're absolutely right," he went on, "they're a couple of . . ." but she cried, "You *named* them! You called them by name! And I've been lying here cudgelling my brains ever since I was told David and Jonathan were out. Joan and Grace! Why, that suits them exactly, Davy! How clever of you."

"I can't take credit for it. Algy and Ellie agreed the names between themselves, and presented me with a *fait accompli*. Seriously, though, I'd like to call them that, if only to please the old couple. Algy's been splendid all the time you've been gone, and I've been pigging it up in the President's room. Since they heard it was twins they've begun to think of them as grandchildren."

"Joan and Grace it is then . . ." but then she yawned, so that he said, "I'd better take myself off. I can look in tomorrow, it's a special half-day for the Devonshire Dumplings match. I'll borrow Barnaby's Douglas again. He's umpiring, I think."

"Please," she said, but sleepily, so he kissed her and stole away, walking down the hill into the evening sunshine and feeling slightly less excited than when he climbed it but more certain, somehow, of the unfolding pattern of his life and hers.

II

There was no doubt about it. The twins and their presence in the crowded little cottage at Stonecross increased his confidence in himself in a way that everyone about him noticed, not only Herries and Howarth, but the more discerning of his boys, especially those that he had begun to think of as friends. Boyer put it into words when David's name cropped up during one of those desultory conversational exchanges the old hands indulged in concerning members of the staff who had joined the family after themselves, thus giving them licence to patronise.

"Y'know, history periods were a crashing bore before Pow-Wow showed up but now they're a high spot. You never quite know what line he's going to take, in or out of the syllabus. Carrington told me he introduced another book of war poems to the Sixth yesterday. By a chap called Wilfred Owen. Bolshie, of course, but that's Pow-Wow, isn't it?"

But no one could accuse him of Bolshievising history in the junior forms although, judged by his own standards, he was prone to revert to old-fashioned methods. The truth was he would use any means to brighten a period, to leaven it with anecdotes, speculations and sometimes doggerel rhymes that he recalled from his elementary school days.

There was a great favourite, designed to jog the memory concerning the string of battles in the Wars of the Roses, dull enough in themselves, maybe, but not the way Pow-Wow presented them, for he used them as a means of teaching the Second and Third Forms the art of war in the fifteenth century, and would even turn aside to sketch bills, glaives, body armour and the early ancestors of the trench mortar on the blackboard. As regards the doggerel, he felt it contributed a little to Irvine's geography lessons, whisking the boys all over England in the wake of the Yorkist and Lancastrian armies. 'All-Boys-Naughty-Won't-Memorise-All-Those-Horrid-Hateful-Battles-To-Bosworth' the Second Form would chant, thus, by identifying the capitals with place names, recalling battles at St. Albans, Bloreheath, Northampton, Wakefield, Mortimer's Cross, St. Albans again, Towton, Hedgley, Hexham, Barnet, Tewkesbury and Bosworth.

It was a great success, as was the old saw to remind them (God alone knew *why* they should be reminded) of the fate of Henry VIII's wives, viz:

> *Divorced, beheaded, she died;*
> *Divorced, beheaded, survived.*

He sometimes invented new ones to raise a laugh, as when he fixed the sequence of the Stuart kings in their minds with—

> *James was nearly blown sky-high,*
> *Charles, his son, knelt down to die.*
> *Charles-the-next hid in the oak,*
> *James-the-next was a bigoted bloke.*

It was all very juvenile, he supposed, but it added to his popularity, for the boys loved to feed upon staff eccentricities and this was one of his. The broad effect of his free-ranging and highly improvised methods had more important results, however, introducing a fruity generality into his periods, and enabling a class to break free of the cast of history text-books and cruise down what he thought of as the main-stream of time.

He had always seen history as the Clapham Junction of education. It opened doors on so many other subjects, not only geography, but English prose and poetry, economics, law, religious knowledge and any number of fringe subjects. A brief study of Edward I's administrative reforms, for instance, whetted the appetite of some—just a few, here and there—interested in the British jury system. An hour or two spent with Lord Shaftesbury's industrial crusades shed some light on the Trades Union movement, and the strikes headlined in the newspapers. In the Fifth and Sixth Forms it was sometimes possible, in his view, to humanise history to a point where he had seventeen- and eighteen-year-olds questioning accepted attitudes concerning the structure of democracy, and the lessons that were to be learned (but rarely were) from the long stalemate on the Western Front.

Here and there, of course, he was challenged. Gilbert, a Tory M.P.'s son, boldly disputed his over-facile analysis of the Russian Revolution, but he dealt with him gently, content to point out that the Czarist regime had been overthrown by the abysmal folly of the ruling class, stoking the fire century by century without once opening a valve to siphon off the steam.

"But surely that's no justification for slaughtering the entire royal family, is it, sir?" Gilbert had argued, and he said, mildly, that it was not, but one rarely looked for justification in human affairs, only the merciless logic of cause and effect. "If the Czar, or rather that neurotic wife of his, had bent a little in 1916, she wouldn't have been murdered in 1918. Over here, thank God, our royal family had more sense, or perhaps more regard for their own skins. Victoria was the most revered monarch in the world when she died in 1901, but as to real political power, she exercised virtually none compared with her uncle, in 1837. That's what I mean by bending, and as a nation we're very good at it, Gilbert. You ask your father if you don't believe me."

Fortunately for David, Gilbert *père* was a left-wing Tory, with a heavy build-up of unemployment in his own industrial constituency. "Like to meet that chap," he told his son during the holidays. "He sounds original for a schoolmaster," and Gilbert Junior obliged, introducing them at the subsequent Speech Day, when they had an amicable discussion on the wisdom of nationalising the coal mines.

This was the way of it, and all that summer and autumn, while Beth was fully occupied coping with the twins in a four-roomed cottage lacking piped water, electricity or even an indoor privy, he was growing into the ethos of the school, so that sometimes it seemed to him he had been here ten years instead of just over three.

It was often difficult, under the circumstances, to continue studying for his degree, but he achieved slow progress and made tentative arrangements to sit for his B.A. at

Exeter University College of the South-West during the forth-coming Easter break. He hated the idea of leaving Beth to cope with two twelve-month-old babies but there was no help for it. Exeter couldn't give him a degree but it was the nearest centre available for sitting the exam. Long before he went, however, something occurred that entrenched him even more deeply at Bamfylde, enabling him to throw down roots that would take a great deal to dislodge.

*　*　*

They were passing through one of their tiresome periods, assailed by snow, then by ceaseless downpours, and finally to-wards the fag end of the Christmas term, by another sharp spell of frost that caused havoc with Bamfylde's antediluvian water supply. On the last day of February Bat Ferguson approached him with news that his aged French mother-in-law had died in Beauvais, and he was obliged to cross the Channel, attend the funeral and clear up her affairs. He would be away a week, he said, and would be greatly in-debted to David if he would live in as resident housemaster of Havelock's during his absence.

It was a confounded nuisance but, having lived there prior to his marriage, he was more familiar with the routines of Havelock's than any of the younger men, and Ferguson invited him to bring Beth and the twins up from the cottage and occupy his quarters for the week. David accepted the chore but Beth declined the invitation to move into the school.

"It'll be an awful upheaval, with all the children's things," she said, "and not worth it for a few days. You sleep up there and come home for lunch every day. I'll be perfectly all right down here, and I can always send a message by Mrs. Ricketts' boy if I need to. You ought to help out, oughtn't you? You always told me the Fergusons were kind to you in their old-fashioned way when you lived with them."

She packed him off with a bag and he took up quarters in his old room, with its view over the rolling moor. Nothing much was to be seen there now, apart from wan glimpses of frozen stubble and a desolate hillside whenever the wind tore rents in the prevailing mists. Shouts, scuffles and the impact of boots on the setts of the quadrangle below were muffled, and even the clamorous notes of Nipper Shawe's bell-ringing seemed to come from far out on the moor.

He called the roll, went the rounds, exchanged a joke with Boyer and Dobson who were Havelock boys, and supervised 'Silence', the five minutes dedicated to private prayer by the bedsides. It was a duty he performed with secret amusement, being absolutely certain that young Skidmore, the Methodist parson's son, was the only boy there who used the interval to commune with the Almighty. After that he followed Ferguson's Airedale, Towser, into the housemaster's study, where he built up the fire and spent a couple of hours brushing up on Central European history as far as Charlemagne's death.

It was a period that had always confused him and his mind kept wandering from the page, isolating irrelevant incidents from his own past rather than that of Charlemagne's. He saw himself fishing with his father in the then untainted stream a mile or so above Pontnewydd. He mused for a moment on the chubby face and clear blue eyes of a girl called Olwen Thomas, who had attracted him when he was at the Grammar School. Errant thoughts of Olwen's smile led him, naturally enough, to a sleepy awareness of Beth and the twins, sleeping as soundly, no doubt, as the seventy-odd boys in the two dormitories overhead. When he heard the duty prefect's step pass on the stairs he roused himself and, telling himself he was entitled to a whisky for leading a bachelor's life for a week, poured a stiff tot from Ferguson's decanter, afterwards re-addressing himself to Charlemagne.

It was no use. Apart from Beth's spell in hospital, this was the first night they had spent apart since their marriage, more than two years ago, and already his body hungered for her, so urgently that he could laugh at himself as he thought, "My God, I wouldn't care to live celibate again in this place . . . I wonder if she's missing me?" and then the unaccustomed whisky (he was a gin or beer drinker when he drank at all) had its effect and he nodded off, the heavy book slipping from his knees and falling with a soft thud beside the indifferent Airedale.

Outside the wind got up, whooping down from the moor like a foray mounted by savage hill-tribes but it did not wake him. What did, some twenty minutes after midnight, was Towser's long, spine-chilling howls, projecting him from the armchair at a bound.

The dog was crouching over by the door, feet braced, head thrown back, every hair on his body standing out like the coat of a hell-hound in a Nordic folk-tale. He shouted, "What *is* it, Towser? What's up, for God's sake?" and the dog stopped howling and began to whine, weaving his muzzle to and fro, as if terror was communicating itself to him by the scent of something gross and evil.

David felt his own flesh crawl as his bemused senses grappled with various possibilities. A ghost? Was Havelock's haunted? If so he had heard nothing of the story, and it would be common currency in Bamfylde, where legends were hoarded like miser's gold. Boys, perhaps, out on the prowl? That was more likely, and glancing at his watch David reached the door in three strides and flung it open.

The stench and unmistakable sounds that assailed him were more frightening than any ghost. Something was burning and, to judge by the volume of smoke billowing in the strong draught on the stairs, it was well alight. Standing there, momentarily paralysed by dismay, he could see a small rosy glow pulsing behind the pall, and hear the soft, menacing crackle of burning woodwork. It was the sound that prompted reflex action, of the kind he had learned over three years of kill-or-be-killed at the Front. Leaping down the stone stairs, with the terrified dog at his heels, he tore open the heavy door of the linen-passage leading to the western arcade of the quad, grabbed Nipper Shawe's bell that stood on a niche beside the post-box, and swung it. Seconds later he was halfway up the second flight leading to the dormitories, where a stream of boys collided with him, some in their dressing gowns, some in their pyjamas, all pouring down the steps in a flood so that he had to grab the iron rail to prevent himself being carried away with the rush.

He managed to grab Dobson, somewhere in the middle of the bunch, and bellowed, "Junior dorm . . . boys beyond? Are they all out?" and Dobson shouted, "Yes, sir! Think so! Ridgeway was there counting them . . .", and then Dobson was swept away as Ridgeway, the duty prefect, appeared just above him bawling, "*Steady*, there! . . . Take it *easy*! The bloody stairs can't burn, you idiots."

He fought his way up level with Ridgeway, a tall, pallid boy, wearing fancy check pyjamas. Odd the things that struck you at a moment like this for he recalled, even as he grabbed Ridgeway by the shoulders, that Ridgeway was the dandy of the Sixth, with his locker full of fancy ties and purple socks. He shouted, "Counted the juniors? They're *all* out?" and Ridgeway wincing, said, "Counted eighteen, sir! That's the lot in there, but the annexe . . .!"

"Who sleeps in the annexe?"

"I . . . I'm not sure, sir!"

"*Think*, man, *think*!"

"The two Kassavas, sir . . ."

"They didn't pass you?"

"No, sir, I'm almost sure they didn't . . . it was one hell of a rush, can't be sure."

He said, between his teeth, "Take the bell. Go on down and line 'em up in the quad. Count 'em again, double-check 'em and send someone over to the head's house to phone the Brigade."

"Yes, sir," and Ridgeway was gone, leaving him alone two-thirds of the way up the stairs, with the smoke thickening, the glow beyond it spreading, and a sound like ten thousand dry sticks being snapped over in the boarded passage on the left of the landing.

He identified this at once as the heart of the fire, a draught funnel running immediately above the linen rooms below, but the identification seemed unimportant. What obsessed him now was the thought of the two Kassava brothers, almost surely cut off in the little annexe just beyond the junior dormitory, two first-termers from India, the sons of a rajah's physician so they said, who slept in Havelock's as spillovers from Outram's, very short of bedspace that term. He thought, with a sickening fatality, "They probably don't even know the geography of the bloody house, but there's nowhere they *could* have gone, except through the junior dorm and past Ridgeway," and clapping a handkerchief to his face he dashed into the disordered senior dorm and down its length to the connecting door. But here, to his amazement, he was checked. There was no hope of going beyond it for the fire seemed to have run along under the floor and burst out of the pipe vents beside the washstands. The junior dorm was blazing from end to end, the fire concentrating at the extreme end, where the annexe lay.

He could not go on but he was terribly unwilling to leave. He stood there dithering a moment, the iron clamour of the bell reaching him from below, a background rhythm to the swelling tumult down there. Then somebody coughed at his elbow and in the light of the flames he saw Boyer, who gasped. "They're out on the roof, sir! Between the two gables ... Ridgeway's shouting to them to move along .. Better go, sir ... before the floor caves in!"

They ran back through the senior dormitory, across the landing and down the two flights of stone stairs to the quad, and as they went Boyer said breathlessly, "Roused the head, sir. Mrs. Herries phoned Stoke Steps and Challacombe. The village team shouldn't be long ... Head's taking a roll-call ..." and then they were in the quad and Ridgeway was pointing up at a steep 'V' between the two gables at the north-west angle of the quad. In the rosy glare outlining the roof he could see two small figures, peering down into the surging quad, and right below them Irvine, chivvying a squad of about a dozen senior boys, ranged around the tarpaulin that covered the cricket pitch on rainy days in summer.

It seemed to him astounding that the tarpaulin could have been located so quickly, and even more so that everybody but the Kassava brothers were right here in the quad, ignoring Ridgeway's shrill commands to go down the passage to Big Hall for a call-over, but staring upward at the two little figures crouched behind the guttering. He understood then, however, that the Kassava brothers would never jump, they that would have to be pushed, or shown some safer way down, and once again his trench reflexes came to his aid, and he grabbed Boyer by the arm, saying, "That rope in the covered playground—the one with the hook ... And the *lighter* rope, holding it to the wall ... we'll have to get them!"

They crossed the quad at a run, elbowing boys out of their way, and in ninety seconds were back with the ropes, a thick one fitted with a brass hook, part of the makeshift gymnasium equipment, and a long coil of clothes-line rope, used for fastening it back when it was not in use. Boyer said, "We could fasten one to the other and throw it up . . . But even if they grab it they'll be too scared to make fast and slide down . . .", and he saw Boyer was right, and that someone would have to carry the lighter coil up to them.

He said, "I could make it from the Remove window . . . There's all that creeper and the drainpipe. Find the head, tell him what I'm at, and keep that tarpaulin team in position. Never mind the bloody roll-call, the fire's confined to Havelock's, no other house is involved yet."

He thought Boyer said, "Come with you, sir," or something like it, but he could not be sure. He was gone by then, pounding up to the steps to the Remove that was situated immediately below the gable ends one storey down. There was plenty of light here, not only from the glare above but from the quad lamps. It took him no more than seconds to join the ropes, force open the tall window and scramble through on to a tiny, lead-covered platform surrounding the braces of the drainpipe.

There was just enough room here to pause and regain his breath. Looking up he saw he was now about sixteen feet from the ridge between the gable ends but the fire beyond the inner gable was spreading rapidly. From this angle it seemed to be on the point of engulfing the gables. He lifted one foot and wedged it into a clutch of creeper, then hoisted himself up another foot or two, the lighter rope gripped between his teeth. He had a curiously intense feeling of isolation up here, as though he was separated from the sea of upturned faces below not by some thirty feet but by the height of a mountain. It was oddly silent, too, despite the steady crackle of the flames and the soughing gusts of wind fanning them. The drainpipe was rusty under his palms but the creeper seemed tough and fibrous, sufficiently so to support his weight, so that he went steadily upward until he could have reached out and touched the two white faces peering over the edge of the guttering.

It would have been simple enough if he could have called to the boys, telling them to stretch out an arm and take the rope but this was impossible with the rope clamped between his teeth and in any case they seemed immobile, wedged there like a couple of gargoyles. So he pushed on over the gutter, its rough edge tearing at his jacket and his outflung hand found a leaded ridge to give him a final purchase. With the rope entangled in his legs he rolled on to the platform, sat back and began to haul, looking over his shoulder for a crevice or leading edge where he could fix the hook when he had drawn it up.

Kassava Major came alive then, moving forward a few inches to help him pull, and between them they hauled in the full length of the lighter rope, and then the hook and a few feet of the heavier rope. It would be too short by a couple of yards, he would judge, but with so many below this was nothing to worry about. The immediate problem, having wedged the hook under the inner window ledge of the annexe, was to persuade the boys to trust themselves to the rope. He said, addressing the elder Kassava, "It's the rope from the gym, strong enough to support a horse. Can you shin down it? If you slip there's a tarpaulin to catch you." Kassava Major's voice seemed steady enough as he said, "I'll do it, sir . . . but the kid . . ." and he left the sentence in the air, spreading his hands outward in what struck David as an oriental gesture of resignation.

He was right, of course. Kassava Minor, rigid with terror, was a child of eleven. Nothing would induce him to project himself over the edge of the drop. He made up his mind on the spot. "We'll have to lower him . . . Explain what he has to do . . . he'll take it better from you," and he hauled on the heavy rope until he drew it in and made a loop of the loose end.

The elder boy seemed to have completely recovered his nerve. Above the roar of the flames he could hear Kassava Major repeating over and over again, "It'll be all *right*, Jimmy . . . Do what Sir says . . . Just *do* what he says," and between them they managed to slip the loop over the child's shoulders and tighten it round his waist, but once that was done they were no farther on, for Kassava Minor clung to the guttering with both hands, and with his full weight braced to the rope David could take no part in prising them loose. He saw Kassava Major's right arm move then, just once and very swiftly, up and then down, and suddenly the rope went taut, and Kassava Minor was suspended below the guttering and he was able to pay out, a few inches at a time, until suddenly the rope went slack and he could haul it up again, finding that in that tiny interval someone below, with their wits about them, had climbed on to the tuckshop roof and untied the cradle, giving him another three or four feet to spare.

There was no time, and no need to peer down to satisfy himself that the younger boy had made a safe landing. Showers of sparks shot from the windows of the annexe and smoke was thickening, masking everything about them but the stark silhouette of the gables and the roof of the head's house immediately opposite. They had little chance of surviving. The orange flames, shooting horizontally from the annexe window, would blast them from the crevice at any minute and send them plummeting down to the quad. He could not see Kassava now, despite the glare, and might not have realised he was alone up here had not the roar from the crowd announced the plucky kid's safe arrival thirty feet below. Then he saw that he must shift for himself and rolled on his belly, testing the anchorage of the rope before projecting himself backwards and outwards, over the gutter. His jacket caught again, ripping clear down the front and he seemed an interminable time going down. Then, inexplicably to him, Irvine was there, and Howarth wearing a bright plum-coloured dressing gown, and old Algy Herries shouting, "Take him inside! Take him across to my house..." and he felt himself half-lifted and swept clear of the press and the next moment he was sharing a sofa with Kassava Major, who was grinning and rubbing the knuckles of his right hand. He said, vaguely, "Where's your brother, Kassava?" and the boy said, almost apologetically, "He's still out cold, sir. I had to do it. He was like . . . like a limpet, sir!" and grinned again, holding up his bruised knuckles for inspection.

III

He played no part in subsequent events, in containing the fire to the top storey by a human chain of bucketeers, senior as far as the first landing, staff and domestics on the flight of steps beyond. He did not see the arrival of the village hand-pump team, or, some twenty minutes later, the crashing descent of the Challacombe brigade, in their new Merry-weather engine. Between them they got it under control by dawn, sending their jets arching across the quad and stopping the spread of flames south to the Fifth form room and his old bachelor's quarters, or north to the Outram dormitories, the covered playground and the labs. The damage was extensive, two dormitories and the linen room gutted, Ferguson's living quarters flooded and all its ceilings down, but it might have been much worse and surely would have been but for so many factors that, looking back, made a pattern on his disorganised memories. The Airedale's spine-chilling howl. Ridgeway's cool performance at the door of the junior dormitory. Boyer's timely appearance through the smoke. Kassava Senior's pluck and resource in knocking his brother cold when he was clinging to the ledge. Carter's cool lead in evacuating the Outram dormitories, and the Herculean performance of the amateur firefighters and their antiquated equipment from the village. But he saw and evaluated none of these things at the time, for the nervous reaction was swift and salutary and he was back again, physically at least, to a time nearly three years before when a single tiresome incident would cause his hands to shake uncontrollably and the nerves in his cheek to twitch. He spent the rest of the night with the Herries; and Beth, leaving the twins in the care of Ma Midden at the farm, came to claim him in the morning. With her on the scene he quietened down and began to come to himself but slowly and uncertainly, like a man snatched from the sea at his last gasp.

He certainly did not see himself as a hero but there were others, it seemed, who did, and he was made aware of this under circumstances of hideous embarrassment when, on the final evening of term, he went into Big School to take prep for the Lower and Middle School. On the instant of his setting foot on the dais everyone stood up and began cheering so that he gazed around as if everyone there had lost his wits. After a moment or two, however, he understood that the ovation was for him, and that it was completely spontaneous, touched off by some hidden spring of emotion in the hearts of the boys who had stared up at him and the Kassava boys on that niche. He raised his hand then and when they did not stop he roared, "Sit *down*! Everybody *sit*! Where the hell do you think you are? At a Cup Final?" and at that they laughed and resumed their seats, and he too sat and pretended to read but found himself listening to the pounding of his own heart as he thought, presently, "I couldn't leave here after this . . . This is the end of the road for me, and for Beth too.

I thought I was home and dry a long time ago, when I brought Beth here and she liked it, when the twins were born. But they were only stages and this isn't. It's a terminus."

But even that wasn't quite the end of the affair. Towards the end of the holidays, when he was spending an hour with Algy Herries on the timetable, Ellie looked in with tea and said, "The post is in. There's a parcel for you, dear boy!" and while he was asking himself who on earth would be likely to send him a parcel, and why it should come to the school rather than the cottage, he saw Algy and Ellie exchange the kind of look parents exchange over a Christmas tree when the family are opening gifts, and fumbled with a small, carefully wrapped package bearing a Delhi postmark that only increased his mystification. Then Algy said, impatiently, "Here, give it to me! You'll let the tea go cold!" and took it, stripping away the wrapping to reveal a square cardboard box. Inside, bedded in blue velvet, was a slim, very elegant gold cigarette case, inscribed with his initials.

He stared at it uncomprehendingly until Algy said, with a chuckle, "Go on, open the wretched thing. Touch the spring and tell us who's playing Father Christmas in April." He touched the spring and inside was a visiting card bearing the name *S. E. Kassava, M.D.(Edin.), F.R.C.S.*, and when he lifted the card there was an inscription above the hinged clip that read, "*In deepest appreciation*", and underneath it the date of the fire.

He said, wonderingly, "It's magnificent ...! But he didn't have to do that ... Why, young Boyer would have shinned up that drainpipe if I'd let him. So would Irvine or Ridgeway or anyone else if they'd thought of it."

"But that's the point, dear boy," Ellie said, her Adam's apple sliding up and down with emotion, "They didn't.

Or not so quickly. Now, Algy, put that horribly complicated-looking timetable aside and have tea. We're supposed to be on holiday, aren't we?"

CHAPTER FOUR

I

1922, 1923, 1924. The years unfolded, season by season, term by term, with a pleasant, almost timeless rhythm, as though Bamfylde, tucked away under a fold of the high plateau, was a planet in its own right, only marginally involved in the rest of the solar system.

Ordinarily, sometimes for months at a time, the planet spun an unremarkable orbit, within the ageless succession of spring, summer, autumn and winter, changeless or so it seemed to David, with its traditional sequences marked off in the school calendar issued to every boy on the first day of a new term.

In the Lent term there were the house matches, the second half of the cross-country season, the Choral Society's Holy Week Concert, the confirmation classes conducted by Algy Herries, the end-of-term examinations for class prizes to be distributed at Speech Day, and the endless shuffle from class to class and period to period, a marathon that took him, in a matter of thirteen weeks, all the way from the Roman conquest to the murder of the Archduke Franz Ferdinand at Sarajevo, in June, 1914, and occasionally a little beyond, as when he asked of the Sixth what they made of the poems of Owen, Graves, Rosenberg and Siegfried Sassoon.

He was invading Howarth's territory here but old Howarth did not seem to mind and was, in fact, grateful for David's English periods in the Second and Third Form. He was glad these had been fitted into the timetable more or less permanently. An hour or so every week, he was able to commune with Goldsmith and Gray, Swift, Tennyson and Blake, airing the corridors of his mind and opening up rewarding cul-de-sacs on the eighteenth and nineteenth centuries. The same applied to trespasses on Irvine's subject, when he would draw a freehand map of Europe on the blackboard of Big School and illustrate, with a cluster of sweeping, south-easterly curves, the dramatic switch of Napoleon's Grande Armée from the Boulogne camps to Ulm and the defeat of the Coalition at Austerlitz in the winter of Trafalgar.

Of his incidental efforts in these directions both Howarth and Irvine would sometimes make common-room jests, as when Howarth said, referring to his introduction of the Middle Third to Goldsmith's 'Deserted Village', "Keep 'em hard at it, old man! With you clearing the ground in that Lower School desert there's that much less sod-breaking for me when The Lump gravitates to Middle School! Not all that much less, of course. Most of The Lump doze through *Hamlet* and Marlowe, damn their churlish souls. But every now and again I find an uncut diamond where I least expect it. Blades is a case in point. Two years ago you started him on mere doggerel, like 'The Ballad of Patrick Spens'. Now he plagiarises Robert Herrick!"

'The Lump' was the staff name for the inevitable group in every new cadre of boys, those odd dozen or so, who clung together in a sullen, unleavened mass, moving up the school at the rate of one shift a year, and finally coming to anchor in the Lower Fifth, where they grew downy moustaches while making successive stabs at school-leaving certificate.

"Autrefois Le Lump, toujours Le Lump," as Ferguson put it, but this wasn't strictly true. Now and again, about halfway up the school, a boy's interest in a subject would quicken, so that he broke free of The Lump and set an individual course. The Lump, incidentally, contributed all

the regulars to Saturday penal drill, where they applied
the same tactics dodging punishment as they displayed
work-dodging in class. It was years before David, who
occasionally took the penal squad, discovered why boys
like Bickford, and his henchman, Rigby, seemed so fresh,
and in good heart, after a double round the buildings. The
command was always, 'Rear rank to the left, front rank to
the right, round the buildings—*Double!*' Old lags like
Bickford would tear round the first corner and wait there
until the greenhorns came puffing past the fives court.
They would then rise from the seat and join the leaders,
nobody having observed to which rank they had attached
themselves at the start of the drill. The Lump, however,
invariably included many of the most amiable boys in the
school, so that David continued to see them as a latter-day
equivalent of the old sweats in the platoon, men who were
always being promoted and then reduced to the ranks for
minor crimes.

The summer term was quite different. For one thing the
weather was much better. For another the thirteen weeks
were starred with a variety of red-letter days. These included Sports Day, Speech Day, the visit of a field officer
from the War Office to judge the O.T.C. drill competition,
and a variety of other functions, including several important
cricket matches. But the summer event David always
enjoyed most was the Whitsun Old Boys' Reunion, when
as many as three hundred Old Boys, a few of whom he
taught in his first two years, would descend on the school
and indulge in an orgy of reminiscence in the old army
hut bar provided for them.

He always felt rather sorry for their young wives and
fiancées, many of them shy and pretty, who drove up with
the impression that Bamfylde was a compromise between
Sandhurst and Blenheim Palace. Once there, however,

they were abandoned by their menfolk and could be seen wandering about rather forlornly, searching for the lavatory, or somewhere where they could sit and take tea.

It was Beth who spotted this unchivalrous deficiency in the O.B.A. programme and tackled Judy Cordwainer's wife about it, so that she found herself appointed hostess to the visitors and persuaded David, as Assistant Secretary of the Association, to give her ten pounds from O.B.A. funds, to be spent on fitting up an old linen room in Nicolson's house as an oasis for bored brides and disconsolate brides-in-waiting.

The Michaelmas term was different again, for it brought a spate of new boys, who were duly invited to the new boys' teas in the cottage garden. The Michaelmas term, in its opening weeks at least, was a time of renewal, with almost everyone settling to a new routine in a different part of the school, with the autumnal running season and rugby football season and, above all, rehearsals for the Christmas Gilbert and Sullivan opera.

Beth was now a regular in the dramatis personae, having already starred in *The Mikado*, *H.M.S. Pinafore*, *The Gondoliers* and *The Yeomen of the Guard*. David never succeeded in making more than the chorus but was sometimes called upon to deputise for Rapper Gibbs at the piano, having learned to play by ear in recreational centres and the officers' mess at Blandford and later, behind the lines in the Ypres sector.

November 11th saw the parade round the War Memorial, where Algy would read the names of the fallen before the two minutes' silence, followed by the sounding of 'The Last Post' and 'Reveille'. David's sour tussle with Carter over the stone cross was forgotten during that first service, in 1920, after watching Algy stumble through the long list of names with tears streaming down his cheeks. So the years slipped away but not without the occasional crisis that would highlight a day, or a week, or sometimes a term.

From the personal standpoint they rarely deserved to be called crises. Once the twins went down with measles. Another time part of the cottage thatch was stripped off in a tearing south-westerly. And twice, during the years when Joan and Grace were toddlers, Beth gleefully announced that she was pregnant again and he made frantic efforts to stake a claim on one of the new bungalows that were being built on an extension of the football field, fifty yards south of the plantation.

He was never able to get one. There was always a queue of men senior to him but in the end it did not matter, for Beth's news turned out to be premature and for a week or two she was down in the dumps. "I so wanted a *son*," she said, when he tried to console her saying they could not really cope with five in the cottage. "I want a son and I'm jolly well going to have one, so just you get used to the idea! It'll soon sort itself out when there are five of us, and there had better be before you spoil those girls to death!"

It was a just accusation, as he was always ready to admit to himself, if to nobody else. For him, and many of the boys, there never had been two children like the twins. They were pretty, biddable, and sharp as a couple of pins, and apart from the fact that Beth insisted on dressing them individually ("I'll not have anyone thinking I'm stage-managing a show-piece wherever we go!") only their intimates, like Ma Midden and her arthritic husband Ben, or Ellie, up at school, could tell them apart. They reminded him more of his elder sister Gwynneth than of himself or Beth, for they were all Celt, with round chubby faces, dark curls and creamy complexions. He even declared he could detect the Welsh lilt on their tongues, especially when they were excited. "That'll be your doing," Beth told him, "but maybe it's just as well. Growing up in this rural wilderness they'll soon be talking broad Devon and we shall have a job finding them anything but pigmen for husbands."

She took this matter-of-fact line with him whenever they discussed the children and subconsciously he understood why. Not only did he spoil them but everyone up at the school did the same, and so did his old mother and Beth's father whenever they got the chance. In this sense, he supposed, it was important they did have another child and they never went out of their way to avoid having one. This in itself was a bonus, as she would sometimes admit in the heavy silence of the moorland night, when they lay still in one another's arms in the main bedroom of the cottage.

"I think we're very lucky this way, Davy," she said, on an occasion quite early in their marriage. "It must be absolutely awful to have to go through a chemist's shop drill every time you want to make love. I suppose people get used to it but I don't think I could."

"You might have to eventually," he said, grinning at the moonlight patch of plaster above the bed. "If I can't bully Algy into giving us married quarters someone will be roughing it in the outhouse and it's not going to be me. I've too much on my plate and need my sleep."

He had, too, for his long-term plans were beginning to mature. They had altered since the days Beth and he had planned how to go about getting his degree. Various opportunities had opened up for ex-servicemen who could claim a spell of teaching experience at a reputable school. He was now working hard for an external London degree, using an Oxford correspondence course that required of the student a minimum of eight hours' work a week. In fact, David was able to put in more, mostly by reading while supervising in class or prep. He was covering British and European history from earliest times to 1900, social and economic history over the same span, one special subject— he chose his favourite fifteenth century—and political theory. There was one other paper, translating a historical extract from two modern languages out of a choice of five, and this required special cramming. His French was adequate, but he knew very little German and had to be coached by Ferguson, a fluent German speaker although he did not teach it. His intermediate was behind him now, taken at Exeter in 1921, when he sailed through in four subjects, including English and European combined history, English literature (coached by Howarth) and Latin, in which he gained a poor pass after some steady coaching by Barnaby.

As the time for taking his finals approached he sometimes wondered whether he would use all this effort as a means of moving on, perhaps applying for a more important post at a better-known school, but it seemed unlikely so long as Herries was around. Even before the incident of the fire he had acquired a special relationship with Algy, whose unconventional approach to education made a direct appeal to him, whereas Beth seemed happy enough, despite social isolation.

Against all probability, she had integrated into the school and come to share his love of the untamed countryside, even in its savage moods. Yet it was not her humour and unswerving devotion alone that played their parts in banishing the final traces of shell-shock, in healing a mind and body that had survived three years on the Western Front. The cure, to his way of thinking at least, had been wrought mainly by regular access to a woman whose approach to him was maternal, in that she was equipped to ease the tensions that had built up inside him, simply by being herself and absorbing him with a directness and merry-hearted innocence. Simply to lie there and watch her undress in the lamplight was a kind of therapy. The sight of her young, supple body, glowing with health and redolent with mystery, even when she was naked, was a demonstration of wholesomeness and flawlessness to a man who had been in such close contact with everything foul and shattered.

He would watch the lamplight play on her breasts and move, like a sensuous lover, over her thighs and buttocks. Sometimes, by way of a laughing glance over her shoulder, she would assess the intentness of his fond scrutiny before pursuing her unhurried way to bed and bestowing on him a few brief moments of ecstasy that would leave him speechless with gratitude for her presence and for her being.

This was her unique contribution, but the other, broader road back to vigour and full mental health was signposted by boys. Boys of all ages and all temperaments, boys who came to represent for him a world of rich and varied promise, that he had assumed lost for all time in hurricane bombardments under Aubers Ridge and Polygon Wood.

They were signposts of variable aspect. Humour was there, and sometimes pathos, and two incidents stood out during that period, so that he thought of them, in after years, as important crossroads.

The funny one, that had the undertones of an outside world's tribulations, was the affair of Paddy McNaughton, the Irish boy who staged a spectacular and convincing show of running amok one wet half-holiday, when games were cancelled, and a group of his peers in the Upper Fourth were passing an idle hour tormenting him about his championship of the Irish Free State. That was in the winter of 1921–22 shortly after Bloody Sunday brought about a final crisis in Irish affairs, and Michael Collins, the Sinn Fein hero, made a clean sweep of British Intelligence officers and Scotland Yard men assembled in Dublin to arrest a number of rebel leaders.

Nobody really resented Paddy's chauvinism. By then it was an accepted fact of the Bamfylde scene, particularly as it was generally known that Paddy's father had been badly wounded serving with the Munsters, in France. But on this particular afternoon Lower Fourth banter over-reached itself and Paddy was collared and thrust into the Big School dust-hole, a relic of the Victorian era, that still absorbed dust and rubbish under the rostrum and was reached by a small trapdoor.

They got him down there easily enough, egged on by Bickford, Rigby, and several other members of The Lump, but their high spirits turned to panic when Paddy re-emerged via a wormeaten section of wainscoting flourishing a large Smith and Wesson revolver, that he used to corner all but one of his persecutors, yelling that he would show them that one Irishman was the equal of a dozen Englishmen.

Half-mad with fright, Bickford and his associates were backed the full length of Big School but Rigby managed to slip away, dashing into the quad and flinging himself upon David, who happened to be crossing the quad on his way to the bandroom.

"Please, sir, come quickly, sir! He'll shoot 'em all, sir! He's in there now, with a damn great gun. Clean off his rocker, sir . . .!" and David hurried in the direction indicated, too late to rescue the hostages but in time to see them herded over the slushy ground in the direction of the swimming pool. He ran after them, a crowd of whipping boys in his wake, but seeing Boyer, now a Sixth Former and trainee prefect, he shouted to him to keep the others back.

He was twenty yards short of the cricket pavilion when he heard a confused outcry, terminated by a series of splashes, and when he burst into the enclosure there stood McNaughton, enjoying the prospect of Bickford and five of his cronies floundering in the deep end.

He walked up to the boy with his hand extended and McNaughton, breathless and grinning, lobbed the revolver in his direction. He caught it and saw at a glance that it was far from being a lethal weapon. It was hammerless and corroded by rust, the relic, no doubt, of a discarded war issue rescued from a rubbish dump.

"What the devil possessed you to play such a tomfool trick?" he demanded, and McNaughton said, cheerfully, "I had to do something, sir. There's a limit to the ragging a man can take. I'll take a beating and no complaints at all, sir. It was worth it, to see 'em cooling off in there, and this no weather at all for a swim, sir!"

He snapped, "Wait here, McNaughton, I'll deal with you in a moment," and leaving the boy by the firing platforms of the miniature range he hurried down to the bedraggled group climbing out of the pool and looking, he thought, extraordinarily foolish as they shook the water from their clothes.

Bickford said, breathlessly, "He's raving mad, sir! He would have drilled us if we hadn't done what he said and jumped . . ." but David said, holding up the rusting antique, "With this?" and the pistol passed from hand to hand with cries of indignation. Bickford said, uncertainly, "He kept telling us it was loaded, sir. He said he'd brought it back from Dublin, and kept it specially for us. We didn't get a chance to get a close look at it. It's . . . it's a real one, isn't it, sir?"

"It was. About the time of the Phoenix Park murders over there. Run on back, strip off and give yourselves a good rub down. Then go down to the kitchen and tell Ned Priddis I said you were to have a pint of hot cocoa apiece. Off with you and don't hang about," and they went, making a cautious circle round the impassive McNaughton as they filed through the gate.

He sauntered back, balancing the weapon in his hand and said, curiously, "Where did you find this McNaughton? And how did it come to be so handy in that dust-hole?"

"I've had it since I was a kid, sir. I found it on a Liffey dump years ago and brought it back after last hols."

"Why, exactly?"

McNaughton hesitated. "Nothing to do with them. The Black and Tans were making house-to-house searches at the time. I didn't want to give them an excuse to shoot the Governor. Even an antique like that could cause trouble over there, sir."

"Ah, so I've heard," David said, and the boy looked at him carefully, as though trying to decide whether the remark was ironic or conciliatory. He said, finally, "My people are neutral actually. My Governor fought for the British and won the M.C. at Cambrai," and then, defiantly, "But the Tans were right bastards, sir!"

"Do you really feel steamed up about asses like Bickford and Rigby?"

"Och, no, sir. Bull Bickford's dim, but there's nothing personal, sir. And the others, well, they just go along. It all began as a lark, sir."

"But got out of hand?"

"Well, yes, sir. But like I said, they asked for it, so they did." Then, doggedly, "I'll shake hands, sir, if Bull and the others will, but there's sure to be a rare shindig now. It'll be all over the school by tea-bell."

"That won't matter, so long as it's handled properly."

"You're saying you'll speak to the head, sir? Tell him my side of it?"

"Wouldn't you prefer to tell him yourself?"

"No, sir. You see—well, I reckon you know about Ireland and the Irish. You must have been in the trenches with people like my Governor. Maybe you could make him see why I blew my top?"

"Very well, leave it to me. As to this gun, what shall we do about it?"

"Throw it away I'd say, sir."

"Good idea. I've seen all I want to see of guns, antique and otherwise."

He nodded and went off towards the plantation, finding a fox earth, stuffing the pistol into it and ramming it home with his boot. He had no intention of punishing McNaughton for what he saw as a justifiable explosion of wrath, and he did not think Herries or Howarth, McNaughton's housemaster, would overrule him. And anyway, by now Paddy McNaughton, with his cool truculence, and his disposition to fight his own battles in his own way, had joined the company of Bamfeldians who had succeeded in forming a strong personal contact with him, a group that already included Cooper and the Sixth Form volunteers of his first term, Boyer, Ridgeway and the Kassava boys, on account of the shared adventure of the fire, Skidmore, now known as 'Preacher', on account of his prolonged bedside prayers, Briarley, the boy he had tried to comfort back in the days of the Big Push, and one or two others, whom chance had singled out for eligibility. There was to be one other before that integration period ended, the boy who now featured in what he would recall as the curious affair of Blades and Julia Darbyshire.

Like most of the episodes that passed as peaks in the terminal graphs it came about by chance, one hot afternoon in late May, when he was taking the long way home over the plank bridge of the stream that ran between two folds of the moor above Stone Cross.

The First Eleven were playing Christow Manor and there had been two free periods after lunch. It was an important match but he had cramming to do and after watching the visitors' innings, he left the field and cut through the plantation to the slope that led down to the Coombe. He had a purpose in mind. A rivulet ran through the cottage garden and Beth had made a water-garden there, planting wild flowers on the margins and hoping for the best. She was now in search of marsh marigolds and he remembered having seen them growing in the river bottom when he had passed this way during the last of the Lent term runs. He borrowed a trowel and a carton from Westacott, the gardener, and decided to see what he could find on his way home.

He had reached the head of a steep path leading to the bridge, half-aware of the distant sounds from the cricket field that carried all the way over here when the wind was in the west, the faint but distant *sn'ack* of a ball hit for a four and the scattered applause, pleasant, summery sounds he thought them and very English in that setting. Perhaps this was why he paused a moment to listen, his back to the school, his eyes on the valley below, a riot of brown and russet, shot through with the vivid green of new growth and, on more open ground, the gleam of celandine showing among the softer hues of lingering primroses and columbine. Rashes of campion grew there and a few sparse patches of bluebells at the top of the wooded slope, a complex that utterly transformed the aspect of this same coombe once summer was at hand.

He was standing there, about twenty yards from the stream, when he heard a woman's laugh and swinging round detected a slight movement among the waist-high ferns. There was no reason why he should investigate. The village women went there to mushroom and collect wood but the sound did not strike him as a local's laugh. It had a light, musical quality that told him whoever was down there was what the moor folk would call a 'foggy-dew' or foreigner. Something else, too. The laugh was associated with dalliance. He thought, shrugging, "Well, I'm no spoil-sport. Nobody tips his hat to a Peeping Tom," and was already turning away when the laugh was repeated, followed by a few indistinguishable words in the voice of a boy, almost certainly a Bamfylde boy, judging by the vowels. He thought, dismally, "Well, that does it. Now I'll have to stick my silly nose in," and moved a few yards lower down, walking on brindled turf, to a point where he could see through a gap in the young foliage to the bank of the stream.

What he saw made him recoil. Sitting against the bole of an ash, her thick chestnut hair unpinned and half-screening her face, was Julia Darbyshire, the new Second Form mistress, who had recently replaced Mrs. Parminter, the motherly soul everybody knew as 'Ma Fender'. And reclining full length, his head on Julia's lap, was Blades, plagiarising the poet Herrick in a somewhat different sense from that implied in Howarth's comment.

There was nothing really startling in the little tableau, framed in the hawthorn and sycamore leaves. On the contrary, if one could have regarded the couple anonymously, it was an idyllic glimpse of a man and his maid, at peace with the world, at one with their pastoral surroundings, oblivious of everything but each other. As he stood there gaping, he was able to identify the source of Julia's laughter, for she leaned forward so that her hair brushed his lips, then drew back with another chuckle but at this Blades roused himself and grabbed a double handful, pressing them to his face in a way that succeeded in checking Julia Darbyshire's merriment. Her face clouded and she said, rather desperately. "*No*, Keith, you promised!"

It was as much as David could stand. He turned and retreated swiftly up the slope, not pausing until he was on the eastern side of the plantation and here, cursing the chance that had involved him in such a ridiculous situation, he took the shortest way home, hurrying along at such a pace that he was sweating when he reached the cottage gate.

Beth called, from the kitchen, "Tea now, or will you wait until Ben brings the twins in?" and he called back, "Now!" and slumped down on the bagged-out armchair, dabbing his temples.

She was beside him in a couple of minutes and even before she set the tray down she realised something was wrong. She said, "Well, what is it? Why the scowl on a lovely day like this?"

"I'm not sure I should tell you, Beth."

"That means you'd rather, so out with it. What's happened up there?"

"The twins are in the farmyard?"

"Having their pony ride. Well?"

"It was something I saw, almost stepped on. On my way home."

"Another adder?"

"No, not an adder. I wish to God it had been." He thought for a moment, aware of needing, if not her advice, then certainly her reassurance.

"It was Julia Darbyshire and young Blades. They were necking, down in the Coombe. They didn't see me. I back-tracked and came home by the road. I went that way to get your blasted marsh marigolds."

She said, slowly, "Necking? How do you mean, exactly? You'd best tell me all you saw, if you want my opinion, that is. If not, we'll leave it there."

"I want your opinion. I'm damned if I know who else's

I can seek, or not without starting one hell of an uproar. Blades is in Carter's house."

He described what he had seen and when he finished she was silent. Finally she said, "In your view, are they lovers?"

"I don't think so. Not from the way it looked, nor from her tone of voice, come to that. My guess is that he's making the running and she's holding back. For his sake more than her own."

"Why do you say that?"

"I don't know. Just a hunch. I saw them and you didn't."

"How old is Blades?"

"Seventeen."

"And Julia?"

"How would I know? About twenty-four, I'd say. I hardly know the woman. Algy appointed a spinster who had been a matron at a school up north but she let us down at the last minute and the agency sent Mrs. Darbyshire."

"She's married?"

"She might be a war widow, I don't even know that. She seems to have made a hit with the Second Form. You've seen her, haven't you?"

"Once or twice, at a distance. Is she pretty?"

"Not pretty but attractive in an odd sort of way. She's got a kind of stillness, not the kind of face at all that goes with playing the fool like this. God damn it, if she was a kid in her teens I could understand it. We had trouble of that kind two years ago with Manners and one of the maids."

"What happened then?"

He grinned. "Old Judy Cordwainer caught them in the shrubbery behind the piggeries. Nearly gave the old boy a seizure. They took a very dim view of it. Manners was sacked, the week before he was due to take Cambridge Senior and the girl was packed off back to Challacombe.

But this is worse. I mean, how the devil can one leave a woman like that in charge of twelve-year-olds? I'll have to tell Algy."

"I wouldn't."

"But damn it, I have to. You must see that."

"Not until you've talked to her and to Blades, if necessary."

He looked exasperated and ran his hand through his hair. "But that's poppycock! I'm a junior master, I can't accept responsibility for a thing like this."

"You can find out more about it before a nice boy like Blades gets kicked out at seventeen. And the woman is put in a position where she couldn't hope for another job."

"She doesn't deserve one, does she? And as for Blades, he's one of the brightest chaps we've ever had. He must have known what he was about."

"He might have, but then again, he might not. How can you know what led up to this, unless you talk to them, separately, and let them know you saw them down there? You owe them that much. *I* think you do, anyway."

He considered, checked by her earnestness but by no means converted to her point of view. He said, at length. "I'm not certain that's loyal to Algy. What makes you so sure there's more in it than meets the eye?"

"Living here. Being a part of it for four years."

"How do you mean, exactly?"

"Look, I'm flesh and blood, and so are you. So is everybody else up there, except one or two who have fossilised, like Ferguson. You've got to make allowances for four hundred boys cooped up in a place like this throughout their entire adolescence, without any contact with women, of the kind boys have in a day school. If half of what you've told me is true there's far worse than this goes on in some of those famous schools. At least this is straightforward, a bright boy, his head stuffed full of romantic poetry, and a lonely

woman, plumped down among God knows how many
attractive young males. It can't go on, I'll grant you that.
But if you take it to Algy Herries and Carter it well end in
something that will do harm out of all proportion to the
harm that's been done. Providing any has."

Her logic began to make sense, or better sense than
emerged from his own reactions. He said, "I'll sleep on it.
Pour me some tea, I'm parched."

II

He took her advice, as he had known he would. Julia
Darbyshire's quarters were two rooms on the second floor
of Outram's, over the quadrangle arch and he knew, more
or less, when he could slip in there unobserved, for the
Second Form had a woodwork class towards the end of
morning school that coincided with his one free period of
the day. He waited until they had trooped in and then
followed Mrs. Darbyshire up the stone steps to her sitting-
room, pausing outside for a moment, summoning enough
nerve to knock. Her "Who is it?" from the far side of the
door, told him a little more about her. She had a very pleasant voice, low-keyed and as musical as the laugh he had
heard in the Coombe.

"Powlett-Jones. Could I have a word with you, Mrs.
Darbyshire?"

She opened the door and stood there smiling at him, a
petite woman, with good features and rather sad grey
eyes. Her hair was her most attractive feature. It was a
particularly fine shade of chestnut, almost auburn, and
she wore it coiled in what they were now calling 'earphones'.
She had a presence that he found difficult to relate to the
woman he had seen teasing a bewitched boy in the Coombe.
It was as though he was looking across the threshold at
two women, with nothing in common except a wealth of

soft, chestnut hair. She said, still smiling, "Well, and
what can I do for you?"

He said, falteringly, "Could I . . . er . . . step inside for a
moment?" and at once the sad eyes betrayed uncertainty
as she said, stepping back, "Certainly," and then, her
fugitive smile returned, "Have you come to give me good
advice, like Mr. Carter?"

"Has Carter been here today?"

"Not today, every other day for the first month of term.
Until I told him I'd prefer to learn from my own mistakes."

It was awkward, her saying that, and in that tone of
voice. He floundered a moment and then made an opening
of the chink she had offered saying, "I'm giving advice of a
kind, Mrs. Darbyshire, but I'm not sure you'll relish it,"
and she replied, seriously, "I will if it's well meant. You're
a very different kettle of fish to Carter."

Her unexpected coolness made it even more difficult than
he had imagined and silently he cursed Beth for putting him
into such a ridiculous situation. Suppose she laughed in his
face? Suppose she denied she had ever been in the Coombe?
Blades would almost surely support her story, and that left
his word against the two of them. Algy would believe him,
of course, but Carter wouldn't, or would pretend not to, if
only to make a score. He said, measuring his words as in
the witness box, "I'm here at the insistence of my wife,
Mrs. Darbyshire. Before I talked it over with her I had
made up my mind to go to the head, and let him cope with
it the best way he could. I say that because I want you to
understand from the first I don't like saying what I came to
say. As a matter of fact, I find it horribly embarrassing. I
was on my way home across the Coombe yesterday afternoon. I saw you and Blades down by the stream."

She flushed, the colour of her cheeks at odds with the shade
of her hair but, apart from that, showed no particular

response. He went on, hurriedly, "You must realise a thing like that can't go on. Sooner or later someone else would see you and if it was one of the boys he wouldn't report it, simply pass it on. From that moment both you and Blades would be in an impossible position ..." He broke off because she had moved away, across to the little dormer window overlooking the quad. It was very quiet down there at this hour, with everybody in class. The noon sun flooded the room with golden light, revealing its shabby paintwork and plaster, despite pathetic efforts she had made with chintzes and a few reproductions, among them Millais's 'The Order of Release'. He noticed something else, a silver-framed picture of a second lieutenant on the mantelshelf and recognised the cap badge as that of the Hampshires. Her voice, when she spoke, was very small, the voice of a child.

"You say your wife advised you to come to me? Does that mean you don't intend making it public?"

"I suppose that depends."

"On what?"

"On all kinds of things."

"On one thing really. Whether we've been lovers." She faced him, bracing herself, as though for a blow. "Well, you can set your mind at rest as to that. We haven't, and wouldn't have been. On my honour, for what that's worth in your eyes."

Suddenly he felt disarmed and very much on the defensive, as though he was at pains to explain to her he wasn't here to pry into her private life. He said, "I believe you."

"Why should you?"

"Partly because I overheard a word or two you said before I backed away. I didn't follow you there. It was pure chance I saw you, and chance again that you didn't hear me coming down the path. But my job, as I see it, is to

consider Blades, and I suppose that's why I'm here. The head
would have to sack him the moment he knew."

"And you wouldn't want that?"

"No, I wouldn't. I've always liked Blades. He's not . . ."

"Not the type you'd expect to imagine himself deeply in
love with a woman eight years his senior?"

"I don't know. I've been at this job since I came out of the
army five years ago. You learn something new every day.
He's the starry-eyed kind, I suppose, but the bright ones
often are."

"Is that frowned upon in a place like this?"

"Not necessarily. The point is . . . I . . . I don't see how it
could have started, how someone as adult as you could
have let it begin, and develop to the stage it had up to
yesterday. You don't have to tell me. I've the right to
question him, I suppose, or Carter has, as his housemaster."

"*No!*" The word was flung at him, more of command
than an appeal. "Not Carter! Anyone but Carter. I can
imagine how he would go about it . . ." And then, with a
gesture of helplessness, "Give me a minute or two. Sit down.
Let me think, just for a moment."

He lowered himself carefully into a small, cane-bottomed
chair. She stood quite still for thirty seconds, then crossed
over to a bureau, opened a drawer and took out some papers.
He said, "If they're his letters I don't want to read them.
God knows, this is complicated enough as it is."

"It's not a letter," she said, extracting two sheets of
paper, "but you asked me how it began. Read that. Then
I'll do what I can to explain. After that we might, conceivably, come to some kind of . . . well . . . arrangement. But
that would be up to you."

He took the sheets and saw at a glance that the top one
was half-filled with a couple of verses by Herrick, copied
in Blades' precise handwriting. It was entirely deficient

of the flourish of a seventeen-year-old, whose hand was not yet formed. He was familiar with the poem, once called *Upon Julia's Clothes*.

> *When as in silks my Julia goes,*
> *Then, then, methinks, how sweetly flows*
> *The liquefaction of her clothes!*
>
> *Next, when I cast mine eyes and see*
> *That brave vibration each way free,*
> *O how that glittering taketh me!*

He glanced up, not yet taking her point despite the obvious one as regards her Christian name.

"Read the other page."

He took the second sheet and read:

> *How easily from there to take*
> *My Julia's hand, and for her sake*
> *Forswear all sleep and lie awake*
> *The long night through,*
>
> *And conjure with a fancy fine*
> *Of making gentle Julia mine*
> *Of seeing in her eyes the shine*
> *Of her love too.*
>
>   *   *   *
>
> *O, I could dream by day and night*
> *Of consummating my delight*
> *At Julia's entrancing shrine.*
> *But how could such reward be mine*
> *For dusting off some musty book?*
> *I've been well paid—by one sweet look.*

"This is his? He gave it to you?"

"He sent it through the post."

"Those last two lines, what's behind them?"

"Nothing very subtle. It was just his way of making sure I identified him."

"You mean this arrived out of the blue?"

"No, I'd been here a fortnight and almost made up my mind to leave. I'll tell you why later if you're interested. I was on my way up here one wet morning when my attaché case burst open and some books fell out. Keith . . . Blades appeared out of nowhere, and scooped them up. When he saw they were muddy he insisted on carrying them up here and cleaning them off with his handkerchief. It would have seemed churlish not to let him."

"And then?"

"He stayed about ten minutes. I had the kettle on and gave him a cup of tea. He began telling me about himself, the way any boy of his age might. What he liked. What he hated. What he wanted to do when he left school. I suppose I encouraged him, partly because he struck me from the first as being a very charming boy. But that wasn't the sole reason."

He looked up at her, but seeing her lip quiver looked down again at Blades' verses. She went on, "I hadn't spoken two words to anyone real for months. Before I came here I'd gone weeks without talking much to anyone at all. I see now how much he read into my eagerness to listen. The next day the poem came."

"You could have ignored it. Wouldn't that have been simpler for everybody?"

"Simpler? Yes, it would have been simpler. But it seemed to me, at that time, that it would have been callous too. At least, that's what I told myself. I realised later it wasn't the truth."

"What was the truth, Mrs. Darbyshire?"

"That I was nearer the end of my tether than I realised. Or anyone else realised. I asked him up here. I honestly meant to tell him he had been stupid and, well a little presumptuous, but to do it as kindly as I could. But then I realised he hadn't written the verses as a joke or a try-on. He intended them to be taken at face value."

"You're sure of that?"

"I'm sure. I daresay you find it difficult to believe, Blades being one of the white hopes at Bamfylde, but it's true. He *is* intelligent. Very. But he's also highly strung and seventeen. Didn't you fancy yourself in love at that age, with the first woman who looked at you as if you were a man?"

"I was seventeen in August, 1914, Mrs. Darbyshire."

"Well, that makes it a little easier. For me, I mean."

She went across the room and lifted the photograph from the mantelshelf. "That was my husband. I say 'was' because the man there is just as dead as the million others in France, even though I'm still married to him. I only had one week with Arthur. What's left of him is still at Netley, and likely to stay there so long as the law regards euthanasia a crime instead of a duty. Maybe you're wondering what all this has to do with Keith Blades?"

He wasn't. Something of Beth's intuitive awareness of the complexity of the situation stirred in him, at least enough to make him glad he had followed her advice.

"Well, there is a link, but Blades didn't forge it. I did, by giving myself away."

"How exactly?"

"I said my piece. It had a hollow ring but I said it. Blades just stood there, waiting politely for me to finish. Finally I did, in a flood of tears."

Somehow it wasn't improbable. Blades being lectured on his forwardness but sensing, behind the rebuke, the pent-up wretchedness of a lonely, distracted woman, deeply touched by his approach, and not knowing how to deal with it.

"It was all he needed. He put arms round me and kissed me. Just once, and on the head. He held me but he didn't say anything. He'll make some girl a wonderful husband one day. I hope it's soon and that she appreciates him. It took me a longish time to pull myself together and everything emerged when I did, all the wretchedness and strain of the last few years, neatly bottled and corked since 1919, when they first showed me the man they said was my husband. Everything else developed from that, you might say."

He got up, not wanting to hear any more. Suddenly he did not give a damn about Blades' involvement. Only hers, and the savage wounds the war had inflicted on her, more pitiless, he would say, than on him and his like. He said, "You don't have to go on, Mrs. Darbyshire. I served three years out there and was pretty well used up myself when I came here, in 1918." A thought occurred to him. "What made you take this job in the first place?"

"I thought it might be a way back."

"It was, for me."

"It wouldn't have been, if you hadn't taken out insurance on a happy marriage. I've not met your wife but she must be an intelligent, compassionate woman. Well, it's that much easier for a man, especially with men in such short supply." She paused for a moment as he stood hesitantly by the door. "I'll tell you something else. That's how I came to see Keith, young as he is—one of the few whole men left on earth. it wasn't to keep it on its original level, tenderness on his part, overwhelming gratitude on mine. Sometimes it was all I could manage to stop myself begging him to take me and he knew it. If it hadn't been for his essential decency you might have had a real mess to sort out. After all, I'm still human, in spite of feeling like a dried-out husk for so long. And it's not as if I've never held a man in my arms. I did, that one week, before Arthur was recalled for the March offensive. Then I had to do a crazy thing like this, surround myself by hundreds of healthy male animals. I should have known myself better."

He was able to smile. "That's asking a lot at our age, Mrs. Darbyshire. Mostly it doesn't happen till we reach the fifty mark."

She looked at him steadily, still holding the framed photograph of the young lieutenant in the Hampshires. "You've been very kind, the sort of man Keith led me to expect. Is it fair to ask you what you intend doing now?"

"Nothing," he said. "I'll leave that to you. You couldn't have been more frank, and I daresay Herries would understand. But Carter and the others wouldn't, and you wouldn't suffer alone."

She said, slowly, "Would you trust me to see Keith once again? I could tell him we had been seen, and that I'd received a friendly warning. Also that I was leaving at the end of term, having decided how utterly stupid it was from his point of view and mine?"

"Would he be likely to accept that as final?"

"He'd have to, the way I put it. I should tell him I'd had better news from the hospital, that my husband was on the mend, and I had to go to him."

"Very well, you do that. I'll go now, before the five-minute bell."

"Could we . . . would you . . . shake hands on it?"

"Why not?"

Her hand was cold, and small as a child's. He clasped it and turned away, trudging down the curving stairway to the quad. The sun was blazing out here but there was no warmth in it.

He was never quite sure how the strange affair worked

itself out during the remaining seven weeks of summer term. Julia Darbyshire refused Beth's invitation to call at the cottage and he understood why. There is no comfort for the sick in taking tea with those who fancy themselves secure in their own immortality. But he did notice traces of her ultimatum in Blades, whom he found himself watching closely through the next week or so. Outwardly the boy gave no sign that he was in despair, a state of mind the very young sometimes find consoling. His work did not suffer and he had always been one of those who liked to walk alone. But one day, after Nipper Shawe's lunch-bell set everyone about him desk-banging and scurrying, he gave himself away to some extent. He sat on, hands deep in his pockets, looking directly at the dais in the Fifth Form but not seeing it. His eyes were clouded and his expression drained. For a moment David was tempted to descend to floor level and have a word with him but he thought better of it.

Instead he gathered up his books, nodded briefly and stalked out, leaving Blades the sole occupant of the big room and its ineradicable smell of apple cores, blotting paper, exercise books, chalk and dust.

PART THREE

THE BELL IN THE BRAIN

CHAPTER ONE

I

Bat Ferguson died early in the Lent term, 1925. He was getting on for seventy, years past retirement age, but had hung on, hating the notion of uprooting himself and seemingly very fit. Yet in the end Bat Ferguson literally flapped himself to death.

He had taught in Bamfylde classrooms for forty years and collapsed at the apex of one of those furious bouts of exasperated energy that were in the repertoire of every mimic in the school. According to the death certificate, simple heart-failure killed him, but the wits put another suspect in the dock, one Dixon, a day boy of the Lower Third. For Bat was in the very act of pouncing on him when he choked, and crashed his length against the blackboard.

Witnesses who tried to revive him affirmed the dramatic truth of Bat's last moments. He had just descended on Dixon, renowned throughout Lower School for his buzz-saw Devon brogue, demanding, at the top of his voice, to be told the colour of the pencil he flourished. Dixon, an attentive boy, knew the word and answered up promptly. '*Le crayon est vert, m'sieur!*'' but because he was Dixon the word emerged as '*verrrrert*' and sounded like a long, half-stifled belch.

It was too much for poor Ferguson, who pranced (this from Archer the Third, who was within touching distance) exactly two feet in the air, descending like a thunder-cloud screaming, "*Vair*, idiot boy! *Vairr*!" It was his final word and Mrs. Ferguson, with Gallic stoicism, received him into her house, where he died ten minutes after Dr. Willoughby's arrival.

Mrs. Ferguson did not find his death incongruous and neither, for that matter, did Bamfylde. Everyone seemed to think of it as a very fitting end, thoroughly in character, a veteran Roman soldier, shouting defiance at a swarm of barbarians. Dixon was rather upset but he cheered up as soon as he realised that a little of the savage splendour of the occasion reflected upon him, a thirteen-year-old who had slain a grown man with a single word, and a foreign word at that. He was given the rest of the day off and cantered his pony home, arriving at his father's farm pale, proud and extremely hungry.

Behind him the machinery of a state Bamfylde funeral went slowly into action, with directives for black ties for all, and special armbands for the boys of Havelock's house. Ferguson, as a stripling, had enrolled in a Paris student corps for the 1870 war, and remembering this Carter moved in on the act and selected a Corps firing-party for the graveside. Mrs. Ferguson produced a tricolour for the coffin and this was thought equally proper, for although Bat had been born in Scotland, of good Scots parentage, he was always regarded as more than half a Frenchman. In steady Exmoor drizzle the long procession wound its way over the half-mile to Stone Cross churchyard where Bouncer, walking ahead in dripping surplice, recited the burial service. This was strictly according to the English prayer-book and some of the dead man's former pupils, remembering how a chance remark in their mother tongue had so often driven the dead man into a frenzy, thought it in poor taste. As Morgan-Smith put it, turning away from the grave and regretting that the solemn occasion prohibited a dash across to Ma Midden's yard in search of apple turnovers, "It was all I could do not to convert the final Amen into *Fin*."

Everybody regretted Bat Ferguson's passing but nobody save his wife mourned him in the real sense of the word. No one, that is, except Towser, his faithful Airedale, who made several careful tours of Havelock's dormitories, passages and linen rooms in search of his absent master. Unable to find him, he slumped in his basket in the Ferguson's living-room and refused to eat until Madame Ferguson, with a French lack of sentimentality concerning animals, shrugged her shoulders and would have ignored him had not David, who came to pay his respects after the funeral, asked how the dog was taking it.

"Very foolishly," she told him. "Three suppers have been thrown away. It is a waste of good meat and my husband would have disapproved. What am I to do with a dog that will not eat, M'sieur Powlett-Jones? I am preparing to leave on Saturday. I am going home to Beauvais, to live with my sister and brother-in-law, and they do not approve of household pets. I shall take the dog to the vet to be destroyed."

"I say, you can't do that, Mrs. Ferguson," David protested, thoroughly outraged. "At the time of the fire Towser's howl saved us all."

"So? I did not hear of that and find it interesting. But what has it to do with a dog that will not eat?"

"Give him to me. I'll coax him to eat. He knows me and I'll soon pull him round."

"But you have a wife and two children in that small cottage of yours. There is no room for a big dog, M'sieur Powlett-Jones."

"We'll find room. We can't let him be put down. He's no more than three or four, is he?"

"I have no record of his age. However, take him, if you wish."

So Towser was led away, to the shrieking delight of the twins, and after a day of their sustained attention he abandoned his suicide bid. Within a week or two, however,

Bamfylde received another grievous blow. Old Judy Cord-wainer, also well past retiring age, followed his colleague to the churchyard, having caught a severe chill standing bare-headed in the rain throughout the service.

"Rectitude killed *him*!" commented the irrepressible Morgan-Smith, "so that day-kid now has two beaks on his conscience."

Once more the long, black-tied procession wound its way to Stone Cross and Algy Herries, quoting Marshal Soult, looked up at the sky as they were returning and said, "I'm beginning to hear the recall up there."

"Nonsense," said David, unable to visualise Bamfylde without Algy's cheery presence, "you're only sixty-two and that gives you a minimum of another three years. Besides, you're the fittest over-sixty I ever saw. Won't you apply to the Governors for a stay when you reach official retirement age? We all hope you will. The place wouldn't seem the same with a new head. And, anyway, what would you do with yourself?"

"Oh, I'll apply for a small, comfortable living somewhere handy," Algy said. "This place will need a face lift by then and not only structurally, my boy. Educational processes are changing as rapidly as everything else. Ferguson and Cordwainer belonged to the old school and could never really adapt. I did, with all you youngsters pushing from behind, but a man can't change to that extent at my age. Hang it all, they taught practically nothing but Latin and Greek when I was a boy here. They welted it into you, too. None of this cosy uncle–nephew relationship that you and Irvine encourage."

"You too," said David, smiling, "so why not own up to it?"

"I've never been one hundred per cent sure," Herries said, thoughtfully. "The average boy has changed, along with everything else. The war did that, I suppose, with that queer chap, Kitchener, sweeping everybody into khaki, and putting them through the mincer out there. Much more individualism nowadays. Don't tell me the Fifth and Sixth don't argue the toss with you every now and again for I know very well they do." He trudged on in silence for a moment. Then, lightly, "How would you feel about taking over Havelock's, P.J.?"

"*Me?* Getting a house at my age? And with an external degree?" He gave Herries a suspicious sidelong glance. "Are you pulling my leg, sir?"

"Of course I'm not," Herries said, grumpily. "What the devil has an external degree got to do with it? You're a born teacher, and I don't mean by that a man with the knack of imparting information. You still have it in mind to move on, haven't you? Well, I daresay you could, and make a go of it in one of these big modern schools, but I don't know that you'd be any better off for it. Except financially, of course. You've come to know my methods, my eccentricities if you like, and you suit Bamfylde. At least, you suit my idea of Bamfylde's true function."

"Can you define that function?"

"Yes, I can. To select what's worth having from the green wood and hang on like grim death to the best of the seasoned timber. I've never been a great advocate of exams, or dedicated scholarship, or even technical education. You know that. Everybody knows it. I've always been more interested in turning out well-adjusted human beings and I imagine you go along with that. Think it over. Discuss it with that nice gel of yours, and let me know by the end of term. For if you don't take it I'll have to advertise for a man around forty, and my guess is I'll have the devil's own job finding someone who suits me."

It was curious that the day of Judy Cordwainer's funeral should prove such a red-letter day for them. There was no question in Beth's mind but that he should accept the offer. Not merely for financial and prestigial reasons—the post carried another hundred a year, plus free living accommodation—but because, much as she had grown to love the cottage, life there in winter left a good deal to be desired. She said, excitedly, "Havelock's is the newest house in the school, isn't it? I'll have much more room over there, and you'll be right in the centre of things. Don't think I haven't realised how difficult it has been to divide your time and energy between the school and us, Davy. And I'll like it too, although I can't really see myself as a housemaster's wife."

"You're better qualified than any woman for miles around," he said, but she laughed, saying, "That isn't the compliment it sounds. There's only about eight of us all told. Seriously, though, I'm absolutely convinced, Davy. You'll be a huge success, you see if you aren't. Not that you don't deserve it. You've worked harder than any of them up there. Won't some of the younger men be jealous?"

"Irvine won't. He doesn't want a house, at least Phyllis doesn't. 'Too much a tie,' she told me, only the other day. Besides, I don't think they'll stay long. She's a town girl, really."

"So am I," she said, but he caught her round the waist, saying, "Ah, but you're different. You threw your cap at a schoolmaster, remember?" and he kissed her, his mind ranging on the vagaries of luck that never seemed to have permanent favourites but played the field, a man-hungry jade. Ferguson had seemed lucky up to now. And Cordwainer, too, in his staid settled way. Both of them too old to get caught up in the war and sticking it out down here, where they were not even obliged to go short of butter. But every now and again your luck ran out, as his had seemed to in the last months of 1917, when he had wished that mortar shell had finished him off, along with all the others in the traverse. Mostly it was a matter of holding on, as Algy Herries had held when he saw an entire generation of his boys killed off in their prime. He was not Anglicised beyond the point where he had ceased to think as a Welshman and caught himself contemplating Bamfylde from a Celtic standpoint, almost as his sisters or brothers-in-law might; "Funny that ... used to think of places like this as proper old snob-factories ... laugh at 'em behind their back, I would. But these hills are as old as ours and the folk holding them are as obstinate as the people of the Valleys ..." And then, as it were, he translated himself, thinking, "If I can emerge as human as Algy in late middle-age, then I'll count myself lucky. He must have had his doubts, pulling this place together when he first came here, but he won through in the end, against the fuddy-duddies, the diehards, God knows how many cheeseparing Governors, and the percentage of failures chaps in our line of business have to accept."

They spent the entire Easter break moving house and settling in, counting themselves lucky that her father and stepmother took the twins off their hands while they did it. For him it was easy enough to adapt, having lived in Havelock's during his first four terms, and later seen large sections of the house rebuilt after the fire. That, Beth said, had been a blessing in disguise, for now she had a modern kitchen with piped water, and the new dynamo they were installing promised electric light. The two rebuilt dormitories had been fitted with a fire escape, a novelty the boys of the other houses professed to despise. Morgan-Smith gave it as his opinion that any potential arsonist among new intakes would naturally gravitate to Havelock's, where they catered for such specialists.

The rest of the staff took it philosophically when news leaked that he was to replace Ferguson. Barnaby, senior to David by several terms, was a little put out, and honest enough to admit it, but he was far too amiable to nurse a grievance, whereas Irvine had been conditioned by his wife to leave his options open. He said, "Best of luck, old man, but it'll bog you down. Phyllis is always nagging me to move on, but it'll bog you down. I've already been on a couple of short-lists. She fancies a prep school of our own, in a seaside town where there's a bit more social life. But we'd need capital for that and I can't see us getting it until her Aunt Faith kicks the bucket. Phyl's her favourite niece and god-daughter, so we've expectations, but there's a snag. We have to spend every Christmas with the old girl, and her parrots and cats, and I can't stand bloody cats."

When Barnaby got over his pique he said, "Old Howarth is delighted, of course, but he's always regarded you as his protégé, ever since you stood up to Carter. They've hated one another's guts for years. By the way, has Carter brought himself to congratulate you?"

"No, he hasn't and I don't imagine he will. Doesn't it strike you as bloody silly, Barnaby, that we wage our little feuds in a place like this, where we've all got to live and work together?"

"It's damned silly but inevitable, old man. The smaller and more isolated the place, the sharper the clash of personalities. You'd find it no different in a firm, a hospital, or government office. Wasn't it the same in a regiment?"

"Not once we came under fire."

"Ah, well, there you have it. Consult your Ovid, old boy! 'Fortuna miserrima tuta est; Nam timor eventus deterioris abest.' Look it up. I took you over it last year," and he floated off, hunching his gown about him in a way that enhanced his counterfeit inscrutability.

David did look it up, finding it in his notes on Ovid's elegies, written during his banishment. 'Tuta petant alii. Fortuna miserrima ...' 'Let others seek what is safe. Safe is the worst of fortune; for the fear of any worse event is taken away.' Like all Barnaby's tags it was apt. Every succeeding generation had to learn from its own experiences. The wonderful comradeship of the trenches, the only solid gain of the war to those who fought it, rested on Ovid's dictum. It was perfect because it was practised by men who had reached a point where they had nothing else to lose. Under those circumstances most human failings fell away. But once the pressure was removed people reverted to what they were and he and Carter were alike in this respect. He thought, "Howarth's wrong and I'm wrong, to persist in this game of 'you-did-I-didn't' with Carter. We're level pegs now, and he can't patronise me as a housemaster. I'll find some way of holding out the olive branch once we're all back for summer term . . ." and he meant to consult with Beth about it but it slipped his mind in the whirl of end-of-term activities.

*   *   *

Looking back on that final period of unclouded happiness he could not recall much but laughter. Laughter, welling from small, insignificant sources, like the ultimate sally of Bickford, in Bouncer's divinity period, one that earned the culprit the standard four penal marks, plus several more on his leathery backside from Bouncer's ill-directed cane, but passed into Bamfylde legend and changed his name to 'Ruby'.

It was a very small joke really, but good enough to be re-told over common-room coffee—how Bouncer, spouting Proverbs to an indifferent Fifth, quoted, 'Who can find a virtuous woman? for her price is far above rubies', whereupon Bickford raised his hand and asked, blandly, "Please, sir, what *was* Ruby's?"

There was laughter among the Orpheans, when Baines Minor, drumming away for dear life one damp morning,

drove both sticks through his soggy drumskin. Laughter in
the Second Form, when Gilroy, a new boy, lacking a nickname, earned one by pausing at the unfamiliar word
'apostrophe' while reading aloud and finally made a gallant
try with 'Apos . . . apos . . . apos-*TROPHY*-sir' and was
afterwards known as 'Strofe' Gilroy. Small, asinine incidents
that yet added something to the texture of life on the plateau.
Nipper Shawe (now launched into the world and said to be
doing well in marine insurance) had surrendered his job as
bell-ringer to a pallid boy called Fogaty, innocuous at work
and play but, given his bell, someone who took on the
gravity and dignity of a town crier. It was thus a joke to be
relished when someone in the Lower Fifth, whose quarters
were situated immediately above the niche where the bell
was kept, bored a hole through the floorboards and attached
a strand of fine wire to the handle, pulling it up the moment
Fogaty reached out to grasp it, so that it began to ring itself.
Then there was Vernon, the amateur ventriloquist, who
threw the entire corps into disarray issuing orders in Carter's
testy voice; Nixon Minor, who got hold of a noxious dye, and
stained the water in the swimming bath the colour of blood,
and Boyer's swan-song as a practical joker, that led to a
confrontation neither Boyer nor David ever forgot, for it
struck a new balance in their relationship and presented
David with his first major decision as master of Havelock's.

Boyer had sobered over the years but every now and again
his extravagant sense of humour shot through the crust of
Sixth Form sobriety like a geyser. His ultimate escapade
was to borrow an Old Boy's motorcycle, disguise himself
in a smock, felt hat and false beard, and ride into the village
where, for a bet, he drank half a pint of beer in the presence
of Barnaby. Barnaby far too much of a sportsman to identify
him on the spot, none the less told David, who sent for
Boyer, demanding to know what had prompted such an

idiotic performance. Boyer said, quite seriously, "I . . . er . . . don't really know, sir. Exhibitionism, perhaps."

"Exhibitionism, my good right boot!" bellowed David. "Don't quote any of those fancy Freudian words at me! I could get you sacked for a thing like that. Kicked out, after how long here?"

"I'm in my ninth year, sir."

"Nearly two more than me, and you in the Sixth. It's the maddest thing you've ever done and by God, that's saying something! Here I was, hoping you'd help play me in as house prefect for my first year."

He was relieved to see Boyer frown as he said, "Does that mean I've been passed over, sir?" and David said, irritably, "I'm hanged if I know! You've got more potential than any other senior in Havelock's. But how the devil can I trust you with responsibility for younger kids when you act as if you were still in the Lower Third?"

"Couldn't we make a bargain, sir?"

"What kind of bargain?"

"Well, sir, you forget my jaunt to the Maltster's Arms, and I'll back you to the hilt until I leave here next spring. The fact is, sir, I've played the fool for so long it's difficult to stop overnight. The chaps . . ." and here he stopped, avoiding David's eye.

"What about the chaps, Boyer?"

"Well, they expect it of you, if you know what I mean, sir."

David knew but was not prepared to admit it. Boyer was the exact equivalent of the daredevil subaltern, the sort who went out into no-man's-land for the hell of it, and finally got himself killed establishing he had guts and initiative. He wondered, fitfully, at his propensity to equate almost everything that happened here with his experiences in the trenches, yet he did, almost as though his time out there had been an apprenticeship for the job.

He said, finally, "Look here, Boyer, against my better judgment I'll take a chance on you. I'll recommend you to take Brandon's place. He's leaving in a week or so, to take that job he wrote after in Rhodesia. But if you let me down I'll see you don't forget it. I ought to give you a damn good hiding but you know I don't even approve of thrashing juniors, let alone a great lout of your age. All I can do is to appeal to you for help, the way I did the night of the fire. I'll keep this last idiocy to myself, and ask Mr. Barnaby to do the same. But it's the last, you understand?"

Boyer, looking more thoughtful than David had ever seen him look, slipped away and that same night David asked Herries to make the appointment. Algy, who had always been slightly bewildered by Boyer's explosive high spirits, said, "Boyer, eh? Well, I hope you know what you're doing, P.J. He's a wild one and no mistake. Sort of chap who might land himself in real trouble one of these days. And without meaning to, for he's got his points. I've always seen him as a chap who took on too much too quickly and went bankrupt. Or a cat-burglar, who only robbed the rich. Nothing the slightest bit vicious about the boy, mind you, just someone who has to let off steam every now and again. What's he got in mind when he leaves here?"

"I don't think he knows himself, sir. That'll depend on the exams at the end of next term, won't it?" but Herries smiled. "Not on your life. Examinations are for the conformists, as I've told many an anxious parent in my time. And nobody could call Boyer a conformist."

They dispersed the next day and holiday stillness descended on the place. In the lull that followed, David, recalling that he and Beth were approaching the sixth anniversary of their encounter on the pier at Colwyn Bay, posted off to Challacombe on the excuse of seeing his bank manager and collecting some curtain materials Beth had ordered. With these errands accomplished he made for Merriweather's, the Challacombe jeweller. He had intended buying her an oval wristwatch as a birthday gift but on entering Market Street he paused outside Marty Lile's car mart, spotting a three-wheeler, with *'For Sale—Bargain'* scrawled on its windshield. Marty, seeing him, waddled out, chafing his hands, in a way exactly mimicked by two generations of Bamfylde boys.

He said, in his broad Devon burr. 'Top o' the marnin' to 'ee Mr. Powlett-Jones! That there motor is a praper ole steal. No more'n dree thousand on the clock. Why dorn 'ee try her out?'' and when David said he was in no mind to buy a car, especially a three-wheeler, Marty said, "Giddon, you and the missus need transport outalong, dorn 'ee? Youm stuck fast half the year round. Woulden it be nice to have your orn means o' poppin' inalong for a visit to the pictures every now and again?''

It would at that, thought David, remembering the long winter evenings, and reminding himself that the twins were due to start nursery school at the village primary in a month or two. "How much, Mr. Lile?"

"Thirty pounds to you, and I'd ask thirty-five to anyone who wasn't up at skuel. Try her, there's petrol in the tank."

He said, taking his seat behind the wheel, "I've never been sold on three-wheelers. They're so easily overset," but Marty denied this, declaring that it only held good when there were two wheels at the front. "Tiz like a triangle, you see," he went on. "Knock un from the apex an' 'er lifts an' stays put. But youm out looking for trouble. How much traffic do 'ee pass 'tween yer an' skuel?"

He drove down to the quay and back, finding the car handled very easily, so that he thought, "Beth would get more use out of this than a watch. I could teach her to drive on the level stretch outside the cottage in a day or two . . ." and after a little bargaining he dragged Marty down to twenty-seven pounds ten, and drove back to Bamfylde in high spirits.

Beth, exasperated with her efforts to adapt the cottage curtains to the tall windows of Havelock's, was delighted. In the first flush of enthusiasm he coaxed her out into the drive and gave her her first lesson, finding that she was a quick learner once she had mastered the gears. "At least we'll be mobile," he said, congratulating her, "and not dependent on bikes. You can pack the twins into the dickey seat, drop them off at school, and then do your shopping in Challacombe. I made it home in twenty minutes and she took Quarry Hill like a bird. I'll give her a good going over when I get time."

But he was short on time just then. Overnight, it seemed, the school was full of boys again, swapping holiday yarns, and Beth was preparing for the first of her new boys' teas in Havelock's, and there were a thousand things to attend to as he began his first full term as housemaster, with a complement of eighty boys, including four first-termers.

And then, just as he was getting into his stride, the Winterbourne divorce had to blow up out of a clear sky, and all his nervous energy was directed towards ensuring that Winterbourne survived what promised to be an extremely unpleasant term and an experience that could, if it wasn't carefully handled, scar a sensitive boy's mind.

II

The news of Viola Winterbourne's divorce reached the school via the Sunday papers, about a fortnight before half-term.

Everybody knew the celebrated Viola Winterbourne, a popular musical comedy actress, currently starring in

Under My Balcony in the West End. She had, in fact, shown
herself at Bamfylde from time to time, queening it over all
the other visitors on Sports Days and Speech Days, for
Winterbourne (nicknamed 'Spats' on account of his sartor-
ial elegance) was in his second year, and currently in the
Lower Fourth.

David had met her, and not been over-impressed, seeing
her as a gossipy, vapid woman, obsessed by her own elegance and popularity, and much given to stage chit-chat
that always headed listeners back to Viola Winterbourne's
career. He had to admit, however, that she was a very
dashing woman and a handsome one too, in yards of flowered
silk and a close-fitting cloche hat, that emphasised the good
bone-structure of her face and brought a sparkle into her
cornflower-blue eyes. She was regarded as the principal
showpiece at Bamfylde functions, whenever she bothered
to attend one, and usually succeeded in relegating most
other mothers to the status of peasants. He did not know
much about the relationship of mother and son but guessed
that Winterbourne, a neat, self-contained boy of fourteen,
was embarrassed by her style and scintillating personality.
Mothers had to be extremely judicious whenever they
appeared at school, striking an exact balance between
elegance and frumpishness. Many boys preferred their
parents to keep their distance or, if they did come, to
remain in the background. Cookson's father, a war profiteer,
owned a Rolls-Royce, but Cookson saw to it, after one visit,
that he left it at home when he called to take his son out for
the day and arrived in a sedate Austin. At the other end
of the scale was Gilroy, whose father, a Challacombe grocer,
sometimes showed up on Sports Day wearing a large, cloth
cap, vintage 1903, and pepper and salt knicker-bockers,
garments that made Gilroy blush for shame, especially as
Gilroy *père* was an excitable little man, prone to rush from

behind the ropes and thump his son on the back whenever
he won a race.

David was aware that young Winterbourne, a member of
his house, was a target for the wags of Middle School, and
this was understandable, for Viola Winterbourne was more
likely to be in the news than out of it. She had been seen
dancing with the Prince of Wales at a nightclub. She
wrote chic fashion articles, almost certainly ghosted, in
women's magazines. She had campaigned for her Conservative candidate and kissed electors in public. She was
always ready to pronounce upon any subject, from the
Black Bottom and birth-control, to survival after death.
Ordinarily a well-conducted boy, Winterbourne had been
known to hit out at those who made jovial references to his
mother, and there had been rumours of a stand-up fight
between Winterbourne and Curtiss, after the latter had
pasted a picture of Viola in a bathing suit inside his desk,
along with a page torn from *London Life*, featuring the
Folies Bergère star, Josephine Baker.

Hints of the approaching divorce bothered David a little,
though not seriously. Divorces, nowadays, were common
enough, and almost everyday occurrences among stage-
folk. Winterbourne would just have to ride it out, like
anyone else with a personal problem. But then the unexpected happened. News came, via the midweek papers, that
Viola Winterbourne's divorce promised to be a particularly
spicy affair, and David at once took steps to prevent the
more sensational papers from being circulated that week.
This was not too difficult to achieve. The papers were
always late, anyway, and were distributed, one to a class, by
the school bursar. On Sundays, when no train stopped at
Bamfylde Bridge Halt, no papers were delivered. David
went so far as to take Boyer into his confidence, telling him
to keep an eye on what the Middle School were discussing

over the weekend. There was always a chance that a boy on day leave, or a servant returning from a Sunday off in Challacombe, would introduce a popular paper into the school. There was not much to be feared from upper school, where a majority would be likely to exercise tact, or indeed from Lower School, where papers like the *News of the World* were not in great demand, but instinct told him boys of the Fourth and Lower Fifth Forms were alerted as to the possibility of a Sunday spread and would keep a sharp lookout for reports of proceedings.

To be on his guard David arranged with one of the domestics to get a copy of the *News of the World* from Challacombe and a single glance at its contents dismayed him. On an inside page was a headline reading ' *"Farmyard Morals!" Scathing Comment by Divorce Judge,*' and below it '*Musical Comedy Star Cited in Divorce Proceedings*'.

The report itself spared nobody's blushes. It was before the passing of the Domestic Proceedings Act, limiting what could be printed concerning cases of this kind, and Viola's private life was hung on the line, the story of her involvement with Victor Manners-Smith, her co-star, being told in detail. There was mention of champagne parties in Paris, and nude bathing parties in the villa of an impresario at Cannes. Even passages from her wildly indiscreet letters were quoted, one describing her feelings about the co-respondent the first time she got into bed with him. Her husband, whom David had never met, had been granted a decree nisi, with costs amounting to over two thousand pounds.

He said, after Beth had read the story, "We've got to keep this from circulating somehow. That kid's life won't be worth living if this is bandied around Big School."

Boyer came to him after the dormitory bell had gone and said that no Sunday papers had been passed around Middle

School and that Winterbourne, whom he had been watching closely, seemed to be taking the scandal in his stride. "I even had a word with him before prep," Boyer said, "and he seems to have himself well in hand. I didn't mention the divorce, of course, but told him he was picked for wicket-keeper in the house match on Wednesday. That seemed to cheer him up no end. Anything else I can do, sir?"

"Not for the moment," David told him. "but keep your eye open for Sunday papers in tomorrow's distribution. I'll warn the bursar and if any show up whip 'em out of circulation," and he left it at that, more or less satisfied that his strategy had succeeded.

It had not, apparently. At precisely six-forty on Monday, about an hour before rising bell when he and Beth were still in bed, there was an urgent rapping on the door and Beth shook him by the shoulder, struggling into her dressing gown. He said, sleepily, "Who the devil would that be at this hour? Get rid of him, whoever he is," and he rolled out of bed yawning and pulled the curtains aside, looking down on the empty quad as Beth crossed to the door calling, "Who is it?"

"It's me, Mrs. Powlett-Jones. Boyer. I'd like to speak to the housemaster at once, ma'am!"

David said, briefly, "Go into the bathroom," and he threw open the door to find Boyer on the threshold looking distraught.

"I'm sorry about the time, sir, but you had to know as soon as possible. Winterbourne's gone, sir. I don't think his bed was slept in, although it was rumpled a bit. I was up early to do an hour's cramming for the exam and I noticed he'd gone. He must have slipped down the fire escape in the night. Do you imagine he's run off to his father, sir?"

"I can check on that, his father's on the phone. That's the

likeliest bet, but he wouldn't be able to get a train to Taunton on Sunday night, would he?"

"There's the milk train from Challacombe, sir. It stops at all the halts to pick up churns. That's about three-thirty a.m. If he hopped it he could be in Taunton by five and catch the fast to London. I've looked at the timetable, sir. There's one gets into Paddington at nine-ten."

He thought, "Thank God for Boyer . . . I was right about him after all . . . !" and said, "Did you think to look in his locker?"

"Yes, sir. It's difficult to be sure but I think he's taken sweater, slacks and stinkers. His two suits are there."

"Why the devil should he run away in plimsolls?"

"He might have planned on covering the distance between here and the next halt, at Crosshayes, sir. I would, knowing I'd be recognised and stopped by Walrus Tapscott down at the station. No one would question him buying a ticket at Crosshayes."

"Thank you, Boyer," David said. "Keep it as quiet as possible. He won't be missed for a bit. Everyone will assume he went out early for a training run. I'll tell the head and do some phoning. I'll let you know what happens."

"Thank you, sir," Boyer said gravely and withdrew as Beth emerged from the bathroom. "I heard," she said. "He can't have gone far, can he? And if he goes home to his father there's nothing to worry about, is there?"

"In that case, no, but it's something we've got to check at once." He threw on some clothes and went down into the quad and across to Herries's house. Ellie, he knew, was an early riser, and he found her making tea in the kitchen. She said anxiously, "I'll fetch Algy. You can find Mr. Winterbourne's telephone number in his address book. It's in the top, right-hand drawer in the study desk."

He got through to Winterbourne Senior with surprising

speed. The Winterbourne house seemed to be a high-pow-ered ménage, with any number of lackeys about, even at this hour. 'Spats' had not shown up but his father did not seem ruffled by his son's disappearance in the middle of the night.

"Probably taken it into his head to go off some place where he had fun in the holidays," he said, as though Spats had been a man in his mid-twenties, with a particularly independent disposition. "Impulsive kid. Always was. Haven't you noticed that?"

"No," said David, grimly, "I can't say that I have," taking a dislike to the flat, impersonal voice. "To be per-fectly frank, Mr. Winterbourne, I've got the impression he's very upset about the publicity Mrs. Winterbourne's been getting."

This seemed to jolt him a little but not much. He said, carefully, "Really? Surprised to hear that. She's made headlines of one sort or another all his life."

Herries bustled in, buttoning his trousers, and David offered him the receiver. The head said, in a whisper, "You deal with it, P.J. The boy's not arrived, has he?" and when David shook his head he frowned. It was not often that Algy Herries frowned and his face seemed to resent it.

"Are you still on the line?" enquired the bored clubman's voice.

"Yes, Mr. Winterbourne. The headmaster and myself think it almost certain he'll come to you. Have you any idea where else he might go? To a relative, maybe?"

"I'll put my mind to it."

"Will you phone us at once if he does show up?"

"Of course."

"Good. Meantime we'll check the railway stations this end. Someone must have seen him. Can I get you on this number any time?"

"No. Ring City 7404 after nine-thirty. My secretary will put you through. I'll leave instructions if I'm in conference."

"Very well."

There seemed nothing more to say so he jotted down the number and rang off, saying, "He's a cool customer, isn't he?" and Herries grunted, "So would you be if your income was twenty thousand a year plus. I've never been able to decide what made a chap like Winterbourne send his boy here. Couldn't trust his wife at Eton or Harrow, I wouldn't wonder."

"I'm beginning to understand Winterbourne's problem," David said. "That chap might have been discussing a lost dog."

"Spats is a bit of a lost dog, P.J., and so would I be if I was his age, and had his home life. Do you know what I think? I don't think he'll go that far. He'll just hang around. Bamfylde has been more a home to him than anywhere else, I wager."

"Then why should he leave it?"

"To think things out, maybe. And let the dust settle."

"Where does that leave us, sir?"

"Under an obligation to go through the motions of the lost, stolen or strayed drill. Get Boyer and four or five of the sharpest seniors in Havelock's. I'll check the stations."

"Couldn't we enlist all the prefects, sir?"

"I wouldn't if I were you," Herries said, calmly. "It's your first term as housemaster. You don't want kindly patronage from all your colleagues at this stage, do you?"

"No, I don't. Thank you, sir," and he went back to Havelock's where Beth was brewing coffee, having first sent for Boyer and four seniors of his choice. They joined him before he had finished his first cup. Boyer said, doubtfully, "We've . . . er . . . got a clue, sir. Not where he is but why he cleared off."

"Well?"

"It came from Johnson Major, sir. He was out with his people yesterday and . . . well, he'll tell you himself, sir." He went to the top of the stairs and bawled Johnson's name and a moment later the boy sidled in, looking, David thought, shifty and ill at ease. He said, at a nod from Boyer, "If Spats . . . er . . . Winterbourne *has* gone off, sir, I might be the reason but I thought I was doing the right thing, sir. I mean, well, sir, he's a good sport, and I didn't want anyone to spring it on him. With that kind of stuff in the papers it was bound to get around sooner or later, wasn't it, sir?"

"What are you trying to tell me, Johnson?"

Johnson swallowed. "I . . . er . . . I saw the paper in the lounge of the Hopgood Arms, in Challacombe yesterday. I didn't want my people to see me reading it, and start asking questions, so I slipped it in my jacket and took it away."

"You're saying you showed it to Winterbourne?"

"Yes, sir. I took him on one side after prep and I waited around while he read it. He asked if he could keep the paper and I said he could. After all, it wasn't mine, sir."

"How did he take it?"

"He was sick, sir."

"Sick? You mean really sick?"

"Yes, sir, there and then, behind the bandroom. I told him to go to matron, sir, and he promised he would, but he made me swear on the Bible not to let on to anyone. I wouldn't have, if Boyer hadn't explained."

"No one else knows, sir." This from Boyer, who looked a little sick himself. "This is the first Dobson and the others have heard about it. Does it mean anything?"

"I think it does." He pondered a moment and then, out of the corner of his eye, he saw the wretched Johnson eyeing him. He said, "Look here, Johnson, nobody holds this against you. I'm not sure you did the right thing but who the devil knows what the right thing is under these circumstances? Clear off now and don't breathe a word of it to anyone, you understand?"

"Yes, sir. Thank you, sir," and Johnson shot away, relieved to be out of it so cheaply.

Herries appeared with one of his half-inch ordnance maps and once again David had a fleeting trench memory, this time of an old, grey-haired brigadier, mounting a company-strength raid on the Boche line. He said, calmly, "I've mapped out the likely routes. He didn't get the train at Bamfylde Bridge and he didn't get it at Crosshayes. Before we start half a dozen hares we'll check the locals. I'll drive over to the Crosshayes area myself and call in one or two of the farms. You take that three-wheeler of yours, P.J. and do the same as far as the Barrows. You others take the routes I've marked and check with any moorman you meet, but make it casual. Don't let them see we're much concerned, you understand?"

"Yes, sir."

"We'll rendezvous at midday under the Clump and pool what news we have. Hold on, you can't comb Exmoor on empty stomachs. Go and get breakfast first. I've told Priddis to serve you before the multitude descends."

They went out and Herries said, "I didn't tell 'em to keep mum, did I?"

"You didn't have to, sir," and he recounted what Johnson had told them. Herries said, "Poor little toad. It's young to have to stand up to that kind of fire, but my guess is he'll do it somehow."

"He's not likely to . . ."

"Do anything silly? Not a chance. Winterbourne isn't the hysterical type. Could that gel of yours spare me a cup of that coffee?"

"Of course," and he fidgeted while Herries sipped the coffee Beth handed him. Over the rim of his cup Herries's sharp eyes caught the movement. "It's all happened before," he said, "and it'll happen again. The important thing is to tread softly, my boy."

*   *   *

They met as arranged at the foot of the knoll, marked on the maps as the Clump, but none of them had anything to report. Winterbourne had vanished and Herries thought it likely that he might be home by now but he was not. There was no message from Winterbourne Senior and when Herries rang the City number he was told the boy had not yet appeared. Herries said, quietly, "We've searched a five-mile radius here and we'll extend it to ten or twelve before dark. If he's still in the district we'll find him, Mr. Winterbourne. Are you prepared to leave it at that, or would you prefer me to notify the police?"

David, standing near the door, heard the calm voice rise to a crackle and saw Herries scowl. "Very well, that's your prerogative, Mr. Winterbourne," and he replaced the receiver.

"Damned codfish," he said. "That's what comes of making too much money, P.J. The word 'police' sent his blood pressure soaring, just as I knew it would. Still, he has a point. The police mean publicity and he's had a surfeit of that. Wouldn't do us much good, either. We'll keep it in the family for the time being."

After lunch they assembled all the prefects and sent them off in couples, nine pairs in all, covering all points of the compass ten miles afield. Those with farthest to go were given bicycles and instructions to phone in.

David pushed his own enquiries as far as Challacombe but when they all met again at dusk no one had seen or heard anything of Spats. Exmoor had swallowed him up.

Herries said, as they picked over a cold supper, "There's no help for it. Publicity or no publicity we'll have to report him missing and I daresay we'll get a wigging for not doing it earlier."

Beth said, unexpectedly, "But you're still not really worried, are you?" and Herries replied, "No, my dear, not to that extent. I'm irritated, and concerned as to his state of mind and my responsibilities. But when you've been at this as long as I have you learn to rely on the barometer in here," and he tapped his hard, round stomach. "Get a good sleep, both of you. We'll turn to again after breakfast tomorrow but I'll discuss it with Inspector Chawleigh at Challacombe before I go to bed."

"But you're worried sick, aren't you, Davy?" Beth said, as soon as Algy's steps had died away on the stairs, and he replied, "By God, I am! Who wouldn't be?"

"Why not trust Algy's instinct?"

"It's not only Winterbourne I'm concerned about," he admitted, with something of an effort. "It's us, you and me. A thing like this, to happen my first term here as house-master. Damn that silly woman and her peccadilloes! Right now I could strangle her with one of her own silk stockings."

She said, "Come to bed, Davy," and he followed her, without much confidence that he would sleep.

And yet he did, a few minutes after she had taken him in her arms, and as he drifted off he thought, drowsily, "She's right . . . I can cope with anything so long as she's around . . . I've been feeling damned sorry for myself all day but I'm luckier than that chap Winterbourne, for all his investments and fancy trappings . . . If he'd had the sense to marry someone like Beth his boy wouldn't be out on the moor feeling the sky had fallen on him." His hold on her tightened, as though he was suddenly aware of the fragility of happiness, how chancy it was and how easily lost.

CHAPTER TWO

I

It had leaked by rising bell the following morning, a heavy, sultry day, with a promise of sticky heat and thunderstorms before evening.

The wildest stories concerning Spats Winterbourne were circulating and there was no stopping them, as Boyer told him after the school had gone into breakfast. Even Algy had lost some of his ebullience and drifted in to tell them Inspector Chawleigh would be making his own enquiries from Challacombe, and was sending a man over to get statements.

"None of these people seem to be able to do a thing without first putting it on paper," he grumbled. "One of these days the entire Western world will grind to a halt, its apparatus clogged with forms, files and memoranda. I had it in mind to comb the south-eastern area today, starting from farther out with Boyer, and one or two others. Will you stay here meantime and cope with that scrivener?"

"Anything you say," David said, feeling that he had lost control of the situation. "Beth planned to take the twins into Challacombe for their inoculations, so I won't have the car until she gets back. I could cancel it, of course."

"Don't do that," Herries said, "that diphtheria scare is still on, I'm told. We had everyone jabbed the first week of term. I was an idiot not to tell Willoughby to do the infants then. I'll phone in around midday and we can exchange news. I daresay Mr. Moneybags will call again. Tell him the state of the poll."

David watched him drive off, his Austin Seven grossly over-loaded with the Sixth Form posse. Ten minutes later

Beth drove the Morgan round from the coach-house with the twins aboard, Joan in front with her, Grace perched in the dickey seat behind. He did not go down and reassure the children about the inoculation. In his present mood she was more qualified to do that, but he waved as they bumbled off down the west drive and Grace waved back. There was no point in going into class. For one thing he couldn't concentrate. For another he was likely to be fetched at any moment to deal with Inspector Chawleigh's man, so he asked matron to show him Winterbourne's locker, sorting through his belongings in the linen room, looking for some kind of clue as to the boy's whereabouts.

There was nothing of any consequence in the pockets and turning them out lowered his spirits a degree or two farther, for he remembered performing this same office for casualties behind Béthune, in the autumn of 1915. A cardboard folder caught his eye and he took it over to the window, surprised to find it contained about a dozen very creditable water-colours, all of Exmoor scenes and signed '*E. W. Winterbourne*', with dates reaching back a couple of years.

The quality of the work astonished him. Spats could not have been more than thirteen when the first of them was painted and, so far as he knew, the boy had had no training. There was one that impressed him particularly, a limpid sketch in bronze, russet and green, of Chetsford Water, where it flows out of the middle moor and passes under an old stone bridge through a desolate area of upland. The autumnal tints of the moor had been trapped by the boy's brush. It had a soft, brooding quality, unrelieved by the width of a sky dappled with those long streamers of cloud that passed in endless procession over the scene at all seasons of the year.

He was still looking at it when Mrs. Gorman, the matron, presented herself. "The policeman is here now, Mr. Powlett-

Jones. Mrs. Herries is showing him into the head's study. Will you be wanting any further help from me?" He told her no, tucking the folder under his arm and going down the slate steps to the quad. The light seemed very queer out here, overcast with a yellowish tinge as if, at any minute, the low clouds pressing on the school buildings would split and empty themselves. From the direction of Big School, where Bouncer was in session, he heard a burst of laughter, and turned in through the arched door leading to the head's kitchen quarters and thence to the study, where a young policeman, looking just as green and uncertain of himself as he had when he reported for his first interview there more than seven years ago, was thumbing his notebook.

II

Venn's lorry-driver, emerging from the quarry two-thirds of the way up Quarry Hill, was aware that something was amiss the moment he levelled out on the gradient, about one in six here but steeper beyond the ash coppices that grew on each side lower down the road. He braked as hard as he dared but the speed of the heavily-laden lorry increased so that he made a wild grab at the handbrake, throwing all his weight on it as the vehicle weaved the full width of the road, its speed increasing with every yard it covered. As he approached the bend he realised he could never make it and acted on impulse, swinging the wheel hard right, mounting the low bank and crashing into the little forest of saplings to cut the corner or, if he was lucky, snarl up on the tangled undergrowth there. His left hand still gripped the brake lever but his right was pressed on the horn, so that his blaring progress could have been heard a mile away.

Old Chuff Greenaway, Farmer Grover's part-time man, was the only witness to the lorry's crashing entry into the wood. He was hedging fifty yards lower down the hill, heard the horn and glanced up just in time to see the vehicle tear into the copse and plough on down the slope, its progress marked by the travelling tumult among the trees that tossed and whirled as though struck by a cyclone. The undergrowth slowed the lorry's progress somewhat but the weight of stone behind it was too much for the ten-year-old growth in the coppice. It shot out on to the road again at about thirty miles an hour, the driver still wrestling with the gears, the horn still trumpeting his terror.

Beth, changing gear to tackle the second stage of the hill, saw it as a looming shadow, bursting out of the woods like a mastodon on the rampage, but she had no real awareness of the impact when the lorry tore into the nearside of the Morgan, crushed it, caught it up upon its front fender, carried it fifty yards or more down the hill and then discarded it before striking the far hedge and overturning on its side. Nothing could have been more sudden, more unexpected or more final. One moment she was addressing a remark to the children about the blaring horn, the next this great thing was looming over her, blotting everything out. She felt no fear or even dismay, only an intense curiosity concerning its sudden eruption from the little green wood on her left.

Chuff Greenaway, panting hard, was on the scene in less than a minute, and what he saw caused him to stand wheezing yards short of the two piles of debris, one big, one small, his mouth agape, his eyes starting from their sockets. Then, with a groan, he turned and tottered back to the farm lane beyond the bend, sobbing out his story to Martha Grover, who was hanging out washing in the cobbled yard.

With a small part of his mind David heard the young policeman's intermittent rumble, something about a terrible accident on Quarry Hill involving Venn's lorry, Beth and the children, but the full portent of what he was saying was too obscene, too monstrous to be absorbed. The man went on mumbling, his big hands fidgeting with his helmet on his knees, but soon David could make no kind of sense at all out of what he was saying and gestured so that he stopped, sitting immobile on the chair David had occupied that first spring day he came here and took tea with the Herries. Then, but dimly, he was aware of several other things, the presence of Ellie Herries who, for some inexplicable reason, was pressing his head to her chest, and a sustained roaring sound in his ears, like the sound of the pre-zero-hour Somme bombardment, and behind it a complex of inconsequential sounds, a distant roll of thunder, the five-minute bell signifying the end of a period, the familiar clatter of boots on the quad flagstones outside, and the shrill voice of Rawlins—it was odd how easily he identified the voice-shouting, "No! Find your own ruddy atlas! You're always scrounging. . .!" as he scuttled past under the window.

He got up, very stiffly, and moved out into the passage, through the arched door to Big School and into the forecourt, instinctively turning half-left and moving up towards the stump of the riven beech, Algy's thinking post. The roller was here again, parked where it should not have been by one of the chain-gangs, very active at this time of year, and he sat on it, grappling with the enormity of the news that the pink-cheeked young policeman had brought. Beth and one of the kids dead. The lorry driver dead. The other twin, he did not know whether it was Joan or Grace, badly injured and rushed by ambulance to Challacombe hospital.

The roaring in his ears increased in volume, blotting out other sounds although he could see, as through the wrong end of a telescope, some of the First Eleven at the nets below the pavilion, and even wonder why they played so soundlessly. One of the groundsmen was poking about the cricket pitch, searching for evidence of his implacable enemy, the mole. It astounded him that life, distorted into an unimaginable nightmare for him, continued to flow so smoothly and unremarkably elsewhere.

His brain was still three-parts numb. It was impossible to absorb a shock of this magnitude. And yet, below the area of numbness, was a terrible rawness that quivered and winced when partial consciousness invaded it. He sat there like a stone carving, hands on thighs, chin thrust forward, seeing without actually seeing, hearing nothing but that dull roaring and then, as unaccountably as Ellie had appeared, Howarth was there, feet planted astride, hands locked behind his back as he sometimes stood in class. He said, "Come up to my rooms, P.J. Come and have a stiff drink, man," and when David did not answer, "The police say someone will have to go to Challacombe. I'll come with you, as soon as the head gets back with transport." And then he did a strange thing, strange that is for Howarth, who had never, in the seven years he had known him, betrayed any emotion other than irritation. His tight little mouth twisted, the eyes behind the prim, pince-nez glasses glittered, and he reached out and placed his arm about David's shoulders, letting it rest there, lightly but firmly.

Away across the field the bell jangled for lunch and a muted clamour reached them. The sounds roused him somewhat. He said, hoarsely, "Do you suppose it's *true*, Howarth? I mean . . . couldn't it be some . . . some frightful mix-up?" and Howarth said, hoarsely, "We'll call in on Doc Willoughby's on the way to Challacombe, David. He'll give you something to help ride out the shock."

It was strange. His brain recorded the fact that Howarth had never before addressed him by his Christian name and this, improbably, touched some hidden spring behind his eyes, so that he began to weep, tears brimming over and coursing the length of his jawline. He even noted that one of them splashed down on the smooth shining surface of the roller, bursting like a star-shell over the lines at night, so that it recalled violent deaths in the past, the very distant past, it seemed, although the wounds those deaths inflicted on him were not healed, as he had always assumed them to be. He said, brokenly, "Out there it was different. Everybody was going to die. It was only a matter of how and when."

"You got through that," Howarth said.

"Not this. *Not this!*"

"*Yes!* Here you've got something to hold on to, make something of. Out there it was just . . . just bloody waste!" Suddenly he became extraordinarily animated, putting both hands to David's shoulders, swinging him round and shaking him. "The people round you aren't numbered for death, the way everyone was out there. You've got thirty to forty years of hard grind ahead of you, doing a job you're uniquely equipped to do and in a way no one else could do it! It won't make much difference for a month, a year maybe, but it will in the end, I promise. A clear purpose always does, and I'm qualified to tell you that."

Something of Howarth's urgency got through to him. Not much, but enough to bring him partially out of his stupor of grief and despair. He said, carefully, "I couldn't go to Challacombe, Howarth. I couldn't identify her. Someone else will have to do that. Killed outright, that policeman said. Crushed by a bloody great lorry running wild . . ." He stood up. "I'm going across the moor. Alone. I can't fight it . . . can't accept it . . . here. Not where *she* was, not where that kid waved goodbye three hours ago. Tell Ellie. Tell Herries when he gets back."

"Let me come with you."

"No! I can only cope with it alone, but it must be away

from here." He glanced down at the great sprawl of buildings, silent again for the lunch break. "This place was a part of her. She's too close here. So are the twins. Can you understand that?"

"Yes," Howarth said, "but for God's sake remember what I said, about using it to hold on to. The place itself, *all of us here*. For there isn't one soul down there who isn't grieving with you, or won't be the moment he knows. That's worth thinking on, David. It's the only thing worth a thought just now."

He stood and watched him go, up past the pavilion, along the fringe of the plantation, then left into the undergrowth. Sullenly he groped for his cigarettes and after three fumbled attempts lit a Gold Flake, inhaling the smoke deep into his lungs. He stood there watching until he saw the tall, spare figure emerge from the far side of the plantation and head for the Coombe. Then, with a grunt, he turned back towards the school buildings, walking swiftly and purposefully, but wondering just how he could explain his sanction of P.J.'s lunge off into the open country, with a more than even chance that he would never find his way back again.

III

David had no awareness of familiar landmarks, or not after crossing the plank bridge over the Coombe, where he had seen Blades and that woman Darbyshire last summer. He walked swiftly but blindly, vaulting stiles, scrambling up and down briar-sown banks, so that often he stumbled and sometimes fell. But he picked himself up with a kind of ferocity and pushed on over miles and miles of upland and across a dozen or more timbered gullies. As long as he could keep walking at this speed he was able to keep at bay the full impact of the blow, to stop it flattening him and leaving him as crushed and broken as Beth and the twins,

wherever they were at this moment. His sole awareness of
the landscape was the curious yellowish light he had
noticed earlier that day and persisted even here, fifteen
hundred feet above sea level. Every now and again thunder
rolled but it was not until he paused gasping, on the crest
of the long, heathery slope leading down to Chetsford
Water, that the storm began to gather overhead and one
or two heavy spots of rain fell on his sweating face. The soft,
yellow glow in the sky dispersed then, replaced by a grey
curtain of rain moving swiftly in from the east, a swaying,
gently undulating curtain, immensely tall and hissing,
coming to meet him like a vast, all enveloping sheet of old
canvas, the sail of some giant galleon torn loose by a
cyclone and running free across the middle moor. He had
never seen its like before. Perhaps nobody had. Perhaps it
was the forerunner of the Apocalypse.

He stood there watching it until it reached him, drenching
him through in a matter of seconds. He was standing in a
particularly open place, two hundred feet or more above
the floor of the valley, where a great belt of brushwood
grew both sides of the stream. There was something vaguely
familiar about the landscape, as though he had seen it in a
recent dream. He recognised the lie of the land, the long
straggle of crouching timber down there, the strangely
even ridges of the hills, like a choppy sea studded with flot-
sam represented by boulders and gorse patches. Great
arteries of forked lightning lit it up in great detail, tearing
jagged rents in the rain curtain and over all, in a succession
of ear-splitting discharges, the thunder rolled.

It was only then that he became aware of the dog and its
presence amazed him almost as much as the spectacle.
It was Ferguson's Airedale, Towser, that must have attached itself to him the moment he left the plantation and
followed at his heels over God knew how many miles of

moorland. The dog was whining, terrified by the uproar, and at every fresh clap of thunder he gave a series of sharp, high-pitched yelps. Finally, getting no response from the man, he ran, still yelping, the full length of the slope to the cover of the brushwood. David did not follow. The cataclysm was a solace, the teeming rain beating over every square inch of his body, a balm. It was the end of the world. He saw it as a kind of climax to the horrors of the day, and, at a farther distance, to days of almost identical uproar in the Salient and the Somme.

And then, just as the dog reached the floor of the valley, he became aware of a figure blundering up the slope, head invisible, shoulders hunched under a yellow oilskin, and with a small part of his brain he wondered who the devil it could be, and what he was doing down there in such chaos. At that moment the whole sky blazed up and, a second or or two later, an explosion of enormous weight burst over him, stunning his senses so that he was only vaguely aware of the arrival of the figure in the oilskin, who seized his hand and began dragging him down, down to the valley until, in the space of a lightning flash it seemed, they were threading a tunnel of dripping foliage leading to a shallow cave in the rock face beside the rushing stream. Inside it was quite dry and the place was clearly inhabited. An array of kit lay about, including blankets and a knapsack. A small fire smouldered under the overhang, obstinate tongues of flame holding out against the hissing downpour.

He sat down then, limp and exhausted, and as in a dream he saw the figure of a boy, tousled and laughing, emerge from beneath the folds of the oilskin and recognised Spats Winterbourne who seemed, for some obtuse reason, to be enjoying himself, for he said, shouting above the uproar, "It's a corker, isn't it, sir? Never seen one like this before!" and then, with concern, "I say, you're drenched through, sir!

Peel off and rub yourself down. There's a towel here somewhere. It's a bit grubby, I'm afraid ..." and David, hyp-
notised by the boy, obediently shed jacket and shirt, and
began towelling himself.

It was extraordinarily cosy in here, a refuge not only from
the storm but from the pitiless world outside, where women
and children were crushed under lorries overloaded with
building stone. Mutely he watched Winterbourne busy
himself about the fire, putting a kettle on a grid and ladling
cocoa from a tin into a thick earthenware mug. What astonished him far more than the coincidence of meeting
Winterbourne here, of having directed his heedless steps to
the very spot where the boy was hiding, was Winterbourne's
identity with the moor, and the impression he gave of being
an integral part of its wildness and remoteness. He had always
thought of Winterbourne as a town-bred boy, dapper and
clothes-conscious, even elegant in a slightly comical way, but
here, in a cave beside a rushing stream he was a gipsy,
moving and doing for himself, as though this was his natural
habitat. A sense of curiosity close to wonder invaded him,
holding his own tragedy at bay, so that he grabbed at it, as
though Winterbourne and Winterbourne's identification
with the moor was a raft in an ocean of misery. He said,
"You've been here all the time, haven't you?" and Winterbourne, with a self-effacing grin, replied, "Yes, sir. I suppose
you were out looking for me."

"Everybody's looking for you. Including the police."

The boy's cheerful face clouded slightly but then he
shrugged. "What does it matter? I'll be sacked, anyway,
won't I?"

He sat crosslegged on his blanket, looking into the fire
and presently he said, incuriously, "You were lost, weren't
you, sir?"

"I was lost right enough," David thought, "but not in the

way he means," and said deliberately, "I hadn't the vaguest idea where I was or how I got here. I didn't even know the dog had followed me," and the boy looked quickly, his woman's eyes sharp with intelligence. He said, "Has . . . has anything happened? Something serious, sir?"

"Yes, but it has nothing to do with you. I'd forgotten you were missing. Forgotten you existed."

The bell in his brain began to toll then slow, ponderous strokes with a repetitive message for him, '*Beth is dead . . . Beth is dead . . . The twins are dead . . . Everything's over . . .*' and he gave a kind of sob.

The boy was beside him in an instant. "What *is* it, sir? What's happened?"

"My wife . . . she was killed by one of Venn's lorries on Quarry Hill this morning."

He heard a long hiss of escaping breath as he bowed his head. He could not bear to talk to anyone who had seen her, gay, carefree and terribly alive. Not even a boy like Winterbourne, who could have known her but slightly.

Winterbourne said, brokenly, "That's . . . that's awful sir. No wonder you . . ." and he stopped. When he spoke again their was a quaver in his voice. "Was she . . . was *she* out looking for me, sir?"

He raised his head. The boy, so heedless a moment since, now looked as scared as a recruit sitting on the forestep awaiting zero-hour. "No, she wasn't looking for you. It had nothing to do with you. She was driving the twins back from Challacombe."

"The . . . the children, sir?"

"One was killed, the other seriously injured. I daresay she's dead by now."

The rain continued to thresh down beyond the fringe of brushwood. The stream before the cave entrance boiled, rushing over the sloping stones in a cataract. Thunder still growled and occasional lightning flickered, but the centre of the storm was moving away to the north-east. The lid of Winterbourne's kettle began to dance and he got up in a single movement, lifted it from the fire, poured water into the mug, and stirred it with the deliberation that attended all his actions. "Drink this, sir. *Please*, you must!"

David took the mug and sipped. The scalding liquid warmed his belly but his hands began to shake in the old familiar way and he had difficulty in holding the mug. The boy was beside him again, as solicitous as a mother nursing a sick child. "Take it easy, sir. Just a sip at a time. But get it down. All of it."

It was impossible to resist his gentle persuasiveness. He finished the cocoa and Winterbourne took the mug, setting it before the fire.

"Shouldn't you . . . we . . . start back, sir? It'll take two hours, even using short cuts, and some of the streams might be too wide to jump. That other little girl . . . you'll have to *know*, sir." He waited, and when David said nothing he went on, "We could make it to Withybridge across the shoulder. There's a phone there in the village store, sir. They could send transport and we could wait for it there."

David said, "You go to Withybridge and call in. Tell them to pick you up before dark. I'll stay here."

"You can't do that, sir."

"I'll do what I damned well like, boy."

"No, sir, I'm not leaving you. We could stay here but then everyone will start looking for you and they wouldn't find you, any more than they could me. They'll think . . . well, it just won't do, sir. You must see that."

After a moment he tried again, in the same insistent voice. "The other little girl. She may need you, sir."

It was a possibility that simply hadn't occurred to him but he gave it thought. A gleam of hope probed the farthest recesses of his mind, an eightpenny torchlight, of the kind boys used to read under the blankets, projecting its feeble beam across a vast belfry, where the one-note bell tolled and tolled in his brain. Was it remotely possible that something—anything—could be salvaged from the wreck of his life?

He reached out and groped for his sodden shirt but Winterbourne anticipated this. "Put this on, sir. It'll be tight but it doesn't matter if it rips," and he began to force a sweater over David's head, struggling with it until it had passed his chin, then smoothing it down so that it fitted like a skin. Out of the corner of his eye David saw a cardboard portfolio, a duplicate of the one he had found in Winterbourne's locker. His mind made the connection, telling why the valley had looked familiar from the crest. He said, "Have you been here often? To paint water-colours?" and surprisingly Winterbourne blushed. "Yes, sir. I didn't think anyone knew. About the painting, I mean."

"Nobody does. I found some of your paintings in your locker. How long have you been coming here?"

"Whenever I could, sir. I found this place by accident, during the Middlemoor run my first term, sir. I didn't tell anyone about it. It was just somewhere to come when ... well, when things got a bit much, sir."

'A bit much.' It was a strange typically English way of summarising the enormous pressures Winterbourne had been resisting, and resisting very successfully he would say, all the time he had been at Bamfylde. A boy with an exhibitionist mother and a cold fish of a father. A child who could never escape the harassment of the one and the inadequacy of the other. It was remarkable, really, how well he had weathered the long, stark terms, retreating into himself, his painting and his integration with the moor, that must have seemed a kind of refuge. Algy Herries had been absolutely correct about Winterbourne, as he was accurate in his assessment of nearly all the boys who passed through his hands. Winterbourne was not really a boy at all but a young and superbly adjusted adult, and somehow, understanding this, David felt the terrible weight pressing on him lift a fraction, as Howarth's words came back to him— "Here you've got something to hold on to, to live for, to make something of. It won't make much difference for a month or a year, but it will in the end, I promise."

Was there anything in that beyond conventional words of comfort? Howarth's astringent way of saying that time would heal, or something equally banal? Winterbourne's private battle seemed to insist that there was, that by submerging body and soul into the ethos of Bamfylde, or some other school with an identical function, he could, in the years left to him, find shape and cohesion in the way he had when he had emerged, equally battered, from an earlier ordeal. They were not the same, as he had protested to Howarth, but in their very difference there might be a chink of hope. For here, in Winterbourne's survival, was a ledge, a handhold that someone with more courage than he possessed, might use to haul himself out of the slough. He said, at length, "About the one in the hospital ... you might be right ... We'd better start back. Now, before the light goes. How long would it take us? To Withybridge, say?"

"Under the hour, sir."

He glanced at his watch, amazed to find that it was after eight o'clock. More than seven hours had passed since he turned his back on Howarth and struck into the plantation. Winterbourne said, "It'll stay overcast and there's no moon, sir, but we would make it the whole way by ten-thirty. It could be quicker that way, providing you don't mind wading, sir."

"Let's go."

He watched the boy pull on his oilskin, damp down the smouldering fire and take a last look round the little cave. He gave the impression of a man taking a final glance at home before emigrating to the far side of the world. They went out, Winterbourne leading, and tackled the long, dripping slope to the crest. The Airedale, subdued now, trotted at their heels. It was still raining but the weight had gone from the downpour. Over in the west there was a small rift in the great banks of clouds and the glint of bronze light beyond reminded him of the glow of a dying fire, or perhaps a few chrysanthemums, glimpsed through a door left ajar. They walked in silence, one behind the other and even under his oilskin Winterbourne still looked dapper and self-contained. He had his mother's easy grace, and perhaps his father's sense of omnipotence, conveyed to David over two hundred miles of telephone cable yesterday. As long as Winterbourne led the trek some kind of purpose attached itself to this silent squelch over miles of seeping moorland.

CHAPTER THREE

I

There were periods during the three years he served at the Front that were lost to him. Weeks and even months, when his senses, dulled by physical exhaustion, anaesthetised by the thrum of shellfire and the sheer boredom of active service in that morass, were expunged from the record of his years as though they had never been.

The period immediately succeeding the calamity on Quarry Hill was such a time, embracing, as it did the dismal aftermath of identification, inquest and double funeral at Stone Cross churchyard where, only a few months before, Beth had stood with him to watch the irascible Ferguson, and then that ageing perfectionist, Cordwainer, laid in that part of the yard that was, albeit unofficially, a Bamfylde preserve.

The news that five-year-old Grace had survived the accident, despite terrible injuries, had no power to cheer just then, for he had to steel himself against tidings that she had followed the others. It did not seem credible that a mite her age could survive a compound fracture of the right leg, a shattered left arm, three broken ribs, severe concussion, and extensive lacerations to the right side of the face, the result of being flung clear from the dickey seat and half-buried by a cascade of stone from the overturned lorry. As yet, as the long, thundery spell continued throughout June, she held on, never fully conscious, and all but invisible in a cocoon of bandages that concealed the whole of her face save for the mouth and left eye. He was not allowed to see her for more than a week and when, at last, he looked down at her, lying there among a grotesque array of cradles and pulleys, he wished he had stayed away. There was something obscene seeing her in that fearful context when he remembered so vividly his final glimpse of her from the window of Havelock's first floor, as the Morgan trundled down the east drive at the start of that frightful day.

He asked Willoughby, liaising with the surgeon, for a frank estimate of her chances and Willoughby, accepting the fact that he was no stranger to violent death, did not hedge. He said that they were fifty-fifty, depending upon factors that could not be assessed at this stage. "She's getting first-class care," he added, "Harvey-Smith, who is in overall charge of the case, regards her as a challenge. If her condition improves in the weeks ahead, she'll have to undergo several more operations, then move on to a London hospital for a skin graft. But there's a chance, a very good one, I'd say. So try and keep that in the forefront of your mind."

It was some consolation, he supposed, or might become one as time went on, but it did not help him to tackle the task of picking up the ravelled threads of his life, and making some kind of attempt to adjust to the bleakness of the future.

He let Ellie persuade him not to attend the funeral. Alone he could contain his grief. He could not share it with four hundred others and there seemed no point in insisting on a private affair when Beth had been so popular with staff and boys all the time she had lived here.

In the event there were two tiny sequels to the melancholy event, one on the evening of the funeral, when he was trying to occupy his mind replying to some of the fifty-odd letters sent him by Old Boys who remembered her, and two more from Cooper and Scrubbs-Norton, who did not. There came a discreet tap on the door and assuming it was Ellie, with some sleeping pills Willoughby had prescribed, he called, "Come in, Mrs. Herries." It was not Ellie but Boyer, carrying two tattered books.

He stood hesitantly beside the desk, sympathy distorting his mobile, amiable features into an unfamiliar and incongruous mould, as he said, with an apologetic cough, "Am I . . . er . . . disturbing you, sir? I can pop in later, I'm duty perk tonight," but David, glad of his company, pushed the correspondence aside and told him to sit down and help himself to a cigarette from a packet on the reading table. Boyer looked startled, as well he might. Smoking was high on what veteran Bamfeldians called the 'watch-it-list', drawn up by Algy Herries when he put into practice his Roman precept of 'Few Rules But Unbendables'. David said, noting the look, "I know you chaps get through ten a day when you can lay your hands on them. This is one occasion when you don't have to climb up among the stacked trunks for a smoke. Don't take it as general, however, or there'll be the devil to pay. For me as well as you."

So Boyer took a Player's from the packet and inhaled expertly, saying, with a fleeting grin, "Er . . . hadn't you better light up yourself, sir? In case someone else looks in?" and when David had stuck a cigarette between his lips, "I actually looked in to give you these, sir. I remembered you quoting from them in the Upper Fifth last year. You said you had them both out there, but lost them with the rest of your kit at Third Ypres."

He passed the books over and David recognised them as old favourites he had read and re-read many times in the last ten years. Fortescue's translation of *The Memoirs of Sergeant Bourgoyne*, and Butler's translation of *The Memoirs of Baron de Marbot*. Boyer went on, "I found them in the Charing Cross Road during the hols, sir. I was going to keep them as a leaving souvenir, but well . . . it occurred to me that you could do with a couple of old friends just now. I've written in them, sir."

David turned to the flyleaves and on each was an identical inscription in Boyer's devil-may-care hand, '*For David Powlett-Jones—In Friendship. Chadwick S. Boyer.*' He said, "That was a nice thought, Chad. I don't think many would have had it. Thank you very much. They were both books I've always been meaning to replace but never did." He sat musing a moment. "I'll tell you something that might sound odd. They were a comfort to me out there. I don't know why, unless it was the reflection that, bad as things were, they were sometimes worse for Marbot and Bourgoyne, soldiers at a time when field surgeons used hacksaws and a pint of raw spirit. No, 'comfort' isn't the word," he knitted his brows, trying to remember when he had last sat in a dugout, and read one or other of the journals by the light of a candle stuck in a bottle. "They had a personal message. Neither man would give up, or even contemplate giving up. They stuck it out and they came through on that account. I suppose I told myself that if they could, then I could. I'll treasure them, always."

Boyer said, with difficulty, "There was one other thing, sir. The perks wanted me to tell you how they felt about it. We all liked Mrs. Powlett-Jones very much. She . . . well . . . fitted in so well, sir, right from the start. I know talking doesn't do a da—doesn't help much, sir. But they wanted you to know. I'll go now, sir," and he crushed out his half-smoked cigarette and rose, abruptly.

David said, "Stay till Silence bell. God knows, I need company," and Boyer sat again, and when Ellie Herries came in with his coffee and pills, he fetched another cup and saucer from the kitchen and poured from the pot. He said, as soon as Ellie had gone, "This is going to take some weathering, Chad. Between ourselves I can't see myself making it."

"I'll bet you will, sir."

"Would you mind telling me why? Without the usual

flannel. The way you might discuss it with Dobson, or some other chum, and I don't ask out of curiosity. I need to know if I'm to stay on and that's doubtful, I can assure you."

He was struck by the boy's crestfallen expression as he protested . . . "But that . . . that's *daft*, sir! I mean it's not *you* at all. . .!"

It occurred to him that one never ceased to be taken unawares by boys. He had always thought of Boyer as an original. A boy who conceived the idea of epileptic fits to beguile a classroom had to be, and, to add to that, he had always seen him as enterprising and possessing above-average intelligence. But he had never thought of him as vulnerable, or having much of what he had come to regard as a boy's poignancy, something nearly all of them had in one way or another. Boyer's distraught look brought to mind earlier encounters. His talk with Briarley, the day Briarley learned of his father's death on the Lys. Skidmore's stiffnecked refusal to bow to the Founder's statue. Blades' lost expression, soon after Julia Darbyshire had warned him off. And, more recently Winterbourne's look when told of the accident. He said, quietly, "I'm not saying I shall end up cutting my throat. Just that I might feel the need to get away from here, where we spent six happy years. Start again, maybe . . .", but he couldn't go on.

"I think you're absolutely wrong about that, sir."

"Why? Isn't it a natural impulse?"

"Maybe, but well . . . I don't know whether I've any right to stick my oar in."

"I'm asking you to."

"All right. You belong here. You have from the first day, sir, and that isn't flannel. It isn't because the chaps like you either, although they all do. It's because . . . well, because you get *through* to them, in a way older masters don't and can't. Particularly in your subject. I never gave a damn about history before you taught it. I mean, it was no more than a string of dates, and dead mutton to me and to most of the other chaps. But you made it . . . well, *mean* something. You showed us how it fits in with today, if you see what I mean?"

It was a queer kind of compliment but it warmed him. He said, however, "Couldn't I do that at any school?"

"No, sir. Or not so well."

"Why?"

"Because . . . well, because you learned the trick of it here, sir. You're part of the place now. The way you teach . . . well, it fits in with Alg . . . with the head's way, sir."

"Are you saying you fellows really understand the head's theories on education?"

"I think some of us do. By the time we get to the Sixth, that is. Some of the chaps have been to other schools, although I never have. I came here as a nipper. They all say the same thing, that this place is different, not just because of the head but because of where it is, up here on its own and with its own way of life. And lately because of you, and the way you try and put the head's ideas into practice. Do you get the message, sir, or am I talking a lot of coc— er . . . rubbish?"

"I get the message, Chad."

"You'll think about it, then?"

"I'll think about it."

* * *

That was the first incident, but there was another a few hours later when, just before morning school, Graves-Jones poked his head round the corner of his sitting-room, holding a bunch of freesias, carnations and maidenhair fern.

Graves-Jones was not a boy one might expect to see presenting a bouquet. David remembered him vividly, from the first day they met in the garden of the cottage, when Beth gave her first new boy's tea-party, and how he clicked his heels, Prussian-fashion, when thanking his hostess. All the way up school—he was in the Sixth now—Graves-Jones had justified Beth's first impression of him, a suave, confident boy, with demonstrably good manners, a little at odds with his generation. He said, without a trace of embarrassment, "I was just going into class, sir, and thought these should go into water. Will you be going to the hospital this afternoon, sir?"

"I'm not sure. I might. Why?"

"Well, if you do, sir, I wondered if you'd take these along? We tipped Westacott to cut them from his patch, and we intended putting them with all the others in the churchyard. But then it seemed a bit silly, sir. I mean, they'll wilt down there, in this weather, and your ... little girl might like them in the ward. I know she can't see them yet but these freesias smell nice, sir."

He reached out and took the flowers wordlessly, too moved to do more than nod his thanks, but Graves-Jones didn't seem to expect thanks. He stepped back gave one of his little bows from the waist, and withdrew, quietly closing the door. David went into the kitchen, filled a vase and put the flowers inside. His hands shook and his throat felt terribly constricted. He wept then and the relief was immediate. He thought, "Boyer's right, of course ... bad enough here, but it would be a damn sight worse among strangers. I'll give it a go. At least until the end of term ..." and he found his gown, shrugged himself into it, and went down the steps just as the bell signalled the start of morning school and his first period with the Lower Third.

II

That was the way of it, not only as far as end of term, and through the summer break, but on through the Michaelmas term to his first Christmas alone.

It was as though his existence, as a man with some useful part to play in life, was a shallow-rooted plant, dependent upon the strength of a cluster of root fibres that ran just below the surface, searching for points of anchorage; another, stronger root perhaps, or an angled rock or a layer of heavier soil. Each tiny fibre was a part of his identity with the place and some ran deeper than others. One was little Grace's survival, of course, and her slow climb back to a point where hope was definite, corrective operations could be attempted, and she could move on to Great Ormond Street for a period of about six months, they said. Another was the close companionship of Herries and Ellie, backed by the unsentimental but solid comradeship of Howarth, and the sympathy of Barnaby, the two Irvines and even, in his bumbling way, dear old Bouncer. A third fibre was the prescribed rhythm of the school, with its succession of red-letter days and self-made entertainments, particularly the Gilbert and Sullivan opera, in which he featured as relief pianist. But much stronger than any of these was his closer integration with boys at all levels, not only old stagers like Chad Boyer, Dobson, Blades, Winterbourne, Skidmore, McNaughton, Graves-Jones and Ruby Bickford, but later arrivals, some of whom had not even known Beth and the twins.

He made the discovery, as the autumn mists closed in, that the ache in his own heart enabled him to take unexpectedly close-range peeps into the hearts of others, so that he began to mellow in a way that suited the new furrows on his face and the touch of grey in his hair. It was as though he had compressed a couple of decades in six months, converting himself into a more youthful edition of Judy Cordwainer, set in a groove before he was thirty. He was aware of this but did nothing to counteract it, or not mentally. Physically he made a supreme effort, refereeing and occasionally playing a practice game with the First Fifteen, and accompanying the cross-country runs as whipper-in. The season of the year helped to acclimatise him to the rapid change in his character, for the moor, in the late autumn, was at one with his prevailing mood. But what really enabled him to come to terms with his loss was a growing sense of usefulness that might, in time, resolve itself into a definite purpose, of the kind he had had when he and Beth moved into Havelock's last spring.

He might have resigned his housemastership, despite clamorous opposition to the proposal, had it not been for Herries' ruse in making him responsible during the holidays, for the group of boys known as 'The Sunsetters', a group nickname Barnaby had invented for the score or so boarders who lived permanently at the school because their parents were scattered about the dominions, the crown colonies and the protectorates. The label was a play on the imperial claim that Britain still ruled an empire on which the sun never set, and was in no sense a gibe, rather a goodnatured joke, aimed at the separateness of boys who looked upon Bamfylde not as a school but as a home. About half of them were coloured, like the Kassava brothers, the remainder the sons of men with overseas posts who, for one reason or another, preferred to have their children educated in England.

For some years now this expanding group lived on the third floor of the head's house but in September, 1925, the second stage of the new building plan was started and their dormitory was converted into a sick-bay. Herries said, when the builders moved in, "My common sense tells me I ought to scatter them to their respective houses, P.J., but they're all very much against it. I suppose they think of themselves as a little house of their own, and don't care to lose their identities. Do you think you could make room for 'em? Take 'em over, lock, stock and barrel? Someone will have to when I put my feet up, a couple of years from now."

David said he would think about it and came up with a plan to extend the junior dormitory at Havelock's by cutting through into the old Remove and the music room beyond. The Remove he said, could be transferred to one end of the woodwork room. One less music room might annoy Rapper Gibbs but was unlikely to trouble anyone else. "I could get twenty beds in there if the builders went about it the right way," he said. "It wouldn't be much of a job. There's no stonework, only partitioning they should have ripped out at the time of the fire but didn't because it was costing so much."

Herries was enthusiastic and at once switched the builder's men from his third floor and set them at work on the new dormitory but before they were finished David had another thought. "Why don't we make a recreation room out of the music room?" he suggested. "The annexe and Remove will give us enough space for beds, and a room of their own will stop the Sunsetters making free with your quarters in the holidays. Besides, only the seniors among them have studies. They ought to have some stake in the place apart from a bed and a locker."

Herries agreed and the conversion was finished before the end of Michaelmas term, giving the Sunsetters a common room where they could keep their array of overseas journals and play their gramophone, a place where 'Massa' Heilbron, a tall West Indian and a very promising cricketer, could strum his ukelele, and little Kilroy, the fleetest runner in Junior School, could massage his calves, against the day when he would be awarded his running colours, and him only fourteen, the youngest colour on record.

Imperceptibly David found himself saddled with the post of holiday uncle to the Sunsetters but the job, demanding as

it sometimes was, proved another fibre binding him to Bamfylde. Even so, when all the roots were down, there were
still moments when the transplant seemed very insecure.

They would steal upon him treacherously, always taking
him unawares. Sharp, poignant reminders, as when he
looked up at the tall windows of Havelock's and saw a
maid shaking a duster in the manner of Beth when they
were settling in nine months before. Or when, coming out
of church, he glanced down the road to the cottage, and
saw snowdrops crowding the patch where she had planted
her rowan tree. The long winter nights were the worst
times, however, when the wind came shrieking down from
Middlemoor, rattling the slates and searching out chinks
in the old window frames, and he would awake and suddenly find himself harassed and sweating, with the sense of
having escaped from a situation in which Beth and the
twins were calling from behind a wall of quarry stones as
high as the plantation. At times like this he would have to
come to terms with the truth all over again.

He broke the habit of Willoughby's sleeping pills. They
left him drowsy and not up to his work, but he found another
antidote. In October, when the nights had closed in, he
dug out his folder of notes on 'The Royal Tigress' and began
arranging them into sections, and during the Christmas
holidays he actually began to work, and was soon able to
lose himself in the surge of Lancastrian and Yorkist armies
the length and breadth of England, and the struggle for the
crown that had given him yet another of his Second Form
tags, viz.,

> In the fight for England's head,
> York was white, Lancaster red . . .

He did not think it would be a very original book but at
least it kept his thoughts occupied throughout the small

hours, and the sleep that followed a session was free of dreams.

He raised another barrier against introspection and self-pity. He had always been primarily interested in post-Conquest history but, via some construes he had made of Plutarch's *Lives* when mugging for his degree, he was led back to the Ancients and tackled, for the first time, Gibbon's massive work on the Roman Empire. Having whetted his appetite, so to speak, he began to study Persian history, from Cyrus the Great to the Alexandrian conquest, so that his small store of Latin was of real service to him and names like Darius, Xerxes and Zenophon emerged as something more than cardboard figures and supplied him with a new source of anecdotes that he could retell to the Third and Fourth Forms.

Barnaby was the first to note this extension into what he regarded as his field and said, when they were sharing a coffee break one morning. "I always took you for a bit of a Philistine, P.J., a chap who thought history began at the traditional starting joint, 55 B.C. I was wrong it seems. Young Hilary, a duffer if ever there was one, came out with something I didn't know about Hannibal this morning during construe. Damned if I didn't think I was hearing Joan of Arc's voice for a minute. Then he admitted you gave them half an hour on the Punic Wars on Thursday."

The incident, trivial enough, had the effect of bringing him and Barnaby closer together. He had always liked the classics master, a very easygoing man, despite a touch of exhibitionism, but he had never quite succeeded in making a friend of him. Now they sometimes took long walks together, or shared a drink in Howarth's rooms, and the association helped, as did the tendency on the part of everyone save Carter, and Molyneux, who had replaced Ferguson in modern languages, to go out of their way to help. There were still two vaguely hostile camps in the common room. His own, that included the amiable Barnaby and was led from behind by Howarth, and Carter's, for Carter, although a stickler for discipline, had a talent for recruiting the younger, pushing men, often with pet theories on education, men who were slightly contemptuous of Algy's refurbished Arnoldian concepts. The rift was deeper than appeared on the surface, dividing those who thought of themselves as progressive-traditionalists, like Herries himself, and those Howarth labelled the Eager Beavers, committed to raising Bamfylde's academic status and attracting a different kind of parent. There was, however, no danger of a flare-up so long as Algy remained in charge, for although he was careful not to flaunt his authority, it was he who charted the school's course and formulated its policies, and his influence with the Governors, some of whom shared Carter's outlook, was very strong after twenty years of steady progress and the lengthy waiting-list he had built up since the war. Sometimes David wondered what would happen when Herries retired, as he was scheduled to do after the summer term of 1927. He would be sixty-seven then, and had already made arrangements to take the living of Yatton-under-Edge, twenty miles nearer the coast.

He did not give it much thought, however, being fully occupied getting his second wind, and in the event it was not until May, 1926, when the shock waves of the General Strike rolled as far as the Exmoor plateau, that the breach was highlighted, not so much between the two factions as between himself and Carter, catalysts of opposing schools of thought.

III

It almost surely would not have occurred had not David chosen that particular week to pay his first visit to Greystoke, the Kent rehabilitation hospital to which Grace, now making very definite progress, had been transferred in April.

He found her in far better health and spirits than he had anticipated. The legacy of that avalanche of stones could still be traced down the dead side of her face, where plastic surgeons had been at work, and in a heavy limp caused, they told him, by the shortening of muscles in the left leg, where three operations on the bone had resulted in a contraction of half an inch. In all other respects, however, she seemed to have made an amazing recovery and Harvey-Smith, who had maintained his personal interest in the case despite the fact that he lived in Plymouth, told him the child would always limp but that the scars on her face would fade a little every year.

"If she had been a year or so older," he said, "say, around eight when it happened, we shouldn't have been so lucky and the limp would have been worse. As it is she'll climb to ninety-five per cent in six months. Apart from strenuous games there's no reason at all why she shouldn't lead a perfectly normal life."

It was a kind of miracle to watch her tackling her formidable exercises in the solarium. He had expected a pale, withdrawn child, heaving herself around on crutches but it was not like that at all. At first she was as shy with him as he was with her but after his third visit they adjusted very well and he was astonished, and a little touched, by her curiosity about the past, asking him all kinds of questions to supplement her fragmentary memories of the last year in the cottage and the few short weeks they had shared at Havelock's.

She said, almost gaily he thought, "I remember bits, Daddy, but mostly it's all mixed up, and there's a lot I don't remember at all."

"Do you remember the actual crash?" he asked, fearfully, and she said she did not, recalling nothing whatever of the final trip they made to Challacombe, not even the inoculation immediately preceding the accident. Her memories, it seemed, were concentrated on the last year at the cottage,

leading up to the move to school and the Easter she and
Joan had spent with Grandfather Marwood, at Elmer's
End. She remembered the last new boys' tea-party Beth had
given, in September, ". . . because it was the day a boy
with glasses upset the teapot on Towser."

"Ah, that was Rowlandson," he said, "he remembers that
too, and will laugh when I tell him you do. How much do
you remember about Mummy and Joan?"

"I remember Mummy bathing us in front of the fire in a
tub, and wrapping the towel round us to look like Indian
girls. And her singing instead of reading a story when we
went up to bed."

"Singing what, Grace?"

"A song with a lot of words, that all came out in a rush.
About a queen it was."

It was like a dart and the impact made him catch his
breath. It had been one of Beth's songs from *The Gondoliers*,
that year's Gilbert and Sullivan, and the laughter behind
her voice came to him now, as clearly as though she was
serenading them from the terrace outside. He steered her
away from memories after that, telling her of his plans for
her when she was finally discharged from hospital, tentative
as yet but sketched over the last few weeks after Harvey-
Smith had said she could be home by the start of autumn
term.

"You'll have my old room overlooking the moor," he
said, "the one I slept in, and used as a study before you were
born. The builders, who are working at school now, are going
to fix it up and make it pretty and Mrs. Arscott, our new
Second Form mistress, is going to give you private lessons
for the time, to help you catch up. You'll have to look after
me at Havelock's, because I'm all on my own there apart
from the boys, and Mrs. Herries says she'll teach you to cook.
Would you like that?"

"I'd like it very much," she said. "Could I give new boys' tea-parties?"

"Why, that's a splendid idea! So you shall, as soon as you're settled in. I've arranged with old Hodge to give you riding lessons too, on that pony of his, the one that used to scrape his hoof at the door for bread crusts. You'll be able to saddle up and ride down to see Ma Midden whenever you want, and over to the village to do the shopping. Granfer and Grandmummy Tilda ('Tilda' was Mrs. Marwood's collie, and the twins had used her to distinguish between their two grandmothers, ever since they were three) will come down here and see you, and take you out once in a while, and I'll come again at half-term. Keep at those exercises, won't you, love?" and he left her, a little hurriedly, reflecting thankfully that she was a cheerful, uncomplicated child, and likely to prove a great comfort to him in the years ahead.

Summer term had already begun when he paid his visit and he was due back on Monday but then, spending Sunday with his father-in-law, the strike was upon them, and there was no hope of returning by rail. He got through, with some difficulty, to the bursar's office, and was somewhat taken aback when the phone was answered by Carter, who happened to be in the office while the bursar was out. David explained the circumstances, asking Carter if he would tell the head he would be back at the earliest opportunity, and was puzzled rather than annoyed by Carter's breezy rejoinder, "Right, Powlett-Jones! Leave it to me." Then, "A case of hoist by your own petard, eh, old man?"

"How's that again?"

Carter said, in what David had learned to think of as his Sixth Form voice, "Nothing, old chap. Only a little dig on my part. After all, you're for the red flag, aren't you? No, that isn't fair, let's call it pink!"

He did not trust himself to answer, having learned something about the art of duelling with Carter over the years, but rang off, glowering through the kiosk panes at two special constables enjoying the brief authority vested in them by their armbands. Then, muttering "Bloody little swine..." he walked down the main road towards Clockhouse.

Carter's gibe, and his own instinctive sympathy with the miners, based on all he knew of the Valleys, conditioned his approach to the strike from the outset. Temporarily stranded, he passed the time talking to anyone who he thought might give him deeper insight into the cause and effect. This included not only members of the British public (as communicative during an emergency as they were uncommunicative when life ran smoothly) but local organisers, who were holding street-corner meetings to promote solidarity. He also read the *British Gazette*, Churchill's broadsheet, impatient with its stridency, and even probed the police point of view from a sergeant guarding a bus driven by an undergraduate.

What surprised him, dismayed him somewhat, was the apparent absence of acrimony on both sides and the inclination of the general public to regard the stoppage as an impromptu national spree. There seemed no way of communicating to the man in the street the reality of the miners' grievances and the unsentimental justice of their claim. As a miner's son he was unable to share the hilarity of the occasion. As a teacher of nineteenth-century history he was all too familiar with hidden factors contributing to the present confrontation. Long hours, backbreaking, primitive conditions above and under ground, miserly pay, the ever present threat of death or mutilationt—these were things that men who hacked a subsistence living from the seams had taken for granted over two generations. What stuck in the craw was the underlying conviction in the heart and mind of the miner that, whereas an approach to some kind of equity was apparent in every other heavy industry since the Armistice, his own had got itself bogged down in a slough of bureaucratic wrangling, Governmental indifference and avarice on the part of the mine owners and drawers of dividends. And behind all was a threat that few ever voiced outside the coalfields, the prospect of technological advances hurrying the industry towards a date when the demand for coal dropped away, a little every year, leaving skilled men, now in their late twenties and early thirties, without such bargaining power as they held today, perhaps without a trade to ply. It was like a huge, ugly boil slowly coming to a head, with everyone watching and no one possessing the wit or the spirit to apply an internal remedy and frustration ultimately drove him to the public library to read some of the debates in Hansard preceding the stoppage.

He found little here he did not know already. There were thousands of words on pay, safety devices, pithead baths and the like, but no one seemed to have commented on the inborn pride in his craft that the miner carried underground every working day. Neither, for that matter, had anyone at Westminster seen fit to acknowledge the modesty of the Miners' Federation's claims made the previous year. It made him wonder, not for the first time, if he had made the most of such brains as he possessed by burying himself on a Devon moor all these years, when he might have played some part in the nation's affairs, either in politics, or as a professional organiser of the Workers' Educational Association, that was striving so hard to improve the education of men and women who had left school at fourteen and younger. But, somehow, illogically, it all led back to Carter and Carter's type, lucky renegades as he thought of them, who had used their superior educations to infiltrate into the lower ranks of the bosses' class. He thought, "I've got to get back there somehow. I've got to see how Bamfylde is taking it and whether anyone down there is trying to see our side of it!" It reminded him how deeply rooted were his prejudices against moneyed interests, that had succeeded in killing his father and brothers, and an entire generation in the years that followed.

"I'll bloody well get there if I have to walk," he told his railwayman father-in-law. "There's no damned sense in what I'm doing, unless I can say my piece at places like Bamfylde," and he went out and bought a knapsack, begging a lift on a milk lorry as far as the Great West Road, where he got another lift in an army lorry returning to Aldershot for more troops.

He walked nearly twenty miles the next day before putting up at a cyclists' hostel and the day after that, following a succession of lifts and tramps, he came down over the moor near Dulverton, riding a market cart. He made short work of the last leg, arriving at school just after dusk on Sunday, May 9th. The strike still had three days to run.

*　　*　　*

He was surprised to learn from Herries that school routine had not been disturbed by more than a ripple or two. They produced their own bacon and vegetables and their milk came from local farms. They had had no newspapers, of course, and Herries was intrigued to hear David's first-hand account, but said, "I appreciate you taking all this trouble to get back here on the job, P.J., but surely you know me better than to have expected it in the circumstances?"

"It was a chance remark that Carter made over the phone that encouraged me to make the effort," and he repeated, word for word, what Carter had said.

Herries said, thoughtfully, "You're very prickly where Carter's concerned, P.J. Too prickly, if you ask me, but that, off the record, applies equally to him. Do you mind telling me why? I wouldn't ask if it wasn't important."

"It isn't important."

"Oh, but it is. To me and to Bamfylde. My guess is that both of you are pretty well entrenched and disinclined to move now that you each have a house. Why the devil do you let him rub you up the wrong way so easily?"

"It's his general attitude. Not to me personally, you can't expect to make a friend of everyone in an enclosed community like this—but he always gives me the impression he's cockahoop at practising a profession, instead of following a trade or craft. That approach is pretty general among men on the way up from nowhere. What bothers me about post-war Britain is that it's getting worse all the time."

"Can you be a little more explicit, old chap?"

"Yes. The gap between the collarless and the fancy-tie brigade keeps on widening and it shouldn't, not after the comradeship they shared in the trenches. I was born into the working class and come from a long line of miners. I'm proud of it. Why the hell should I have to apologise for it to a chap like Carter?"

"But my dear chap, you don't have to," Herries said, with one of his cherubic smiles. "And it isn't your background that bothers him."

"Then what does?"

"Your war record. He hasn't got one to speak of, and he was quick to notice the difference it made to you when you started here."

"But the war's been over nearly eight years! Nobody here gives it a thought any more."

"Except you," Herries said.

"I find it hard to forget. Is that so wrong?"

"It's neither right nor wrong, old son. It's inevitable. You witnessed those eighty-odd Old Boys of mine blown to bits, and you won't ever forget and forgive."

David said, with some difficulty, "Does that imply you don't approve of me keeping it in front of the boys? You saw those boys die, too. You knew nearly all them by their nicknames. I'd say they were still very fresh in your memory."

"One has to strike a balance," Herries said. "That's what education is about. Rationality, tolerance, give and take, call it what you like. Carter has his faults. So have you, and all the rest of us. But he's a first-class man at his subject, and very sound as a housemaster. He's exam mad, of course, and almost certainly thinks me an old fool for not being, but he has a point. Life *is* getting more competitive and we have to have a modern side here and might do worse than Carter, judging by some of the science men I've interviewed in my time. This is what it boils down to. I'll be gone in just over a year and some new man will move in. My bet is the Governors will appoint a modern man, but whoever he is he'll have to learn to lean hard on you and Carter. So my advice to you is to call a truce."

He took Algy's advice. His first impulse had been to buttonhole Carter and challenge him about the phone jibe, but he thought better of it. A few days after his return he was approached by Bamfylde's sole Free Stater, Paddy McNaughton, now a leading light of the Sixth. "I'm in a rare fix, sir," he said, with the conspiratorial grin that had been common currency between them since the incident with the pistol. "I volunteered to present the T.U.C. case at the Society's debate tomorrow and I don't know the first thing about it. Can you brief me, sir? The proposition is, 'That the Trade Unions were justified in supporting the Miners' Federation in recent strike action'."

David grinned. "You're backing a lame horse, aren't you?"

"Oh, sure I am, sir," said McNaughton, "but why not? It's a chance to take another crack at The Oppressors. You know the drill, sir. Anyone heaving a bomb at Westminster is welcome in Ireland. I only volunteered for devilment, but now I'm stuck with it."

"Who's opposing?"

"Sanders, sir. He's hot stuff, and does his homework."

"I'll brief you," David said, "and it's lucky you came to me. I was in London last week, and Sanders isn't the only one who does his homework."

He gave McNaughton several lines of argument to pursue and when the boy had jotted them down he said, "Er . . . would it be asking too much to get you to second, sir? We could pull the pants off 'em, between us."

David had taken part in several Sixth Form debates but never on a controversial subject. He said, doubtfully, "Would that be fair on Sanders?" and McNaughton replied, "Sure it would, sir. The seconder only has five minutes. All you need do is sum up."

There seemed no harm in it and secretly he relished an opportunity of speaking up for the miners.

"Very well, then, but only in support of the arguments you put forward, so don't go off at the tangent. You Irish have been doing that for centuries!"

The debate was a cheerful, innocuous affair. Sanders, son of a Conservative candidate in a Liberal-held constituency, was Bamfylde's most accomplished public speaker and had obviously had a briefing from his father. He trotted out all the old saws in reply to McNaughton's passionate defence of the workers, loss of trade, breach of working contracts, readiness to put the nation in jeopardy for a shilling, and so on, but coming from a pleasant chap like Sanders the arguments sounded harmless and David saw them as no more than an exercise in schoolboy polemics. His own speech was brief and to the point. He stressed that the mining community was defenceless against the owners and that their work, vital to the nation, deserved a good working wage and better working conditions. The strike was the only weapon they had against exploitation. He or Paddy or both must have converted some among the audience. The motion was lost, certainly, but by the narrow margin of four votes and Paddy claimed this as a victory.

The sequel was not slow in coming. The next day, entering class to take the Sixth on the Reform Bills of the eighteen-thirties, David found a newspaper cartoon pinned to the blackboard with a thumb tack. It was a particularly lurid one, depicting a leering Bolshevik fishing in British industrial waters, using a bag of bait ticketed '£400,000 Bolshevik subsidy'. The sea in the drawing was marked '*British Coal Dispute*'.

It was the kind of prank that he, and every other master at Bamfylde (with the exception of Howarth and Carter) was expected to take in good part, but somehow, in his present mood, that was asking too much. He said, "Who owns this sheet of toilet paper? I'm not asking who put it there. Who owns it?"

Sanders rose, looking a little apprehensive. "It was mine, sir."

"Where did you get it?"

"Where?"

"Yes, where? It's a simple question, isn't it?"

"My ... er ... my father sent it. With some other news-clippings. After I'd written home for material on the debate, sir."

Boyer rose from the back, looking, David thought, very glum. "Nothing personal, sir. Just a joke and we were all in on it, even the chaps who voted with you and McNaughton last night."

The flicker of anger that had stirred in him subsided but the ember glowed. He waited, getting himself in hand, before crumpling the cartoon and tossing it into the waste-paper basket. "Right. I don't find it all that much of a joke but I suppose I'm expected to make allowances in the Sixth and I will. However, while we're on the subject let's jump a couple of generations from the Reform Bills and I'll tell you something you might not know. As far as I'm concerned very few here do know, for I've never made a parade of it, and I wouldn't now if you hadn't sat up and begged for it. I'm a miner's son. I was born and grew up in a Welsh mining community. I saw, at first hand, the kind of deal those chaps get, and have been getting, ever since the English moved in and made a midden out of their valleys. Most of them bring home fifty shillings a week for a five-and-a-half day week underground, where they might die at any moment. From a fall, from fire-damp, from flooding. There are no pithead baths in most of the pits. The absentee owners drawing royalties on seams thousands of feet below the surface are too damned miserly to instal them. So the men wash in tin baths before the fire, scrubbed by their womenfolk. Think about that. Fifty shillings a week, for a man with a wife and family and it costs around four-ten a week to keep one of you fellows here for eight months of the year. But that isn't all, not by a long chalk. When I was a kid younger than anyone here I went off to school one morning leaving behind a father and two brothers, working early shift—four a.m. to midday. When I got home that same night my father and brothers were dead. Their bodies were never recovered. Ewan, my younger brother was sixteen at the time. Now let's get back to the syllabus."

They were silent and attentive during the remainder of the period. Nobody approached him afterwards, as he half-expected they would, but he felt much better for having blown his top, as he described the outburst to Howarth that evening.

Howarth was mildly amused and said, at length, "You got quite a kick out of that, didn't you, P.J.?"

"Yes, I did. But I don't fool myself I got through to anyone."

"You might have. One or two. But I'll give you yet another piece of advice if you care to have it."

"To work a bit harder at cultivating the Englishman's stiff upper lip?"

"On the contrary. To blow your top more often, and give the Celt an airing every now and again. You'll feel the better for it and it won't do them any harm. Or the rest of us either for that matter. Have a drink."

It was over and done with as far as David was concerned, but there was an unlooked-for sequel that made nonsense of his outburst in class. A day or so later he was standing before the open window of his own kitchen quarters, looking out on the quad, when he saw a Third Former, Watson Minor, emerge from the arch with a tuck parcel and call across the quad to Vosper, one of his boys. "I say, Voss! . . . There's been a balls-up in parcel handout. This isn't an Outram parcel, it's for Kidbrooke. He's in the Kremlin, isn't he?" Vosper, taking the parcel, made no comment except, "I'll give it to him," and disappeared into the main entrance to Havelock's.

David called across, sharply, "Hi! You there! Come over here, will you?" and Watson turned on his way back through the arch and sauntered over. "Me, sir?"

"You used a certain word just now, in respect of Havelock's. What was it again?"

Watson looked bewildered for a moment but then he grinned. "A certain word? You mean . . . er. . . 'balls-up', sir?"

"No, I don't mean that, although that isn't King's English according to Mr. Howarth. I meant 'Kremlin'. It *was* 'Kremlin', wasn't it?"

"Oh . . . yes, sir."

"That's new, isn't it? I've never heard Havelock's called 'Kremlin' before."

"Well, no, sir, but it is now, sir. In Outram's that is, and in some of the other houses I think. Is there anything wrong with it, sir?"

Watson, not a particularly bright boy, had already enlisted in The Lump. It would take him four more years to get as far as the Fifth, if he ever did. "Just what do you know about the Kremlin, Watson?"

"I don't know anything about it, sir."

"Then why did you say it just now?"

"Well, it . . . it sort of came out, sir. Like I say, the chaps are calling Havelock's the Kremlin."

"All right, that's all, Watson. Mere curiosity on my part," and Watson, relieved of the tiresome necessity to rack his brain, trotted off.

After prep that evening David found Boyer and told him of the encounter. "Did Sanders coin the phrase, Chad?"

"No, sir. It wasn't Sanders."

"I didn't think it would be. Who did originate it?"

"You're asking me, sir?"

"I'm asking you."

"Well, as a matter of fact, it wasn't a boy at all. I heard it was one of Mr. Carter's. It cropped up when someone in the Lower Fourth made a mess of something they were doing in the lab and caused a fearful stink. Mr. Carter said something about 'Stinkbombs being the prerogative of Havelock's, otherwise known as the Kremlin'. I thought it was a bit thick, sir, but it was just a joke and seems to have stuck, the way some of them do. Like nicknames."

"That's about it," David said, "a nickname. Well, thanks for telling me, and for your information I'm going to follow it to source right now. Don't worry, I won't involve you," and he strode off through the quad arch and up the short flight of steps into Outram's.

* * *

Carter was just dismissing Sanders, his head prefect, with laundry lists and other notices for the board. David waited until the prefect was out of earshot before saying, "Can you spare a minute, Carter?"

"Certainly. About Saturday's house match? Come inside, old man," and he led the way into his ground-floor study. His affability, as always, was deceiving. He was the kind of man who used forms of address like 'old man' and 'my dear chap' as camouflage. David followed him inside and closed the door.

"It's about a remark you made in the lab a day or so ago. You referred to my house as the Kremlin."

Carter's red-rimmed eyes blinked rapidly. For a moment he seemed baulked but he made a quick recovery.

"I did? Well, what of it? Don't you make jokes in class sometimes?"

"Not that kind of joke, Carter."

"What the devil are you driving at?"

"You know bloody well what I'm driving at. It was a personal gibe at me, on account of the part I took in the Upper School debate. Or maybe what I told the Sixth two days ago."

It was being challenged in his own den that nettled Carter, so much so that David saw him as he had never seen him during all the years they had sparred together. His jauntiness fell away and with it that shrewd command of tongue that usually enabled him to get the better of their skirmishes. He jumped up, red in the face, stuttering and shouting, "How *dare* you bully me in my own house! I've always thought you a bounder, Powlett-Jones, but there are limits— *limits*, you hear? And you're exceeding them!"

"Doesn't it occur to you that you did just that in the lab? You as good as accused me of being in Russian pay. And within the hearing of boys I have to teach!"

"I did *no* such thing! I made a small joke at your expense. How many have you made at mine since you came here? I . . . I won't continue this discussion, d'you hear?"

"I can hear. They can hear you across the quad, I daresay. But you will continue it, until I get an apology. Just what is it about me that makes you behave like a police stooge?"

He had never thought to see a man so beside himself with rage and the streak of malice he had always nurtured for this one man at Bamfylde enjoyed the spectacle, one that would have embarrassed him in different circumstances. "God bless my soul, you're the right one to come in here talking like that, I must say! Ever since you set foot in the school you've tried to foist your filthy principles and . . . and disloyalty on the boys. I'm not alone in thinking so, either!"

"Who else, Carter?"

"Alderman Blunt, for one, and other Governors and parents I've talked to. I'm hanged if I know why you haven't been asked to resign before this! You wouldn't stay here ten minutes if I had my say!"

"So long as you haven't I'm in no danger. But at last we seem to be getting somewhere. 'Filthy principles' you said. And 'disloyalty'. Disloyalty to whom, Carter?"

"Why, to the country, to the type of parent who sends his son here to get an education. Your entire approach to your work is . . . is slanted, twisted in favour of class hatreds and destructive forces. But I'll not stand here and . . ."

"You'll stay until we've had this out, Carter. You'll do it if I have to pin you down in that tinpot throne of yours. Disloyalty, is it, eh? Was it disloyal on my part to spend three years in those bloody trenches, fighting for trench-dodgers with gammy knees? That knee of yours came in handy, didn't it? It enabled you to play soldiers when there was a real war on your doorstep."

He hadn't meant to go that far and regretted it the

moment it was out. It was not that he failed to view Carter
in this light. He had heard too much about 'gammy knees'
and 'faulty tickers' to believe Carter's explanation of his
discharge on the eve of his draft crossing to France, but it
was a cheap, easy gibe, of the kind he would have despised
in the mouth of another opponent. It lit another fuse under
Carter, however, who began to dance with rage, his little
tripping movements bringing him closer to David, who
was standing with his back to the door. And then, to add to
the absurdity of the scene, Carter began pushing and he
pushed back, so that neither of them heard or saw the door
open and close again. When they circled, however, there
stood Herries, watching them from just over the threshold,
and it seemed to David that he had materialised through the
ceiling or floor-boards.

"For God's sake! Pull yourselves together both of you!
I heard you from the Founder's statue and I daresay others
did too, apart from the boys in your house, Carter!"

They separated, a couple of admonished Second Formers,
caught scuffling in the dormitory after silence bell. Then
Carter began to bleat, and it seemed to David he was
very close to tears.

"It was Powlett-Jones, Headmaster . . . he came in here
making the vilest accusations . . . I told him to go but he
wouldn't . . . wouldn't . . ." and suddenly, to David's dismay, he did crumple, slumping down in his chair, whipping
off his pince-nez glasses and pretending to polish them with
a piece of tissue.

Herries said, "Take yourself off, Powlett-Jones. We'll go
into this later," and David went, out of the study, down the
passage and into the quad that was empty, so that he guessed
prep bell had gone, although he did not remember
hearing it.

As a housemaster he was exempt from prep-taking, unless

deputising for a colleague, so he went straight upstairs to his living-room and poured himself a whisky. He was pouring another, and wondering wretchedly about the outcome of this extraordinary scene, when there was a tap on the door and Herries entered in response to his gruff invitation. Algy said, bitterly, "I'll take one myself if you're making free with them," and sat heavily on the padded window seat. David poured the drink, adding a touch of soda.

"You don't have to tell me," he said. "I know it if Carter doesn't. We both made damned fools of ourselves and if he'll accept an apology I'll offer one," and when Herries, sipping slowly, made no reply, "Did he tell you his version of it?"

"About that crack in the lab? Yes, he did, and made the same offer as you in that respect."

"It was about even," David said, glumly. "We both behaved like Second Formers. Did anyone else hear us?"

"If anybody did you can wager it will be all over the school by dormitory bell." He looked up, knitting his shaggy eyebrows. "Not so good for discipline, is it?"

"Not good at all," David said, resisting an insane impulse to chuckle.

"It was that final taunt of yours that did the damage. You hit him where it hurt like the devil, and you had no excuse for it. I warned you about that the night you came back from town."

"He made some pretty wild accusations himself."

"Why the devil didn't you go when he asked you? Why didn't you write him? Or come to me? How is either one of of you going to bury the hatchet after this? I'm hanged if I know why I should be that concerned, I've only a year or so to go."

"But you are concerned."

"Good God, man, of course I am! This place is my life.

I've put twenty-three years into it. Given it all I've got!
Do you think I can turn off my love for it like ... a
tap?"

"I know you can't, sir. What's to be done then? Do
you want my resignation? Or his? Or a matched pair,
maybe?"

"You know better than that," growled Herries. "Any other
bright suggestions?"

"I could apologise in writing. Admit I lost my temper, and
make no reference to the Kremlin business. That would
smooth his feathers, if I know Carter."

"It would still leave yours ruffled."

"Yes, it would. But I'd do that much for you after all
you've done for me. And mine."

He saw the older man's expression brighten a little as he
said, "Well, that would be a start. Seems to me a bit one-
sided but you're young enough not to bother about that.
Yes, I know, Carter's only a few years older, but he's always
seemed to belong to my generation more than yours. I
don't know why, but he has. You write that letter, and send
a boy straight over with it. Then we'll see what happens."
He sighed. "It's all so childish when you think about it.
People say schoolmasters end up by treating all adults like
Third Formers, and dim-wittted ones at that, but it isn't
really so. The truth is, most of 'em revert to Third Formers
in their forties. Sometimes they don't even wait that long."

"Suppose I took the letter over myself?"

"You'd probably find Outram's out of bounds and senti-
nels posted. He's not so resilient as you, P.J."

He got up, nodded and drifted out in that soft, floating
way of his. David sat for a long time looking out on the
orange sunset over the moor but without appreciating it.
Presently, he got up and went across to his desk. On a sheet
of Bamfylde paper he wrote,

My dear Carter; I behaved like an ass and present my apologies. We could have talked this out like adults. The fact that we didn't was my responsibility, not yours. Very sincerely, David Powlett-Jones.

As soon as end-of-prep bell rang he went out on to the landing and caught little Hobson scurrying up to the junior dormitory, telling him to give the letter to Carter personally but not wait for an answer. Then he went down and out across the cricket-field, half-shrouded in violet dusk, and heady with the scent of grass cuttings, wondering if Beth would have approved his back-down, or merely laughed at them both, saving her sympathy for Algy Herries. It was imponderable, but he did recall what she had said on the occasion of a previous quarrel, about 'there being a Carter in every school, office or factory, from here to Land's End'.

By the time he got back for supper Carter's reply lay on his desk. It was as brief as his own but more guarded. It said:

My dear Powlett-Jones, I accept your apology. I should not have lost my temper in that fashion. It was unprofessional on my part, as was my remark in the laboratory. Sincerely, Trevor S. Carter.

Unprofessional. It was a curious word to use in the circumstances. He stood by the window, watching summer darkness fall across the moor. It was not a reconciliation on either man's part. More of a truce, each agreeing to stay within his own lines.

CHAPTER FOUR

I

The bell in his brain, tolling an intermittent knell for some sixteen months now, was stilled by Grace's homecoming, in the first week of the Michaelmas term, 1926.

The intervals between its clamour had been lengthening all summer, not because he missed her the less, but because there was always so much to do, so many claims upon his attention, so that he saw the wisdom of Herries's insistence he stayed on as housemaster, and even enlarged his responsibilities by adding the Sunsetters to the Havelock roll.

Grace's return took priority over everything that September, when summer lingered on into autumn, and a record number of thirty-eight boys arrived, eight of them coming to Havelock's, but there were partings as well as greetings. He would miss Chad Boyer badly. Of all the links he had formed with boys who had come and gone in the last eight-and-a-half years, Boyer had forged the strongest, and would be the most difficult to replace after he went up to University to read modern history and economics.

"I'll keep in touch, I promise," he said, when he marched off to summer camp at Tidworth Pennings with the Corps, on the final day of term, and David hoped he would. It might prove useful to get Boyer's private opinion of any innovation he had in mind. Having spent nine years on the moor, Boyer was as dedicated a Bamfeldian as Herries himself.

Helen Arscott, the businesslike Second Form mistress who had replaced Julia Darbyshire, took a fancy to Grace on sight and Grace responded, perhaps because, in the child's mind, her manner matched so many 'let's-brush-our-teeth' sisters and nurses of the last sixteen months. She still limped, and was under orders to persist in her exercises, but the surgeon's prophecy regarding her facial scars was fulfilled. They were hardly noticeable now, no more than a flattish area of tissue, spreading from below the eye to the sweep of the chin—Beth's chin, as he noted, swinging her joyously out of the station taxi and hugging her close.

Ellie Herries wept, as he knew she would, and they all trooped in procession up to his old bachelor quarters, overlooking the forecourt, where Grace was ceremoniously installed. She seemed a little overawed by her reception, but soon settled down under the sharp, no-favourites eye of Helen Arscott, who promised her seven hours' tuition each week.

David found the child's gravity very appealing. Months of dragging pain, and a longer period of convalescence, had left its mark on her, but in a way that one soon came to accept. Somewhere along the line she had acquired the patience of a serious-minded child twice her age, offset by a rather comic dignity, that showed in her determination to do everything for herself and break out of the invalid cocoon. Her approach to him was almost maternal, as though someone had coached her in the need to fill the gap in his life and sometimes, watching her slyly, David was reminded of a string of Victorian heroines: Beth in *Little Women*, Little Nell, in *The Old Curiosity Shop* and Eva, in *Uncle Tom's Cabin*. She was going to be pretty, despite the terrible mauling she had received in the accident. Her hair was a glossy black, curling at the ends, and her eyes as large and brown as Beth's, with identical high cheekbones and dimpled chin. And yet, in another way, she reminded him of his Rhondda nieces, for she was Celt in complexion and build. She had a Celtic imagination too, with a whiff of Beth's Cockney humour added, not the irreverent humour of her mother, but what Herries called 'the stand-off-and-chuckle' brand. "That's the Welsh in her," he added. "You Taffys can laugh at yourselves more than most, even when you're singing."

In no time at all she became a tremendous favourite with the boys. Paddy McNaughton, the Irish boy, was a friend of hers because he treated her as an equal, but of all the boys in Havelock's she seemed to favour Winterbourne, perhaps because Winterbourne took such an active interest in her, dating from a premonition in the cave beside Chetsford Water, that she had survived and needed help.

The first time David became aware of this relationship was one evening when he looked in to say goodnight, and found her sitting up in her dressing-gown, sketching. She was hard at work on a crayon sketch of old Hodge's pony, the one selected for her first riding lessons in their cottage days. The background of the drawing was recognisably Hodge's broken-down stables, on the eastern shoulder of Stone Cross Hill, and he exclaimed, "Hi, where did you learn to draw as well as that? In hospital?"

No, she told him, shading industriously, Winterbourne had taught her one wet afternoon, when a house match was cancelled and he called in search of David.

"I always thought Spats buried his talents. He's very good at it but I got the impression he thinks it's something a boy shouldn't do at a place like this."

"I think that's silly," Grace said, "for he ought to be proud of it. I would be, if I was a genius like him."

"Well, he's got a genius for teaching," David said, and later sought out Winterbourne, thanking him for giving the child a new interest, for time hung heavily on her hands when everyone was in class. Winterbourne said, unexpectedly, "But she's got a gift, sir. I saw that at once. She sees all the stronger lines in her head, before she starts scribbling, the way all kids do. Er . . . could I make a suggestion, sir?"

"Of course."

"Get her a really good box of paints, an old easel, and some of this paper, sir. She'll never be bored then and she'll teach herself far more than I could teach her." He produced a roll of stiff cartridge paper from his desk and David noted that its sticker bore the name of a Challacombe stationer. "It comes in largish blocks, sir, but be sure and get Marker to sell you a professional watercolourist's outfit. Don't tell him it's for a little girl or he'll fob you off with rubbish."

"I've got a better idea," David said. "How much would such an outfit cost, together with the paper?"

"Oh, around fifty bob, sir."

"Well, here's three pounds. When you go into Challacombe, for the match on Saturday, buy it for me. If there's an easel small enough for her to cope with order that too. Would you do that?"

"I'd like to, sir." And then, shyly, looking over David's shoulder in that self-contained way David had noticed the day he got to know the boy out on the moor, "She seems bonnie enough now, sir. Will she . . . grow out of that limp?"

"I rather doubt it, Spats. It'll certainly become less pronounced but it'll always show."

"Does she mind it all that much, sir?"

Did she? He had no idea as yet but he imagined she might come to mind it as time went on, and she mixed with other girls at school. "I just can't say, Spats. She's intelligent enough to learn to live with it. More than that who can tell?"

Winterbourne said, "Would you mind if I spent a bit of time working with her when she gets her kit? You can't teach anyone painting, sir, but well . . . I think she's a real tonic, and that's a fact! I mean, most kids that something as bad as that had happened to would be floored, wouldn't they? Or the smart ones would start trading on it."

Not for the first time he found Winterbourne an uncomfortably perceptive boy but it was clear that Grace had struck some chord in him. On the following Saturday evening he appeared with an impressive-looking paint-box, ten blocks of paper and an easel. "I've paid for the easel, sir, and I'd like very much to make her a present of it. I left the blackboard behind. She'll see more than enough blackboards round here, won't she, sir?"

It was the first time that he had ever heard Winterbourne make the smallest joke, so he let him pay the extra and give Grace another lesson before prep. He thought, seeing their heads draw together over the paper, "She's got her mother's way with men. I wonder how her sister would have turned out? Would she have been a contrast, in spite of them being twins?" It was odd, his memories of Beth were sharp and clear but he was finding it difficult to remember anything distinctive about the child who had died with her. Somehow he had never seen them as two people, not since the moment Stratton-Forbes had panted up to the long-jump pit, shouting news of their arrival and qualifying on the spot for the nickname, 'Nun'. And thinking of Stratton-Forbes, David made a decision he had been putting off for days, the choice of a head house prefect to replace Boyer.

Stratton-Forbes was no longer the smallest boy in the school. He was now the fattest; a droll, cumbersome figure with all that flesh, and the squint they had never been able to correct. He was nearly eighteen now, and the most promising Latin scholar Bamfylde had ever had, according to Barnaby. The classics master used him as a junior master in the Second and Third Forms whenever he could be spared from his effortless studies. But despite his reputation as a swot, despite his flabbiness and malevolent squint, Nun was well-liked, enjoying that gratuitous popularity often granted a butt. Far too overweight for any active game, he had brought his impressive powers of concentration to bear

on musketry, down at the long range, and had twice cap-
tained Bamfylde's team at Bisley. The squint, that had
so worried his parents when he first arrived at Bamfylde
did not inhibit him as a marksman. Discarding unnecessary
glasses he practised shooting with the single-minded fanati-
cism he brought to the classics and was soon the pride and
joy of his fellow enthusiasts. For all that David hesitated to
appoint him Boyer's successor. Popular or not, he was still
a butt, even with Lower School boys, and a job of that kind
sometimes demanded a strong hand.

He took his problem to Howarth, an acknowledged expert
in these fields, who decreed that the appointment be made
without delay. "A boy as self-disciplined as that will suit
your book admirably," he said. "Stands to reason, doesn't
it? Anything Stratton-Forbes sets his hand to he accom-
plishes and the same will apply to any responsibility he's
given. He'll keep far better order than Boyer, you see if he
doesn't! Besides, I hear he's staying on for extra cramming,
and that'll save you the trouble of replacing him next year."

David took his advice and Stratton-Forbes was appointed
head of the house, proving his worth at once, for he came to
David within the week with a problem that a less conscientious boy would have shelved.

It concerned the perennial nuisance of bed-wetters in the
Junior dormitory, where Havelock's had two, Lowther
Minor and Grindling. Persistent bed-wetters were not un-
common and all the usual expedients were resorted to, but
with the pair berthed side by side at the far end of the dormitory the problem was seemingly aggravated.

Stratton-Forbes appeared in David's study one night
looking more than usually serious. Not being given to finesse
he went straight to the point. "It's about Lowther Minor
and Grindling, sir. I think something will have to be done
before one of the others writes home on the subject."

"Why on earth should they do that?" asked David, innocently, and Nun said, without a flicker of a smile, "They are calling the space between their beds the Hellishponk, sir!" and David, turning away, muttered, "Ask a damn silly question . . ." But there was nothing funny about it to the boys concerned, as he well knew. "Tell them to come and have a talk with me in the morning," he said. "Lowther before morning school, Grindling immediately after, but Nun . . ."

"Sir?"

"Let 'em know in advance I'm taking the medical approach. I don't want either of them upset. Do you think you could manage that?"

"Well, in a way I already have, sir. I read it up, and then asked around a bit."

"*You read it up?* Bed-wetting? Where?"

"There's a book in the library that goes into it very fully, sir. I don't know how it got there and it isn't catalogued, but it's there, sir. It's in my study now."

He looked at Stratton-Forbes with reverence. "Drop it in on your way to bed, will you? What conclusions did you reach, if any?"

"Well, sir, it's generally recognised now as a psychological problem. In most cases, that is. There were quite a few words I had to look up in a medical encyclopaedia, but I decided that both our cases come under the heading of emotional stress, sir."

"They do?"

"Yes, sir. In Lowther's case it's the old story of divorced parents, but in Grindling's case it's pure funk, sir, this being his first term. I daresay we could iron them out in time but it might be as well to check up with Dr. Willoughby first, wouldn't you say, sir?"

"It would indeed, Nun, and I'm uncommonly obliged to

you for the research. On second thoughts, don't mention the matter to either of them. I'll read that book myself, and check up with the doctor in case we go off on a wrong tack."

"Yes, sir," and Stratton-Forbes left, with the polite unconcern of a gardener who had been discussing early tomatoes with an attentive but ill-informed employer.

He read the book and had a long telephone conversation with Willoughby on the subject, after which he sent for Lowther's elder brother, currently one of the bloods in the Upper Fifth. Lowther Major, vice-captain of the Bamfylde First Fifteen, was aggrieved when David broached the subject. He said, dismally, "The kid's been that way for long enough, sir. It's a frightful bore, isn't it? I mean, it lets a fellow down, wouldn't you say?"

"I didn't bring you in here to cry on my shoulder, Lowther. What's behind it? When did it start?"

"When? Well, about the time the pater took himself off, sir. The kid was about ten then."

"Can't you be more explicit? I don't want to pry into family matters but it's very important to your brother. If we can do anything to help it might save him a lot of grief."

"Well, sir, he was closer to pater than me. They were both a bit—well, highbrow, sir. My Governor is nuts on Shakespeare and that kind of stuff. He used to take the kid to the theatre a lot."

He implied, somehow, that father and brother had conspired to go to the devil in consort. "Then the pater got a job abroad and breezed off to Canada and the kid started brooding. Mater seemed to think that coming here early would take him out of it."

It struck him then, by no means for the first time, how damnably unfair life could be, how effortlessly cheerful oafs like Lowther Major could coast along when weaker, more sensitive vessels were caught up in cross-currents and thrown about like matchboxes. He said, "Look, Lowther, you ought to help out in this. That kid needs encouragement and you're the best one to give it. I'll do what I can, and so will Stratton-Forbes, but you've got to back us up, do you understand?"

Lowther Major blinked, "Well ... yes, sir, but how exactly? I mean—well—he's seen doctors before and we all assumed it was just a leaking tap—a weak bladder, sir."

"Dammit, boy, it's very little to do with his bladder! Once he gets over the shock of being separated from the one person in life who meant anything to him, he'll stop wetting his bed. You can take my word for it. And Doc Willoughby's. In the meantime look out for him, spend time with him if necessary and that's an order."

"Yes, sir," and Lowther Major left, about as puzzled as he could be.

Grindling was something else again. David had him in after Willoughby, on the excuse of a routine chest examination, had had a talk with the boy.

"What did the doctor have to say, Grindling? You're not going into a decline, are you?"

"He said I've got an above-average expansion, sir. He had me go up the ropes in the gym and I did it in nine seconds."

"Nine seconds, eh? That's very lively. Keen on gym?"

"Yes, sir."

"What else are you good at?"

The boy hesitated. "I like playing the piano, sir. I've started with Mr. Gibbs, but it's difficult to practise properly here. I mean, there's generally a queue for the music rooms, and you don't get time off as it's an extra subject."

"Oh, I think we could fix that if you're really keen, Grindling. Would you like me to have a word with Mr. Gibbs?"

The boy relaxed a little. His head went up and his mouth,

pressed in a nervous downward curve, straightened out. "I'd like that very much, sir."

"Then take it as done. How's your voice? Can you sing?"

"A little, sir. My father . . ." and he stopped, his crest-fallen expression returning.

"Well, what about your father?"

"He's a pro . . . professional, sir. He's singing baritone, in an opera company touring South Africa, sir."

"How would you like a try-out for this year's opera? We're doing *Pinafore* again."

The boy hesitated, "I'm still treble, sir."

"Half the chorus is treble. The head likes to rope in everyone he can get for the girls. It's a lot of fun, believe me."

"Very well, sir."

He forced himself to come to the point. "Look here, Grindling. I know you're finding it a bit difficult to settle but there's nothing odd about that. Most first-termers do. Did myself, for that matter, but it soon wears off, once you start taking part in things. As to that bed-wetting business, the important thing is to stop worrying about it. A lot of kids your age go through that stage, for one reason or another and you'll shake it off in no time, providing you don't see it as—well, put it like this—as a permanent handicap you're lumbered with, like a wooden leg. Do you follow me?"

"I . . . I'm not sure, sir."

"Well, think it over and if you have any other problems, go to Stratton-Forbes about them. That's what he's there for. And if he can't sort 'em out, I can."

"Thank you, sir," and Grindling slipped out, glad to be gone no doubt but very relieved, David thought, judging by the way he tackled the stairs and dived across the quad to scrutinise the day's parcel list. The campaign must have had some effect for around about half-term Stratton-Forbes reported a great improvement in both cases, even though, from then on, the far end of the junior dormitory was stuck with the name, 'Hellishponk'.

II

The new boys' tea, presided over by Grace, was a tremendous success, reminding David a little of a stylised gavotte, with everyone present on their dignity. His own thirtieth birthday fell on St. Luke's Day, so Grace decided to combine tea and party in one event, and decorated the cake baked for him by Ellie Herries with thirty candles.

She went about her preparations so seriously that David, fearing an anti-climax, summoned all the new boys an hour or so in advance and laid his cards on the table.

"Now, listen here, you chaps. This tea is an old custom at Havelock's, but it's very special this year and I'll tell you why. My daughter, Grace, just out of hospital, remembers her mother giving these teas and although she's only six, and you might find it all a bit solemn, you'll have to play along, you understand?"

Bristow, boldest of the new boys, spoke for all of them. "How do you mean, sir? Help her pour out?"

"No, by George! Quite the reverse. Let *her* do the pouring. *And* all the passing round. That's her job as hostess. Just keep the conversation going and don't laugh, whatever you do. If she thinks any of you find it funny she'll be very upset and I don't want her upset. She's been through a very rotten time." He hesitated a moment, then took the plunge. "Do any of you here know what happened a year or so ago?"

Most of them looked blank but Bristow spoke up again. "I do, sir. There was a motor-smash on Quarry Hill and Mrs. Powlett-Jones was killed, sir."

"My wife and Grace's little sister. Grace was badly knocked about but she pulled through."

They stared at him with embarrassed sympathy. Then

Grindling said, with an effort, "Er . . . just leave it to us, sir."

And he did, to such good effect that, ever afterwards, he had a particularly soft spot for the Michaelmas intake of 1926. Grace sat at the head of the table and poured, looking like a tiny grandmother entertaining a flock of grand-children on their very best behaviour, but then, Bristow, already qualifying for the role of Second Form humorist, made everybody laugh describing an adventure he had in Boulogne that summer, when he had lost his way and talked French to a gendarme. Then Grindling played 'Autumn Ride' on the upright piano Mrs. Ferguson had left behind, and made them laugh again by declaring that the piano needed tuning, and Grace limped around the circle with a bowl of crystallised fruits and everybody seemed genuinely reluctant to leave when the prep bell went. Bristow, he noted with approval, bowed from the waist in Grace's direction, and thanked her very politely on everyone's behalf, and they all went off with a slice of his cake wrapped in paper napkins.

"That was absolutely splendid!" he said, as soon as the door had closed on them. 'You did it just as well as your mother. I'm only sorry Winterbourne wasn't here to see it," and she replied, mildly, "Oh, he would have felt silly among boys that age." She said it as if Winterbourne would soon be up here celebrating his own thirtieth birthday.

* * *

So the days sped along, to half-term and onward to the Michaelmas climax, the opera, staged in Big Hall two days before break-up. A rather sad occasion this, for it was Algy Herries's last. "Twenty-three in a row!" he crowed, as they were wedging him into his First Lord's uniform. "That's a run, if you like! Only D'Oyly Carte can equal that and this role is my second favourite. I've always had a weakness for Ko-Ko."

David, sitting in as understudy for Rapper Gibbs at dress-rehearsal, had a surprise in store for him, however. At the given moment in marched four marines, sent to their stations downstage by a piping command of a midshipman, and it was as well he wasn't accompanying at the time for, from under the band of the flat white cap, peeped Grace's dark curls and the try-it-on-the-dog-audience cheered, presumably all in on the secret. Young Masters, it seems, cast as the midshipman, had gone down with a feverish cold, and Algy, taking Helen Arscott into his confidence, had coached Grace to take his place. She had no words to learn, other than the command, and among all those white bell-bottomed trousers her limp did not show. But David had a bad moment, remembering Beth as Buttercup, in 1921, and it took him a minute or two to recover. It was reckoned a great joke to play on a member of the staff and Algy, apologising afterwards said, "I daresay it gave you a jolt but it tickled her no end and the audience too, as you noticed. She's a great favourite, they tell me."

She was too, more of a favourite than even Algy knew, for besides having Winterbourne to teach her to paint in water-colours, she now had 'Sax' Hoskins teaching her the Charleston and the lyrics of all the dance hits that were crossing the Atlantic in a flood just then.

'Sax' was the current Bamfylde jazz enthusiast. His five-piece band played at all the weekly dances, and there were even rumours that he would begin training as a professional when he left. He was a noisy, uninhibited chap, with no other interests or attainments to his credit, and approached David one day after seeing Grace at her exercises.

"Excuse me, sir. It might sound daft but couldn't we make that drill of hers a bit more interesting? I mean, if she is supposed to exercise the muscles in that way, wouldn't dancing help?"

"Dancing? What kind of dancing? Folk dancing of some kind?", but at this Hoskins looked outraged. "Good Lord, *no*, sir! *Real* dancing. Modern steps. The foxtrot, two-step, and waltz. Even the Charleston, if she's up to it!"

David said, chuckling, "Well, I don't see why not, so long as she doesn't overdo it," and Hoskins said, "I'll watch that, sir. After all, she'll want to learn ballroom dancing in a year or so. They all do, sir. My kid sisters are absolute dabsters, and they're not much older than Grace."

So it was done. Hoskins carried his portable gramophone up to the living-room at Havelock's and put on a number he described as 'just the job'. It was called 'Crazy Words, Crazy Tune', and David looked on as Hoskins taught Grace how to shuffle her feet this way and that, and cross over, and perform all manner of ritual hand gestures while doing it. She seemed extraordinarily quick to catch on so that Hoskins pronounced her 'a natural'. "She's quicker on the uptake than my sister Margaret," he said, "and Miggs won a box of chocolates for shimmying at a concert."

One way and another it was a memorable, rollicking term, and for once he was sorry to see them depart six days before Christmas when, in the period between first light and nine a.m. the place emptied and then, magically, was still.

The next day the station taxi called to take him and Grace to catch the Bristol train for Wales, where they were spending Christmas, this being 'Granmam Powlett-Jones's turn'. Some of the Sunsetters helped load their bags and as the battered old Belsize ran over the frosty surface of the east drive, and swung left to pass along under the playing-field hedge, Grace voiced a thought that had occurred to him while he was making the early morning tea. She said, "It'll be fun seeing Granmam and Auntie Gwynneth, and Uncle Ewart and Auntie Megan. But I'll miss everyone here, won't you, Daddy?"

"Well, let's say I shall by the day they all descend on us again," he said. "Let's see, when *is* that exactly?"

"January the nineteenth," she said. " 'New boys arrive the day before'."

You could never catch Grace out on any Bamfylde milestones.

PART FOUR

AVE ET CAVE

CHAPTER ONE

I

Few among those acclimatised to Howarth's glacial classroom expression would have spotted anything amiss with him that particular morning, some halfway through the tight-rope term, that is to say, towards the end of February. But David, who looked upon the dry old stick as friend and counsellor, noticed it as he helped himself to his bacon and eggs from the side-table in Big Hall.

It was not that Howarth looked more disdainful than usual, or more likely to erupt in the quiet, deadly way he reserved for the fool and the chatterer. He picked at his food with his customary air of distaste, and crumbled his toast with the air of a man disposing of an unpopular relative's ashes, and all the time kept his deceptively neutral gaze on his customary focal point, namely the kitchen hatch at the far end of the hall. Yet David noted something particularly wary about him, and something supremely world-weary too, as he raised his coffee cup and sipped as though sampling hemlock, then set it down again, noiselessly, for Howarth hated racket above all Bamfylde's shortcomings.

David's eyes rested for a moment on a buff, typewritten envelope, neatly slit, lying at Howarth's elbow and presently, speaking very quietly, he said, "Not bad news, I hope?" Howarth's bleak gaze turned on him and he saw that he was right. The face of the man under its frigid mask was deeply troubled as he muttered, "Doing anything tonight?" and when David shook his head, "Come up and take a gill

then. After prep bell," and got up abruptly, striding down
the centre aisle between the massed tables and out. He took
the letter with him but left a barely tasted cup of coffee and
most of his rasher and toast.

He was in command of himself again several hours later,
and had the tray of drinks and his usual box of Gold Flake
set before the fire when David joined him at eight. "Must
have given myself away. Wouldn't have said so but evi-
dently I did."

"Not to anyone but me. What's up?"

Howarth got up and crossed to his tidy desk, opening a
drawer and taking out a large silver-framed photograph, of
the type usually kept on a piano or mantelshelf. It was a
studio photograph of a girl about twenty, wearing a style of
dress popular about twenty-five years before. The features
were very delicate and the small, slightly prim mouth sensitive. The hair was fluffy and looked very fair. David studied
the photograph, recalling a chilly confidence on the bench
under the fives court more than eight years before, when
Howarth had mentioned the girl who turned him down for
a stockbroker. He had never referred to her since and was
not a man one questioned on personal matters.

"Was the letter from her?"

"It was about her. She died, six months ago."

"You didn't know?"

He said, petulantly, "I haven't kept in touch with her.
She had a son nearly as old as you!"

It was curious how certain David was of the closeness of
the link between news from some matter-of-fact executor,
and Howarth's ravaged look at breakfast and somehow the
circumstances were uncharacteristic. He had always thought
of Howarth as a man proof against deep feelings. Yet here
was evidence of another kind. Clearly there had never been
any other woman for Ian Howarth.

"I'm sorry. It's hit you pretty badly."

"Like the very devil, but don't ask me why. Haven't set eyes on Amy Crispin since the spring of nineteen-hundred and six."

"You keep her photograph handy."

"Out of sight. You've never seen it before, and nobody else ever will. Not until they poke around my things and wonder what the hell to do with it. Keep me company, P.J.," and he poured two more pink gins, larger ones than usual.

David said, carefully, "You want to talk about her?"

"I don't know. There isn't a day when I haven't thought about her. But talking, that's different. As you must know to your cost."

It drew them closer somehow. Not much but a little. Himself nursing a half-healed wound, with its unpredictable ache and Howarth, outwardly the eternal bachelor, mourning a certain Amy Crispin, lost to him a quarter-century ago. Howarth said, at length, "What the devil can it be to you, anyway; a man at the receiving end of a real tragedy?"

"Beth and I had six years together. They were very happy years."

"That's a point of view," Howarth said. "I wonder if Amy or I could have said the same."

"Were you engaged?"

"For more than a year. Do you know what they paid an usher in '03? And you think we're underpaid now! I was getting a hundred and thirty a year at Beckworth Grammar School, and I was twenty-four. It was late to change horses and in any case I had no mind to, then or later. If I have a vocation it's teaching. Like you, my friend."

"I daresay she could have waited."

"For how long? Five years? Ten? She wanted children and went elsewhere for them. I never held that against her."

"Was she happy?"

"I always assumed so." He sat thinking a moment and then, with a grunt expressing protest at his own sentimentality, he took out the letter and passed it across the table. It was the lawyer's letter, but its content was arresting, perhaps on that account. Howarth had been left the sum of eight thousand pounds by the late Amy Hodgson, née Crispin, together with his pick of the library at a house called Clearwood Court in Sussex. There was a brief footnote to the letter. Seemingly in an agony of embarrassment the lawyer had added, in his own handwriting,

"I feel it my duty to quote the relevant passage from my client's codicil, relating to the bequest, viz. 'To Ian Howarth, whom I remember with the greatest affection'."

It explained, David thought, so many things. Not merely Howarth's bleak and hurried exit from the dining-hall that morning but the threads that made up his entire personality. It was as though, somewhere around 1903, eleven years before the world went raving mad, a young, love-sick schoolteacher in a provincial grammar school, had sentenced himself to self-petrification, a penance that had, in the end, transformed him from an eager, dedicated youngster, into a wry, ironic husk of a man, racing towards middle age and the ultimate pedantry that awaits all but a very few of the profession. It was a personal tragedy, in its way as much a tragedy as the loss of Howarth's generation in Flanders, and yet, as David acknowledged at once, the petrification had never been wholly achieved. Somewhere, under the ice of the simulated personality, the original Howarth was still there, trying hard to get out, and once in a while almost succeeding.

"Eight thousand pounds! That's a small fortune. What will you do now?"

"What should I do but leave it in the bank? Money never interested me. If it had, I shouldn't be here, any more than you."

"But, damn it, man, you could retire now if you cared to. Properly invested that would provide an income double the pension you can expect."

"I don't give a damn about the money," Howarth said, savagely. "It's discovering, this late, that I could have married the girl if I'd had the nerve. You can't buy back the fruits of your own folly and cowardice with eight thousand pounds! She must have been miserable with that bloody stockbroker!"

He took another drink and his gin began to mellow him. "Let this be a lesson to you, P.J.! Get married again if you can. Don't play the little gentleman, as I did."

"I'm not looking for two lucky breaks, Howarth. Most men don't get one. You didn't, it seems."

"Well, then, what will you do with your life? Don't fancy you can live celibate, my friend. Or not without corroding your personality. Some could, but you aren't made that way and it's my opinion you know it."

He wondered if this was true. In the last twenty-two months he had not been aware of physical yearnings, of the kind Beth had satisfied so gaily and so graciously, but who could say whether this was permanent? A time might be approaching when enforced celibacy developed an itch, to be scratched at all costs, or bottled up until it began to warp him, the way he had noticed among ageing bachelors and long-term widowers. In the strictly personal sense the prospect of holding a stranger in his arms was vaguely repugnant to him but would it always be so? He was only just thirty; all things being equal he had another forty years ahead of him. Curiosity nagged him, encouraging him to risk a formidable snub. "What did you do about women all these years, Howarth?" and Howarth, draining his gin, got up and crossed over to his bureau again where he extracted another photograph. From a different drawer, David noticed. It was an enlarged snapshot, featuring a very different woman, a big, blowsy, cheerful girl about twenty-five, with bold eyes and a wide mouth daubed with too much lipstick.

"I know her, don't I?"

"You should. She keeps the Unicorn, over in Challacombe. She didn't when that photograph was taken. It was partly my money that set her up. Before that she was the barmaid for ten years."

"You still call on her?"

"No, but I could do. She's a generous soul. She probably wouldn't charge me nowadays."

On the face of it it seemed incredible. Howarth, the dry, irascible symbol of rectitude, utterly dedicated to his job, feared and respected by almost everyone at Bamfylde, slipping away to a chintzy bedroom at the Unicorn every now and again and paying cash down for a few moments' frolic. It occurred to him that Howarth was tacitly offering him solace if he needed it. Not in a spirit of leeriness, like two men drinking and talking women in a pub, but as a sincere gesture of friendship.

He said, deciding to make a joke of it, "Well, thanks for the tip. I'll bear it in mind," but Howarth replied seriously, "There's something more important you should think about. If you mean to spend your life here, and not move on if you get the chance, then it's time you began planning, my friend. Herries will be gone in a few months, and so far there's been no serious attempt on the part of those idiots on the Board to replace him. Why not put in for the job?"

"For Algy's job? As headmaster here? You can't be serious, man."

"I assure you I am. You've taken to this place and it seems to have taken to you. The most hopeful sections of it, that is. Well then, since you've committed yourself to soldier on to the point of no return why not try to ensure it's run your way, and not the way of some other officious new broom. Replacing Herries won't be easy. Whatever this place is it's his creation and he's stayed too long to give it flexibility. Someone who had worked under him would have a flying start."

"But good God, Howarth, you're senior to me by twenty years. Why not you?"

"Can you see me assuring mothers that their little darlings won't be corrupted by the writing on the lavatory walls? Or that Bloggs Minor, solid from the neck up, is a future Cabinet Minister? Don't talk bloody nonsense, P.J."

"Well, then, Carter, although God forbid. Or Barnaby, for that matter. He was upset when Algy gave me Havelock's after Ferguson died."

"Barnaby's a pleasant chap but he isn't headmaster material. He's too amiable and too close to his subject. Administration and real authority would send him out of his mind. How does communion with the Ancients qualify a man for the job of modernising this place, without converting it into a factory, of the kind Carter and his ilk regard as essential? And speaking of Carter, he's already backing himself for the job."

David had heard a vague rumour to this effect but Howarth's positive statement shocked him into reassessing his own future. He could never work here under Carter, or anyone like Carter. Their methods, theory and practice were too opposed, and suddenly what had so far proved a fireside chat with an intimate ran him into an impasse. He said, sullenly, "If Carter was appointed I'd resign. I wouldn't even wait until I found another billet."

"You don't have to tell me that. Well?"

"What are his chances?"

"Only fair. He's got Alderman Blunt in his pocket, and can probably win over one or two of the fence-squatters, men too timid to jump down until Herries is out of the way."

"Suppose he got it, what would be his line?"

"Overnight modernisation, with the emphasis on science and technical education. New labs, I daresay, and men like yourself replaced with nonentities. History and the classics don't cut much ice with Carter."

"But Bamfylde isn't that kind of school."

"A school is what a headmaster makes it."

"But there are several Old Boys on the governing board. They wouldn't stand for a complete reversal of policy."

"They mightn't see it as that. Who knows? Maybe Carter is right. This is 1927, and Herries's conception of the place is 1907, or earlier. Don't forget he was a year old when Prince Albert died."

"Bamfylde could be brought up to date without making a bonfire of everything Algy brought to it."

"By someone like you, someone with imagination plus drive. Not otherwise."

"I've been here eight years, and I'm five years younger than the most junior headmaster in the country, discounting day-schools. What chance would I stand?"

"About the same chance as Carter. I'd say you were about even at the moment. It would mean canvassing, of course."

"You mean soliciting votes among the Governors?"

"In the nicest possible way."

"I don't think I could do that."

"You'd have to, old boy. And you jolly well would if it meant keeping Carter out. You could begin on Brigadier Cooper. He's very partial to you, I hear. Converted by that son of his, no doubt."

"Will Herries have any say in it?"

"Officially, no. Unofficially, quite a lot."

He sat pondering a moment, his thoughts centring on the likely reaction of both Brigadier Cooper, 'Warrior' as older Bamfeldians thought of him, and Algy Herries. Headmaster at thirty. Headmaster of Bamfylde. In authority over men like Howarth, old Bouncer Acton, Rapper Gibbs, Barnaby and even Carter if he didn't resign. It was preposterous and yet, if it meant a choice between him and Carter, he couldn't stand aside without a fight, even if it was only a token fight. He said, "I'll think about it. No more than that, Howarth," and then, with a slightly baffled expression, "You'd serve under me?"

Howarth permitted himself the luxury of one wintry smile. "What choice would I have, so long as I stayed on the job? I'm well past the point of no return. Besides, I daresay you'd need your Eminence Grise!"

Down in the quad the end-of-prep bell jangled. On its final, jarring notes, the hum of the manumitted rose to a subdued uproar. David got up. "Thanks for the gin, Howarth. And thanks for your trust. I'll think about it, I really will."

In fact, he did rather more than think, broaching the matter to Brigadier Cooper when he saw him emerge from Algy's house one afternoon a week later.

Howarth must have been a shrewd judge of character. The Warrior was surprised but delighted, making no bones at all about his dislike of Carter or, for that matter, his apprehension concerning the appointment of anyone likely to change the style of the school. In fact, his extreme conservatism left David a little doubtful of his choice of patron. "We don't want a Clever Dick prancing about here with God knows how many damn silly modern theories," he growled. "All I ask of the place is to turn out chaps who can speak up,

play up and look anyone straight in the eye. Some of the
Governors have been naggin' poor old Algy for years, 'Get
the scholarship level up and never mind Kipling's "If",'
they kept telling him, but he never took a dam' bit of notice,
bless him. He knew what he was about and kept the flag
flying, didn't he? As to that feller Carter, he's not the type
either. We used to regard chaps like him as oddities in my
time here. Called 'em 'Stinks' and they were very small
beer then, I assure you. Not saying we haven't got to watch
the science side, mind you, but he'll do well enough right
where he is for my money. Have a crack at it, young
feller-me-lad. Why not? What have you got to lose?"

"My job, sir. I couldn't serve under Carter. We'd be after
one another's scalps from the word go and no matter who
won the school wouldn't."

It was a situation the Warrior obviously relished. He said,
rubbing his long nose with a nut-brown forefinger, "Tell you
what you do. Leave the reccy to me. I'll sniff around and
flush something out before the next monthly meeting.
Carter's application is in, and they're already whittling
the first batch down. Nothing definite yet, of course. They'll
leave it all to the last minute, if I know 'em. Wish to God I'd
had a few of 'em under me in S.A. and Mespot."

He went off, growling to himself, the traditional Blimp and
a Godsend to the cartoonists but still a man to be reckoned
with. He had won his V.C. at the Modder River more than
a quarter-century ago, and later served four sweltering years
in Mesopotamia, Palestine and Salonika when he was
recalled from retirement. David had intended asking his
advice on approaching Algy if he hadn't marched off so
abruptly. As it was, he decided to delay that until he got
some idea of the amount of support he was likely to receive.

He did not see the brigadier again before the end of term
but on the first day of the holidays the old chap wrote saying

David could be sure of three votes, including his own. Three wasn't many out of a Governing body of eighteen, but it insured him against ignominy. The brigadier added that the short list was now almost complete, and that it included at least one headmaster, of a school roughly equivalent with Bamfylde. The passing of information, he supposed, was very unethical but Cooper was not a man to worry on that score. It had the effect, however, of preventing David from confiding in Algy. The approach would now have to come from him, as soon as the news leaked that he had applied. In the interval David took Grace off to London to spend the Easter holiday with Beth's people. It would provide a change for her, Beth's sisters having daughters about her age. "She'll grow into a boy if I don't change her diet now and again," he told Ellie. It did not occur to him, as the Taunton–Paddington express pulled in, that he had reached a point where he needed a change himself.

II

He had almost outgrown cities and city amusements but he liked to visit the theatre when the opportunity offered and with Grace in good company took himself off to the West End one afternoon to see a matinée at the Globe, in Shaftesbury Avenue. The play did not impress him overmuch and he was emerging into the crowd of teatime shoppers, heading for the Coventry Street Corner House, when he heard his name called and turned to see a smartly dressed woman waving excitedly in his direction. At first he could not be sure and hesitated but then, with pleasurable surprise, he identified her as Julia Darbyshire, who came up very much out of breath, saying, "You always were one for stepping out! I saw you in the foyer and almost lost you ..." then stood back, letting her glance run over him as she said, "You're looking well, P.J.! Better than I expected. Wuther-

ing Heights must agree with you. All I really wanted to say
was ... well ... how terribly sorry I was when I heard
what happened, and how many times I thought about writing but didn't. Why? Does one ever know whether letters
of that kind are welcome?"

She stopped, looking a little confused, so he came to her
rescue, telling her he would have liked to have heard from
her, and was pleased to see her looking so pretty and cheerful. She coloured at this, but then smiled and said things
had taken a turn for the better. Her husband had died a year
ago and it would be hypocrisy to regard that as anything
but a mercy. Later she had landed a job as manageress of
a fashionable teashop, in Old Bond Street. "The pay is a lot
better than Bamfylde's," she added, "and the waitresses
are a nice bunch of kids. I get a free hand running it and
every now and again celebrities drop in and that gives me
the illusion I'm back in the swim. The wide open spaces were
never for me, P.J. I was an idiot to ever imagine they were.
As for Arthur, well, to be frank, I was relieved when he
died under an operation. Glad for both of us but especially
for him. There was absolutely no hope and he was never
free from pain. Your loss was very different. I couldn't
get you out of my mind, and you've no idea how glad I am
to see you looking fit and ... well, more or less yourself again.
Not surprised, though. You always had plenty of guts."

"Don't let's stand here," he said, embarrassed by her
directness. "I was popping into Lyons' for tea. Won't you
join me?" and she said she would be delighted for it was her
day off, and everybody she knew in town was at work. He
said, as soon as the Nippy had taken their order, "How did
you come to hear about it, Mrs. Darbyshire? I had no idea
you kept in touch with Bamfylde. I always had the impression you were thankful to scrape the mud from your shoes."

"Keith Blades wrote. Don't worry. Just once, and only

about you." She hesitated a moment. "You see, I told him about your part in it. I thought I owed it to both of you, but don't worry, he's a very discreet boy. I'm quite sure he's never mentioned it to anyone and probably won't until he finds a nice girl, marries her, and lays his murky past on the table, the way men do once they've sown their wild oats."

He had always respected her for her courage and integrity but now he found himself enjoying her company, partly as a fellow traveller but also as a smart and attractive woman, who had faced her troubles and side-stepped self-pity. Everything about her indicated a cheerful ability to get up and try again, and again after that if need be. She had taken great pains with her appearance, and although he knew she was the same age as himself she could have passed for a woman in her early twenties. She had what he thought of as 'the West End look', and her forthrightness was much at odds with the Julia Darbyshire he had confronted in that shabby little sitting-room above the quad. He could see now how entirely possible it was that an imaginative boy like Blades had persuaded himself that he was madly in love with her. She had charm and high spirits, as well as good looks, but more than enough femininity to captivate an adolescent romantic, especially one isolated in a male community. Algy, he thought, should have had more sense than select her, even as a stop-gap. There was magnetism here, and promise too. It was a wonder there hadn't been a dozen boys mooning after her during her brief spell as Second Form mistress.

He told her the facts of the accident, then how he had succeeded in adjusting to it, partly on account of Grace's survival, partly because of the stimulus and comradeship offered by the staff and boys. He told her how the boys competed to spoil the kid, how Winterbourne was teaching her to paint, and Hoskins to dance. "It seemed to me I owed it to everybody to make the effort," he admitted. "It was like being at the receiving end of trench comradeship, with everyone in the unit reaching back to give you a hand. Does that sound fanciful?"

"Not from you it doesn't. I don't suppose I'm telling you anything you don't know when I say you're so *right* for that place. It wouldn't surprise me, thirty years from now, to hear you had spent your entire life down there, and enjoyed every moment of it, even your feud with Carter."

Her mention of Carter reminded him of their present rivalry and he was surprised to note how even the remote possibility of him replacing Herries excited her. "Why, that's perfectly splendid, P.J.! I can't think of anyone who would make a better job of it and the boys will be rooting for you. Is it likely? I mean, you're very young for the job, aren't you? Or they'll think so, won't they?"

"I'm only a few years younger than Carter," he said, "and he's applying. He's down there right now, canvassing like mad if I know him."

"Oh, they'll never give it to *him*," she said, so emphatically that he felt encouraged. "If it isn't you it will be a stranger, someone in his late forties, you see if it isn't. Would you be terribly disappointed?"

"No," he said, "as a matter of fact I think I'd be relieved, providing he was the right chap, of course, and didn't play merry hell with Algy's legacy. It's a very special kind of school, Mrs. Darbyshire. It's difficult to say why or how, but it *is*, you know. It's got so many of the good things about the old-style public school, a kind of steadiness, continuity, and a touch of genuine idealism, but it also has—how the devil can I put it?—post-war optimism, and a broadening of out-look that's been achieved in all kinds of ways since people got the war into perspective. Put it this way, it's a kind of launching platform for kids moving out into a world that's still doing precisely what you and I have been doing this last year or so."

"And what's that?" she asked, smiling.

"Licking our wounds, and preparing for another go. That's Algy's doing, of course. He's a bit of a genius really, especially when you consider he was born at a time when they were still hanging people in public and schools like Bamfylde were a cross between a gaol and a four-ale bar! We'll all miss him but we'll survive, given half a chance. Mind you, the setting has something to do with it. It's so . . . so permanent, so English if you like. But the best of England."

He broke off, laughing at his own enthusiasm, but she said, "Go on, P.J."

"Well, Algy and the surrounding countryside complement one another. There's Exmoor, looking just as it did when your tribe and mine were wearing skins and painting themselves blue, and there's the grab-your-girl-grab-your-cash world outside. And smack in the middle, like an adjudicator, is old Algy, doing a weighing-out act to make sure one doesn't swamp the other."

"That's a pocket sermon," she said, "with the smack of the Welsh about it, but then . . ." and she stopped, smiling.

"Well?"

"I was only going to say that every time you get enthusiastic about anything, I remember you're a Taffy who has decided to throw in his lot with the English. Do you ever regret doing it?"

"No," he said, chuckling. "The English have got their points. An ability to organise is one of 'em that we lack. The truth is I had my faith in the future handed back to me at Bamfylde. The place saved my sanity, so naturally I'm prejudiced."

She said, with conviction, "You're one of the sanest people I've ever met, P.J. You'd have steadied up somewhere but I see what you mean, nevertheless. Well, here's hoping those Governors see it too, and give you the chance you deserve. Why don't we drink to that somewhere? I might be the very first to wet the new headmaster's head."

They went out and she piloted him expertly through crowded side streets to a pub she knew, where they drank three gins and he listened to her for a change.

After leaving Bamfylde, she had gone to Southampton, taking an office job in a solicitor's to be near her husband. After his death she had been lucky enough to land the managerial job at the Old Bond Street teashop. It was an American firm, and paid above average for good executives. The owner, who spent half his time over here, was a genial middle-aged New Jerseyman called Sprockman—"Hiram Ulysses Sprockman, believe it or not," she told him, "and a real sweetie, in a ponderous, teddy-bear way. He takes me out to dinner sometimes, and even asks my advice on buying pictures and Regency furniture. He's a terrific Anglophile, all set on becoming a New England squire when he's tired of making money, but that won't be until he's in his dotage if I'm any judge. Once Arthur's estate was cleared I could afford a flat to myself in Camden Town. It's very handy and I've furnished it myself with pieces my mother-in-law left me." She paused a moment. "Look, why not come back and let me cook dinner for you? I'm far better at cooking than teaching."

"Let me buy you dinner in Soho," he suggested, but she shook her head. "Not on your life, P.J. Their menus look appetising but I've seen the inside of some of their kitchens and prefer to poison myself. Are they expecting you back early?"

"No," he said, excited at the prospect of being entertained by her. "Grace is sleeping out at her aunt's tonight and I said I'd be late back. I thought about taking in another show. The Aldwych, perhaps."

"Nothing worth seeing," she said, "and I've had a look at most of them. Come back to my place and let me cook you something. Time somebody fussed you a bit. The way your wife did when you'd been fussing over those boys all day. Or is that taking things too much for granted, P.J.?"

"Don't you believe it. I can't think of a better way of rounding off a very pleasant reunion."

*   *   *

She was better than her word. It was a long time since anyone had pampered him and she prepared a very appetising meal, carrying on a conversation with him through the door of the kitchen while he sat before the fire. She was much more relaxed in a house, reminding him more of Beth coping with the unpredictabilities of the cottage stove, but there was nothing of that kind here. Someone, Julia or her parents-in-law, had excellent taste. All the furniture was antique and well-cared for, each individual piece being the work of an eighteenth- or early nineteenth-century craftsman. There were one or two valuable paintings, among them a Crome, and a display of Rockingham china in a china cabinet. The neighbourhood outside was rackety but the flat was in a cul-de-sac, backed by a high wall beyond which, she said, was a market, unused at this time of day.

After the meal he helped her wash up and she brought coffee into the big living-room, where he felt so relaxed that he had no inclination to leave and make his way via tube to Charing Cross. Here, on her own ground, she was very easy to talk to and when dusk fell outside, with an accompanying drizzle, she drew the curtains and came and sat beside him on the sofa, kicking off her shoes and shooting her legs towards the fire so that once again he had a sense of renewal, as if they had known one another intimately, had been separated for a long time, and met again under congenial circumstances.

He said, after praising her cooking, "This is the most enjoyable afternoon and evening I've spent since it fell on me, Julia," and as he said it he became sharply aware of her nearness and her easy-going approach to him ever since her initial hail encouraged him to take her hand. He would have thought he had outgrown his early shyness with women but he had not, or not entirely. When she turned her head he felt as young and inexperienced as young Blades must have done, and then, as though to explain away his impulsive gesture, he said, "I haven't touched a woman since it happened . . . was hardly aware of them again until lately."

"And now?"

"Now? I'd be a prize-hypocrite if I said I didn't want to kiss you, Julia."

She said, evenly, "I'd be a worse hypocrite if I didn't admit I was rather hoping you would," and took the initiative by kissing him, gently but assertively, as though she was experimenting, and he was encouraged to take her in his arms and kiss her properly, not as he recalled kissing Beth, on that last occasion he had held her in his arms the night after Winterbourne went missing, but as they had kissed in the earliest days of their association.

He was not disposed to let her go then and there was no occasion to, for she seemed content to stay with her head on his shoulder, looking into the shifting coals. They sat like that for what seemed to him a long time before she said, "Two years, David. It's a long time, for a man as lively and imaginative as you. Beth was a very affectionate girl, wasn't she?"

"Very," he told her, "from the very beginning. It's not

that I haven't begun to think of women again, particularly in the last few weeks. Sometimes I had half a mind to go out and look for one. But with me . . . well, it sounds damnably stuffy, but there has to be a personal relationship of some kind. The fact is, I had very little experience with women before I married and it wasn't wholly on account of the war. Somehow a casual relationship, after Beth died that is, would have seemed . . . well . . . too damned clinical for my taste." He had to laugh at himself then, adding, "By God, I sound as pious as Skidmore, the parson's son, telling me why he wouldn't make the new boys' bow to Founder's statue in the quad."

He wondered if she would remember Skidmore but she made no comment and seemed, in fact, to be pondering memories of her own. Presently she said, "Listen, David, I'm going to take a big risk. Big, because I've got a hell of a lot of respect for you, and I wouldn't care to have you leave here with the wrong impression. If you hadn't said what you said just now it wouldn't have occurred to me but here it is, without a lot of fancy talk. You're very welcome to stay the night if it would help. I wasn't in love with Arthur, not in the way you and your wife were in love. I didn't have time to discover whether or not we would have made a go of it after the war. Frankly I doubt it. I was very young then, and as full of silly ideas about love and marriage as most girls growing up with a war on. When we married Arthur was very much the extrovert, keen on games, and making a good impression on people who didn't matter. When he did come back he wasn't anything at all. Just a hulk, and that was that, for both of us."

"And since then?"

"Since then I haven't been Goody Two Shoes. I tried now and again, wanting very much to be a real woman, instead of something and nothing, the way it had to be all that time, but . . . well, nothing sparked. The few men I met wanted to use me, and I soon came to the conclusion that I would be using them, and that wasn't me, for roughly the same reasons as you held off."

"You mean it might be different with me?"

"I know it would be. You don't need me in particular but you need affection even more than I do, and that's saying a hell of a lot. Well, there it is, except that you can say 'Thanks very much but . . .' and walk right out of here, with no hard feelings."

He noticed then something that touched him deeply. Her voice was very level but the hand clasping his as his arm rested on her shoulder, shook in a way that was painfully familiar to him, the tremor betraying the careful flatness of her voice. He said, kissing her cropped hair, "I should like to stay very much, Julia. And I wasn't fishing for it, if you can believe that."

The hand stopped shaking, and she lifted her face to him, laughing like a girl. "You never went fishing in the whole of your life. You wouldn't know how. Give me five minutes," and she got up, turned off all but the centre light, and put the guard in front of the fire.

He gave her ten minutes, then went across to the bedroom and knocked. She was sitting up in bed, the pinkish light of the bedside lamp glowed on her white shoulders and neck, throwing a shadow across her full breasts in a way that made him catch his breath. He said, standing looking down at her, "Why did you get your hair shingled? You had lovely hair. It was one of your best features. The first thing I noticed about you."

"You didn't notice me at all until you convinced yourself I was seducing one of your ewe lambs."

"That's what you think. Well?"

"It was the fashion. Up here you have to stay in the fashion.

It cost me a pang or two, until I got used to it. Shall I turn off this light?"

"No," he said, "not for a minute," and he sat on the edge of the bed, took her face between his hands and kissed her gently on the lips. He noticed aspects of her that seemed new to him, the clearness of skin, the vivid flecks in the grey eyes, the regularity and delicacy of her features that added up to a stillness and dignity that was singular and striking. There was character behind her prettiness, but warmth, too, and fleetingly he remembered his wife but without guilt.

She reached out and extinguished the bedside light and he undressed in the glow of the street lamp outside but when he laid himself down beside her and ran his hand across her breasts, she seemed to hesitate a second and said, turning to him, "You're sure, David . . .?" and he said, impatiently, "I'm sure. We've both had more loneliness than anyone deserves," and then her arms went round him and she came to him not merely joyously but with a spontaneity that confirmed his guess about her desperate loneliness over the years. He said, when they were still, "You've been through as tough a time as me and learned more."

"Tough, David. But not as tough as yours."

"With me there was always someone around to lend a hand," and the admission had the effect of redoubling the tenderness he felt for her at that moment.

*   *   *

It was a bright day when he awoke to find her smiling down at him, with a breakfast tray resting on her forearm. She was wearing an Oriental dressing-gown, embroidered with dragons and pagodas. "What time is it?" he asked, sitting up.

"Why should you care what time it is? That dreadful bell is out of earshot." She gave him the tray and sat on the bed.

"God, how I hated that damned bell! I always thought of it as the equivalent of a prison siren," and he laughed, saying one got used to it in time.

"I don't think I would, not in a century. But then, you like a well-regulated life, don't you?"

He considered, stirring the excellent coffee she had brewed for him. "I suppose I do. I hadn't thought of it but I like predictability and you get plenty of that at a place like Bamfylde. Within a framework of chaos, of course."

"By God, they'll be fools if they don't grab you while they have the chance, Davy! Dr. Arnold, in the splendour of his youth! What more could they ask?"

"Arnold died getting on for a century ago," he said. "All his disciples are dead too, and I sometimes wonder if there's any place in the post-war world for their gospel."

She leaned back on her hands, relaxed and smiling. They might have been lovers for years instead of hours. "What exactly *was* that gospel? Was it the academic version of Victorian muscular Christianity?"

"No," he said, "that's only how the cynics think of it . . . Carter, and all the other modern pushers. It was more fundamental than that. Algy Herries both understood and practised it, and he laid it out for me, the first day I met him. The war was still on then."

"But what *was* it exactly?"

"In its day it was an entirely fresh approach to the word 'education'. Or a rediscovery, maybe. Two thousand five hundred years ago the Greeks had the golden key, but it was lost, somehow, when their civilisation crumbled. I suppose it concerned itself with a search for truth. Not simply truth about the universe but about us—ourselves. To see things and ourselves as they and we really are, not as fashionable trends and fashions project them, generation by generation. Get that across to kids in their formative years and there's hope for everybody. It always was important but now more than ever."

"Why now particularly?"

"You ask me that? After what the war did to you?"

"Then it's teaching the young how to learn from the mistakes of the past?"

"That's part of it, an important part, but you can't begin searching out truth until you know yourself, and getting to know yourself demands a reasonable amount of self-discipline."

She was laughing at him now but not in a way that he resented.

"You shouldn't have much difficulty in that respect, Davy."

"As much as anyone else. That's why professionals have to lean heavily on a system, symbolised by that bell you hated. There's got to be a system, an organisation, a chain of command. Like the army, the church or a well-run business, come to that. And you have to work within that system, even though it's far from perfect and needs adjustment all the time. Here, what the devil am I doing? Pontificating at this time of day, and with you sitting there half-naked? You aren't thinking of taking another teaching job, are you?"

"God forbid!" she said, and got up, hitching her dressing-gown.

"Take the tray and come back to bed," but she said, "I'm sorry, Davy, I'd like to very much but I can't. I'm off to work as soon as I'm dressed and I'm late now. How about you?"

"I'd better go home, I suppose. They'll wonder what I'm up to and fear the worst. But I can see you again, can't I? I'm here for another ten days."

"Do you want to?"

"When are you going to get it through your head that my

bones aren't chalk and there's no watered-down ink in my veins?"

"Oh, I never did suppose that," she said, kissing him swiftly and relieving him of his tray, "even before you accepted my invitation last night." She laughed again. "I say, I really have seduced Bamfylde this time, haven't I?"

"Never mind that. Where do we go from here, Julia?"

"That's up to you, Davy. I'd love to see you again, so long as you're on the run from that gaol on the moor. But how about your little girl?"

"I planned to take her to Hampton Court on Sunday. Why not come with us? I'd like you to meet her, and you'll find she's very easy, growing up among all those ruffians. In any case, I have all my evenings free and we could do a few shows. You don't have to catch up on what's happening in the outside world, but I do. What are your hours at that teashop?"

"Nine-thirty to six, with Wednesday afternoons off. Look in and have tea about five today and I'll go through the theatre guide and find something you'd like. I'll take you up on that Hampton Court invitation too; in fact, we could strike a bargain. You pilot me round the tourist spots, guide services thrown in, and I'll show you post-war Gomorrah."

"It's a deal," he said, climbing out of bed. "See you at five. What's the place called?"

"The Maypole," she said. "Very significant, don't you think? I'll have to fly now. Bathroom's over there but watch the geyser, it's temperamental. Let yourself out. I'll be gone by the time you're ready."

He caught her by the arm as she turned, whisking her clothes from the dressing-table stool.

"Julia!"

"Well?"

"No regrets?"

"None at all. Quite the contrary. And you?"

"That's a silly question."

"No sillier than yours, sir!" and she plumped herself down before the mirror, applying make-up at what seemed to him phenomenal speed.

III

It was one of the gayest intervals of his life, certainly the most carefree since the time he and Beth and the twins had moved into Havelock's, after Ferguson's death.

Julia and Grace got along splendidly, and he was quick to notice that Julia adjusted almost at once to the maturity of the child and did not make the mistake of talking down to her, as some of his relatives were inclined to do. He enjoyed himself so much that he spent the entire Easter holiday in town. Every Wednesday and Sunday the three of them made excursions, to Hampton Court, the Tower, down the Thames to Greenwich on a launch, and to St. Paul's for morning service. Every evening, save for an odd one or two he spent with Beth's folks, he took her out somewhere, and on several occasions he called in at her sedate teashop where, on one occasion, he met the owner, Hiram Ulysses Sprockman, taking an immediate liking to the breezy, outward-looking man of about forty-five, with his genial approach to all his employees, even the junior waitresses, but what seemed to David a steady admiration for his manageress, whom he treated with elaborate courtesy. On one occasion he took Sprockman to Westminster Abbey to show him the Coronation Chair, and the tomb of Elizabeth, renowned for the superbly modelled hands on the effigy. Sprockman had an enthusiastic approach to all things English and said he had half a mind to retire here. "My part of the States has a past," he said, ruefully, "but not beyond the late sixteen-hundreds.

I never forget what that guy Rupert Brooke said, when he paid his first visit to the American continent."

"What did he say?" David asked, and Sprockman seemed mildly shocked that he had to ask. To him Rupert Brooke epitomised England. He quoted, " 'The breezes have nothing to remember and everything to promise. There walk, as yet, no ghosts of lovers in Canadian lanes . . . It is possible, at a pinch, to do without gods. But one misses the dead.' "

"That's pretty good," David said. "I'll try it on the Upper School when I get back. We've got two Canadian boys in the Sixth." It was easy to see why Julia Darbyshire liked Sprockman, and why she had found security and repose in her job.

They were lovers on several other occasions, rather dismally on her part the night before he was due back to Bamfylde for Algy's last term, but by then he had quite made up his mind, remembering Howarth's advice on the subject of remarriage. Physically she attracted him very strongly but he knew himself well enough to admit that he was not in love with her, that he could never love as he had loved Beth. But he had no doubts about their compatibility, and tremendous respect for her courage and fundamental honesty, towards himself and everyone else. His one lingering doubt, involving Grace, was erased by the pleasant, undemanding relationship they formed during their jaunts about town. Grace, for that matter, could adjust to anyone who gave her half a chance. Growing up among four hundred boys, all of whom she knew by their Christian names and nicknames, she was the most adaptable seven-year-old in his experience.

They were half-dozing in front of the fire when he proposed, very soberly in the circumstances, for they had been in one another's arms a few moments before and this time, aware that there was no prospect of seeing him until July at the earliest, she seemed as fully committed as himself. It was this that helped as he said, "Julia, suppose I land that headship. Or if I don't, and aim higher at some bigger school, would you like to think about marrying me? I don't expect you to decide right away, of course. You've made your own life here, and it's a very pleasant one, so long as you work for Sprockman. But you've made all the difference in the world to me and I'm sure you and Grace would get along fine." But, to his dismay, she did not even wait for him to finish, saying sharply. "No, Davy, my dear! That's something I don't have to think about. I'm very fond of you, and always will be, but marriage . . . that simply wouldn't work, not for us."

"But why not? I'm not saying it would ever be quite the same for me again. I'd look after you though, and I daresay we'd have a lot of fun together. Children, too, if you wanted them. And neither of us are beginners, so we'd each make allowances. At least think about it until I come up again at the end of the term."

She said, with shattering finality, "As I say, Davy, there's no point in that. For two reasons. In the first place, you're not in love with me . . . and bed isn't the kind of love that's essential to you."

"What's the other reason?"

"I couldn't come back to Bamfylde and you'll realise that if you think about it."

He was harassed enough to misunderstand her. "Good God, woman—that nonsense with Blades? Nobody knows about it except the three of us. And even if they did what the hell does it matter now? Knowing you, I see it wasn't even important at the time."

"I wasn't meaning that. Something else that's very important to both of us, if we were stupid enough to confuse our physical needs with all the other essentials."

"But I could leave Bamfylde and get another school . . ."

"Any school, no matter where it was, would be the same for me and the same for you. You're as dedicated a man as I ever saw. But me . . . ? A job is a job, a means of getting the things I want, and keeping boredom at bay. No matter how much I cared for you or you for me I wouldn't make out as a housemaster's wife, still less as wife of a headmaster. I'm the wrong material, Davy. I'd hold you back and you wouldn't be held back and we'd fight. We'd fight like hell. The job, and the boys, would always take precedence with you, and I might come to accept that. But I'd fall down on what was expected of me and in the end you'd have a straight choice—hating the sight of me or compromising, as most husbands have to when they've made a bad choice and are wrapped up in their jobs. That would be damnably unfair and I'll have no part in it."

She was so explicit that there seemed no point in arguing with her just then, so he said something about writing as soon as he got back, and of putting it all on paper, but this only made her laugh. She said, kissing him, "Now don't go off down to that barrack on the moor looking like the wrath of God. Everyone will think the cares of headship have settled on you in advance. And don't spoil our last evening, either."

"You don't know me if you think I'll give up that easily. I'll see how that application of mine fares and if I'm lucky I'll pop up in that teashop of yours when you least expect it."

"You do that, Davy," she said, equably, "but face the risk of wasting your railway fare. I mightn't be there to-wards mid-summer."

"You're not thinking of switching jobs again?"

"Sprockman has been talking about sending me to the States. He's hoping to open a chain of Ye Olde English Tea-Shoppes in New Jersey, Maine and Connecticut."

"You mean you might be gone permanently?"

'No. He just wants me to survey the towns and report on sites and locations. And why not? Do you know, I've never been abroad in my life? Not even across the Channel. I thought it might be fun."

"How long would you be gone?"

"Oh, not all that long, five to six weeks, maybe."

He tried to extract more information but failed. There were areas of Julia Darbyshire she preferred to keep fenced off and he left her with a sense of complete bafflement. But then he took a more philosophical line, thinking how much good she had done him in the last four weeks, and telling himself that one had to make allowances. Bamfylde was not an ideal place for a woman like her, city-bred, and earning good money (more than he earned, he suspected), at the hub of affairs. Clearly Julia Darbyshire and Bamfylde, as it existed, would not mix, but this was not an insurmountable obstacle to marriage. If he got the headship he could do a great deal to improve Bamfylde's image in her eyes, refurnishing and redecorating Algy's quarters, and buying a car that would give them local mobility and easy access to the tourist areas in the West. If he was rejected, as he felt certain he would be, then he would assault the agencies for a post in a more civilised area, and wait until she was disenchanted with a five-and-a-half-day week in the West End. Such a time would come with a woman as mercurial as Julia and there were advantages in delay. He had no doubts but that she approved of him as a lover, and could also evaluate the security he offered as a husband. She was not the kind of woman who could do without a man for long, the little she had told him concerning her previous relationships indicated that. As for himself, he was more and more certain as the days passed, and he picked up the rhythm of his life, that he stood in sore need of her cheerfulness and

brisk common sense. The memory of her lying in his arms
unsettled him and made him impatient with fools, and the
guerilla tactics of The Lump in Middle School, so that the
more observant boys began to notice a tetchiness about him
that had not been there in the past.

It was Winterbourne, who missed very little, who reassured them all concerning Pow-Wow's uncertain temper
as the term got into its stride, saying, "Go easy on him. He's
tensed up these days, on account of Algy leaving and a
new man taking over. They're all on edge, he and Carter
more than the others, seeing they're both lined up for the
job."

For it was now common knowledge that there was a
possibility of Algy being succeeded by the housemaster of
Outram's or Havelock's and, to a degree, the tension spread
downwards as far as the Lower Fifth, where Collier, a
barrister's son with a penchant for colourful metaphors, said,
"This bloody place is like Pompeii this term. Everyone is
waiting around for the lid to blow off. Even Algy's lost
some of his bounce. He's trotting around looking as if he
might run into the Press Gang behind the piggeries."

The Governors seemed to take an interminable time to
come to a decision, and it was Howarth who, for all his air of
detachment, was invariably the best informed of the staff,
who advanced sound reasons for the delay. He told David
one evening, when they were taking their constitutional
round the cricket-field, "There's something of a deadlock,
I understand. Short list of six, and you and Carter both on it.
Of the other four only two are in the running. A man from
Repton, and the former head of a school in Cape Town, who
retired and settled over here last year. They're both highly
qualified, both around the fifty mark. Actually, I believe
everybody's waiting for Sir Rufus Creighton to show up."

David had heard a good deal about Sir Rufus Creighton

but had never met him. He was an ex-Indian judge, a County Councillor and notable educationalist, who owed his seat on the Board to Bamfylde's status as a direct grant school. Having taken it into his head to go on a world cruise, none of the other Governors felt disposed to make the appointment without his guidance. On Howarth's advice, David stayed clear of his sponsor, Brigadier Cooper. "Won't do to compromise him," he said. "He's tamed tribesmen on the North-West Frontier and knows more than you and I about in-fighting."

And so, for David, time stood still. May passed, and half of June, long, sunny days that ordinarily he would have enjoyed but in the circumstances, and for the first time since settling here, seemed flat and stale. Apart from one letter in reply to his four Julia had not written and was incommunicado, for her trip to the States had materialised and she was living a life of rapid movement up and down the eastern seaboard. He read and re-read her letter until he knew it by heart. It was breezy and friendly but gave no hint that she had changed her mind, or was likely to, only that she was finding America an exciting, stimulating place, that parts of New England reminded her of Devon, and that she had resorted to remote hypnotism of the Bamfylde Governors in order to influence their choice of candidate. She was likely to be home in early August if everything went according to plan. She addressed him as 'Dearest Davy', and concluded 'All my love to you, dear.' He recalled then that the odd letter from Beth had always been starred with crosses, schoolgirl fashion, but there were no crosses here and the impersonality of the letter bothered him a little. At a deeper level, however, he did not devote a great deal of thought to Julia. The looming possibility of triumph or failure absorbed most of his nervous energy.

And then, catching him offguard after weeks of suspense,

the summons came. All short-listed candidates were to be interviewed on the following morning by a specially convened meeting of the Governors in the school library, that had done duty for a Board Room ever since it was built in the first years of Herries's reign. Both he and Carter were spared the embarrassment of a waiting period, in the company of the other four applicants, who were interviewed swiftly, one after the other, the last of them during morning coffee break. The two local men were asked to present themselves at eleven-thirty a.m., when the others had been taken to the head's house for refreshment. On the way across the quad, David caught a glimpse of two of them, a tall, slightly stooping man, some twenty years his senior, with a high-domed head and thick, greying hair, and a much younger man with quick, nervous movements, who looked as though he was convinced he had missed the boat, for he scowled at the Founder's statue as though he entertained the same feelings for it as Skidmore. David thought, "One down and one to go, but I don't like the look of that beetling chap. The old place is in for a shake-up if they settle on him ..." But then, surprisingly, Carter touched his elbow, betraying his own extreme nervousness by saying, "I say, Powlett-Jones, this is a bit of an ordeal, isn't it? I mean, being quizzed by the whole bunch of them on our own ground. I've got the most appalling indigestion, damn it!" The brief encounter did a little to resuscitate his own confidence as they went up the steps together and took two of six empty chairs ranged along the wall of the duty-librarian's office, reminding him of a row of chairs in a dentist's waiting-room, a dentist who wasn't doing so well.

He said, gritting his teeth, "Well, good luck, Carter. Don't let 'em rattle you!" and Carter, blinking nervously, made his first and only joke in David's presence, saying, "When I get in there I know just how I shall feel. Like that smug little brute in the picture, 'When Did You Last See Your Father?' "

There was no chance to cap Carter's joke. The head's part-time secretary, Miss Rowlandson, from the Old Rectory in the village, appeared and said, in a hushed voice, "You now, Mr. Carter . . . !" and Carter rose, straightening his tie, smoothing his wet-rust hair and lurching towards the door like a felon summoned by the hangman.

It seemed very strange sitting there alone, in a room that was as familiar as his own bedroom. His thoughts ranged back nine years, to the days he had first poked his head into the library, finding it a hotchpotch of books, most of them tattered legacies from Old Boys and including, surprisingly, a full set of G. A. Henty's. He tried to concentrate on something inconsequential, the gable end of the roof where Havelock's met Outram's, the perch where the Kassava brothers had taken refuge on the night of the fire. It seemed a very long time ago, an incident in his childhood, like the day he came home from school to be told that his father and two brothers had died in the pit, or that bright summer dawn on July 1st, 1916, when he had waited, mouth parched and heart hammering, for the second hand of his watch to move up to zero-hour. But then he tried to think of something more cheerful, selecting Julia Darbyshire at random—Julia Darbyshire, stark naked in the faint glow of the street lamp the night they became lovers in her flat, and this focal point was more rewarding, for at least it stopped him trying to make sense of the indistinct murmur beyond the door. He thought, gloomily, "I wouldn't give a damn if she had been here, or even accessible. I could have put through a trunk call tonight and laughed it off, but the only one handy to serve as a buffer is old Carter. Queer him being so nervous, and coming out with that joke. Not such a bad joke, either. Howarth will swear I've

made it up when I tell him . . . By God, they need some new
linoleum in here—this is shredding away . . . hasn't been
renewed since Queen Victoria died . . . What the devil
am I yawning about? Haven't yammered like that since I
was in a dugout under bombardment . . ." And then, his
nerves taut as trip wires, "I was an absolute bloody fool to
let Howarth talk me into this, curse him! He made sure he
kept well clear of it himself. Damned if I can recall having
been more embarrassed in my life . . ." But he was more
resilient than he realised. A moment later his thoughts took
a new turn: "To hell with them all, boyo, Julia included!
If I miss out, as I'm certain to, I'll drift, and give the new
man a sporting chance . . . Grace is settled here and so am
I in normal circumstances . . . Wouldn't care to start all
over again, and lose touch with young Cooper, Chad
Boyer, Skidmore, the Kassavas, Briarley, Keith Blades and
all the others . . . I already feel as if I'd attained my century.
What you need right now, Davy, is a good stiff gin, so damned
if you don't go looking for Howarth the minute we're
finished in here . . ."

And then the door opened and Carter came out, so red in
the face that he looked almost apoplectic, but before he
could say a word Miss Rowlandson appeared again and
said, in the same empty-church voice, "Mr. Powlett-Jones?"
and he tried to grin at Carter and slipped past him across the
threshold.

CHAPTER TWO

I

He remembered reading somewhere that a man awaiting a verdict on a capital charge could assess his chances the moment a jury returned to the court. If they looked at him he was acquitted. If they avoided his eyes he was guilty.

There must be something in it, he decided, for the same applied here. His known sponsors, Brigadier Cooper, and his two converts, Birley, the Challacombe grocer and Newsom, another Old Boy, glanced up and smiled. The brigadier might be said to have winked. About half the remaining fourteen kept their eyes on the blotters, Carter's backers no doubt, but the Chairman, a little brown nut of a man, looked at him quite impersonally when inviting him to take a seat.

There was a little shuffling and throat-clearing and then Sir Rufus took him gently through a formal application check—full name, age, degree, and so on, until David began to wonder whether the whole thing was rigged, either in favour of Carter or one of the other candidates, and that his presence here was no more than a polite ritual. Then Sir Rufus asked him about his war service, what regiment he had served in, and where, and what part of the line he was occupying when he was buried by a mortar shell. He answered briefly, almost impatiently, until the brigadier said, "You were awarded the M.C., Powlett-Jones. Would you care to tell us about it?"

"I'd prefer not, Brigadier Cooper. You were out there, and you know how many chaps earned decorations and didn't get them," and Brigadier Cooper twinkled again, implying that this was a perfectly satisfactory answer and one he had expected.

Newsom, an apple-cheeked man in his fifties, said, vaguely, "You've ... er ... been happy here, Mr. Powlett-Jones? Apart from that dreadful business on Quarry Hill, of course," and then chewed his moustache, as though he regretted raising the matter.

"Very happy," David said, "and that's mainly why I applied. I realise there are men senior to me, of course, but I made sure none of them wanted the post before I filed an application."

This seemed to nonplus them a little but the brigadier rallied and mentioned the fire, addressing his colleagues as though David wasn't present.

"Dam' fine show he put up on that occasion," he said. "Been a shambles if he hadn't been up to the mark," and he glared around as though others were denying the fact.

There was an awkward pause then until Sir Rufus said, "I understand you took an external degree while serving on the staff, Mr. Powlett-Jones. Wouldn't it have been more satisfactory to take advantage of the shortened University course for ex-officers?"

"Possibly, sir. But it would have meant a two-year break with Bamfylde. I was married then, with two children to support, and would have had to chance getting back here." He wondered if this was the real reason and decided it was not. "The fact is, Sir Rufus, Bamfylde was rehabilitating *me* at the time. I wanted to take full advantage of it."

The qualified answer interested the little man. He screwed up his face so that eyes and mouth were all but lost in a maze of wrinkles. "Would you care to elaborate on that a little?"

"Sharp as a damned needle, he is," David thought, checked for a moment, but then he said, deliberately, "I was in very bad shape when I came here, in 1918. The hospital specialist decided a job would be the best therapy. I didn't take him seriously at the time. I did later, as soon as I'd met Mr. and Mrs. Herries, and made friends with some of the staff."

"Weren't the boys something of a strain in the circumstances?"

"No," he flashed out. "No! . . . Not once I'd let them see I wasn't to be fooled around with. I got the measure of them in less than a week."

There was another awkward silence. Still nobody else spoke, and the interview seemed likely to resolve itself into a wary dialogue between himself and the little Indian judge. Sir Rufus said, carefully, "To sum up, Mr. Powlett-Jones, what, in your view, is the most essential factor of a school like Bamfylde?" and David heard himself say, "I can answer that straight out. A happy atmosphere. If that's there everything else falls into place."

That, at least, resulted in a shift of glances of the committed and neutral groups. Fourteen pairs of eyes moved as one to his level, then half of them were lowered to the doodle-starred blotters on the table.

Sir Rufus said, quietly, "Thank you, Mr. Powlett-Jones. That's all, I think, unless any other member of the Governing Body would like to ask a question." There were no questions and after a lapse of a few seconds he got up, bowed towards the chair and walked out.

Back in the little lobby he found he was sweating freely. He said, aloud, "By God, I need that drink!" and went in search of Howarth and his decanter.

Hoskins, whom he thought of as Grace's dancing professional, came up to the living-room a few minutes after lunch and David, brooding in his study with the door open, heard Grace's squeal of delight as he said, "New one here, real hot number, Tuppence! You must have heard it on the wireless but this is the first recording to reach the Outback!"

"Put it on! Put it on, Sax," he heard 'Tuppence' exclaim but Hoskins, briefed in these casual visits, said, "I'll have to ask your father first. Is he around?"

"I'm in here," David called. "Play the damned thing. I shan't get any peace if you don't," and Hoskins called back, "Thank *you*, sir! Just the one side," and in a moment later the half-familiar rhythm of "Bye, 'Bye, Blackbird' grinding out of the portable, followed by the thuds and squeals that invariably accompanied a 'lesson' in the latest ballroom craze.

It was not by any means soothing music but it helped and he found himself humming the lively refrain.

> , . . *So, make my bed and light the light,*
> *I'll be home, late tonight,*
> *Blackbird, 'bye, 'bye!*

There was a small oval mirror immediately above the desk and David watched his own grin, thinking, "Do I really give a damn whether they turn me down or not? What the hell does it matter on what terms I stay? I belong here. Grace belongs here. Beth and Joan are still around somewhere, and so are all the names on that war memorial outside . . ." and then he heard the gramophone needle screech to an abrupt halt and Hoskins say, "I'm sorry, sir, just trying out a new one. Yes, he's in the study . . ." and after that whispering and the sound of the door closing on Tuppence and her instructor.

Algy's white head showed round the door. He looked like an elderly, pink-eyed rabbit, tufted and slightly scared, as he said, "They're through, P.J. I volunteered to come up with the news." He came in, shut the door, and stood with his back against it.

"Well?"

"It's ... er ... good and bad, though I shouldn't say it, not to someone with his hat in the ring. I wouldn't either, if I hadn't started packing and that lets me out. You and Carter broke exactly even. No one would budge an inch. That's why they've been closeted up there for nearly three hours. Haven't even lunched. Scared someone would get at them, no doubt."

"Who is it, then?"

"Neither of you. Sir Rufus gave his casting vote for Alcock. He wouldn't have, or so he hinted, but for the long-term risk of having either of you serving under the other, and he has a point there. Suppose you or Carter had got it, and the other had decided to soldier on? It wouldn't have worked, would it? School would have been split down the middle in no time at all. As it is, you're both level pegs under a new man, with impressive qualifications. He'll have to lean equally on the pair of you."

He felt no real pang of disappointment. Rather relief that Carter had not succeeded in pipping him. He had not exchanged a word with Alcock, the bowed, beetling man from Cape Town, so he could form no opinion how he was likely to set about following an institution like Algy Herries. 'Better the devil you know ...' they said, but it wasn't true in this case. Carter would have made a shambles of Algy's carefully erected edifice and as things had turned out Carter wasn't getting the chance to monkey with the place. That was a gain, he supposed, and his mind raced ahead to a point when, conceivably, today's ordeal might be repeated, for somehow he couldn't see himself leaving Bamfylde now.

He said, "How old is Alcock, sir?" and Herries said, "Fifty-three. Late for it, I'd say. He could stay seven or twelve years, depending how he feels, or how well off he is. I think he's pretty well fixed for cash and will likely put his feet up at sixty. There's one other thing. Nothing to do with today's business."

"Yes, sir."

"For Heaven's sake call me 'Algy' to my face from here on. I've always had a very soft spot for you, P.J. So has Ellie."

David turned away, looking down on to the forecourt through the window he had last seen Beth drive off in the three-wheeler, and had raised his hand in response to Grace's wave. He said, at length, "I'll never have another friend like you, Algy. That goes for most of us here, I imagine," but Herries said, fruitily, "Oh, come now, old sport, don't talk as if I was tucked away at Stone Cross, with Ferguson and Cordwainer. I'm only in the next parish but one, and I'll be over here at least once a month, I promise you."

"Well, I'm glad to hear that." And then, "What sort of chap *is* he, Algy?"

"Alcock? Difficult to say. An activist, judged on his record. He could have done much better than Bamfylde if he'd been ten years younger. Very quiet. No nonsense about him. Not much sense of humour, either, and that'll hinder him unless he develops one. However, we might have done worse. As for you, I'll risk offence by telling you something no one else would, not even Howarth. I admire your pluck for trying but you weren't ready for it. It would have been a gamble, and Bamfylde isn't something I'd care to stake in a lottery, even with the dice loaded in my favour. Can you take that, David?"

"Why not? It's true."

"Then come on down and I'll introduce you. The others have gone off in high dudgeon, all sharing a taxi. Carter's already made his bow. The king is dead. Long live the king!"

They went out, passing the side table where Hoskins'

new record, arrested in the middle of a chorus still lay on the portable.

"' 'Bye, 'bye, blackbird'," David said, and when Algy muttered "What?" he said it was nothing, just a private joke for Sax Hoskins and Tuppence.

"In a place like this, distinguished for nicknames you ought to find a more dignified one for that mite," said Algy.

II

The letter came by the afternoon post, an innovation since the Challacombe sorting office had acquired a van for its country round.

He saw it lying on the tray on the landing when he came up from afternoon classes to make himself a pot of tea before devoting an hour or two to the final chapter of 'The Royal Tigress', now standing in a foot-high pile on his desk and crowding all his other correspondence to one side.

He saw at first glance that it was from Julia and that she was still in America. With a feeling of elation he carried it into the living-room, and settled to read it slowly, relishing every line. But then, his eye leaping down the page and catching a phrase, he read swiftly, imbibing its contents like a draught of bitter medicine:

. . . They tell me it takes about eight days door to door for a letter to cross The Pond, Davy. So, by the time you get this, I will have been married. Mrs. Hiram Ulysses Sprockman, no less. Sonorous but . . . well . . . rather sweet once you get used to it. This will come as a shock to you, but I'm not apologising for that. I'd apologise to a little man but you're not a little man. Given a few years you'll be the biggest one Bamfylde has ever seen. Everything I said to you the night you asked me to marry you still holds good. I would have been a terrible flop as a schoolmaster's wife, worse even than as a parson's wife, for parsons, these days, are often anxious to get in on the act and keep up with the latest fads and fashions. A good schoolmaster isn't so daft. He tends to adapt with more dignity. I'll always remember your proposal as the greatest compliment anyone ever paid me. Much greater than Arthur's and Hiram's, for neither really knew me as you did. But that wouldn't make it right in anything but the purely physical sense and as regards that I give you full marks. Ten out of ten, for loving. It would do for most men but again, not for you, not since you've matured and distilled all you learned and suffered in France into a kind of—how can I put it?—a rejuvenating elixir. For the exclusive benefit of generations of Bamfeldians.

That elixir would have been watered down if I had been around when it was being mixed, stirred and seasoned, and I don't mean by this you shouldn't ever think of marrying again. You should. Given the kind of luck you once had, and deserve again, you'll make some lucky wench a wonderful husband, providing she has the sense to give you your head, and not go for the old impossible—changing a man into her image of what she thinks he ought to be.

As to me marrying Hiram, well, I'm not pretending I'm in love with him and I've told him so, over and over again. I didn't tell you but he had already proposed twice when we met again by chance that time. But Hiram doesn't need your kind of wife. He's been married to commerce ever since he discovered what fun it was to make money. What he needs—what he is getting—is a mistress-cum-manageress. Apart from that, he's kind and considerate and intelligent, as you were quick to notice.

Well, there we are, Davy. I've cut the knot for you and left you free to push on and I still don't know whether or not the Governors gambled on you or kept you in cold storage. Touching that, will you let me give you one last piece of advice? *Stay where you are, no matter what.* I couldn't say why but I *know* Bamfylde is right for you, and whilst you'd do a good, conscientious job elsewhere it wouldn't be an inspired one.

My best love to little Grace. I adored her. She'll grow up to be a credit and a solace to you.

My love to you, too, Davy. I'll never forget you and if you care to write and keep in touch I'd always be happy about that, although I leave this entirely to you.

Very, very affectionately,

Julia.

He drifted across to his study and sat down at his littered desk, trying hard to come to terms with the new situation. Julia married. Julia's cheerfulness and stimulus denied him. And this, on a day when he had to begin all over again and practise his trade under the cold eye of a stranger.

His first reaction was one of bitterness but almost at once resentment was reduced to indignation that she could have been so damned secretive and left him half-hoping, despite her unqualified refusal of marriage. But then, looking out on the moor, shimmering in the heat haze as far as the lip of the plateau where he had walked into the thunderstorm the day another woman was lost to him, a spring of common sense welled out of his resentment. It wasn't really ruthlessness on her part. Behind it was discernment, of a kind not vouchsafed to many women, with their eye on the main chance. As man and wife they might have made it but not as consorts, for a woman like her would never have been able to get Bamfylde into his kind of focus. In the end, she would have lost patience, first with it and then with him, and there would have been, as she had warned him, compromise on an ever-enlarging scale. A man shouldn't compromise with his search for personal fulfilment. He could only compromise with a creed, Carter's kind of creed, that was really no more than a set of prejudices.

Well, that was that. Now, all that remained, he supposed, was to decide on an approach to their relationship in the future and he found the answer to that almost at once. What was the point of keeping up an intermittent correspondence? Where was there sense in torturing oneself with sensual images of a vigorous, clear-skinned body stretched on a bed, the kind that would come to mind every time he sat down to write to her? Howarth had probably done that with the memory of Amy Crispin and what had it brought him but hardening of the emotional arteries, and a constant reminder of wasted years? He cleared a space on his desk and wrote, on a sheet of Bamfylde notepaper:

My Dear, I didn't get the headship. We have a new man ... not Carter, thank God. I'm staying on here indefinitely, partly because I can't be bothered to change, but mostly, I think, because I still have a notion I owe the place something. Congratulations to both of you. You made a neater, swifter job of pulling out of the Sargasso Sea than I did, and you're clearheaded enough to stay out. Good luck always, Julia dear. Very affectionately, Davy.